JUST PLAYIN'

SHANDI BOYES

Edited by
MOUNTAINS WANTED PUBLISHING
Photography by
**FURIOUS PHOTOGRAPHY

COPYRIGHT

Written by: Shandi Boyes

Photography: Furious Photography

Editing: Mountains Wanted Publishing

Proofreading: Lindsi La Bar

DEDICATION

To Ann, and my beloved Uncle Larry,

Heaven gained another two angels way too early, but love is strong; it lives forever. Just as you both will in my heart.

Shandi xx

WANT TO STAY IN TOUCH?

Facebook: facebook.com/authorshandi

Instagram: instagram.com/authorshandi

Email: authorshandi@gmail.com

Reader's Group: bit.ly/ShandiBookBabes

Website: authorshandi.com

Newsletter: subscribepage.com/AuthorShandi

ALSO BY SHANDI BOYES

Denotes Standalone Books

Perception Series

Saving Noah *

Fighting Jacob *

Taming Nick *

Redeeming Slater *

Saving Emily

Wrapped Up with Rise Up

Enigma

Enigma

Unraveling an Enigma

Enigma The Mystery Unmasked

Enigma: The Final Chapter

Beneath The Secrets

Beneath The Sheets

Spy Thy Neighbor *

The Opposite Effect *

I Married a Mob Boss *

Second Shot *

The Way We Are

The Way We Were

Sugar and Spice *

Lady In Waiting

Man in Queue

Couple on Hold

Enigma: The Wedding

Silent Vigilante

Hushed Guardian

Quiet Protector

Enigma: An Isaac Retelling

Twisted Lies *

Bound Series

Chains

Links

Bound

Restrain

The Misfits *

Russian Mob Chronicles

Nikolai: A Mafia Prince Romance

Nikolai: Taking Back What's Mine

Nikolai: What's Left of Me

Nikolai: Mine to Protect

Asher: My Russian Revenge *

Nikolai: Through the Devil's Eyes

Trey *

The Italian Cartel

Dimitri

Roxanne

Reign

Mafia Ties (Novella)

Maddox

Demi

Ox

Rocco *

Clover *

Smith *

RomCom Standalones

Just Playin' *

Ain't Happenin' *

The Drop Zone *

Very Unlikely *

False Start *

Short Stories - Newsletter Downloads

Christmas Trio *

Falling For A Stranger *

One Night Only Series

Hotshot Boss *

Hotshot Neighbor *

The Bobrov Bratva Series

Wicked Intentions *

Sinful Intentions *

Devious Intentions *

Deadly Intentions *

<u>Coming Soon</u>

Nanny Dispute *

Protecting Nicole (November 23)

AUSTRALIAN GLOSSARY

Jumper – Sweater

Tinnie – Can of Beer

Thongs – Flip Flops

MCG – Melbourne Cricket Ground

Cricket – Sport played in Australia, India, and the UK

Stubbies – Super-short men's work shorts—Google search it for a visual!

Canteen/Tuckshop – Cafeteria in schools and at sporting events

Wanker — A real idiot

Tosser – See above

Scull – Drink quickly

Mate – Anyone of any gender as long as they aren't your friend

Lounge-room – Living area

Milo – Like hot chocolate but different

Vegemite – A yeast spread a lot of Aussies eat

Tim-Tams – A really yummy chocolate biscuit. (Biscuit, as in a cookie, not those weird things you think are scones)

Buckaroos – Money

Bob — See above

Footy – Football

John Farnham — Australia Music Icon

Peter Andre — Also an Australian Music Icon, just slightly different. You might need to Google this one

AFL - Aerial pingpong. Not really, it's a sport played here that I know nothing about!

NRL - National Rugby League

Bogan - An Aussie who usually wears flannel shirts, thongs, and swears a lot. Sometimes the male version comes with a mullet

Sneakers — Running shoes or otherwise known as tennis shoes

Map of Tasmania — Region on a girl between their thighs, often called a vagina

State of Origin — Three game football competition between New South Wales and Queensland played once a year

Golden nugget — Something worth remembering for later use

Dob me in — Rat me out, tell the cops. Tattletale on someone

Rort - A scam

Breaky – Breakfast

Undies — Male or Female undergarments: Panties, Boxers etc

Cheerio — A small red sausage, think mini hot dog Weiner

Wardrobe — Closet

CHAPTER ONE

Willow

"Nope."

I step away from my roomie/quickly-becoming-best-friend, Skylar, with my hands in the air and my nose screwed up. I could never be accused of being overly girly, but even this is below me.

"I don't care if we're sitting in my loungeroom back home sipping Milo through Tim-Tams, you'll never catch me wearing anything remotely like that."

Skylar's brow cocks in utter confusion.

"You'll understand when we backpack Australia during summer break. You'll be wearing thongs on your feet and slapping vegemite on your toast in no time."

The bullshit expression I'm wearing jumps onto Skylar's face. "You'll never sell me on vegemite. The thongs though…" A frisky wink finalizes her sentence. No matter how many times I tell her thongs aren't floss for her backside, she doesn't believe me.

After slathering a second layer of orange glitter on her cheeks, Skylar lifts her blue eyes to mine. "Come on, Willow. You're dying to show me all the great things Australia has to offer, yet you're unwilling to get on board with an American tradition. It's Show-down Saturday. You can't get more traditional than this."

"I can appreciate tradition without all *that*." I wave my hand at her navy blue and orange-painted face, super-tight 69er jersey, and giant No. 1 foam hand.

I wish her visible getup was the end of her craziness.

Unfortunately, I saw the streamers she stuffed into my backpack when she thought I wasn't looking. Skylar is what we normal folks like to call "football obsessed." If she could lift her leg above her head, I have no doubt her fanfare would extend past the bleachers. Alas, the squats she does at precisely five o'clock every morning have nothing to do with agility, and everything to do with the latest curvy butt craze.

Unlike me, Skylar doesn't have natural curves. Bar the areas she pays careful consideration to, she's tiny. Her belly doesn't hold the rolls mine do. Her arms don't wobble when she waves goodbye, nor does she wear elastic-waisted pants so her backside can squeeze into her favorite pair.

I have what is known as an hourglass figure: big breasts, tiny waist, large hips, and cellulite dinted thighs. My granny thinks my "womanly figure" makes me classically beautiful. I think my curves are annoying beacons that attract the wrong type of man.

Men these days want it all: a pretty face, large breasts, and a bootylicious ass on a petite frame. Even the drastic advancements in mankind haven't clued them in on the fact that the likelihood of a woman having both a booty and a tiny waist is virtually impossible.

Corsets went out of fashion in the 1900s... *along with most men's realistic beliefs on an ideal woman.*

Snagging a throw cushion from the couch, I take its spot before using it to hide the bulge my stomach gets any time I sit. "Maybe I should stay here? I have exams at the end of the week and a recital coming up."

I love the kids I teach hip-hop to every Thursday afternoon and Saturday morning. Their mothers... not so much. Skylar and I reside in a region of America with more trophy wives per capita than any other place. God forbid the occasions their children's sporting endeavors clash with their nannies' one week of holidays they're approved to take every three or so years.

When I started teaching, I never thought it would be the parents' cells I'd be confiscating mid-lesson. Their eyes shoot daggers at me every time I enter the room, but poodle perms, botched manicures, and which housewife has a new set of boobies can wait until they're outside my dance studio walls. I may not teach the classical ballet they wish their daughters would learn, but the values I instill in my students are still important.

Skylar clicks her fingers in front of my face, breaking me from my mommy-hating trance. "Nope. Nuh-uh. You're not doing this again, Will. You chickened out of the last game."

"I had the measles!" I throw my hands into the air.

She glares at me, but I can't take her seriously with all she's got going on. She looks like Bozo the Clown, but instead of a tear drop on her cheek, she has the number of her favorite player scrawled there in thick navy ink.

"My mother was dilated to ten centimeters but instructed not to push until the final whistle was called."

"Because only an insane man would pretend his wife wasn't in labor so he could watch the playoffs," I murmur under my breath.

Pretending I didn't speak, Skylar continues, "She scheduled her contractions to arrive only during commercials so neither she or my father would miss a single moment."

I gag, sickened she thinks her parents have an ideal marriage.

"And..." She pauses, building the suspense as if I haven't heard this story a million times since I commenced studies in the US three years ago. "Not only did the game go down in history as one of the greatest sporting events of all time, our team won."

"All because your momma closed her legs?"

Even though I'm asking a question, Skylar ignores it, preferring to continue with her somewhat obsessive rant on how American football is why God created mankind.

"That's the part you don't understand, Willow. This is bigger than anything you've ever experienced." She points to her cheek. "This is not paint on my cheek."

"It isn't?"

She shakes her head. "No. It's my heart, my honor, and my pride. It's what I live for."

I'd laugh if she weren't being serious.

She spreads her hand over her heart as if she is about to recite the Pledge of Allegiance "Perfection is not attainable. But if we chase perfection, we can catch excellence."

"Babe Ruth?"

Squealing, she moves to our makeshift kitchen to gather her keys from the bowl we cook our noodles in every night. "Babe Ruth played baseball—another great American sport, by the way—but it doesn't come close to football. That was Vince Lombardi: player, coach, executive of the National Football League, and inductee to the Hall of Fame in 1971."

After throwing on her 69er-emblazoned jacket, she nudges her head to the door. "Move it or lose it, Will. I don't care if I have to drag you to the stadium kicking and screaming. We're going to eat hot dogs and drink lukewarm beer from a can while watching twenty-two men get hot and sweaty."

I hold my hands out palm-side up. "Why didn't you start there? You can have the beer, but hot dogs and sweaty men..." My leap off the couch covers my fake eagerness.

I love spending time with Skylar, but I'd rather do it without thousands of like-minded footy fanatics.

The closer our train chugs to the stadium we're about to waste three precious hours at, the less loony Skylar seems. Our cart is brimming with people dressed similar to her. There's an even mix of 69er supporters and the team I'm not allowed to mention. They're rivals, but their love of the game is undeniable.

They come in all shapes and sizes too. The guy on my left has a face full of piercings and a blue and orange mohawk that nearly took out my eye when the jam-packed train caused my breasts to land in his face. He wasn't jumping in fright, more hopeful for another collision than anything. On the right we have a bunch of kids whose dads never got drafted dragging them away from the books for the night with the hope their love of football will rub off on them.

Then there are people like me: the lunatics with plain clothes, unpainted faces, and lack of team colors making them stick out like a sore thumb. If Skylar had warned me my contempt for donning all things 69ers would mean I'd be gawked at like a freak in a sideshow act, I wouldn't have been so opposed to the idea.

Ha! Who am I kidding?

Even a million buckaroos couldn't convince me these people are normal. There's only one occasion I'll don a face full of paint and florescent clothing—it is when I'm on stage, grinding off calories to the latest hip hop track.

I stop picturing the kids' faces when I reveal the outfit I've organized for the beginning of the season dance off when Skylar stands from her seat. She found a seat because her waist is half the size of mine, but her chest is nearly as voluptuous. Even my cleavage being all-natural didn't award me any extra brownie points.

"Ready?"

I scan the frantic crowd making a beeline from the train platform to the stadium before nodding. "As ready as I'll ever be."

Damn, I thought the fans in the trains were nuts. They have nothing on the thousands of people filling the stadium. Skylar laughs when I ask if she has earplugs. I'm not joking. The roar of thousands of people cheering at once is near deafening. The last time I heard such a ruckus was when New South Wales finally conquered Queensland in the State of Origin after eight years of consecutive losses.

Now that's what you call football. State versus state. Mate versus mate. There are no shoulder pads and helmets. Pure muscle and speed are the only things needed to play Australian Rugby League... and perhaps a lack of brain cells. I wouldn't necessarily say it's a dangerous sport, but it's not for the weak at heart either.

"This is us."

A wolf whistle parts my lips when I drink in the bleachers next to us. Leather-lined, extra-wide seats mere inches from the action. Money couldn't buy such a prime spot... so how the hell did Skylar afford them? She's not broke, but she isn't rich either. Unlike me, her studies are being funded by her parents. I'm on a paid scholarship that thankfully wasn't withdrawn when my knee buckled upon landing a near perfect grand jeté.

I'm drawn from reminiscing about the good old days when Skylar huffs, "These aren't our seats. This is our section." After pointing to the very top of an extremely long set of stairs, she says, "*Those* are our seats."

The thirty pounds I've put on since my prima ballerina dreams were squashed by a knee reconstruction hasn't affected my fitness. I climbed the 9351 steps to our seats—*yes, I counted*—without stopping to chug a beer gifted by an unknown admirer during my climb.

That hideous display of bad sportsmanship falls solely on Skylar's shoulders. For someone "dying to smell the testosterone of Saturday night football," she's seconds from passing out. Her face is as red as a beetroot, and she's gripping the armrest of her chair so firmly, her French-tipped nails are close to snapping.

"You. Here," she commands a man to her with the wiggle of her finger and two breathless words. "Two root beer floats, four hot dogs, and one of whatever that is."

The man's eyes drop to the assortment of food in his hands. "My fried PB&J?"

His reply resurrects Skylar from her death. "They sell fried peanut butter and jelly sandwiches here?"

Pretending her girly voice didn't pierce his eardrums, the man nods. "That they do... in the *cafeteria*, where I picked these up."

With a wink that reveals he's struggling not to ask her for her number, he takes his seat four rows down from us.

Skylar slumps into her chair with a sigh. "God. What happened to the good old days where hot dogs were delivered to your seat, and your beer wasn't room temperature from hiding it in your cleavage to deceive security?"

Her questions coincide with the removal of the beer cans she snuck down her shirt seconds before our bags were checked. It also has me wondering if I got stuck in a time-warp that delivered me back to Australia. The whole "hiding your beer from security" was a trick my dad did at the cricket, except he used his beer belly as a cover for the extra lumps in his stubbie shorts. Non-Australians won't understand the effort he went to scull a beloved tinnie at the MCG until they Google the original stubbie shorts of Australia.

Let me paint you a picture: short-hemmed, elastic-waist cotton shorts that leave *nothing* to the imagination. Up until this day, I still haven't worked out how he hid an entire six-pack down his pants. It defied logic—in more ways than one.

"No, I'm good," I assure Skylar when she tips a can of contraband my way. "I'll stick with water."

After ensuring memories of my dad didn't wet my cheeks, I wave my hand in the air like the students in my class do when busting to go to the bathroom. I'm vying for the attention of the vendor who is serving a group of college cheerleaders a dozen rows down from us.

When he fails to see my wildly flapping arm, I plonk into my seat with a grumble. I get extra angry when I'm hungry.

Skylar bumps me with her shoulder. "It will be quicker—and a shit-ton more hygienic—to go to the canteen." She winks, happy she worked some Aussie bogan into her sentence. "If the angle of his cooler is anything to go by, you don't want to touch anything he's selling. He cools his balls in there after every shift."

"Eww!"

"What?" She laughs. "It's true. Look at his face. Guaranteed he has a raging boner right now."

A little bit of vomit creeps up my esophagus when I take in the vendor's parted lips and hooded gaze. He has the same dirty geezer expression Todd Richards had when he asked if he could touch my boobs in the sixth grade. He told his mom he fell off his bike when he ran to her crying after I punched him in the face.

Six years passed before he grew the courage to ask me again. My response that time around was less violent. Todd was the handsome surfer who befriended everyone, and I was the awkwardly shy dancer who spent more time counting calories than amassing friends.

A lack of social life shouldn't have factored in my decision, but unfortunately, it did. Between ballet lessons and the many gym sessions needed to keep my weight at "industry standards," I didn't have time for boys. Todd offered me a no-strings-attached deal. It worked well for us until I chose to attend a university eight thousand miles from our hometown.

While recalling Todd's lazy smile and glistening baby blues, I stand to my feet before swinging my eyes to Skylar. "Do you want anything at the tuckshop?"

After storing away another Aussie slang golden nugget for a rainy day, she gives me a look that speaks volumes.

"Two root beer floats, four hot dogs, and whatever the hell that disaster the cutie in row 3875 is letting go cold because he's too busy ogling all of this." I circle my finger around her beautiful face before pointing to the man who's spent the last ten minutes watching Skylar instead of the two dozen scantily clad cheerleaders on the field.

With a giddy clap, Skylar nods. I'm not sure what she's more excited about: the food or the fact she's added *another* admirer on her long list of many. If her fumbling as she searches her purse for notes is any indication, I'd say it is the latter. She can't take her eyes off the dark-haired hottie for two seconds to rummage up some coin.

"It's okay. I've got it," I assure her when she attempts to thrust two crumpled bills and a handful of quarters my way.

I wish I weren't so generous. Even with the Australian dollar having a recent resurge, the price of a hot dog is highway robbery. Who in their right mind pays eight dollars for a hot dog?

An idiot trying to fool people into believing she doesn't live paycheck to paycheck.

Just as my hard-earned money is about to be torn from my grasp with a bucket-load of tears and perhaps even a tantrum, I spot a food van outside the stadium walls. There's no line-up like the one I'm about to join, and the cracked neon lighting assures me they'd never charge eight bucks for a sausage in a bun.

With a smug grin and my pocket only twenty dollars lighter, I make my way back to my seat. My intuition on the food van was spot on. The dogs are a little floppy, and the buns a little stale, but at a savings of four dollars a pop, my taste buds will suck it up.

I'm halfway back to my seat when reality dawns. I forgot Skylar's fried sandwich. I could tell her they sold out, but I can't lie even if my life depends on it. Furthermore, she may be a little crazy, but she's been there for me way more than I can count the past three years, so the least I can do is get her her heart attack sandwich, retake my seat, and feign interest in a game I have no clue about.

My stomps back down the four thousand stairs I just climbed are brutal enough to turn the root beer floats into milkshakes.

Thirty minutes later—*I kid you not*—I'm finally heading back to my seat. Skylar's kiddie sandwich is a massive hit amongst the locals, meaning I had to wait for a new batch to be fried. If I hadn't forked out twelve dollars before they advised me of the wait, I would have said, "thanks, but no thanks." Regrettably, they saw me coming from a mile away. It's not hard to spot a sucker in a crowd of many.

With the players now on the field, the crowd is super buzzed. Their roars set my hearing back a decade as they race to the barriers to get a picture of their favorite player warming up. I have to push and shove just to reach the stairwell where my seats are located, and even when I break through the human jungle, their animalistic tendencies don't stop. They look like men the morning after a bachelor party—drunk, randy, and boisterous—there's just thousands of them.

"Whoa! What the hell?"

My squinted eyes stray from a can of beer resting at my feet to the direction the flying can came from. Just as my eyes land on a blond man with a tank top so tight, I can't testify it isn't body paint, from the corner of my eye, I witness a person not nimble enough to dodge his second flung beverage. A crushed can of beer smacks her right in the nose, instantly dribbling droplets of blood onto her extensively pregnant stomach.

"Oh my god, are you okay?" I rush to her side to steady her movements the best I can since my hands are overloaded with food and a slush that once resembled root beer floats.

The pretty brunette peers at me with wide, shocked eyes. "Umm... I think so?"

She doesn't look okay. She's handling her injury well, but the shock of being struck is draining the color from her cheeks as quickly as it fills mine with anger.

Peeved as fuck, I return my narrowed gaze to the man responsible for her injury. "Look what you did, you dipshit!"

The A-grade moron suspends high-fiving his friends to shuffle to his feet and face me. The wide width of his pupils indicates he's highly intoxicated, but the sneer on his face reveals he was an asshole long before alcohol laced his veins.

"What was that, sweetheart? I couldn't hear you over all that blubber you've stuffed between us."

My mouth gapes. "Excuse me?"

His response annoys the shit out of me, but it's not uncommon. The instant you no longer wear single digit-sized dresses, you're classed as a fatty. It's beyond wrong, and it frustrates the hell out of me, but society's ideal body type isn't my fight this time around.

Manners, though... I'm more than happy to show him what happens when you leave them at home.

"Perhaps you should pull your micro dick out of your ass and use it as a Q-tip, then you'll be able to hear me."

The crowds roar nearly drowns out what he says next. "My dick only shrank when my eyes landed on you. Look at you, little miss piggy, you can't even put down your food to help your friend. What's the matter, did you lose your trough?"

Anger works from my stomach up to my throat when he makes pig noises. His squeals are so loud, they gain us more than a few spectators. They stop watching the game to focus on something just as ludicrous as men fighting over a leather-stitched ball.

The stranger's pig grunts stop when I growl, "I'd rather be fat than have a face that looks like a baboon's ass. I can lose weight, but you'll always be ugly."

When he fails to return my one-hundred-percent accurate taunt, I nudge my head to the pregnant lady standing next to me. She is still dazed, but her cheeks aren't as white as they were before I defended her. "Apologize to my friend—"

"Or what? You'll sit on me until I buckle in fear for my life?"

The crowd surges closer to us when I sneer, "I could slap you, but then I'd be charged with animal abuse."

"Look who's talking." He recommences squealing like a pig.

I grind my back molars together, aware that retaliating to bullies is just as wrong as instigating bullying, but I'm unable to hold back. "You're the exact reason gene pools need lifeguards. We've got to do everything we can to stop the uglies from breeding. Have you looked in the mirror lately? You're so hideous, if being ugly was a crime, you'd be serving a life sentence."

His lips twitch as he struggles to formulate a comeback. When he fails to find one, the mob circling us stomp their feet in euphoria, awarding me the win for our showdown. I don't relish the victory. All I'm feeling is guilt. I should have been the bigger person—but I guess that's what started our confrontation to begin with?

"Come on, let's get some ice for your nose." After dumping the food I spent nearly an hour gathering, and several hours working to pay for, I curl my arm around the pregnant lady's shoulders and guide her toward the cafeteria.

Not willing to accept the invisible white flag I'm waving, the fat-shamer continues to taunt me. He calls me several crude names between loud pig grunts. I take his belligerent rant in stride, knowing not even an exemplary bill of health would convince him I am just as fit and healthy as the men he's here to marvel at. I may have rolls on my stomach and dimples in my thighs, but I work out daily, eat a balanced diet, and have a heart so strong, his hurtful comments don't constrict it in the slightest.

I am good, balanced, and happy... until he switches our exchange from a verbal altercation to a physical one.

I miss a step when something hard smacks me square in the back. I don't need to peer over my shoulder to know what hit me. The hushed whispers of the crowd are enough of a clue, let alone the evidence teetering back and forth between my feet. He threw a can of beer at me—a full can of beer.

While reminding myself that I can't stamp out violence with more violence, I suck in numerous deep breaths. But the more he goads me, the more my tether snaps. He hit a pregnant lady in the face, yet he doesn't see the need to apologize.

What the hell is wrong with these people?

Worked up and slightly hormonal, I gather the beer in my hand then pivot around to face the unnamed aggressor. The arrogant sneer he's wearing doubles when I toss the can into the air like a bowler does on a cricket pitch while strategizing how to bowl out his opponent.

He wouldn't understand my Australian analogy, but he can't miss the threat on my face. "What are you going to do? Hit me with—"

His words fall short when I hook back my arm to hurl the can through the air. My throw is so accurate, it smacks the blond right between the eyes not even two seconds later. He stills as his hands dart up to cradle his face like his victim did minutes ago. There's just one difference this time around: blood doesn't trickle from his nose...it drains from a large gash in his forehead.

With his eyes rolled into the back of his head, he collapses onto a row of hard plastic chairs. He's knocked out cold, and I'm once again seeking the closest exit.

CHAPTER TWO

Presley

Teammates slap my shoulders as sweat rolls down my back. The cheers from the boisterous crowd are still ringing in my ears, but their excited hum from our win isn't loud enough to drown out the one ringtone I'd give anything not to hear.

She's calling me—again. She does the same thing at the end of every game. She congratulates me before asking how much longer it will be before I come "home."

She says "home" like she's waiting for me at a ranch with horses, a handful of milking cows, and a couple of pigs. It's not close to that. Her "home" may be a jungle; it's just not one I'm planning to scale anytime soon.

To Lillian, home is the hustle and bustle of New York City, the town that never sleeps. Lillian—or Lily as her friends call her—is my ex-fiancée. The "ex" part of her title wasn't my choice. She thought our nine-year relationship was "wearing her down" and that she needed some time to "reenergize her inner Lily."

I thought that was what Josue and she did during their daily Bikram yoga classes. I realized my error when my physical therapist got stuck in gridlock traffic twelve months ago. Josue was teaching

Lillian the downward dog, just minus the clothing most instructors wear.

It's funny how things ended up. The tabloids had a field day with our breakup. Unfortunately, they didn't see Lillian as the lying two-faced bitch she is. They saw a man angry his career was cut short during his golden days, one who reached for the bottle more times than he hit the gym. They believed Lillian's affair was a desperate call for help—that by hurting me, she'd help me.

In a way, that's precisely what she did. I left her in our high-rise apartment in the middle of Manhattan to "rejuvenate" while I relearned who I was in my hometown of Ravenshoe. I surfed and drank with high school buddies. I even hooked up with a few girls I never had the chance to seduce because Lillian was always there to cut back their attention with the intensity of a weed-wacker on crack.

It was a good six months.

The following six weren't as pretty.

Doctors, lawyers, even hairdressers often say they exceed in their field of expertise because they were born to do it. The same can be said for athletes. I was bred into the rowdiest, grubbiest, and big-hearted football fanatic you could imagine. It didn't matter what was on, or the importance of the occasion, if it occurred during game time, it didn't exist. Nothing on this earth will ever supersede football on the totem of importance to my dad. Not weddings. Not anniversaries. Not even the birth of his first grandchild lifted my dad's backside from his favorite couch during a game.

He often tells people he's inspired me to return to my glory days. I'm not so quick to issue him the same praise. Yes, he loves football. Yes, he was ecstatic when I secured the number one draft pick after four years of college ball. But he didn't run me through drills while it poured down rain. He didn't even pick me up after my high school games. Until I went pro, my father had never seen me play.

Some say that's why I fell for Lillian's "trophy wife" trick so quickly. She was so interested in everything I did, I truly thought she cared about me. It was only after I walked in on her with Josue did I realize I was wrong. She didn't count my calories because she knew the leaner I was, the faster I ran. She was keeping her piggy bank well-stacked. The fitter I was, the better I played. The better I played, the more endorsements I secured.

I thought the record-breaking amount I secured for a five-year contract with the 69ers was impressive, but it had nothing on the sponsorships I negotiated off the field. I was bringing in so much money, I could practically roll in it.

Then it all came tumbling down.

My illustrious career was struck down by a supposed "non-rehabilitation" injury. I canceled my wedding with Lillian because I refused to roll down the aisle in a wheelchair, and the endorsement money I anticipated living on after I spent my fortune on a twenty-three million-dollar penthouse in New York went up in smoke.

I was left with nothing but the clothes on my back, the support of my fiancée, and the occasional gig she brought in being the face of a clothing company no one had ever heard of.

I should have seen Lillian's affair as a blessing. If I had, my share of our penthouse would have helped me start a new life. Instead, I funded Josue's retirement in the Caribbean. He's a twenty-six-year-old yoga instructor living on a yacht. If that doesn't show you how fucked up life is, I don't know what will.

With that in mind, I hit decline on Lillian's call. She'll leave a voicemail; I'll pretend I never got it, and the vicious cycle we've been playing the past six months will remain on course.

Unsure if I am amused or annoyed, I stand to my feet to gather my belongings. Only the slightest smidge of disdain crosses my face, but from the way Danny arrives at my side two seconds later, you'd swear I was howling in pain.

"How's your back? Any twinges? Spasms? Do you want me to get Amara to give you a rubdown before you head off?"

I lift my milk-chocolate eyes to Danny. "Amara? The Italian with more hair on her top lip than me?"

He smiles a cunning grin. "It doesn't matter what she looks like. Her hands are worth a million bucks."

I give him a look. He can say that since he has no interest in discovering what Amara has going on underneath the white masseuse dress she dons daily. He's too busy sneaking peeks of the players exiting the showers to let female anatomy deter his mission.

"It's good. I'm good. I don't need Amara..." My words trail off when I stuff my clothes into my gym bag, and Danny's eyes land on numerous bottles of pain medication stacked in the back corner.

"Don't," I warn when his lips twitch with the telltale sign he's about to begin one of his infamous lectures. "I haven't taken any pain meds in months. They're from an old prescription."

A sprinkling of blond hair falls in front of his eye when he slants his head to the side and widens his eyes. He's going for the innocent, *I'm your friend more than your agent* look. It's not a look he can pull off. "Then why don't we throw them out?"

I snatch his wrist when his hand darts toward my bag. My hold is weak enough not to hurt him, but firm enough to indicate he's overstepping the bounds of the job I pay him to do.

"I said I haven't taken any. That doesn't mean I won't need them at a later date." I scan the locker room to ensure we're alone. Happy we are, I drop my eyes back to Danny. "They're backup. Just in case."

When I spot my teammate/best friend Dalton darting past the locker room, I use his whitening face to my advantage. Danny and I have held the same conversation numerous times the past six months. We always reach the same outcome. My meds are there just in case I need them. I don't use them. They're merely reminders of how far I've traveled since my injury—well, mostly.

"Hey, Dalton. Wait up."

Dalton freezes just outside the door being buckled by eager sports reporters wanting interviews with players of the winning team.

"Everything alright? You look like you've seen a ghost."

My brows furrow when he replies in a hurry, "It's Becca. She got assaulted in the bleachers."

"Hold on, what?" I grab his shoulder, pulling him back before he's swallowed by player-eating journalists. "She got assaulted—here? On our home turf?"

Surely I heard him wrong. The 69er fans are a rowdy bunch, but they love all aspects of their team—wives and girlfriends included.

Dalton's comment makes sense when he adds, "She lost her ticket. With her ID left on the kitchen counter along with her baby brain, she bought a ticket from a scalper. He failed to mention her seat was in hostile territory."

"Is she at the hospital?"

Dalton groans then shakes his head. "No. You know Becca: as stubborn as she is beautiful."

A chuckle vibrates in my chest. I've known both Dalton and Becca for over a decade, but their friendship was proven without a doubt after I was injured. They were the only couple who stuck by me through thick and thin. Becca even went as far as offering me a job with her design firm when I was released from my contract. I'm not exactly sure what she wanted me to do, but just the fact she offered reveals what a standup woman she is. Dalton got lucky when he stumbled upon Becca. All I got was hives from my college relationship.

Noticing Dalton has an Uber app open on his phone, I ask, "Do you want a lift? I'm about to head out anyway."

He raises his eyes from his phone to me. "Don't you have an endorsement meeting tonight?"

"Nah," I lie. "They need proof I'm sitting at a zero body fat percentage before they'll let me sell their sugar-loaded drinks—as if they won't have their customers shitting out of the eye of a needle within a minute of drinking them."

Dalton's face screws up. "Thanks for the mental image."

I slap him on the back, accepting the praise he never meant to give before directing him to the parking garage under the stadium. "Car is this way."

While leading him away from the throng of reporters who'd give their left nut to capture the quarterback aspiring to return to his glory days, and the captain of a three-time state championship team on the same reel of tape, I send Danny a message.

ME:

> Family emergency. Cancel appointment with pharmacy rep.

Danny either anticipated my text or he's sitting on his phone. I'd say it is a combination of them both. He's rarely seen without an electronic device attached to his hand, but being my friend more than my agent means he felt my unease during our talk with a pharmaceutical company last month. They want me to endorse a diet shake they've created. I've always been a firm proponent of fueling your body with a good nutritious diet, not gunk that makes you so sick you can't eat.

As Dalton and I push through a set of double doors, I answer my ringing phone. Danny breaks into a conversation without issuing a greeting. "We discussed this. Until you've proven yourself, the amount on your contract will be disbursed in minimum scheduled payments. By minimal payments, they mean not even enough to cover my salary. That's where endorsements come in. No true sports star makes all his money on the field, Elvis..."

His words waver at my growl, but his scorn doesn't lessen in the slightest. "You need this deal. Let an attack of the conscience eat you alive once you're back on your feet."

I sit on my reply for a couple of seconds to contemplate. I know the right thing to do, but I also understand Danny's viewpoint. In this town, you're nothing without money. If you have it, you're expected to flaunt it. If you don't, you fake it until you do. My $200,000 leased ride proves this more than anything.

Needing more time to deliberate, I reply, "I do have a family emergency."

"Okay. That's fine. We can reschedule." Danny's hurried words expose his relief that I'm not pulling out of the deal entirely. "What about tomorrow morning before you fly out? Say 8 AM?"

After pressing the lock button on my 2017 Aston Martin V12 Vantage S, I nudge my head to the passenger seat, suggesting for Dalton to begin the awkward maneuver it takes for men our size to squeeze inside. It's no easy feat. We're both over six-foot-two with shoulders wider than the Aston's leather seats. Its cramped insides are smaller when Dalton's shoulder squashes mine as I slam my door shut.

Giving up in defeat, I hum, "Reschedule the meeting, but don't give the reps any indication I'm interested in their offer." Dalton chokes on his spit when I say, "A little bit of disinterest may see their five million dollar offer climb to ten."

"Just turn up and leave the rest to me. I'll get you more than ten."

In his eagerness to get negotiations started, Danny disconnects our call.

"Agents," Dalton grumbles. "Can't live without them, but it'd be a whole lot easier if we could."

I laugh. It will be a long time before he goes down the "I love my agent" route. Only eight months ago, he fired his "ball-crusher" agent for using work events to place strain on his relationship with Becca. Amy thought the more she distanced Dalton and Becca with endorsement meetings, contract talks, and any other bullshit she could find, the more fragile the relationship would become.

She underestimated the love Dalton has for his wife, and in some ways, she helped their relationship blossom. If she hadn't scheduled Dalton on the latest flight possible to attend the wedding of a mutual friend of both his and Becca's, he would have discovered he was becoming a father the old-fashioned way—by being handed a pee-loaded stick.

Thank fuck his schmoozing wrangled him a flight an hour earlier—because no man should *ever* be handed something a woman peed on. I get you're excited, truly I do, but if it requires a toilet at any stage during usage, I don't want to see it nor touch it. You can keep that shit to yourself.

Our trip from the stadium to the home Dalton shares with Becca reveals how different my life could have been if I had taken better care of myself. Don't get me wrong, I'm not poor by any means. I just don't have an eight-bedroom house with no mortgage and a paid-for-in-cash Maserati and top-of-the-line Range Rover in the driveway.

My crash pad is a few blocks from here. It's one of those housing developments techies hide out in while waiting for their app to hit the big time. It has two full-sized tennis courts, three pools, and I was lucky enough to snag one of only two condos with a hot tub in the courtyard. It's modest but not in a way its two million dollar price tag can hide.

Dalton flings off his seatbelt then locks his eyes with mine. "Coming up?"

A "no" sits on my lips, but a niggle in my gut shuts it down before my mouth can deliver it. Only once has my stomach cautioned me like this. It was when I told my physical therapist to head to my apartment instead of her office. It was two miles closer than our arranged meet-up point, and she wouldn't need to go through an accident scene that had traffic backed up for miles.

If I hadn't listened to my gut that day, I wouldn't have discovered the extra-curricular activity Lillian was participating in every afternoon between two and three.

"I won't stay long. Just long enough to check if Becca is okay."

Dalton slaps my shoulder, wordlessly advising me he appreciates my support before clambering out of my car. It takes even more effort for us to peel out of my sardine can than it does for us to enter it.

The further we descend down the path separating Dalton's four-car garage from his mega-mansion, the more my brow perks. There's a female voice in the distance. From how one-sided her conversation is, I can only assume she's talking on the phone. Her numerous apologies for "skipping the shit-fest" gains my attention, but the sexiest accent I've ever heard utterly seizes it. She's either Australian or South African. I often get their accents confused.

A smile tugs on my lips when the voice in the distance snarls, "From the way you're acting, anyone would think I instigated the incident." Her friend clearly believes that when she barks out only two seconds later, "He assaulted a pregnant lady with a can of beer."

I love the way she says "can of beer" like they're a rarity.

"He should be grateful I didn't shove it where the sun don't shine." She murmurs a throaty moan of agreement. "Oh it was, but

I would have made it fit. Men with attitudes like his don't have much dangling between their legs. Why do you think he was such a prick? Because he doesn't have one!"

Hearing the chuckle I fail to stifle, the unnamed brunette spins around to face us.

Holy fucking cupcakes!

Wavy brown locks fanning a flawless heart-shaped face, eyes that are either really light blue or gray in color, and a rack a Viking could feast upon for a year and never go hungry.

What? You can't see what I'm seeing. The fact her boobs were the third thing I noticed should award me some brownie points. I've never seen a more impressive pair of tits in my life.

I'm not a religious man, but I'm praying to God now, hoping he'll unknot the thin strip of material keeping his greatest creation contained. Her breasts are seconds from exploding from her top, and my tongue is hanging out of my mouth in anticipation.

Swallowing harshly, the brunette's eyes widen. "I have to go," she squeaks into her phone, her words breathless.

I want to pretend she's struggling to breathe because she perused my body as readily as I did hers, but the fret in her eyes weakens my hypothesis. I'm confident she likes what she sees, but the daring glint in her eyes verifies she's not the type of girl to let a chunk of man-meat steal her smarts.

As her eyes dance between Dalton and me, she murmurs into her phone, "No, Skylar, truly, I have to go. This isn't a ploy to skip the celebration." Her dated cell phone presses close to her fleshy, nude lips before she whispers, "The feds are here to arrest me."

Her friend squawks down the line when she lowers her phone from her ear. After pushing the end button, she slips it into her jeans, which are struggling as hard to contain her sweltering curves as her shirt is.

I could imagine her hips being gripped during raunchy, explicit sex, and her mouthwatering thighs look capable of surviving a marathon fuck session. She's got more curves than I've handled before, but her ripped jeans, chunky wedge shoes, and tight shirt embrace her voluptuous frame in a way that stimulates more than a bit of interest out of me... *and my cock.*

Wary of my prolonged gawk, she holds her hands into the air, then takes a step back, her skin growing pale . "It was an accident, I swear. I didn't mean to knock him out; I just forgot instruments like cricket balls are dangerous weapons in the wrong hands."

Cricket balls?

Her reply piques Dalton's brow as much as it does his interest. "You're the girl from the YouTube video?"

YouTube video?

As confused as me, the brunette replies, "Yes, I'm Willow... or Will, as my friends call me." It takes several swallows to dislodge the lump in her throat before she continues, "And I know I have a baby face, but I swear I was legal when that video was filmed."

My heart thrums against my ribcage as Dalton does a double-take. "You have multiple videos uploaded to YouTube?"

Thank fuck Dalton jumped back into the conversation because I was two seconds from whipping out my phone, snapping Willow's photo, and going on a Google hunt. These days, Willow is a common name, but that won't dampen my eagerness in the slightest to discover what tape she *thinks* we're referencing. I'm not a dirty old man who trolls the web for naughty pics of college students, but if they're out there for the world to see, its fair game as far as I'm concerned.

Furthermore, I'm dying to discover if her tits are real. Her video may give me the answer I'm seeking without making me appear seedy... *for the most part.*

If only I could lift my jaw from the ground, then maybe she'd stop staring at me like I'm a contestant at a freaky Friday competition.

The hang of my jaw doubles when Willow asks, "That's what you're thinking, isn't it? A... *somewhat* risqué YouTube clip?"

Although panicked, she's got a smart head on her shoulders. By keeping our interest on the footage, she's hoping we'll forget her confession about knocking someone out. I'm not as willing to let it slide. She's young—*so young I shouldn't be looking at her as I am*—but her youth has unlocked something inside of me I haven't unleashed in years: my naturally engrained playfulness.

When Dalton attempts to relieve Willow's worry, I stop him. He eyes me with suspicion but doesn't break my cover when I say, "First-degree assault is a very serious charge, Ms..."

"Hart," Willow fills in, her voice quivering.

My arched brow grows and grows until she succumbs to its pressure. "Fine. It's Underwood. Willow Reed Underwood. U.N.D.E.R—wood. As in the wood your pants struggled to contain when I spun around to face you."

Spit flies out of Dalton's mouth when he fails to smother his chuckle. I don't know if he's chuckling at Willow's reply or the horrendous name her parents bestowed upon her. Whatever it is, I'm laughing right with him.

"Your name is Willow Reed Underwood?"

When she nods, I laugh even louder. "Your parents aren't environmentalists by any chance, are they? Tree huggers? Forrest lovers?" My voice crackles more with each word I speak. "Let me guess, your sister's name is Aspen, Maple, or Birch. It's Birch, isn't it?"

Unimpressed, Willow folds her arms under her chest. I really wish she wouldn't. One thrust of her boobs and my brain turns to dust.

"Alright, asshat, you've had your fun; now get on your bike."

Her sexy accent eradicates any chance of me taking her threat seriously. Her straight lips and narrowed eyes have me laughing so hard, the timber decking beneath my feet shudders. Their vibrations are so fierce, Becca sprints out the door separating the deck from her massive kitchen, panicked about an earthquake.

Considering she's eight months pregnant, her mad dash doesn't just steal my laughter, it has Dalton's fist getting friendly with my gut.

After a stern finger point, Dalton devotes his attention to his wife. "Are you alright? I saw the footage on YouTube. What were you doing in that section, Becca? You know how crazy those Marshall fans are. You should have gone home."

I barely hear Becca whisper, "I wanted to see you play your final home game before the baby comes," before a scent too sweet to be innocent secures my attention.

Willow is standing next to me. She still has her arms folded over her chest, and her nose is screwed up, but the fire in her eyes has dulled from witnessing Dalton's attentiveness to Becca.

"If she's married to a fed, how did she get such an impressive house?"

Although she's asking a question, she doesn't give me a chance to reply.

"Ohhh. I mistook your Tweedledum, Tweedledee outfits. You're not feds! You're hitmen who'll pop the guy I knocked out." She peers up at me, her short height made more noticeable by the long crank of her neck. "If I knew you wanted him dead, I would have loosened up my muscles before taking my swing."

"You hit the man who struck Becca?" Surprise resonates in my tone. She's got fighting spirit in her eyes, but she appears to be more of a lover than a fighter.

"What? No!" The front of my pants tighten when she flashes me a mischievous grin. "I just returned his missing beer can."

With that, she paces away from me to interrupt Becca and Dalton, her steps as seductive as her gorgeous face.

CHAPTER THREE

Willow

You know that weird sensation your tummy gets when you're lowering your parents' closed bedroom door handle? You know you don't want to see what's happening behind the door, but the weird noises coming out of their room are too loud for a nine-year-old to ignore. That's how I'm feeling right now as I approach Becca and the man I mistook for a federal agent.

My error can be easily excused. It's not every day you have two men approach you in matching navy suits without warning, much less after you fled the scene of a crime. If that wasn't suspicious enough, their shoulders are as wide as I am tall, and the bulkier of the two has a black eye and a cut lip.

Alarm bells were ringing.

Unfortunately, a warning siren wasn't the only one their arrival set off.

The slimmer of the two is handsome. He has a defined jaw, pillowy lips, and cheekbones that sit a shit-ton higher now than they did when he arrived. I guess his wife's constant reassurance that she's fine gives him a good reason to smile.

His friend, on the other hand is rough, rugged, and so damn

wickedly sexy my panties filled with moisture long before my eyes did. The split in his top lip enhances his wonky smile; his stacked shoulders reveal he'd have no trouble pinning a woman to a wall and fucking her until her legs gave out, and the most deliriously sexy dimple rests in the middle of his chin. You have no idea how hard it was for me not to whack my chest and say, "You Tarzan, me Jane," upon spotting him.

It was a close call. The only thing that stopped me was recalling how long it took me to calm Skylar down from "dumping" her at the game. I had left Becca unaccompanied for over twenty minutes, giving her plenty of time to dob me in to the cops.

Becca is as sweet as pie and was extremely convincing when she said I could hide out in her palatial home until the heat died down at the football stadium not too far from here, but I've been fooled by pretty faces before.

Not many rich people are nice. It's not their fault. They're just so hungry from the constant diets they're on, they can't help but be cranky. I'm not putting down skinny people; I'm talking facts. I was the crankiest bitch on the planet when I followed my strict *no more than 1,000 calories a day* diet, so wouldn't it be the same for everyone else? We are, after all, cut from the same cloth.

Realizing I'm letting my hunger get the better of me, I tap Becca on the shoulder. "Hey... ah..." *Come on, Willow, you've been able to talk under water since you were nine months old.* "I'm gonna head off. The sirens have settled, and your man is here now, so you don't need me hanging around anymore."

Although I used Becca's offer of shelter as a way to flee prosecution, for the most part, I wanted to make sure she was okay. She copped a nasty sting to the head a month out from giving birth. I would have felt really bad if she was left concussed and alone.

"Don't go. Please. I was going to order Chinese before cracking open a bottle of wine... for you and Willow," she adds on in a flurry when the dark-haired hottie plastered to her side growls. "Please, Will. At least let me buy you dinner for everything you did."

Her plea is cute as fuck, but I'm not a five-year-old. The pouty lip, *I'm the answer to all your dreams* look doesn't work on me.

If she were the brute eyeing me from afar, different story. I don't run after any man, but this bitch might powerwalk for him.

"I'm sorry, I really have to go. My friend isn't happy she's been left to celebrate the victory by herself." My eyeroll is relinquished halfway. I had no clue the pain associated with acting like a bimbo. I won't make the same mistake twice. "I'm just glad you're okay." Because my reply is sincere, it sounds that way. "That's all the reward I need."

"If your friend is upset about missing the game, I can arrange for replacement tickets for both of you—"

"No!" I scream, interrupting Becca's husband mid-offer. After lowering my voice to an acceptable volume, I add on, "That's real nice of you, but *completely* unnecessary."

I thought I said my comment politely, but a grumble from behind my shoulder indicates it may not have come out as sincerely as I hoped.

"Not a fan of the 69ers? Or do you just hate football in general?"

"I like football." I spin around to face the hunk of man-meat who makes my lady parts tingle as rampantly as he agitated my nerves by picking on my name. "*Real* football."

"Real football." He paces closer to me, making the quiver of my pulse descend to a dark and extremely moist region of my body. "What's *real* football?"

The split in his top lip widens when I clarify, "Australian football."

"As in the aerial ping-pong game they play on a circular field?"

I gag. "No. That's AFL."

"*A*ustralian *F*ootball *L*eague." He emphasizes the first letter in each word he speaks.

"I meant the NRL. No shoulder pads. No groin protection. Not *I'm such a Nancy, I'll run the ball but don't dare ask me to tackle anyone* football. *Real* football. Blood, sweat, and tears football."

I nearly roll my eyes at the pompousness in my voice, but recalling my earlier pain stops me. Instead, I fold my arms under my chest and purse my lips. My dad would have been proud as hell about the rant I just delivered if he were still here.

As quickly as memories fill my eyes with moisture, silence falls around me. After uncrossing my arms, my eyes drift between three pairs staring at me in shock.

"What? This can't be the first time you've heard of the NRL. It's pretty well known back home."

"It's not that we haven't heard of it. It's just—"

Becca's husband gets cut off by Tarzan slicing his hand through the air. He's stunned by his friend's request for silence, but also amused by it.

"Is that it? Or do you have more words of wisdom on a sport that grips the nation numerous times a week?"

"Hmm." The tap of my index finger on my lips lessens the arrogance on the stranger's face, but only by a smidgen. "Just the players? Or the rort as a whole?" When confusion replaces some of the irritation in his eyes, I explain, "Rort means a fraudulent or dishonest practice."

My thighs wobble when he spits out, "Whatever you feel comfortable with, *Will.*" He sneers my name the same way Skylar did when she answered my call. "Instill us with your knowledge."

I nudge my shoulder up. "Alright."

If he thinks his livid glare will scare me into submission, he's shit out of luck. I only dispelled half the annoyance bubbling in my gut from the fat-shamer earlier tonight, so I've got plenty left to dish out.

"First, the players get paid too much. They run around a field, fighting over a ball you can pick up at any store for five bob. It's not rocket science, so why are they paid as if they're curing diabetes?"

Becca burrows her flaming cheeks into her husband's neck, losing me one set of bugged eyes. Unfortunately her surrender doesn't weaken the intensity brewing between Tarzan and me. If anything, her early departure from our conversation makes the intensity grow.

Never one to back down when challenged, I continue, "Second, what's with the whole defense/offense thing? If you can take a tackle, you should be able to give one."

Excitement trickles into my veins when Becca's husband nods as if he's agreeing with me. I must be getting through to him. I'll have him jumping the fence entirely once I've fattened the purse.

"And third..."

Fuck! I'm stuck but I have to give them something—because everyone knows, whether good or bad, everything comes in threes.

I nearly dance on the spot when my third annoyance crashes into me. "Their hot dogs are too expensive. The supporters already fork out a fortune for body paint, jerseys, and a ticket to the travesty, but no, that's not enough; let's slap them with an eight-dollar charge for a wiener in a bun. There are hookers in Vegas who charge less, so why the hell is something that doesn't even give you thirty seconds of satisfaction so expensive?"

I stop, impressed with myself... and perhaps a little embarrassed. Compared to the men's expensive suits and Becca's casual yet designer outfit, I already look like trailer trash, much less sound like it.

With a wave and a spin, I mumble, "And now that I've made a total fool of myself, I'm out."

"No, no, no, please stay." Becca chases me down, halting me before I can gallop down the concrete stairwell at the end of a deck with views for miles. "I wholeheartedly agree with you. Ask Dalton. I complain about the price of hot dogs at every game." She slings her eyes back to her husband. "Don't I, Dalton?" She gives him a look that warns he better agree with her.

"Yep. Every single game." His low mouse-like squeak doesn't match his big, burly frame.

Smiling like the cat who swallowed the canary, Becca returns her eyes to me. "And don't get me started on the players' salaries, or we'll be here all night."

Feeling more comfortable, I allow Becca to spin me back toward the door she rushed out of in a hurry only minutes ago. I really should leave, but with curiosity guiding my steps, I'm more reluctant to go than stay. I like Becca. She gives off a vibe that reveals our differences in age and wealth won't stop us from forming a friendship. For some inane reason, she likes me.

I highly doubt her male companions agree with her viewpoint.

"That's perfect, Willow. Thank you. Just leave it on the counter, and I'll bring it out when the dumplings are ready. "

Becca's praise makes it seem as if I hand-whipped the cream instead of using the fancy electric thingamajig every knocked-up wife has. With a mischievous grin, she barges me out of the kitchen with more gusto than an eight-month-pregnant woman should have.

"Why don't you go see what the boys are doing in the den?"

Before I can announce I'd rather eat uncooked liver, she pushes me into a room that's bigger than the entire floor of my college dorm. The den looks like a playful space... if you're a man stuck in the Stone Age. Bulky leather seats take up one corner of the room, surrounded by walls of liquor that extend from the floor to the ceiling. A black billiard table sits to my right, and a poker table is in the middle of the room. It's only just visible through the blinding rays of a mammoth TV that's playing highlights of the game I *unfortunately* missed tonight.

That's where Dalton and the still unnamed man sit. They're playing cards and smoking cigars while watching reruns. If that doesn't prove I'm out of my element tonight, nothing will.

With their focus rapt on some man sprinting down the sidelines, I mosey to the side of the room to summarize my evening so far. Although it has been odd, it's also been fun. Becca's personality is exactly how I envisioned. She's friendly, slightly kooky, and she loves her husband with every fiber of her being.

Dalton has a similar temperament to her. He dotes on his wife, but in a sexy, *makes me want to drool* type of way. He has a smoking-hot southern accent, and has laughed off my clumsiness as if it isn't the first time he's handled a ditzy college student.

Then there's the mystery man...

Who knew it was possible to sit down and share a meal with someone without their name being mentioned once? I know not all conversations start with, "Hey, blah-blah, can you pass me a napkin?" but politeness usually dictates an introduction—especially after they so rudely scorned the tree-hugging name your parents slapped you with. But nope, his name has been as safely guarded as his personality.

I honestly don't know if he thinks I'm funny or a complete nutter. If the suspicious glances he's given me from beneath lowered lashes many times tonight is any indication, I'll say he's five seconds away from calling the psychiatric ward to ask if any patients named Willow escaped tonight.

Spotting me lingering awkwardly at the edge of the vast space, Dalton lifts his dark eyes to mine. "Oh, hey, Willow, why don't you join us?"

See? He has no trouble saying my name, so why is he keeping quiet on his friend's identity? Seems a little suspicious to me.

When Dalton raises a brow, prompting me to answer him, I murmur, "It's okay. I'll wait for Becca. She mentioned something about dessert."

Good one, Will, bring up food like a piggy who didn't just scarf down two plates of Chinese without coming up for air. It wasn't my fault. I hadn't eaten since breakfast, and their Chinese was incomparable to the packet noodles I consume most nights. I swear, I nearly orgasmed when the honey chicken hit my taste buds. It was *that* good.

Not wanting to overstay my welcome, I hook my thumb over my shoulder. "I should probably call a taxi. It's getting late."

"It's barely eleven," Dalton scoffs at the same time the mystery man asks, "What's up, buttercup, afraid poor poker skills will make you lose more than your hate of all things American?"

Buttercup? Should I be pleased he's awarded me a nickname so quickly or annoyed? I'm not often given a nickname, so I'm inclined to swoon, but this one's double-meaning has me sitting on the fence. In theory, it sounds sweet, like a cupcake topped with delicious buttercream icing, but in reality, he could be insulting me.

Buttercup flowers are deadly when consumed by cattle and people. He is aware my parents gave me a tree/plant name, so did he nickname me Buttercup because he believes any man who devours me will learn from their stupidity by dying? Or...

Certain I'm looking too deeply into this, I answer, "No. I'm a good poker player. I just have limited funds on me." *None. I have none. Bar a few pennies in the bottom of my bag, I'm flat broke until Tuesday.* "I depleted my cash at a food truck outside of the stadium. Their pretzels were worth the splurge. They were only the teeniest bit stale."

I curse in my head when the man with the unamused brown eyes says, "You left the game for food? Wow. I thought maybe you just hated the players, but I'm quickly learning the error of my ways. You don't just hate the game, you hate American sports in their entirety."

"I didn't leave *during* the game. I left before it started, *thank you very much.*" My last words are only for my ears, but he can have the daggers firing from my eyes. "And I like sports. Just none that morons with half a brain play."

All my daggers miss their mark when he smirks. He has a really nice smile, even when it's delivered with a scowl. "Oh... sorry. I didn't realize your research extended to the players' academic capabilities. Please, excuse me. "

Not even Dalton can miss the sarcasm in his tone. "Elvis," he drawls out in a growl. "Play nice."

With the tension in the room at a stifling point, you'd think I would have more pressing matters to attend to than clenching my thighs together. I'm not doing Kegels because Elvis's narrowed eyes make his dark and brooding features even sexier; I'm doing everything in my power not to pee my pants.

My bladder full of wine stays where it should, but the girly shrill rumbling up my throat like thunder makes it hard to play it cool. I sound like a hyena seconds from gorging on a wildebeest. I'm in pure, man-meat heaven from karma slapping Elvis hard in the face.

After coughing to clear the laughter trapped in my throat, I ask, "Your name is Elvis?"

When his eyes narrow to barely a squint, all attempts to hold in my giggles are lost. I laugh like a lunatic, my chuckles coming out with the occasional snort from my lungs' brutal fight for air. I swear, I've never laughed so hard in my life. Tears roll down my cheeks unchecked as my almost bursting bladder holds on for the frightening ride.

"And here I was thinking they were keeping quiet on your identity because you're famous, but that wasn't it at all, was it? It's because your name is *Elvis*." I say his name with the disgusted gag every teen uses when forced to dissect frogs in science.

"Oh my god!" I take in several laugh-calming breaths to ensure he can hear me before asking, "Is your last name Presley?"

A completely unladylike bellow roars from my throat when Elvis throws his cards onto the tabletop.

"It is, isn't it?"

When he fails to deny my claims, I slap my knee. The chuckles bubbling up my chest are so boisterous, when I release them, I'm certain half the state can hear them.

"Don't get *All Shook Up*, Mate. There are worse names in the world. Like..." Even with my eyes watering from how hard I'm cackling, I stare Elvis dead set in the eyes before declaring, "Nope. I've got nothing. That's the *Devil in Disguise*. You can't *Return to Sender*. It's *Stuck on You!*"

Clutching my stomach, I bend in half. I really shouldn't have drunk all those glasses of wine Becca handed me, because right here, right now, I'm not just on the verge of peeing my pants, I'm acting like a drunken buffoon.

Elvis isn't to blame for the hideous name his parents lumped him with. If karma weren't in play, I'd act more respectfully, but unfortunately, payback is a bitch.

Only once my lungs warn of an impending asthma attack does my laughter lessen.

Elvis perches his kissable lips high in the air. "You good?"

"Yep." My chuckles find a second wind when I imagine Elvis's broad shoulders, thick biceps, and large frame being squeezed into the famous white sequined jumpsuit I saw at a museum last month. "In a minute."

I suck in three big breaths before forcing them out in a long, vibrating exhalation. "Okay, now I'm good."

My shuddering frame exposes I'm a lying piece of shit. The

video-like images rolling through my head are too much. I've never seen such a hilarious thing in all my life, and it isn't even real.

When Elvis stands to his feet and heads my way, I assure him, "I'm not laughing. I'm just coughing—repeatedly."

My giggles settle in an instant when he stops to stand in front of me, but nothing can fix my flaming red face. Have you ever laughed so hard your cheeks ache? That's me right now. They're burning even more than my ass did after the hundred squats I did this morning.

"Alright. I've got this now. I promise." I wipe under my eyes before straightening my spine. "I didn't mean you any disrespect."

I stomp down my foot like a child, hating that I'm about to cave. I'm not bowing out of the fight because Elvis's stare has more than just my pulse quickening; it's because I can't lie. That's why I have no filter. If my brain thinks it, you'll hear it, no matter how nuts it makes me appear.

"Okay, I did! I just thought maybe if you felt as humiliated as I did earlier, you'd go easier on me next time."

Half of my comment is for Elvis; the other half is for the scorning I didn't expect to be handed earlier tonight. I want to pretend my ego is big enough to sustain the most brutal blows, but that would be like saying Elvis's dark locks, thick lashes, and ruby-red lips are hideously ugly to look at. The stranger's comments dented my ego. It's only a slight bruise that will heal in a few days, but it's still big enough for me to feel its sting.

I don't realize my chin is balancing on my chest until Elvis raises it back to its original position. His hand is barely touching my chin, but his yummy smell makes up for his lack of contact. He smells freshly showered with a hint of a tangy cologne... and freshly cut grass.

Huh?

My eyes bounce between his somewhat icy, somewhat amused chocolatey eyes when he asks, "Next time? Did you not get enough of my brooding, moody silence tonight that you want a second round?"

Pretending I can't feel a flare of hope igniting in my gut, I reply,

"That's not what I meant. I was referring to Becca and Dalton. For some insane reason, Becca wants to be my friend. If I'm friends with Becca, that automatically makes me a friend of Dalton's, right?"

"I guess," Elvis agrees, peering down at me.

"Well, if I'm their friend, and you're their friend, at one stage we're bound to cross paths again. Right?"

He's not so quick to agree this time around. He remains quiet for several long seconds, his silence adding heat to my still flaming cheeks. There's just one difference: this is needy heat, not an amused heat.

My lungs start accepting air again when Elvis finally relents. "I guess that could occur. *Occasionally.*"

"You don't have to sound so disappointed." I throw my fist into his stomach. Bad move. This man is as impenetrable as the friction bouncing between us, but I'm confident I can get the ball back to my side of the court. "If you stay out of my hair, I'll stay out of yours. Deal?"

I thrust my hand toward him. He leaves me hanging by spinning on his heels and stalking across the room. After retaking his seat, he raises his eyes to me standing dumbfounded. "No deals are made in this house without a wager being placed, right, Dalton?"

"Uh..." Dalton grapples for a response, seemingly lost. "That's right?" His unease makes his confirmation sound more like a question.

My chest rises and falls in rhythm with the vein in Elvis's neck when he negotiates, "If you win, I'll agree with your deal. If you lose..."

I peer over my shoulder when his words trail off. There's no one behind me, so there's no reason for his sentence to fall short as it did. It seems like he doesn't know what he wants if he wins.

My theory is proven accurate when he says, "We'll discuss the fine print later." With a smirk that reveals there's a lot more to him than the brooding, muscle-loaded shell he's been displaying all evening, he asks, "Peanuts or plain?"

I'm confused... until I peer down at the poker table. They're not betting with money. The tabletop is covered with M&Ms.

I pace closer to them. "Are peanut M&Ms worth more than their skinny counterparts?"

When Dalton shakes his head, I say, "Then I'll have plain. Everyone knows you get more candy per packet since they're smaller."

"But they don't taste as good," Elvis interjects.

Smiling, I nod. "True. But I'm not here for the candy." I take the empty seat next to him before leaning into his side. "I'm here to keep your mitts out of my hair."

It could be the alcohol heating my veins, but I swear displeasure is the first thing to cross Elvis's face during my confession. My breath can't be blamed for his ghastly response, either. I steered clear of any dishes that included ginger or garlic. Don't ask me why. I've already lied once today, so I'd hate to break your trust for the second time.

CHAPTER FOUR

Presley

"You're lying! That can't be right. I have a straight. How can a bunch of random cards beat a straight?"

Willow stares at me with wide, glassy eyes. She's confident I'm lying but aware I have no reason to. The final eight M&Ms she went all in with won't be missed in the massive stockpile in front of me, but she's not giving in.

Becca and Dalton bowed out nearly an hour ago, but Willow played a good, logical game... until she thought she had a winning hand.

"I have a flush—"

"Your cards aren't in any order." She waves her hand over my cards. "They just have hearts on them. I have a straight. Three, four, five, six, seven." She counts out her usually impressive hand onto the felt with force. "I win."

She stops dragging a massive pile of rainbow candy to her side of the table when Becca grimaces. "Elvis is right, Willow. A flush ranks higher than a straight."

Willow slumps into her chair, the candy only halfway across the table. "Really?"

I scoff, peeved she believes Becca in an instant. I shouldn't be shocked. I could tell her I'm allergic to peanuts, and she'd stuff peanut M&Ms into my mouth to test the theory. I guess I somewhat deserve her distrust. I did make out I was planning to arrest her when we met. I also did a stellar job of acting annoyed at her description of ballers.

I'm a little annoyed, but not enough to display it to a stranger. To be honest, it's nice hearing someone's open rawness for a change. Dalton and I are surrounded by people paid to kiss our asses. Dalton escapes the madness by returning home to his wife who keeps him grounded. I don't have access to the same crutch.

Even when I was engaged, Lillian didn't bring me back to earth. She stroked my ego so much, I thought I was invincible. When the doctors told me I had broken my back, I didn't believe them. I was Presley Carlton: number one draft pick, star quarterback, and captain of the world-renowned 69ers. I was not a cripple.

I lived in that bubble for the eight weeks following my accident. It only burst when I attended my first physical therapy session after surgery. Even with a brace designed to hold my back in exact alignment, I could barely take a step. I was out of shape, pissed at the world, and blaming everyone but the man responsible: me.

I drank a fifth of bourbon before getting behind the wheel of my flashy sports car.

I raced through the streets of New York at an excessive speed.

I plowed into a multi-passenger van without my foot touching the brake.

And it was me who nearly ended an entire family's existence faster than I could snap my fingers.

But do you know what? They weren't mentioned in any of the reports that circulated after my accident. They weren't brought up when Lillian sought advice on my case from spinal specialists from around the world. No one spoke a word about them until I woke up screaming because the weight on my chest finally grew too much for me to bear.

It wasn't the brace pinning me to my sweat-drenched sheets.

It was guilt.

I was told over and over again that I didn't do anything wrong.

That the accident wasn't my fault even with my vehicle being cleared of any malfunctions. They said what they thought I wanted to hear instead of the truth.

So, having someone like Willow call it as it is isn't just amusing to watch, it's refreshing.

I'm snapped from dark and dreary thoughts when candy crunching sounds through my ears.

"Are you eating my candy?"

Willow's light blue eyes lock with mine. "No." The smears of chocolate on her teeth reveal her lie, much less the brown dribble pooling in the corner of her plump lips. "I'm eating *my* candy. I don't care what any of you say, a straight *always* beats a flush."

Stealing my chance to reply, she stands from her seat and makes her way across the room. I had wondered earlier if the wine she had with dinner added to her sultry walk. It didn't. She hasn't had a drop of alcohol in over three hours, yet her walk is still sexy as fuck.

I stop staring at the generous sway of her ass when she renegotiates our deal, "Best out of three. Winner takes all." She nudges her head to a large billiard table.

I'm fucking wrecked. I was up at six this morning for a PT session to loosen my muscles before I was assessed by the team doctors at eight AM to ensure I was fit to play, but not even drooping eyelids will make me decline Willow's challenge. I don't back down when challenged. Not even when the odds are stacked against me.

My imminent return to my glory days will be undeniable proof of that.

◆

"I thought you said you've played before?"

Willow attempts to roll her eyes. They only get halfway around before they do a weird twitchy *I look like I'm having a fit* spasm. After returning them front and center with a shake of her head, she narrows them at me. "I have played before... *just not on a table this big.*"

"Not accustomed to handling big things?"

Cocking her hip, she spreads her hand across its generous swell. She looks like she wants to say something, but she can't. She walked straight into that one, and she knows it.

After a few seconds of deliberation, she finally unearths a comeback. "I've handled my fair share."

Even though she's a terrible liar, anger is the first thing to pummel me. *Or is it jealousy?* Whatever the fuck it is, I shouldn't be feeling it. Willow's not here for a long time. She's the post-game entertainment Dalton and I skipped tonight to check on Becca. She's full of fun, but only recommended in minimal doses.

Pissed—more at myself than Willow's inability to hit a cue ball—I head to her side of the table. "You need to hit the white ball."

She glares at me. "I know that, you nincompoop. It's working out how to reach it when it's in the middle of the friggin' table. Unlike you, I don't have octopus tentacles for arms." She snaps her eyes to Becca and sighs. "Why did you partner me with him again? I thought we had sisterhood vibes going on."

Becca smiles before cuddling into Dalton's side. She's not cozying up; she's holding him down so he can't retaliate to her reply. "Dalton doesn't like watching me play with other men's cue sticks."

"Damn straight," Dalton agrees without pause.

I wish they were joking, but not even the giant baby bump separating them can come between Dalton's possessiveness of Becca. How do I know this? I may have used his neurosis against him a handful of times the past nine years. The first time was during a competition similar to this. It was the night Dalton was smacked on his ass by a brunette way out of his league. He and Becca have been inseparable ever since.

With that night on my mind, I put my cue stick in its rack before moving closer to Willow. She watches me with the same doe-eyed look she's been giving me all night. It's not a shy look. It's more uneasy than anything. She can't read me, and it's frustrating her as much as my cock's numerous meetings with my zipper any time she purses her lips has frustrated me. She has a mouth men can't help but pay attention to, because there's no way lips as fleshy as hers wouldn't give good head. They're too meaty and erotic to belong to a good girl who'd never get on her knees. That'd be a grave injustice to mankind. God would never be so cruel.

Pretending my dick isn't once again consulting with my zipper, I say, "You need to brace your arm better so your stick doesn't bow no matter how loose your hold is."

I adjust one of her hands until it's halfway down her cue before moving her other one to the very bottom. "Gentle, Buttercup. Do you strangle a cock when you caress it? Or do you apply just enough pressure it feels both nice and firm?"

My zipper bites my cock when she replies, "Depends. Some guys like it rough."

With a wink revealing she didn't just return my serve, she ended our game altogether, she arches over the billiard table. Her shirt clings to her skin when I place my hand on the small of her back.

"You're not waiting for him to climb aboard and take himself for a ride, Willow. You're meant to ride him as much as he rides you." Ignoring the fact her ass is in prime position for me to whip out my cock and drive home, I growl, "Lower."

Willow drops her ass an inch.

"Lower."

She bobs down another half-inch.

"Even lower."

Becca giggles when Willow roars, "Jesus Christ, Elvis! Am I fucking the table or is the table fucking me?"

Not thinking, I lean over her shoulder to fire off a retort. Since she's so tiny—I'd guess a maximum of five feet, four inches—every inch of her is swamped by my body. Not even Dalton and Becca's prying eyes can see her. My nostrils flare as I suck in her scent. She smells pretty, like candy and sugar and a wicked naughtiness that derails my train of thought in an instant.

"The only thing about to get fucked on this table is you if you don't make this shot."

Either turned on by my threat or scared, Willow's spine snaps straight. Since she is holding her cue stick away from her body, it sails into the air. When it collides with the light suspended over the billiard table, she yanks it back with force. Every bad deed I've ever done is answered for when the butt of her stick, along with her fist, slams into my crotch—my extended crotch because of the syrupy scent of her hair.

With watering eyes and the groan of a man crawling to his death, I stumble backward. I've been tackled more times than you can count, had three ribs broken by a bull when I visited Dalton's ranch for his bachelor party, and survived a head-on collision with another vehicle, yet this is by far the most painful thing I've ever experienced.

I fall to the ground with a thud, my hands unsure whether they should protect my face or my crotch. They go for the latter, confident it can't endure anymore pain. I don't feel any wetness on my cheeks, but that doesn't mean I'm not crying. This fucking hurts. *It hurts sooo bad.*

"Oh my god. I'm so sorry."

Incapable of speaking through the pain shredding me to pieces, Willow takes my silence as a call for help. After dumping a half-consumed bottle of wine from an ice bucket on the bar, she upends the soggy slop into a napkin that is powerless to hold its wetness, drops to her knees, then presses her makeshift ice-pack to my crotch.

Now matters are ten times worse.

The napkin crumbles within a nanosecond of absorbing the soggy remains of the ice bucket, so nothing but a few shards of ice separate Willow's hands and my crotch. The only good that comes from this highly embarrassing situation is confirmation she hasn't permanently injured me. My cock is inflating so quickly, I can feel its pulse over the pain strumming through my veins, and I'm not the only one noticing it.

"Oh no, you're swelling up. Maybe we should call an ambulance?"

I stop Willow from grabbing her backpack at the same time Becca and Dalton lose their shit. They howl in hysterics, not the least bit concerned their best man is down for the count in their den.

"I don't need an ambulance."

"Are you sure?" Willow's wide eyes bounce between mine before they return to my crotch. "What if you sustain permanent damage... *down there*? I'll never forgive myself if *he* stops working." Her words grow weaker with every one she speaks.

"I'm sure he'll be okay..." My assurance ends with a groan when I attempt to stand. Who could have known a girl as short and as pretty as Willow could take down a man my size? "I'll be fine. I just need to walk it off."

"That's right, Elvis. Walking it off will help." Dalton's southern drawl is colored with both laughter and remorse. "If it doesn't, Willow can always borrow Becca's naughty nurse outfit to ensure that type of swelling is normal."

Snagging a pool ball off the table, I peg it at his head. He's standing next to his heavily pregnant wife, but even with crushed nuts, I'm confident in my throwing skills. I didn't sign a thirty-seven million dollar contract fresh out of college for no reason. I'm the best quarterback in the industry... Well, I will be when they clear me to play in that position again.

Not as annoyed by Dalton's sneer as me, Willow says, "I can take a look, if you want?" She waves her hand to my saggy trousers that are clinging to my frozen crotch.

My teeth grit when I drop my eyes. I look like I pissed my pants.

Once again taking my silence as a cry for help, Willow steps closer to me. Her eyes float up from my crotch when I say, "It's okay. I've got a handle on things."

I glare at Dalton when he snickers, "You sure do. You're *hand*ling things mighty fine right now." He swallows several times in a row when he's subjected to my fury, but his smile doesn't fade. "What? I'm just looking out for you."

I take back every nice thing I've ever said about him. He isn't the best wingman there is. He's shit. The worst on the planet. Proof? I asked him to keep my focus off Willow and her fantastic tits, not encourage the stupid thoughts in my head. Willow is too young for me to mess with, so young, I'm beginning to wonder how dated the YouTube video she mentioned earlier is. It could have been recorded last week for all I know.

After taking in the cue ball-sized hole next to Dalton's head, the dangling light above the billiard table, and the indent in the carpet from where I fell like a bag of shit, I realize it's time to call it a night.

When I announce my decision, Willow agrees with me. "Good idea." She gathers her backpack before shifting on her feet to face Becca. "What cab services come out this way?" She has her cell-phone at the ready to call a taxi.

I linger at the side, pretending I haven't spotted Dalton's numerous head nudges to Willow. I like her; she's quick-witted, smart, and sexy as fuck yet completely unaware of her beauty, but a whack to the nuts is the only warning I need that I've delved too far into murky waters tonight. Her calling a taxi may be the only life vest thrown my way, and I'm not giving it up for anything.

"Stop it," I half-whisper/half-mouth to Dalton when he adds a snarl to his head nudge. "She wants to go home in a taxi. Let her go home in a taxi."

He performs a gesture no thirty-year-old male should, but it relays his thoughts with crystal clear precision. He thinks I'm playing with myself.

We can only hope after the jab my balls just endured.

When Willow shadows Becca into the kitchen to see what car services are operating this late at night, Dalton stops using gestures. "You're a fucking idiot, Elvis. Offer the girl a ride home."

I continue my stubborn stance by folding my arms over my chest.

It doesn't faze Dalton, though. "Why the fuck would you turn down an opportunity like this? There is so much heat between you two, I would have made Becca leave the room if she weren't already pregnant. You two are the very definition of immaculate conception."

I would laugh if he wasn't being serious. There's an abundance of attraction between Willow and me, but it's not happening. Not tonight. Not next week. Not even next month.

When I tell Dalton that, he yells, "Why. *The. Fuck.* Not?"

I throw my hands into the air. "Because of what you said earlier.

You said 'girl.' I've got enough shit to swim through; I'm not adding fooling around with a minor to the mix."

Dalton glares at me. "Don't treat me like an idiot. I saw you watching her when she was pretending not to watch you, and from the number of times you've adjusted your crotch, I'm reasonably sure you know she's a woman."

He steps closer to me. Guilt is lining his face. "But just to be safe, I took a peek at her license when she went to the bathroom. She's twenty-two." He grimaces as if his next set of words are arriving with a bucket load of vomit. "In a few weeks... perhaps months."

"Which is it, Dalton? Weeks or months?" I'm tired, dealing with throbbing nuts, and having inappropriate thoughts about a girl who is either eight or nine years younger than me.

Eight I could be okay with. Nine... I'm not so sure about that. That's bordering on gross old man/daddy issues to me.

After scrubbing the stubble on his chin, Dalton murmurs, "It's months, but only four—"

My brows rocket up my face. "So I'll be thirty-one for a few weeks while she's *only* twenty-one? Fuck, Dalton. That's wrong. So very *very* wrong."

Dalton screws up his face. "No, it's not. Age doesn't matter when sparks are flying."

"Says the guy married to a woman who's only sixteen days younger than him."

"We're not talking marriage, Elvis. Just a bit of fun. A little playtime to loosen the tight strings you've been controlled by the past twelve months."

I smack him in the chest before giving him a stern finger point. "If you ever use a word like 'playtime' around me *ever* again, I'll rearrange your face." I check that the coast is still clear before asking, "Besides, who says she wants me? You heard her. She thinks football players are dumb fucks who get paid to chase a ball around a field."

"We do get paid to chase a ball around a field," Dalton's reply reveals whose side he's on. He's not my wingman anymore; he's Willow's.

Fucking traitor!

I halfheartedly shrug, my attitude at an all-time high. There is a bro-code no man should ever cross—Dalton just crossed it.

"You might get paid to fuck around, but I don't. I earn every penny I get."

Dalton's arched brow reveals he doesn't believe a word I'm speaking, but he remains quiet on that matter, preferring to take up his first campaign. "Come on, Elvis, admit it. You like her as much as we do because she brings out a side of you no one has seen in years."

His comment shows he's including Becca. Even though she's not in the room, she's still a part of our conversation.

"Tonight was the first time in a long time I saw the man who stood at my side when I married the love of my life. There were points during the past decade I thought you'd never come back."

I won't lie, his words get me a little choked up. I know what he's saying—*whole-fucking-heartedly*—but there is more at stake here than just the resurrection of a personality.

"Things are complicated."

Dalton nods in full agreement. "I know, brother, I know." He slaps my shoulder before giving it a squeeze. "Just like I knew Lillian wasn't good for you, and Willow quite possibly could be. But you'll never make any sense out of it if you don't take a leap of faith."

Those are the exact words I spoke to him when his feelings for Becca took him by surprise. He was scared. Rightfully so. They had the world against them, yet they still made it out of the storm without a drop of rain on them.

"She's ten years younger than me—"

Dalton purses his lips. "Nine, but who's counting?"

I continue crossing off my objections as if he never spoke. "She's nothing like Lillian—"

He makes a *duh* face. "Like that's a bad thing."

"And..."

I flex my fists, lost on another objection. Dalton was right on the money when it came to Lillian. He called her a blood-sucking leech on many occasions—long before we became a couple. Did I listen to him? No, I didn't. Did I pay for my error? Yeah, in more ways than you'll ever understand. Have I learned from my mistake? Up until ten minutes ago, I would have said no. Now... now I'm just praying I get out of tonight alive.

"Fine. I'll drive her home." Before Dalton can fist bump me, I warn, "But if things go south, I get naming rights for your kid."

Not giving him the chance to reply, I enter the kitchen. Stupid ass nerves grown men like me shouldn't have settle when Willow watches me cross the room. She's pretending to peruse a taxi pamphlet. Her acting skills are so top-shelf that if her syrupy smell didn't intensify with every step I take, I would believe she hasn't spotted me.

It's a pity for her I'm smarter than she thinks.

It's also a pity her good deed is about to be rewarded in the most controversial way.

CHAPTER FIVE

Willow

"Are you sure you don't mind? I'm happy to take a taxi home."

Although I'm giving Elvis an out, latching my seatbelt shows my eagerness to stay. It isn't that I'm hopeful something magical is about to occur between us. I just want a chance to apologize for announcing his erection to his friends as if it were a gross deformity.

It was far from gross—quite the opposite actually—I've just never handled so much... *man-meat* I was petrified I had badly injured him.

I give up waving goodbye to Becca and Dalton when Elvis lies, "It's fine. My apartment isn't far from your university."

I know he's lying because Becca mentioned his apartment was only a few blocks over numerous times when our evening began. That's the only snippet of information she disclosed on him in over eight hours. Apparently, my legendary interrogation skills aren't as stellar as I had hoped. Bar his name and impressive crotch size, Elvis still remains a mystery.

Aiming to ease my curiosity, I ask, "Investment banker?"

His mysteriousness has me so twisted up in knots, even with it being past 4 AM, I'm a live-wire. My veins are thrumming with excitement, and sweat is beading on my top lip. It's lucky the confines of his car are dark, or I'd look like one hot-ass mess.

When Elvis smirks before shaking his head, I guess again, "Stock broker?"

His smile picks up, as does his shaking head.

"Insurance consultant?"

His eyes stray from the nearly deserted road to me. "What about any of this..." When he drags his hand down his body, I pretend I wasn't already ogling it by following his hand's descent, "... screams soft cock with a stick shoved up his ass?"

"Your hair." I slap my hand over my mouth, mortified I said my comment out loud. I'm not really embarrassed. I just don't want Elvis to think I'm a total bitch.

"Oh, okay, now my hair is an issue?" His tone is more playful than grumpy. He's got the uptight, brooding personality down pat, but I can see a glimmer in his eyes that reveals he's got a mischievous side he's yet to expose. "And exactly what is wrong with my hair?"

"It has that messy look, like you just got out of bed." *Like a woman ran her fingers through it while you ate her out like you hadn't eaten in a week.*

My inner thoughts annoy me more than they please me. Elvis's hair is so thick and luxurious, I have no doubt I'm not the first woman to fantasize about gripping it while he goes down on me. Add his messy locks to his chiseled jaw, piercing brown eyes, and undeniably fit body, and you've got the perfect package to have women's heads in a tizzy.

I'm extra woozy just from sitting across from him the past five minutes. I thought my flighty response was because our shoulders touched when he entered his flashy yet compact car, but now I'm not so sure. The sweat beading on my lip isn't the only sticky situation I'm handling right now, and no, I'm not referring to my undies... sorry, let me correct that, panties. I'm so hot, I wind down the window, hoping some fresh air will settle my erratic heart rate.

"You alright?" Elvis drags his eyes over my sweat-beaded face before dropping them to my cleavage. He's not checking me out

—*unfortunately*—he's taking in the drenched edge of my low neckline. "Bedhead gets you that upset?"

"It's not that..." I stop speaking as my stomach makes a noise it should never make, much less when I'm sitting in a very small car with a very handsome man. "Please hurry."

Elvis flattens his foot to the floor before my two short words leave my mouth. It could be the clamping of my hand over my mouth advising him to hurry, or the horrid smell vaporing between us. My stomach is churning so badly, pockets of gas were bound to be released at some stage. Unfortunately, they didn't wait for me to give them permission.

Elvis peers at me in disgust. "Jesus, Willow, is that you?"

"No!" I doubt he can hear my denial over the loud grumble making its way from my stomach to my back entrance. "That smell isn't me! It's coming from outside."

I'm such a liar. I didn't mean to fart; I just had no choice. My stomach was cramping so intensely, it snuck out before I knew it was coming.

Elvis slides down his window before angling his head so his flaring nostrils catch the night air streaming past. "Oh sweet lord. That's not natural. You really should get that checked."

I punch him in the bicep, unappreciative of his humor. I'm five seconds from dying, and he's laughing like he's at the Comedy Club.

When we brake at a red light, the couple in the car next to us glare at me with their brows pulled together. Elvis's head is hanging out the window like a dog enjoying a late afternoon drive in summer. There's just one difference: he has plugged his nose.

Not the least bit embarrassed at the attention we're gaining, Elvis waves at the couple with his spare hand. They don't wave back.

"Please stop. They're looking at me funny."

My words arrive with a barrage of giggles, making the tightness in my stomach even more noticeable. I can't do this. Just like it isn't possible to have both a big bust and a tiny waist, it's impossible not to giggle and fart at the same time.

I clutch my stomach with all my might, praying that whatever is in there stays put until I make it back to my dorm. "Just go, please!"

"It's a red light." Elvis's deep timbre is muffled since he's still protecting his nose from the horrid stench lingering between us. "I can't run a red light."

"Yes, you can. I'll pay the fine if you get one..." My words taper off when the most unladylike noise rumbles from my stomach to my throat. It may be only a burp, but it's as unpleasant as the sneaky fart I released two minutes ago. "Please, Elvis. Please, please, please, please, please."

I stop begging when his dark car slips through the intersection at a rate fast enough we don't collide with any cars that have the right of way, but not fast enough to miss the flash of a red camera light. I'm as broke as a pregnant hooker, but I'll find the money to pay his fine. I'll work extra shifts, or force Skylar into a rant that will have our swear jar brimming with one dollar bills. I'll do anything... once I've brought myself out of the trench I plan on hiding in for eternity.

Elvis's eyes stray from a row of buildings on our right to me. "Which one is yours?"

"Any. The closest. Just pull over!"

Not waiting for him to heed my demand, I fling open his door, toss off my seatbelt with so much force I nearly whack him in the head, then hightail it to the closest dormitory. All the buildings in my university are configured the same way. They have a lobby with two guest toilets. One of them better be free, or I'm about to gain a new nickname.

"Shall I call you?"

I'm clutching my butt cheeks together as forcefully as vomit is racing up my esophagus, but nothing will stop me flipping Elvis the bird. He didn't ask his question with genuine interest. It was brimming with hilarity, like my embarrassment is the most entertaining thing he's ever encountered.

Wanker.

CHAPTER SIX

Presley

I wait for Willow to enter the dorm she's charging toward before slipping into my car. My body is shuddering so hard, my chuckles have coated my skin with a dense layer of sweat, and my stomach is aching.

I'm an ass for laughing, but my god, when Karma comes to play, she leaves no survivors. Willow is a hoot; she speaks it as she sees it and doesn't hesitate to put people in their place, but even she was left speechless by the smell her body was excreting. The stench was so thick, you could cut it with a knife. It reminded me of when the guys and I went on a spinach diet to shed the chub before our championship weekend. Seventy eighteen-year-old males doing a cleanse with only eight toilets. The odds were stacked against us from the start.

After dragging my hand across my nape to remove the sweat sitting there, I latch my belt. Its click sounds familiar, but the noise coming from my stomach is brand new. I've never heard my gut make such a disturbing noise. It's usually as solid as iron—nothing affects it.

"Oh sweet Jesus," I murmur to myself when pain shreds

through my midsection so hard and fast, I nearly fold in two. "Oh, no, motherfucker, you're not doing *that* here."

Burning rubber lingers in my nostrils when I slam into reverse and tear out of the parking spot I barely made it into before Willow evacuated my car as quickly as my stomach's contents are attempting to exit my body.

Guilt for laughing at Willow slams into me as I race through the isolated streets at a speed too fast to be safe. The pain is intense, almost as extreme as when she rammed her cue stick into my nuts.

I make the usual twenty-minute trip to my apartment in under eight. The light traffic aided in my race, but so did my foot's love of the gas pedal. A plume of gas follows my track up the stairs to my front door. Every step is the equivalent of having a knife stabbed into my rectum.

What the fuck is this, and why is Karma biting my ass? I behaved tonight... for the most part.

"No!"

I hold my finger in the air, suspending Danny from breaking into a conversation when I enter my home. He's camping on my sofa while his place is being fumigated. Little does he know he's about to face a brand new type of fumigation. My charge across the living room should advise him of my urgency, much less the tight grip of my jaw.

I've been in the bathroom for nearly ten minutes before Danny risks death to knock on the door. "Are you alright? Do you want me to light a match?"

I groan, hating the mirth in his tone but understanding it. I thought it was hilarious when this was happening to Willow. Now I feel like a dipshit.

"I'm never eating Chinese again."

"Oh..." I can't see Danny, but I can imagine his face screwed up in thought. "There's an all-night pharmacy around the corner; want me to go grab you something?"

My lips perk. When Danny asked if he could sleep on my couch, all I saw were negatives. I never thought it could benefit me.

"That would be great."

Danny's shadow stops moving away from the door when I shout his name. "While you're there, can you do me a favor?"

CHAPTER SEVEN

Willow

My bare feet shuffle along the floorboards as I make the eight steps between my bed and my door. I feel like death warmed up. Last night was... I don't have words. Horrendous. Disgusting. I'm never *ever* eating Chinese food again. If it isn't bad enough I passed wind in front of a stranger, my dormitory only has communal bathrooms. It's been a horrible five hours, and I'd give anything to restart—minus the gobbling of uncooked chicken.

After gripping the doorknob with a sweat-coated hand, I swing open my door. "It's 9 AM on a Sunday; what the hell do you want?"

A man I'd guess to be early to late-twenties balks when he sees me. It's not his fault. I'm braless, shoeless, and pants-less. I can barely see through the bags swelling under my eyes, and the minute bit of mascara I had on yesterday is smeared on my cheek. I can't see it, but I can feel it.

"Yep. That's vomit," I murmur through a gag when his eyes zoom in on a blob of brown I was too woozy to handle at 6 AM.

I rest my head on the doorframe before raising my bloodshot eyes to his. "What do you want?" I think that's what I say. I can't be certain, though. My pulse is thumping into my ears too loudly to be confident of anything.

"Ah..." His wide eyes drop to a clipboard in his hand. "I have a delivery for a Willow." He returns his eyes to me. "Is that you?"

"Yep." I do a one-handed clap, demanding he cough up the goods.

When he fails to immediately jump to my command, I attempt to snatch the bag out of his hand. He yanks it back with barely a second to spare, his dramatics too much for my thumping head.

I take back my hate of his theatrics when his high-pitched tone drills through my eardrums, "You're the third Willow I've approached this morning, so I've got to be certain it's you before I can hand over the goods."

I shove him backward by his fancy-schmancy satin shirt. "Look, mate, just keep it. I don't care what it is. It's yours. I've got dying to do, so I don't have time for this shit."

He's saved from having my door slammed in his face when he asks, "Do your... *farts* smell like a potato chip sandwich you forgot to take out of a gym bag at the end of the semester?"

His question resurrects me from the dead. "Excuse me?" My girly voice is as high as his perfectly manicured brow.

"I'm just reading what it says here." He spins his clipboard around to face me then taps on a handwritten sheet attached to it. After turning it back to himself, he continues reading, "It's not a fresh chip sandwich smell. It's the acidic scent you get when you open the moldy packaging to inspect the watery contents at the bottom, because you're stunned something that was once a solid mass has turned to mush."

He raises his eyes to mine, his expression deadpan. "Is that you?"

I have no clue how he's keeping such a straight face. Mine is flaming with embarrassment, because no matter how much I wish what he's saying is inaccurate, it's spot on. That's exactly what the horrible stench expelling from me last night and most of this morning smelled like.

"What's in the bag?"

Hearing the threat in my tone, the sassy-faced man takes a step back. "I can't tell you that without proof you're the intended receiver."

"Oh... you want proof?"

Finally, his gills green. It isn't my attitude that reeks of pompousness causing his whitening cheeks. It's me turning my bloodshot, *I'm minutes from barfing on your hideous shirt* eyes to the vomit bucket leaning against my single bed. My room is dark, but not dark enough to hide the tragedy that occurred here last night.

"It's fine!" he swears, halting my steps to the bucket mid-stride. "I'm satisfied you are who you say you are."

I return my eyes to his like I'm a zombie seconds from sucking out his brains. "Are you sure? I don't mind giving you proof. I'd hate for you to get in trouble."

He thrusts a bag of goodies into my chest. His shove is so forceful, I topple a few steps back. "It's fine. We're good."

He charges down the hallway so fast he's nothing but a blur. My steps back to my bed are nowhere near as brisk. I stomp the eight paces like I'm an elephant, and the paper bag filled with *god knows what* is my trunk.

I flop onto my mattress headfirst. I sweated so much overnight, my pillow is damp, but I don't care. Clean sheets, showering, and all those other basic hygienic things people do every day can wait until I'm not dying.

If only my curiosity could be cured as quickly.

With a groan, I raise my head off the pillow and shift my eyes to the bag I dumped next to my spew bucket. It's not a standard grocery bag. It's a little smaller and a bit thicker. While blowing a strand of curly brown hair from my eyes, I gather the bag in my hands. It feels heavier now than it did when I stomped it across the room, probably because I have my elbow propped on my mattress.

When I pull open the stapled bag and peer inside, a long, sickening sob tears from my throat. The contents inside should be a godsend to a woman in my condition, but it's knowing only one person in the world could have purchased these for me that has me whining. They're products to alleviate gas, stomach cramps, and the many other bodily functions I endured last night. There's even a packet of gum and a scented candle.

I flop back onto my bed, my hand darting up to cover my mortified eyes. This is ten times worse than when Tracy Skulski broke wind halfway through our routine at a dance competition when we were in kindergarten. It took eight years for her to live down her infamous Stinky Skulski nickname. I don't want to be called Windy Willow until I'm thirty. It might have been cute when I was three, but no one over the age of thirteen wants a nickname—not a farting one, anyway.

The bag landing on the floor with a thud coincides with my room door being flung open so forcefully it indents the drywall.

"Oh my fucking gawd!" Skylar saunters across the room, her hips swaying like she didn't drag her ass out of bed four hours ago to start her day doing boxing with a hottie all the girls at our college clamber out of bed at 5 AM to ogle.

I'd usually be there with bells on as well, but I'm dying, remember?

"You're an internet sensation! You're everywhere. *TMZ*, *The Late Show*, you even had a feature on *Good Morning America* this morning."

"W-w-what?" My stammering heart is heard in my reply. "What do you mean?"

"Your video is everywhere." She plants her backside on the edge of my bed, her nose screwing up when the duvet riles up the smell circling the vomit bucket. "Over two million views every hour."

"An hour?" I shoot up so fast, my head grows woozy. "Which video? Does Todd know? We were just playing; it was never supposed to go viral." My words come out in such quick succession, even I have a hard time understanding them.

"Todd?" Skylar takes a moment to read the confusion in my eyes before shooing it away with a wave of her manicured hand. "Not your dancing videos, silly, the one from last night."

"Last night?" I swallow numerous times in a row, my mouth suddenly burning. "Someone took a video of last night?"

Not spotting my wide eyes and panting chest, Skylar nods. "Uh-huh. There are multiple copies, but this one is getting the most attention—it has the best angle. Don't worry, even under the circumstances, you look sexy as sin."

Images of Elvis's head hanging out the window with a plugged nose flash before my eyes. *How could that ever be considered sexy?*

"Here. Look. This video alone has twenty-three million views."

She swivels her iPhone screen my way. I suck in my first breath in nearly a minute when I realize the video isn't about the *incident* that occurred last night. Well, it is, just not the one where I farted in front of God's gift to women. It's my altercation with the drunken idiot at the football stadium.

"Someone recorded the entire event and uploaded it to YouTube, making you an overnight internet sensation."

My shocked gaze dances between Skylar's bright baby blues. "A sensation? Or..." I leave my question open for her to answer how she sees fit.

"Sensation..." She screws up her nose. "For the most part."

"What does that mean?" My voice is too high and too loud for a woman on her death bed.

Skylar runs her hand down my sweaty arm in comfort. "Most of the comments are good, but you know what some keyboard warriors are like." She scrolls through the thousands of comments displayed under the now still video. "There's a handful of people not happy you retaliated, then a few who agree with the tosser."

Her use of one of my favorite Aussie slang words lightens the tension between us.

"A majority are with you, Willow. The praise far exceeds the occasional gripe."

She scrolls slowly, allowing me to see a handful of the comments.

BETSY2517

You showed him, girl!

KATEMBRIMGINTON21

I didn't think superheroes existed anymore
until I stumbled upon this recording.
Whoever this woman is, she's the new
Wonder Woman.

MARCSINTOWN

Call me. I want to prove not all men are like
him. You're so fucking beautiful, I get hard
every time I imagine what your lips taste like.

My eyes rocket to Skylar after reading the last one.

She laughs at my shocked expression. "That's one of *many* invitations. Last count was thirteen proposals, fifty-eight requests for a date, and you don't want to know how many are praying for a booty call. That dry spell you've been having the past three years is about to become the Nile."

"I can't go out with these men."

Skylar bows her brow. "Why not? No one says you have to sleep with them... but you can order the most expensive steak on the menu." Waggling her brows, she stands to her feet and crosses the room. "Leticia suggested holding out when you're approached for an interview. The more disinterested you seem, the higher their bid will be."

"What are you talking about? What interview?"

She removes her gym shirt and hideous sports bra before pivoting to face me. "This is huge, Will, like massive. You're going to be broadcast around the world." She latches a lacy bra around her tiny frame before moving to her half of our closet that is brimming with clothes. "With you not being the owner of the video, you won't make any profits from the marketing it brings in, but that doesn't mean you won't see any money. The world is your oyster, if you want it to be."

She stops rummaging through her clothes when I murmur, "What if I don't want it to be?"

My question stumps her for all of two seconds. "Why wouldn't you want this? You wanted to be famous—here's your chance."

"I wanted to be a prima ballerina, not an internet sensation who rides her five seconds of fame all the way to the bank." I clutch my stinky pillow to my tummy while my eyes drift to the ground. "This doesn't feel right."

The guilt I felt yesterday returns stronger than ever. I was as much of a bully as the man who confronted me. I also assaulted him. I don't want that broadcast to the world. I'd rather be happy and poor than rich and nasty.

After slipping a flirty dress over her slender thighs, Skylar moves back to my side of the room. "You can do as little or as much with this as you want, Will. The choice is entirely yours."

A small grin tugs at my lips. "Thank you."

Her wink tells me my praise wasn't needed, but the press of her lips to my sweaty temple shows she appreciated it. "You're still warm. Are you sure you don't want me to run down to the drug store and pick something up?"

The concern in her voice warms my heart. "Thanks, but I'm okay. I got everything I need right here." I nudge my knee against the brown pharmacy bag.

"You went out?" Not waiting for me to answer her, Skylar snaps down to gather the bag in her hands. "Jesus, you've got an entire medicine cabinet in here." She raises a box of Gastro Stop tablets in the air before spinning around to show me the price on the back. "You went for the good stuff." Her eyes bug out of her head. "Where did you find thirty-eight dollars for a box of colon cloggers?"

"I didn't. They were bought for me."

Hearing something in my voice I didn't mean to express, Skylar slaps away my hand before it gets within an inch of the bag. "Someone bought these for you?" Her perfectly manicured brow inches high on her face when I halfheartedly nod. It matches the generous curve of her top lip. "That wouldn't happen to be the same man you swear you're never speaking to again?"

"This isn't fair, Skylar. You know the barf rules. Nothing said during barf-time is to be repeated the following morning."

She bumps her knee against mine. "That may be true when it's drunk-puking, but it doesn't count for food poisoning. Anything you said last night—*whether delirious or not*—will and can be discussed." She whacks my knee for the second time, this one harder than her first. "Now scoot, then spill."

"There's nothing to spill. I told you *everything* that happened last night." I'm not lying; she knows it all—embarrassing bodily functions and all.

My mattress squeaks when she flops next to me. She's as light as a feather; my mattress is just as dated as me. "Are you sure you didn't miss something? Because I don't see any rando going out of his way to deliver vital necessities if he had no intentions of a second meeting."

"He's just being nice."

Skylar's shoulder touches her ear. "Maybe." Her chest deflates when she exhales slowly. "But then why would he leave you his cell phone number?"

My stomach rolls. For the first time the past six hours, it's a good churn. "He left his number?"

Nodding, Skylar hands me a business card, allowing it to answer my question on her behalf. It's a pretty basic business card. White with black print, no details bar a name and a number. There's just one odd thing—the name and number attached isn't for Elvis. It's for a guy named Danny.

Spotting the confusion crossing my features, Skylar flips the card over. My heart matches her brutal flip when I see a handprinted cell number and name on the back. It's from Elvis.

"Maybe he's still just being nice."

"He could be," Skylar agrees, her tone as hopeful as mine. "Or... he could be hoping for a chance to prove he isn't an ass." Her dress scrunches up around her thighs when she scoots off my bed. After returning her hem to its rightful spot, she pivots to face me. "I guess there is only one way for you to find out." She nudges her hand to the card I'm clutching for dear life. "Call him."

CHAPTER EIGHT

Presley

The hum in the locker room is nearly deafening. We had a good training session tonight, and the excitement bouncing off the players is palpable in the air. It's been my first full session back after the worst case of food poisoning I've ever experienced in my life.

Thank fuck Becca didn't touch any of the chicken products we consumed, or my guilt would be double. On the recommendation of her doctor, she only consumes chicken she has prepared herself to ensure it is fresh and thoroughly cooked. I'm not pregnant, but I'll be taking her obstetrician's advice from here on out. I swear, I lost five pounds over the weekend, and even more in muscle conditioning. I've never been more ill.

I lift my chin up in thanks when our head coach, James Maloney, praises, "Good session today, Carlton. Keep up that level of intensity, and we might get you back into your favorite position sooner than scheduled."

I keep a cool head even with my insides freaking out like a hooker on crack. "Sounds good."

When Coach James rounds the corner of his office, I throw my fist into the air. This is what I've been working toward the past six months, and I'm beyond stoked that I'm another step closer to returning to the position I was born to play.

My excitement doesn't linger long. The ringing of my cell phone quickly nips it in the bud. There's only one person who calls me after a training session. It's the same person who relentlessly nags me after every game. My ex—Lillian.

The tightness in my jaw weakens when I dig my hand into my locker to pull out my phone. The name flashing across the screen isn't who I was anticipating—far from it.

With a wonky grin, I swipe my finger across the screen before pushing it to my ear. "I nearly fired Danny when you didn't call within the first two weeks. Figured he must have forgotten to include my number in your package."

"Uh... yeah, sorry about that." Willow doesn't sound sorry—not an ounce of coyness has invaded her sweet Australian twang. "I got caught up with life. You know. Busy and all that."

The honesty in her tone has me wondering how long it was before she lost the bucket I had attached to my hip the five days following our meeting. I was a little greedy with the Chinese, so it's only fair I paid the highest penalty.

I'm snapped back from my thoughts when Willow asks, "Do you remember me saying there may be instances where my forming friendship with Becca and Dalton may cross over with your stale-ass relationship with them?"

She can't see me, but she must intuit my head bob because she continues not even two seconds later, "This is the instance I was referring to."

Half of her words are drowned out by someone groaning in the background. If it sounded anything like a pleasurable groan, I'd be pissed, but this doesn't sound anything like that. It sounds like a groan of pain.

"Becca is in labor, and I can't get ahold of Dalton. I've been ringing his cell phone non-stop. He ain't answering." She sounds as anxious as the panic roaring through my body. "I don't know what to do, Elvis. This isn't what I signed up for when I became Becca's friend. I like her and all, but this is above my paygrade."

She continues blubbering as I race through the locker room. I assure her everything will be fine when she takes a much-needed breath. "Just keep Becca calm until I get Dalton to her."

"You're with Dalton?" The relief in her voice can't be missed.

"No, but I know where he is."

I burst through the door where Dalton is holding a press conference about our upcoming game. He must see something on my face because he leaps to his feet faster than I can snap my fingers. Cameras and the reporters behind them follow his race across the room.

"What is it?"

"Becca."

I only say one word, but its breathless delivery speaks volumes.

I pull into Dalton's driveway five minutes later. Our travels from the stadium to his house were made as if I'm not on the verge of losing my license. The citation I got for running a red light three weeks ago already gained me points, much less the speeding ticket that arrived in the mail along with it. The red camera citation is on Willow's shoulders, but I'll accept the speeding ticket. It was snapped during my mad dash home.

"Thanks."

Dalton flings off his belt with the same force Willow used three weeks ago before he races up the stairs. I swear to God he returns not even ten seconds later with an ashen-faced Becca under one arm and a bursting-the-zipper suitcase under the other.

Just as he veers to the left, a sight more beautiful than the excitement on his face enters my vision. Willow is following his gallop down the stairs. She's wearing a shirt similar to the one she had on the last time I saw her, but her jeans have been cut off to expose inches upon inches of her tanned thighs.

Not noticing my bugged-out eyes, she ushers Becca into the passenger seat of Dalton's Range Rover before assuring him she'll lock up everything before leaving. I'm not shocked when Dalton gives her his immediate trust. He has a good knack for reading people. It's why I should have listened to him when he warned me to stay away from Lillian. He knew in under a minute what took me nine years to figure out.

Once Dalton's taillights blur in the distance, Willow spreads her hands across her hips, flips her head back, then closes her eyes. She takes in numerous deep, relieved breaths before they slowly flutter open. When she spots me gawking at her like a freak at a peek show, she shyly waves before mouthing, "*Thank you.*"

Wanting more than unspoken words between us, I switch off my ignition and clamber out of my car. The more I struggle to extract myself from my vehicle, the more worry leaves Willow's face.

By the time I'm standing in front of her, she's smiling broadly, and I'm sweating like a pig. "I think it's time for a bigger car."

Her teeth graze her sexy-as-fuck lips as she nods. "It's fun to watch at a circus, but you've got to have more than one trick up your sleeve if you want to make it big."

After squeezing my nose and making a *honk* noise, she pivots on her heels and climbs the stairs.

I follow after her. "So I take it your friendship with Becca is going well?"

She flashes me the most adorable smile over her shoulder before nodding. "Away from Dalton, she's great. But them together..." A gag finalizes her sentence. "I haven't seen so much PDA since the last time I saw my parents."

I laugh. My mom and dad aren't much better... except when football is on.

I shadow Willow as she makes her way around Dalton and Becca's house like she's familiar with the floorplan. She shuts all the windows on the lower floor before moving upstairs to partially crack the window Becca keeps open every night for natural filtration. Once she has everything locked up as Becca and Dalton do each evening, she moves to the kitchen to gather her backpack and keys from the kitchen counter.

She punches a six-digit code into their security system while I say, "You've certainly made yourself at home."

She smiles, loving the snippet of envy in my tone. I've been friends with Dalton for over a decade, but I don't know his security code.

Traitorous bastard!

My eyes stray to Willow when she asks, "Jealous?"

When I nod, she winks before heading for the main entrance. Once again, I follow her like a lost puppy. The low hang of my jaw triples when she places a freshly cut key into the deadlock to secure Dalton's front door.

"You got a key too?"

Acting like I didn't whine like a bitch, Willow gallops down the stairs of Dalton's house. She adjusts her backpack before pivoting to face me. The late afternoon sun bounces orange hues off her springy locks, making them look more auburn than they are.

"It was nice seeing you again, Elvis."

With that, she spins on her heels and heads down the sidewalk.

"Where are you going?" Curiosity rings in my tone. There's nothing but a bus stop and a few vacant plots of land in the direction she's heading.

When reality smacks into me, so do my back molars. "You're not catching the bus. It will be dark before you get home."

Like I need any more reminding I shouldn't be gawking at her ass like I am, Willow says, "It's okay, old man, I know how to handle myself."

My look shows my disdain for her nickname. "Even if you can, let me give you a ride."

Not looking back, she continues down the path. "Once bitten, twice shy. I'm good."

"Come on, Will." I purposely use her nickname, hoping she'll believe I'm her friend and not a creep looking to be gassed for the second time in my life. "It's a ride, not a wedding proposal. It's on my way anyhow."

That stops her.

She fiddles with the straps on her backpack while connecting her eyes to mine. It's the fight of my life to force my eyes to follow her eyes' lead. It isn't my fault; I'm a man and her backpack straps are displaying her impressive rack in the most brilliant light. If I were a cartoon, my tongue would be hanging on the ground, and my eyes would be bulging out of my head. Her body... *schwing!* When you combine her sexy curves with her beautiful face, what do you get? Me continuously adjusting my crotch.

When my eyes finally find Willow's, she asks, "It's on your way?"

I angle my head to the side so my head bob could be misconstrued as a shake.

She doesn't buy my half-hearted response. Snarling, she pivots on her heels and keeps walking.

"Fine! It's not on my way, but I'm hungry, and there's a pizzeria near your college I'm dying to grab a slice at."

My heart stops beating when her feet stop pounding the pavement. "Which pizzeria?"

She doesn't spin around to face me. She keeps her eyes front and center, confident she doesn't need to look at me to know I'm lying. She'll hear it in my tone.

I shouldn't like that she *thinks* she can read me so easily, but I do. "Mickey's."

She cranks her neck back to peer at me. "On West 37?"

Smiling, I nod. "Best pizza on this side of the country."

"More like best pizza on the planet." While bridging the small gap between us, she asks, "And you're going there tonight?"

"Yep!" *—I am now—* "It's right across from your university. I don't even have to pull into the parking lot to drop you off. You can just get out at Mickey's and walk across the street. What do you say? That sounds fair, doesn't it?"

She rocks on the balls of her feet while contemplating. I really wish she wouldn't; every rock forward brings her fantastic tits within touching distance. If she doesn't hurry up and make her decision, I'm about to face charges for sexual misconduct.

After what feels like an eternity, she finally relents. "Okay, but..." She takes five seconds to settle the redness creeping up her neck before murmuring, "If you at any stage hang your head out the window like a dog, I'll do more than slam a cue stick into your balls."

My nuts tuck inside myself, the threat in her tone too ominous to ignore.

Confident she has me scared, she returns to Dalton's driveway, slides into the passenger seat of my car, then closes the door without the slightest bang. My entrance is nowhere near as sleek as hers. The panic buzzing in my crotch has me on high alert, and it's weighing down my movements.

Unfortunately it also has me thinking recklessly.

Willow stops fiddling with her belt when I ask, "Before we head out, can I ask you something?"

Her brows furrow in confusion, unsure what has caused the crackle in my usually smooth timbre, but she nods all the same, too curious to let a flare of panic stop her from discovering what's caused the quick change in my composure.

I bet she wishes she weren't so damn inquisitive when I ask, "When was the last time you ate Chinese? The new car smell is finally returning, and I don't want to risk ruining it."

CHAPTER NINE

Willow

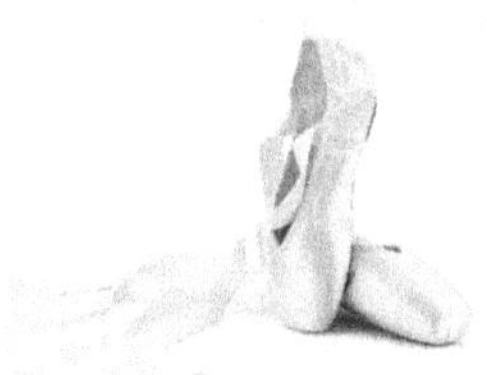

My attempt to peel myself out of Elvis's chub-holding car is thwarted by him splaying his giant arm across my chest. His arms are so long, his fingertips could brush the window next to my head, but he'd rather use them to pin me in his car, so he keeps them curled around my side boob.

"I'm just playin'. I know, poor timing, but I swear I was only trying to lighten the mood."

"Lighten the mood... or intensify it?"

When my eyes lower to his inappropriate grope of my breast, Elvis's eyes bug out like they did when they took in my body earlier.

"Oh fuck, sorry." He yanks his hand back to his side of the car as if scorched by my touch. "I wasn't going for a feel. I'm not like that. I'd ask before grabbing. I don't just help myself."

Realizing he's rambling like a pimple-faced virgin, he pushes the automatic start button and reverses out of Dalton's driveway. We travel the first five miles with his eyes forward and his mouth tightlipped. I don't mind the silence. It gives me a chance to settle my erratic heart rate from his closeness.

I thought the patter of my heart against my ribs was because of Becca, but it didn't taper when she left with Dalton. It grew astronomically. That could only mean one thing. Elvis is the cause of my heart's stutter.

I don't know whether to be pleased or annoyed by my notion. Elvis's cell phone number has been burning a hole in my pocket the last three weeks, and just when I thought I had a hold of the situation, it blows up in my face.

Don't get me wrong; I wanted to call him—only to thank him for the products that helped me emerge from hell days earlier than I expected—but my pride wouldn't let me. I've never been more mortified than I was the night he drove me home, and I've had some ripper blunders in my short nearly twenty-two years. Add that to the fact everyone at my university watched my video on YouTube, and I simply ran out of time. The last three weeks have been a blur. Not necessarily a good haze, but a blur nonetheless.

It's funny how people enter your life at the right time. If I hadn't defended Becca three weeks ago, I wouldn't have a video on YouTube with close to two hundred million views, but then I also wouldn't have needed her maturity to keep my head out of the clouds the past three weeks.

Skylar has been great, but Becca was the only one who remained quiet regarding my supposed "stupidity" for not accepting the numerous requests for an interview. No one but Becca could understand why I didn't want the publicity. She understood my worry about how quickly the tables can turn, and how it would feel if I were the one on the receiving end of the backlash, so she constantly reminded me no monetary amount could replace my values when the offers grew exceptionally with everyone I rejected.

That's why I was visiting Becca today. She was helping me draft a letter to have my details removed from the original video that started this all. I love the messages of support I receive multiple times a day, but they do little to soothe the sting of the handful of hateful ones I get.

Loathing the silence between Elvis and me, I attempt to end it. "What do you think Becca will have?"

Any tension left brimming between us ends when Elvis answers, "I'm hoping a baby, but who knows these days."

"Ha ha, smart ass. I meant a boy or a girl. Becca said they kept the gender a surprise."

I swivel in my seat to face him head on, taking in his casual yet scrumptious jeans and fitted shirt as he discloses, "It's a secret to Becca, but Dalton knows."

"What? How!"

I give him a sympathetic look when my squeal shreds his eardrums. He's not concerned. His chuckle has my nipples paying him as much attention as they did when his arm was splayed across my chest.

"He bribed the sonographer for the results. Becca was happy to wait until the birth, but Dalton is an impatient ass. He would *never* wait to find out something he could know months earlier."

"So he's known their baby's gender the entire time, and he's never told Becca?"

I'm truly astonished. I've spent a lot of time with them the past three weeks, and up until a minute ago, I would have happily declared they keep nothing from each other.

Elvis nods, then grimaces. "Well, he hasn't directly said it, but—"

"Ohh... the giant teddy in the nursery. He bought that, didn't he?" When Elvis nods, I tap my feet on the ground. "I told Becca his fur wasn't aqua. That's straight up *baby boy blue* fur!"

I sink deeper into my seat, loving the excited butterflies taking flight in my stomach. Becca and Dalton will be great parents, and, if I'm being honest, I'm dying to meet the little person they created together. I don't have any siblings, so until I marry someone with a shit ton of brothers and sisters, this is as close to an aunt as I will become. I'm also not the one about to squeeze a watermelon through a lemon-sized hole, so I'm feeling great right now.

I'm still buzzing with excitement when Elvis pulls his fancy sports car into Mickey's Pizzeria's parking lot. This early at night, it's more deserted than usual.

My eyes stray to Elvis when he says, "Grab a bite to eat with me." His tone reveals he isn't asking, but he's not demanding I eat with him either. He's giving me a suggestion and letting me choose whether or not to run with it.

Although it will most likely make me even more embarrassed, I ask, "Do you not recall what happened the last time we ate together?"

A ghost of a smile raises Elvis's cheeks. "Are we talking about the cue stick or our trip home?"

I give him my *take your pick* look.

His faint grin turns into a full, blistering smile. "I'm safe either way. One, Mickey's doesn't have a pool table. And two, your campus is right over there." He points to a row of buildings, unsure which dormitory is mine. "I don't need to drive you anywhere. You can walk your sorry ass home."

I rake my nails down his pec like all the super-hot chicks in the movies do. Regrettably, I don't have the French-tipped nails required to pull off the sultry tease. I kept mine clipped when I played netball in my teen years, and habit has kept them that way.

My breath tickles Elvis's jaw when I lean in close to his side. "The only thing sorry about my ass is the fact it's failed to gain your attention."

Confident my lack of flirty moves was made up for by my sassy tongue, I peel out of his car. It could be hope making me hear things, but I swear Elvis murmurs, "Your fine ass was the first thing I noticed about you," before he begins the acrobatic routine it takes for him to leave his car.

"So Becca arrived with a date in tow but left with Dalton?"

After downing a gulp of his soft drink, Elvis nods.

"No way. How did her date handle it?"

He swallows before locking his eyes with mine. "He didn't have much choice. Dalton wasn't leaving without her."

"That may work in fiction, but that's not the way things happen in real life." I drag a napkin over my saucy lips before scanning the room. "If I were interested in the crew-cut, *spank my monkey three times a day just to dispel half the testosterone pumping through my body* brute two booths over, just because you tell him I'm leaving with you, doesn't mean I have to."

"Yeah, it does." I can't tell if his voice is self-assured or pig-headed. It may be a combination.

Hooking my foot under my bottom, I angle myself closer to Elvis. "But who I go home with isn't up to you. It's my decision. If I want to mess the sheets with Dog the Bounty Hunter's son, that's my prerogative."

He dumps his half-empty glass onto the table before leaning his elbows on it. The sauce from the pizzas we've shared fans my lips when he asks, "Do you want to smear the sheets with him?"

His sexy scent of pureed tomatoes, garlic, and a manly cologne is messing with my senses because I swear he sounds jealous right now. I shake my head to rid it of my stupid thoughts. The past two hours have been awesome; we've talked like lifetime friends, shared two whole pizzas, and he gave me an update on how he and Dalton met before he "forced" Dalton to work up the courage to approach Becca.

It's been amazing, but our time together has also revealed how rusty my dating skills are. Not only have I continually misread Elvis's comments as flirty one-liners, but I've taken the occasional brush of his thigh against mine as a signal he wants to play Naked Twister with me beneath the sheets. I know that isn't the case. I couldn't compete for his attention on my best day, much less against all the attention he's attracted tonight. Even with him requesting that we be seated in the far back corner of the restaurant, he's gained many admiring glances.

I'm not even angry. Elvis is too handsome not to encourage a second look. I'm just grateful I don't have to strain my eyes to drink in all his features. It's not often I say I'm lucky, but I am tonight because I have the best seat in town.

The silly thoughts in my head shift to naughty ones when Elvis's deep growl rolls through my core. "Willow?"

When I peer at him, shocked by the anger drawing his dark

brows together, the conversation we were having only seconds ago smacks back into me.

We're discussing women's rights, not my womanly needs.

"No, I don't want to sleep with him, but that's not the point. If I *wanted* to sleep with him, I *could* sleep with him, and there's nothing you could do about it."

The thick stubble on Elvis's top lip digs into his nose when he twists his lips. "That's true."

I gasp, surprised he's conforming to my ways so quickly. He doesn't give off pushover vibes. From the stories he's shared tonight, most of the alpha machoism Dalton exhibited the night he met Becca was learned from Elvis, so I expected more fighting spirit, or, at the very least, a sneer.

I get both when his lips tickle my earlobe and he snarls, "Just like if I *want* to drag you out of here over my shoulder, kicking and screaming, I *could*, and there's nothing you could do about it."

Jesus—how can I misconstrue that? The need in his voice is so extreme, a bead of sweat rolls down my back. It's absorbed by my panties, which are just as sticky.

Before my chest can bristle in confusion, Elvis adds stacks of wood to the fire he's building. "Now follow me outside before I go all caveman on his ass."

I slant back far enough I can see his eyes. They're narrowed with anger and blistering with a glint I can't quite identify.

Although I'm a mix of confusion and excitement, I can't help but say, "You're being a buffoon. He's not interested in me. I just used him as an example."

While scooting out of our booth, Elvis digs his wallet out of his pocket. He tosses a bundle of crisp notes onto our recently delivered bill, then his eyes stray to the gentleman in question. "Oh, he's interested alright. He's nearly busting a nut just looking at you. I think the schmuck needs to be taught a lesson about what happens when you mosey in on a girl while she's on a date."

Date? When did this become a date?

When Elvis heads in the stranger's direction, I remain frozen, too shocked to move. I'm usually pretty clued on, but tonight I'm utterly dumbfounded. I guess the plot within minutes of the start of a movie; I know who the killer is long before the on-screen detectives do, and I knew I was going to crush hard on Elvis well before I spun around to face him, but this is a one-eighty I never saw coming.

Elvis is a brute of a man with enough testosterone to light the city, but I never pictured him as the jealous type. He was so laid-back tonight, I was beginning to wonder if he had a competitive bone in his body. Then I realized my error. You don't need to be competitive when there's no one to compete against.

When Elvis's long strides end next to the man I used to make a point, I snag my backpack from my seat and race his way. I'm reasonably sure he won't do anything, but considering tonight is only our second meeting, I'm not willing to test out another theory. The throbbing veins in Elvis's arms are concerning enough, so I don't want more mess thrown into the shitstorm I'd like to avoid.

"The pizza was great. Thanks for the wonderful service," I mumble to our waitress before hooking my arm around Elvis's elbow and dragging him toward the exit.

It's lucky I skipped weights this morning because it takes all my strength to move him, and even then, I still feel like I'm lugging a crane. At this rate, I'll need to exchange some of the medication Elvis purchased me last week to buy hemorrhoid cream.

"Holy fishcakes, are you a lunatic? Who goes all jackrabbit crazy like that so quickly?" I break away from Elvis's side when we reach the gravel parking lot at the back of Mickey's. "Did you forget to take your medication today? I don't recommend doubling up, but I also wouldn't recommend skipping your loony pills tomorrow. You went from normal to fucked up in under three seconds. Who does that?"

My belligerent rant is abandoned when Elvis asks, "But you left with me, didn't you?"

I still as commotion stirs in my gut.

He smiles, loving my stumped state. "That was the point, wasn't it? You wanted proof of how Becca arrived with a date but left with

Dalton." He waves his hand to the glass door I just barged him through. "Evidence submitted. Case closed. I won."

"Oh. My. God!" I pace closer to him, unsure whether to kiss the mirth off his face or smack it off. I settle on words instead of a physical response. "You're an asshole. I seriously thought you were going to deck him."

His face does a weird twitchy thing. "It was close, especially when he handed me this."

My mouth falls open when he thrusts a Mickey's Pizzeria napkin my way. It has a name and number scrawled across it.

"Wow, he has bigger balls than I thought. He's either very brave or extremely stupid to hand a man his number to forward to his date."

Elvis flops his head to the side in a seriously cute way. "Date?"

"Oh, puh-leeze. You can't go there, as you said 'date' first." I begin pacing to my university by walking backward. "But if this isn't a date, and we're just friends sharing a slice, cough up the napkin, because this girl has *needs* that need to be taken care of."

Elvis looks seconds from having a coronary when I grind my hips in a way only a stripper should while running my hands up my body. Although he doesn't react to my tease, the scrunching of the napkin and its plonk into a trash can on his right is answer enough.

"Nice shot." The balled napkin didn't even hit the rim; it just glided between the silver circle, his shot a perfect three-pointer.

Elvis's wink is as flirty as the smile on my face. While bridging the gap between us, which takes him all of two seconds with how long his strides are, he digs a cap out of the back pocket of his jeans and sinks it down low on his head. I nearly gag when I see the emblem on the top. It's a 69ers cap.

"Do you often bring a hat to a *date?*" Yep—I'm going there. In this very instance, I'm in love with the word, and I don't care if the world knows it.

The moonlight glistens on his teeth when he smiles a sultry grin. "Not often, but I didn't know this was a *date* until an hour ago."

"An hour? *Wow.* You knew a good fifty-nine minutes before me." I bump him with my hip before crossing the patch of weedy grass between Mickey's Pizzeria and the border of my university. "But in all seriousness, what's with the cap?"

I end my sentence in just enough time, saving me the embarrassment of expressing what I really want to ask: *why would you ever hide a face that sexy?*

"It's been a few years since I've stepped foot on college grounds. Don't want the dean thinking I'm an old geezer looking to bed some college girls."

His reply elevates my curiosity of the past three weeks. The difference in our maturity proves he's older than me; I'm just lost on how many years separate us. I'm not bothered either way. Age is just a number, and with him tossing the napkin in the bin, his number is the only one I have in my phone right now.

"If you're worried about the dean getting upset, you clearly haven't met him. He is a dirty old geezer wanting to bed college girls himself. He'll only be angry about you mowing the lawn he's been watering the past six months."

Elvis throws his head back and laughs. It barely lingers for ten seconds before the entirety of my statement smacks into him. His head returns front and center as his mouth snaps shut. "Watering with the hope of mowing? Or is he already mowing it?"

Happy I have him on tenterhooks, I jog the last ten paces between us and the stairs at the front of my dorm. The fun we've had tonight is all over my face, and it doesn't reflect half the excitement tingling in my stomach... *and a region a few inches lower.*

Elvis stands in the middle of the footpath as his suspicious eyes dart between Mickey's and me. "You live next door to a pizzeria?"

I grimace. "Yep! And it's as torturous as you're picturing. My ass has never been more thankful for a lack of student funding."

My screwed up nose and furrowed brows jump onto Elvis's face. "Ah, the good old college days. I've not touched a ramen noodle since the day I graduated."

"And how long ago was that?" Just because I said I don't care how many digits are between us, doesn't mean I'm not curious.

Elvis's head bobs side to side as a blinding smile stretches across his face. "A while..."

I climb two stairs so we meet eye to eye before asking, "As in, more than a decade, or is it closer to two?"

"Jesus H to the fucking Christ, how old do you think I am?" His playful roar gains us the attention of a handful of students milling around.

"I don't know? It's hard to gauge without an *in-depth* investigation, so you either need to fess up and tell me..." I drag my eyes down his body in a long, dedicated sweep while murmuring, "... Or show me."

Damn, I've never been overly good at flirting, but I've got the moves tonight, and I'm not even drunk. Usually, that's the only time I dust off the cobwebs and break out the one-liners that will either have the guys in a fit of laughter or purring at my feet.

I really hope Elvis is a giant kitty under all those layers of muscles.

After pulling his cap down even further on his head, Elvis places one foot onto the step separating us before tilting his torso close to mine. Pizza, garlic bread, and a smell that's even yummier than them all combined smacks into me when he whispers, "I'm old enough to know I could get in trouble for this, but young enough not to care."

Any reply I am planning to give is swallowed by his mouth.

Elvis... *I don't know his last name...* is kissing me. It's a blood-warming tingle from the top of my head to the tips of my toes, *I'll never eat pizza in the same light again* kiss. He devours my mouth with slow licks and playful nips while drawing me closer with his big hands gripping the generous swell of my hips.

I spread my hands across his chest to make sure I don't topple to the ground. The firmness under his shirt worsens the wooziness in my head. His pecs are amazing—and heaving. He's as breathless by our kiss as I am shocked that we're kissing. I daydreamed about this exact moment many times the past three weeks, but I never believed it would actually happen.

When I pull back to catch my breath, Elvis tugs me closer. "No, not yet. Need more."

After nipping at my lower lip, he spears his tongue between my gaped, kiss-swollen lips. He drags it along the roof of my mouth, tasting and sampling me before dueling with mine. I can feel him against me, as hot and heavy as the heat his kiss elicits from me. He's not even rolling his hips, yet I feel every inch of him. Every. Perfect. Inch. When he threads his fingers through my hair, I melt into his embrace. I respond to the strokes of his tongue as if this isn't the first time we've engaged in a tender embrace of tonsil hockey.

I am right there with him, every step of the way. My tongue is as courageous as his, my hands just as wild, and he's loving every minute of it. He smiles against my mouth, happy he's getting as good as he's giving. His kiss is greedy and hard, but tender and loving at the same time. He takes control, but only as much as I'm willing to give.

Seconds from melting into a puddle of pleasure, he relinquishes my mouth from his. It isn't that he's had his fill. It's the cat-calls and shouts for him to "give it to me" killing his mojo.

"I was right. Your mouth is as sweet as your face but as naughty as the glint in your eyes."

I smile a blistering grin, adoring that I'm not the only one who's fantasized the past three weeks about us kissing.

"Now I better leave before things get difficult." He looks pained, as if his words were as bitter for him as they were for me.

He leans in to press a peck to my tingling mouth before spinning on his heels and walking down the cracked path. We must have put on a real show because not only does he get slapped on the back numerous times during his short commute past bystanders, he also has his picture snapped.

I wait until he's gobbled up by the darkness before entering my dormitory. Since my room is on the first level, it doesn't take me long to push my key into the lock. My heart rate is so high it takes several attempts to open the door, and don't even get me started on my wobbly knees, but nothing—not a single friggin' thing—can stop my little boogie when I enter my room.

I'm so shocked and deliriously happy, I groove around my room like I'm in the middle of a night club. I shake my booty and pump out my chest to the imaginary song in my head. I may even do a few lassoes with an invisible rope. I wiggle and shake until all the food and drink in my belly becomes slop, my thighs ache, and my cell phone rings.

My hip thrust suspends mid-air when I realize who is calling me. It's Elvis. After wiping the sweat from my brow, I push my phone to my ear and play it cool. "Hey."

The frenetic quiver of my pulse triples when he replies, "Hey." His short reply can't hide that he is as breathless as me, and just as excited.

With my clothes clinging to my body, I pace to the window, needing some air. I've worked up such a sweat, I'm seconds away from entering a wet t-shirt competition.

I've yanked the window up halfway when Elvis asks, "Are you hot?"

Suspicion runs rife through my veins. I sprayed fish oil on the tracks of my window only last week, ensuring its creaking wouldn't wake Skylar any time I sat on the windowsill to take in a starry night.

"A little." I keep my reply short, hoping Elvis will fill in the gaps.

He follows along nicely. "Was it our kiss that made you sweaty, or that bump and grind routine you just performed?"

Spinning, I take in my room, from the dowdy, paint-peeled walls covered with posters, to the near-inch gap at the bottom of my door from the RA shaving off too much wood when the door warped after the homecoming party last spring.

I only stop twirling when the flash of headlights beam into my room. With my hand clutching my throat, I angle my body to peer out my window. I die a thousand deaths when my eyes lock in on a flashy sports car in the parking lot of Mickey's. The hood of Elvis's parked car is pointed right at my bedroom window—the same bedroom window I just shook my tuchus in front of.

"Willow..."

I swallow down the uneasiness creeping up my throat. "Yeah?"

He waits long enough I think our call has been disconnected. "Don't ever change. You're fucking perfect just the way you are."

CHAPTER TEN

Willow

J'm still reveling in the high of Elvis's comment as I make my way to the studio to set up my space for this morning's dance lesson. It's a beautiful day. The clouds of the past week have lifted; I slept well, and my workout last night under Elvis's unknown watch meant I didn't have to drag my ass out of bed at 5 AM to go to boxing with Skylar. I'm feeling great!

It must be evident on my face because many eyes turn my way as I stroll down the campus footpath. I haven't been gawked at this closely since the morning the "Beauty Pummels the Beast" video was uploaded to YouTube.

"Hello."

I return a blond stranger's greeting with the wiggle of my fingers and a smile before continuing my trip.

"Nice day."

"It is," I agree to another handsome, yet unfamiliar man only a few paces away from admirer number one.

I pivot on my heels and walk backward when another gent decked out in a football jersey and muddy running shorts adds, "Looking good, Willow."

"Thank you..."

"Ted," he fills in.

"Thank you, Ted."

Eager to get away from the freaks suddenly hoping to be my new best friend, I spin back around then increase my pace. I have over forty minutes before my lesson starts, but I'd rather watch the lesson before mine than continue my odd morning. It was a good day; now it's wack.

By the time I make it to the building my dance studio is in, my skin is clammy from my brisk walk, and I've been approached nearly a dozen times. I've heard sex gives your eyes a sparkle you can't get anywhere else, but Elvis and I only kissed, so this type of response is ridiculous.

Just as I fumble through the double glass doors, a little sob whimpers through my ears.

"Oh, sweetie, what's wrong?"

There is a girl I'd guess to be nine or ten huddled in the corner of the foyer. She's wearing a pale pink leotard and a matching tutu. Her straight blonde hair is shielding most of her face, but I can tell she is crying.

"It's okay." I crouch down in front of her before lifting her tear-stained face to me. "Are you lost? Do you need me to help you find your mommy?"

"No." She clutches my arm so firmly, I'm certain she'll leave a bruise. "Don't tell her; she'll be mad."

Her big blue eyes look up at me in a plea, praying I won't dob.

"Okay, I won't say anything." She exhales, relieved. "But you need to tell me why you're crying." When fresh tears roll down her cheeks, I wipe them away as gently as possible. I hate seeing anyone cry, let alone a little girl with a face as adorable as hers. "It can't be that bad, can it? You've got a pretty leotard and a brand new tutu; what more do you need?"

Her lips quiver when she replies, "I want to dance."

A giggle leaves my lips as they part into a smile. "That's good. That's why you're here. This is a dance studio." I wave my hand at the big "dance studio" sign spread across the front windows. "You can dance here until your heart is content."

My hand falls to my side when she whimpers, "But Ms. Francesca won't let me. She said I can't be in her class."

"Why would she say that?"

When she burrows her tear-stained face into her knees, I peer through the cracked-open door she's huddled outside of. My heart rate breaks into an unnatural rhythm when I spot the class inside—a ballet class full of perfectly slender children and an even more svelte instructor.

My heart cracks when my eyes return to the little girl. She is beautiful. Flawless hair, a milky-white face without a single blemish, and the cutest little dimples in her rounded cheeks, she's just wearing a leotard a size or two bigger than her dance partners.

I kneel down closer to her. "Do you know what? I used to be a ballerina."

"Used to be?" She wipes the tears from her cheeks when I nod. "You're not anymore?"

"No, I'm not." Disappointment blisters in her eyes. "But I'm still a dancer. I have a class every Saturday morning just like yours. There's just one difference. We don't wear tutus and leotards. We wear leather jackets, bright pink pants, and sneakers painted with glitter."

"Sneakers?"

"They're kinda like running shoes, just flashier and more Australian."

My heart soars when she giggles.

"Do you think you'd like to dance in clothes like that?"

Nodding, she removes the last of the tears on her cheeks before sitting up straighter. Just as quickly as her excitement arrives, it's swiped out from beneath her. "I can't. My mom said I have to do ballet. She was a ballerina, and so was my sister, so I have to be one as well."

"Is that what you want? If it is, I'll march straight into that lesson and rip Ms. Francesca a new butthole." She giggles again.

"But if you just want to dance, I have a dance class that would *love* to have you."

"What about my mom?"

You can tell I'm years away from being a parent when I say, "What about her? You arrive here every Saturday at eight, right?" When she nods, I add on, "Then I'll meet you here every Saturday at eight."

"You'll do that for me?" She seems genuinely shocked, like no one's ever had her back before.

I nod. "Of course I will. It will be my privilege."

"And you won't tell my mom?" she double-checks.

"No. She pays the dance studio good money for you to dance; we're just making sure she gets her money's worth."

Excitement beams out of her.

"Good?"

"Yes. Thank you." She throws her arms around my neck so quickly, she nearly bowls me over.

"You're welcome. Now how about you head into the studio and warm up? Then I'll update you on some routines before the rest arrive."

Eager to get started, she springs to her feet and charges into my unlocked studio. I wait until she is out of earshot before entering the room next to mine. Francesca eyes me beneath lowered lashes when I cross the room, pretending she hasn't heard my furious stomps.

"How dare you treat her like that. She's a goddamn child!" My hiss is violent but not loud enough for any of the children in Francesca's lesson to hear over the music they're practicing arabesques to.

"Child or not, you know the rules, Willow." She instructs the children to switch to pliés before turning to face me. "Diet and nutrition are directly linked to agility. The lighter the dancers are, the easier they'll float across the stage. You know this, Willow, because it is a regime we've abided by our entire lives..." She rakes her eyes down my body before correcting, "You *once* abided by."

I would smack her if there weren't twenty-four little pairs of eyes watching us. Instead, I use words. "Someone's weight has nothing to do with their passion. You can have skills in abundance, drive by the bucket load, and more knowledge than you know what to do with, but without passion, you'll never reach the pinnacle of success."

With my dad's words ringing in my ears, I leave the studio with my head held high and my heart weighed down.

CHAPTER ELEVEN

Presley

"What the fuck was that, Elvis? You were on fire tonight." Foster walks away from me with his hands shaking like they're on fire.

"He's not joking, great game tonight." Another teammate, Mitch, slaps my shoulder before making his way to the showers.

I'm awarded the congratulations of another three players before their celebrations switch from the locker room to a VIP box only a select few have access to after every win. Even with my team playing without our captain, tonight's game was good. Coach James was hesitant about me stepping into Dalton's role while he is on daddy-to-be duty, but his hesitation eased after my first three throws. I'm not bragging when I agree with Foster. I was on fire tonight.

I want to pretend the hype surrounding my return to quarterback was fueling my on-field performance tonight, but that would be a lie. I'm still basking in the glory of last night. God—Willow... *fuck*. Her mouth. Her body. Her over-the-top attitude. I hardly slept a wink last night as I took it all in.

I wasn't planning to kiss her, but, my fucking god, am I glad I did. I've never experienced a kiss like that before. It was like a fireworks warehouse exploding in the dead of the night, awe-inspiring and ten times better than I could have ever predicted. One kiss had me wanting another. And another. And another.

I could have kissed her all night. I would have if I didn't feel the familiar eyeball sensation I get anytime I'm in public. I already secured a number of unwanted watchers at the pizzeria, but I brushed off their interest because I couldn't be certain it was all focused on me. Willow gains as much attention as I do when I enter the room, but she just doesn't have a job title to thank for it; she just has her sexy-as-fuck face.

I'm drawn from my thoughts by Darris when he asks, "You coming?"

"Yeah, I'll be up in a minute..." My words trail off when my phone rings. I'm equally hopeful and pessimistic when I dig my cell out of my gym bag. I'm hopeful it's Willow calling, but pessimistic it's most likely the leech who can't get the hint.

I'm wrong on both parts when I recognize the number flashing across the screen. "Hold on, boys, we might have another reason to celebrate." I hold my finger in the air while climbing onto the bench in front of the lockers. "Dalton is calling."

This is the first time anyone has heard from him since he left his driveway in a hurry over twenty-eight hours ago.

"And?" I ask after swiping my finger across the screen of my phone and raising it to my ear. "Do we have a future linebacker in our midst?"

Dalton laughs, his joy uncontained. "We have a girl!" He doesn't sound disappointed. Far from it. "Becca paid the sonographer to steer me in the wrong direction."

"Ha! I told you she's always one step ahead of you." When our team circles me, waiting for an update, I cup my phone before shouting, "Drinks are on Dalton! He's the proud daddy of a little baby girl!"

The energy in the room triples as the guys shout their congratulations into my phone. A few even offer their commiserations— they're the ones who have already fathered daughters. By the time everyone has passed on their well-wishes, twenty minutes have passed, and the stadium is deserted except for the players and their management teams.

After returning my ass to my seat, I push my cell into my ear. "How's Becca?"

I can't see Dalton, but I can hear his smile. "She's good. It went a little longer than she would have liked, but she handled it like a real pro."

"I have no doubt, man. That girl of yours is strong."

I can picture his smile when he murmurs, "She sure is."

A rustle sounds down the line followed by a coo. I never thought I'd get misty-eyed over a baby, but I can feel a little dampness sliding across my corneas. It's not much, but enough to relay how proud I am of Dalton and Becca. They've been waiting for this day for years.

After telling Dalton I'll drop by the hospital tomorrow, I call Willow.

"A girl! Can you believe it?" She squeals down the line before I can issue a greeting.

"He called you—*before me?*" You can't miss the jealousy in my last two words.

Willow laughs, loving my unease. "No, Becca updated me while Dalton called you."

I screw my nose up. "They joint-dialed us?"

She giggles and murmurs something about me being a dork before saying a little louder, "Better than them drunk-dialing us like I am you."

I jackknife back. "Hold on, what? You're drunk-dialing me? Didn't I call you?"

Her third laugh in under a minute answers my question on her behalf. "Oh, yeah, you did."

"Where are you?" I scan the locker room, wondering where the fuck that alpha-macho *I'm about to go on a rampage* voice came from.

There's no one in the locker room but me.

My attention reverts to my phone when Willow says, "Skylar dragged me to a sports bar." She gags, weakening some of the tension in my jaw. "While she watched the game on the big screen, I found a much more entertaining way to occupy my time." I can picture her brows waggling.

I swivel my tongue around my mouth before easing out my next set of words. "You watched the game?"

She makes a weird *eh* noise. "I pretended to watch it, but if it weren't for Skylar galloping around the bar on a broom, I wouldn't have the faintest idea who won."

I exhale the breath I didn't realize I was holding. I don't like being deceitful, but it's been over eight years since I've been looked at like Willow looks at me. Not once have I seen money signs flash in her eyes as I have numerous times the past decade.

Furthermore, whatever we're starting is new, as fresh as Dalton's daughter, so I have no clue what to expect. If there's even the minutest possibility this is a flashbang relationship that fizzles as quickly as it heats up, the longer I keep it out of the public eye, the better it will be for all involved.

My entire relationship with Lillian was lived in front of the cameras. I learned from my mistakes. I won't do that *ever* again. I've been on the wrong side of the media. It was fucking vicious, and even though Willow appears to have a hard shell, I refuse to sit back and watch them try and crack it. So until I know what "this" is, I'm going to keep quiet about what I do for a living.

"Are you planning to stay at the bar? Or did you wanna..." I leave my question open for Willow to answer how she sees fit.

She's not going to let me off the hook that easy. "Or do I wanna..."

I stuff my sweaty jersey, shoulder pads, and cleats into my bag, hook it over my shoulder and spin around. Mid-pivot, I ask, "Are you hungry?"

I freeze halfway across the empty locker room when Willow replies, "Do my nipples have breasts?" She snorts before correcting herself. "I meant, do my breasts have nipples? Oh my god, I should probably cut back on the vodka." She cups her phone, meaning I barely hear her murmur, "I was joking; fill her up. I've got all night to drink and all of next week to regret my decision."

"What happened to your lack of funds?"

Vodka isn't pricy... until you're a college student drinking at a bar. Then it's the equivalent of top-shelf liquor.

"I'm not buying them." She giggles like a school girl worried she's about to get in trouble. I understand why when she whispers, "I didn't even bring my purse."

The slurring of her words reveals her level of intoxication, much less the return of my tight jaw. "If you're not paying, who is?"

"Umm..." She cups her phone again before whispering, "What were your names again?"

I feel my blood pulsate through my veins when a male voice replies, "This is Tim; he's Bryce, and I'm your new best friend, Archer."

The dumb fuck doesn't even attempt to hide the innuendo in his tone. If Willow isn't already sitting in his lap, he's praying she will be within the next five minutes.

Not on my watch, asshole!

"Thank you." Willow moves her hand away from her phone, and the buzz of drunk patrons grows louder down the line. "Archer, Tim, and Bryce have been generously supplying my drinks. They're really nice—"

"Willow?"

I hear her swallow harshly before, "Yeah?"

"Which bar are you at?"

Her breathing picks up as the sound of her teeth raking her lip flows down the line. "Umm... Mister M...Mister M..."

"Mister Mystra? Is there a cartoon of a chubby Chinese man holding a football on the front window?"

She giggles a throaty laugh too sexy to be heard in public while surrounded by drunken idiots hoping to get in her panties. "Yes, it does. How did you know that?"

Ignoring her question, I say, "I'll be there in fifteen minutes."

As I drag my cell from my ear, I hear her take in a sharp breath, but she fails to protest, assuring me I'm doing the right thing.

My steps down the abandoned corridors of the 69ers home stadium are long and efficient, only halved when Danny unexpectedly steps into my path.

"Hey, you ready?" He tugs down the collar of the shirt I threw on haphazardly before attempting to lick and spit my messy locks into submission.

I step back to avoid his saliva-coated fingers while bouncing my eyes between his. "For..."

"For the pharmaceutical reps."

He nudges his head to the door he just walked through. There are four suit-clad men huddled around a table and a lady in a fierce-looking three-piece suit helming the meeting.

"We scheduled this weeks ago; how can you not remember?" Danny leans closer to me, ensuring his words are only for my ears. "We're looking at closing on the ten million you requested. If you can't memorize a calendar, surely you can remember a figure that high?"

His words are whispered, but they leave no doubt of his annoyance. He's been working his ass off the past four months to secure the astronomical figure I wanted because he knows as well as I do endorsements are where the money is.

"I've got somewhere to be." My eyes fall to my watch. Five minutes have already passed since I spoke to Willow, add that to the fifteen minutes it will take me to get to Mystra, and that gives douchebag Archer an extra twenty minutes to convince her he's worth more than the vodka he's plowing into her. "Can it wait 'til tomorrow?"

"Please, for the love of God, don't do this to me again." Danny rakes his fingers through his hair to give it a rough tug as his chest displays early signs of a panic attack. "I did as you asked, I schmoozed the fuck out of them to get this deal to the amount you requested, but if you walk away now, they aren't coming back, Elvis. The deal will be done. Swiped from the table. Given to one of the many agents waiting for me to fuck up this deal."

He bends in half, his dramatics not unusual. If he gets so much as a papercut, he demands 911 be called. He's as far from an agent as you can imagine, but that's why I asked him to be mine. I needed someone out of the industry, someone I trusted to put my interests before anyone else's. Danny has done that. He renegotiated my return to a game he knew nothing about with the skill of a man in the industry for decades. He's profited much more than at the insurance firm where he used to work, but like every man in the world, he wants more.

His prima donna routine is tucked away when I ask, "How long are we talking?"

He gives me his best puppy dog eyes while murmuring, "Five... twenty minutes tops."

His eyes widen when a growl rumbles between us.

"Ten? Can you give me ten?"

My eyes return to my watch while my brain calculates how fast I could reach Mystra's if I ran every red light. It would be pushing it, but I think I could trim it down to eight minutes.

Danny's brows furrow when I ask, "How many points do you have on your license?" When he looks at me, stumped, I add, "Enough to cover the handful of fines I *may* incur tonight by attending this meeting?"

"If it gets your ass into the meeting, I'll reinstate my MetroCard before calling it a night. Scouts honor." He crosses his heart and hopes to die... I can't remember the rest of the pledge he usually makes. It's something about kissing boys—or other parts of their bodies.

When Danny thrusts his hand toward mine, I accept it. "Deal, now let's get in there and make me some money."

Then I can offer Willow something fancier than a cheap-ass bottle of vodka.

Our meeting was over in three minutes, meaning I don't need to run the one red light I've been slowed by the past thirteen minutes. The swiftness of our meeting shouldn't be surprising. It was the standard one every company has while forking over a heap of money to the superstar they want recommending their products.

"Sign here, here, and here." They then toss the encyclopedia-sized contract into their briefcase, lock their hands with mine, and say, "We're very excited to work with you, Mr. Carlton."

I then leave the meeting with an armful of their products—which will get tossed into the coat room in my condo, never to been seen again—while my agent works out all the minor details such as filming location, scheduled in-store appearance and anything else they want me to do to have them handing over the amount we negotiated.

I don't like this side of my industry but understand it's a major part of it. I'm not just an athlete; there is a lot more to this industry than running onto a field once a week. I have nutritionists, coaches, physical therapists, and muscle conditioning instructors, just to name a few. There is an entire field of people behind me, which means I need a lot more than a standard man's income.

Love it or hate it, that's where endorsements come in.

I lower the revs on my Aston Martin when the neon lighting outside Mister Mystra's enters my vision. This place was my old hangout when I played college ball. Its beers were under three dollars, and their TV was bigger than the computer monitor-sized one Dalton and I had in our dorm room, so it wasn't just ideal for two broke-ass students, it was like our second home. The only places we spent more time at than here were the field and class, which we took the bare minimum hours needed to maintain our sports scholarships.

Mr. Mystra passed away four weeks before my final college game. Rumors are he was so excited about the upcoming playoffs, his heart couldn't function with the massive surge in his blood pressure every season. He was a great man, and it was only right his devotion to the game was honored during championship week. Both teams, home and away, wore black armbands to mark their respect, then the game ball signed by the captain of the winning team was donated to his family. It sits proudly in a glass cabinet at the back of the bar.

"Hey, man, you can't park there. That's a tow zone."

I toss the key to my car into the cautionary teen's chest before jogging around my idling vehicle. "I'll only be a minute, and if you stop it from being towed, I'll show you my gratitude with a freshly printed Benjamin Franklin."

He smiles like I just told him I'm paying his tuition for the next four years before he dips his chin in silent agreement. While he moves to guard my driver's side door, which I leave hanging open, I enter Mystra's.

The number of drunk college students filling the space is eye-numbing. The bitter scent of beer filtering through the air and the tangy smell of too many people in one place reveal nothing has changed the past eight years, not to mention the chatter of patrons as they slap down their glasses on the beer-soaked bar. This place is as packed and as happening as it was when Mr. Mystra was alive. I'm glad to see his legacy is being kept alive, just like the ink I scribbled across his football all those years ago.

When I reach the bar, the bartender greets me like Mr. Mystra always did—she's just forty years younger and nowhere near as short and pudgy. "You haven't aged a day."

She nudges her head to the display cabinet the winning ball and team photo is displayed in before locking her eyes with mine. The sparkle of attraction in her hooded gaze would usually have my cock paying very careful attention, but he's not even twitching tonight.

Don't get me wrong; the barmaid is attractive with her long, dark locks, pulse-quickening green eyes, and a rocking body; my cock just has his sights on an even more appealing brunette than the one giving me all the right signals at the completely wrong time.

"I'm looking for my friend, around five-four, curly brown hair." I project my voice to ensure the bartender can hear me over the hum of patrons, but she still appears lost. Unsure if she's confused by my lack of interest or my description of Willow, I try another tactic. "She's been plied with vodka by three douchebags hoping to get in her panties."

"Oh." Now she's clued in. "She's over by the jukebox." She sets down the glass she's polishing before pointing to the far left-hand corner of the room.

I jerk up my chin in thanks before taking off in the direction she's pointing.

"If it doesn't work out, you know where to find me. My shift finishes at twelve…"

If she continues talking, I wouldn't know it. Her sultry voice was swallowed by the roar of the crowd watching re-runs of Foster's third touchdown of the night.

I make it three-quarters of the way across the peanut-shell-coated floor before my dimpled chin, carved cheekbones, and trade-mark wonky smile give me away.

"Hey, it's Presley Carlton. Great game tonight!"

"Oh my god, my dad is going to flip! Can you sign my cap?"

"Mr. Carlton, do you have any tips on how I can improve my game? Coach has been riding my ass all season, but I'm still not meeting targets. If I don't shape up, he'll ship me out."

I smile at the first greeter, haphazardly sign the 69er's cap the second shoves into my chest, then lower my eyes to the beer the third accoster is clutching before swinging them to the mountain load of empty glasses on his table sitting next to an open packet of cigarettes.

Enough said.

"I'll quit right now." He fumbles his words just like his hands when he dumps his half-chugged beer on the table before submerging his cigarette pack into the liquid. "There. Done. Thanks, Mr. Carlton."

I smirk, wishing it was that easy before continuing to cross the room. I find Willow a few seconds later. Her back is flattened against the jukebox as she attempts to get as much space between her and the asshat who is crowding her as she can. She doesn't seem impressed with whatever he's whispering in her ear. Her shoulders are high in annoy-ance, and her fitted shirt has no chance in hell of hiding the thrust of her chest. She's not just annoyed, she's quite possibly frightened.

I rush over to save her, but my liberation comes too late. Willow's knee becomes friendly with the man's groin before I get within an inch of her. He topples to the ground like I did weeks ago, his screams as tormented as the ones I shredded when I felt seconds from death.

When Willow leans over his fetal-curled frame, I expect her to offer him the same assistance she gave me. She doesn't. She lays her boot into his ribs, her kick firm enough to cover his sports blazer with peanut shells.

"John Farnham is a national icon! How dare you compare him to Peter Andre!"

She makes a gagging noise, like everyone within a five-mile radius understands who she's talking about. We have no fucking clue. The dozen or so people surrounding her are peering at her with as much blankness in their eyes as my face is holding.

"So no, Archer-Mac-Farcher, I don't want to show you my map of Tasmania. Australia has enough droughts to contend with without adding the dryness your tacky 'I'll make you so wet you'll fill a river' line caused the area between my legs."

After a final sneer that includes an incredibly cute screwed up nose and prolonged stare, Willow steps over a writhing Archer to head back to the bar. She makes it two steps away before she notices me at the side, gawking at her. I expect her sass to continue, to give me as good as she gave Archer, but she does no such thing. She withers like a picked flower left on the windowsill in the midday sun before racing toward the exit.

Her race through the crowd is made with ease. I'm not so lucky. I'm stopped and asked for autographs multiple times, and the ones without a Sharpie hover close to pat me on the back in silent congratulations on the supposed "great game" I had.

By the time I make it outside, my car is getting a boot placed on it, and Willow is halfway down the block.

"I'll be back." I give the parking attendant a severe finger point before taking off after Willow.

A squeak pops out of her mouth when I band my arm around her waist, tug her into my torso, then spin her around. I probably just scared the living hell out of her, but with my car seconds from being towed, I don't have time to offer an introduction.

"Please not tonight, E. My stomach is swirling, and your car just got back its new car smell. Do you really want to risk it?"

I tug her into my embrace a little tighter, loving that she called me "E." Elvis is the annoying nickname I was given by a football camp coach who had an obsession with the "King of Rock." Like everything when you're seventeen, it spread through camp like wildfire. By the end of the day, everyone was using it.

Unfortunately, even those closest to me knowing how much I hate it hasn't stopped them from using it. Thank fuck I'm mostly referred to by my last name. It's the name commentators and fans scream when I'm sprinting down the sideline or throwing a perfect ball to the receiver, so for the most part, Elvis is an alias only those closest to me use. But I like "E." It has a nice ring to it. Especially when it's voiced by an inebriated Australian girl who could read the dictionary and make it sound sexy.

Willow sags into my chest when I ask, "Did you eat anything before you went out drinking? Or did you chug them down like a novice on an empty stomach?"

I take her groan for an answer.

"I'd rather extract half a bottle of vodka out of my interior than a doner kebab loaded with tzatziki sauce."

"Mmm, a doner kebab sounds mighty enticing right now."

I continue walking us back to my car. My steps are slow since Willow's dangling legs are swaying precariously between my splayed thighs. The last thing I want is another whack to the nuts.

"We'll look at a greasy kebab tomorrow—when you're begging for something to soak up the leftover slosh in your belly."

When we reach the passenger side door of my car, I swing my eyes to Mister Mystra's. "Where's Skylar?"

I scan the crowd seeking the blonde bombshell Willow painted in painstaking detail last night. Her description was so vivid, I was convinced I had met Skylar before, but it didn't take me long to realize the errors of my ways. We had never crossed paths; Skylar is just the quintessential American college girl. Long blonde hair, big cornflower blue eyes, and a body that apparently makes men drool.

If I hadn't heard the pride in Willow's voice when she described her friend, I would have thought she was jealous, although she has no reason to be. Willow might not be a typical, everyday girl, but she has plenty going for her. Enough that several men on the sidewalk are more than happy to sneak a peek at her thighs when her unladylike slide into my car causes her skirt to ride up well past her knee.

I slam the door shut, nearly drowning out Willow's reply that Skylar left twenty minutes ago. I'm about to go on a rant about safety in numbers at college hangouts, but my front tires lifting from the road surface forces it to the backburner. I don't just have a boot on my tire, but my car is being towed.

"Come on, man, you can't take my car. Look at my friend; she's nearly passed out in the passenger seat. If you tow my vehicle, I'll have no way to get her home. Do you really want that on your conscience?"

The parking officer's hand looks like a duck jabbering away before he continues filling in the citation he is planning to give me. "This is a red zone. Red does not mean stop. It means you can't park here." He talks to me like I'm an idiot, as if my skills on the field are the only skillset I have. "Your vehicle will be impounded at the Walter Street impound lot. Once you've paid your fine and the impound fee, it will be returned to you. It opens at 5 AM."

He rips off my citation notice before pivoting around to face me. I've never been more grateful for a recognizable face than I am right now. He stammers backward, his eyes widening with every fumbled step he makes.

"You're... You're... *Oh. My. God!*" His last three squealed words shred my eardrums. It was worse than any female fan I've heard in my life.

Before he can blow my cover to a curious Willow watching our exchange with an eagle eye, I pace closer to him. "Hey, I'm Presley Carlton; it's a pleasure to meet you. Have you been a 69ers fan for long?"

He looks seconds from passing out as he answers, "Only my whole life. My dad is a 69ers fan; his dad is a 69ers fan; hell, even my granddad's dad was a 69ers fan."

"That's awesome, man, really great. So I take it a pair of season tickets wouldn't be of any interest to you, would they?"

His pupils turn massive as sweat beads on his top lip. "Season tickets?"

He's certain he heard me wrong.

He didn't.

"Yep. I've got a few passes lying around, not doing anything. They're yours, if you want them?"

"Oh, please, sir, yes, sir, I'd love them, sir." His hurried words remind me of Oliver Twist asking for some more gruel.

"Alright, great. Can I borrow your pen to write down where you need to pick up the tickets?" He shoves his pen into my hand even faster than he did my fine. "I'll give you the ticket agent's name and number, then all you need to do is hand him this, and he'll give you the passes." I nudge my head to the citation in my hand. "Where should I jot down the information he needs? On here, perhaps?"

I give him a look, one that says we won't be exchanging any details without him giving as much as he's receiving.

It takes him a few seconds to understand, but when he does, his head bobs up and down. "Yeah, that will be great. While you do that, I'll get that pesky boot off your tire."

"Perfect."

I flash him my trademark smirk before filling in the details as requested. Every letter I scribble increases Danny's imaginary whine in my ear. Season passes don't come cheap, but if it saves my cover being blown and a pricy impound fee, I'm happy to lose a few thousand from my bank account.

Once the boot is removed from my tire, I hand the parking officer my fine. "There you go, all set. It was a pleasure doing business with you."

He stumbles out a hundred apologies in one sentence. I only catch half of them since I'm too busy sliding into the driver's seat of my car and hightailing it down the street before Willow catches on to what our exchange was about.

I shouldn't have bothered. She's fast asleep, her faint snores barely audible over the healthy purr of my engine.

CHAPTER TWELVE

Willow

I wake with a grumbling tummy. Its frantic moans aren't due to the copious amounts of liquor I chugged down last night. It's the delicious scent of frying lamb and fresh-cut lettuce instigating its gripes.

I sit up slowly, anticipating more than a hungry tummy. I'm shocked when only a slight thump drums my temples. With the exception of my horrid morning breath, I don't feel any different today than I do every other morning.

As my mouth works through its dryness, my half-asleep brain demands that my eyes open. With my hangover not as bad as I expected, the need for a greasy breakfast isn't dire, but nothing will keep me from unearthing where that smell is coming from.

The thumping head I was predicting rolls in like a vicious thunderstorm when my eyes finally follow the prompts of my brain. I'm in a room much too fancy to be a dorm. There's steel, wood, and manly features as far as my weary eyes can stretch. It's a sexy room with an industrial, loft-type feel to it, but it's not a room I belong in.

Cringing at my first walk of shame in over three years, I snatch the bedsheet close to my body before slipping out of the ginormous bed I'm sprawled on. With the plain white T I'm wearing hitting my knees upon standing, I soon ditch the bedsheet.

Years of ballet classes come in handy when I tiptoe across the vast room to gather my skirt, shirt, and sky-high heels from a large wood chest. After peering over the steel and wood railing to the floor below to make sure the coast is clear, I slip the unknown man's shirt over my head before throwing on the clothes I wore last night.

The clean scent of body wash lingering out of the bathroom on my right makes me wish I had time to shower and brush my teeth, but the happy whistle of the man downstairs assures me I'm out of time. While tugging my skirt up my trembling thighs, I try to recall who I went home with last night. I really hope it wasn't Archer; that guy was a creep. Tim wasn't too far behind him, and although Bryce was cute, he had those nervous fumbling hands. I'm sure the only zippers he has unclasped in his life are his own.

Whoever it is, the lack of ache between my thighs makes me grateful for my blank thoughts. As my grandma always liked to say: "If you don't feel them the next morning, they didn't do their job." I'm not feeling anything.

With my heels in my hand and my purse tucked under my arm, I commence my painstakingly slow tiptoe down the spiral staircase separating the loft bedroom from the main residence. If my hungry tummy had its way, I would take a left at the bottom instead of a right. I don't know what my unknown host is cooking, but it smells good.

I swivel around, ready to make a break for it, when the quick glimpse of a profile sneaks into my sight. So much muscle, so much height, so much scrumptiously delicious man-meat on display, my foot misses the final step. I try to regain my balance. I flap my arms around like a recently beheaded chicken and stick out my ass like it will counterbalance the many pounds I carry on my chest. My efforts are useless. I'm going down, and I'm going down hard.

As my cheek skids across the floor, my skirt creeps up my thighs so high, if it weren't for my boobs, it would asphyxiate me. My shirt becomes a mid-riff top, and my only hope of coverage goes skidding across the wooden floor with a clatter. My heels' brutal *dong, boink, dong* routine sounds like Santa galloping across a hot tin roof in the Australian outback. It's loud and unmissable.

I've barely concealed my panty-covered backside when a deep voice on my right says, "Serves you right for trying to sneak out."

While I attempt to muster up a lie, Elvis takes a giant bite out of a loaded doner kebab. When white sauce dribbles down his chin, my pussy recreates the scene. It doesn't use tzatziki sauce as its liquid of choice, though.

As I stand to my feet, without any assistance from Elvis, my eyes shift past the wide span of his shoulders. The mess in his kitchen reveals his delicious-smelling brunch wasn't picked up at the store. He made it. The chopped lettuce, diced tomatoes, and sliced cucumber are proof enough, much less the seasoned lamb still sizzling in the pan.

My lip drops into a pout when I return my eyes to Elvis. I didn't need any more proof on how cruel life can be, but if I did, the very definition of unfair is standing right in front of me. This isn't fair—he isn't fair! You can't have a perfectly structured face, panty-wetting smile, cooking skills, and a body that defies both logic and my panties' ability to hold moisture.

Elvis doesn't just have a six pack, he has eight. His serratus muscles are so defined, it looks like he has fingers on each side of his abs, and his Apollo's belt is so perfectly carved, his hips are in direct symmetry to the trail of hair leading from his belly button to an area I'm certain is as stacked as his spectacular body.

I freeze as a disturbing notion rolls through my head. Minus the frantic quivers his naked torso, bare feet, and sultry smirk has caused my pussy, it's still void of any feeling. There's no ache of exhaustion or a snippet of the sensation you get after being stretched.

There's nothing.

Zilch.

Sweet fuck all.

A whine creeps up my esophagus when the truth smacks into me. That's why he's so incredibly handsome. He got double the looks because he only got half the deal downstairs.

Elvis looks at me like I'm batshit crazy when I demand, "Stick out your tongue."

"What?"

"Tongue, E. Stick it out."

He smiles a grin that reveals he loves his nickname as much as I do before doing as requested. He has a nice tongue. Nice pink coloring, wide, and nicely curved at the tip, and his reach is undisputable when it hits his chin once it's fully extended.

"Alright, good. That's great. Now your fingers."

"What the fuck are you doing..." His words trail off when I snag his hand with mine, un-ball his fist, then mentally measure the length of his fingers.

There are no issues here. Not a single one. His fingers are longer and girthier than some men's penises, meaning we are more than fine, we're great. I can live without penile penetration if the rest of the package can take up the slack.

Feeling much better, I drop Elvis's hand, side-skirt him, then enter his kitchen. I make myself at home by whipping up a lamb kebab. I should be going home, but my excitement at discovering I spent the night with Elvis instead of one of the three musketeers I was hanging with last night is too thrumming to ignore. Even my run-in with the teary-eyed girl yesterday morning and Skylar's demand we watch football couldn't dampen my happiness yesterday. Our kiss was the highlight of my entire day, so if I'm presented with the perfect opportunity to recreate it, I'm not giving it up for anything.

Elvis watches me from the side, not the least bit confronted I'm taking over his domain. From the grin on his face, anyone would swear he's loving my command of the reins. I can see him changing his mind when I start grilling him.

"What happened between us? First, second, or third base?" I take a big bite of my recently rolled kebab before raising my eyes to his. "I didn't fall asleep halfway through, did I? That's only happened once before, and I was adamant I'd never let it happen again, so please tell me I gave as good as I received."

Praying it will hide the mammoth smile stretching across my

face from the lowering of Elvis's eyelids, I take another bite of my kebab. He's so worked up right now, the vein in his neck is pumping as hard as the buzz keeping my clit firm.

That's why I'm stirring him. I either tease him or climb him like a tree. Considering I have no clue how I got here, or what he thinks of me right now, the former is the safer option.

Elvis answers my question without words by nudging his head to the left. There's a white sheet sprawled over a two-seater couch—a couch much too small to sleep a man as tall as him. Even I would struggle sleeping on it.

Grimacing, I return my eyes to Elvis. "So no sleep for you, then?"

"No." He looks at me with twinkling eyes while popping the last piece of his kebab into his mouth. "The couch wasn't the issue, though." I'm about to ask what was, but he puts me out of my misery before I can. "Your snoring was."

Spit-covered lamb flies out of my mouth when I make a *pfft* noise. "I do *not* snore."

My teeth rip through my kebab like I'm a savage animal, wordlessly advising Elvis what will happen to his package if he continues with his snoring accusation. His sausage is about to be cut in half for the second time in his life.

Elvis shrugs off my warning, not the least bit worried. "Your snoring is worse than a freight train." He makes noises identical to the ones I heard when Skylar recorded me sleeping to prove her theory on my supposed "drunk snoring issue."

"Are you sure you weren't being kept awake by your own snoring? Scientists have proved every man on the planet snores."

Elvis rounds the counter to prop his hip next to mine, interested to hear the theory he sees in my eyes. When he folds his thick, bulging arms in front of his chest, I enlighten him with my profound knowledge, "When men lie on their backs, their balls fall in front of their butthole, causing a vapor lock. With one hole blocked, their only remaining one has to double its production. Digestive fumes, beer gas, even weed gas is vented out of their mouths. Hence the snoring."

I vibrate my lips together, making a *neigh* noise. It turns into a squeal when Elvis snags a damp tea towel from the kitchen counter and uses it to whip me. As I charge across his large, yet still homey loft apartment, I shove the last two bites of my kebab into my mouth.

He's on my heels in under a second, the hotness of his breath causing more excitement to my stomach than his delicious culinary skills.

•

"You don't think you should tell her mom?"

I lean back into my chair, the glass of wine I'm nursing balancing on my partially bare thigh. "I suggested it to Chelsea, but she's adamant she doesn't want her mom to know."

Elvis tucks his still bare foot under his backside before swiveling to face me. Thankfully, a cool afternoon breeze forced him to put on a shirt. Unfortunately, a cool afternoon breeze forced him to put on a shirt. It's good because the more he covers up, the smarter I appear, but bad because only an idiot wouldn't want to ogle all he has going on.

My eyes relinquish their missile lock on Elvis's biceps when he asks, "But is Chelsea really old enough to make that decision? She is only nine."

"She's ten next week," I argue, hating that my good deed might not turn out so good.

I spent the last thirty minutes updating Elvis on the events of yesterday. He agreed with me that Chelsea should have never been excluded from ballet because she's didn't have the usual ballet body type, but I could see the caution in his eyes when I told him I had accepted Chelsea into my class without first gaining parental permission.

"You should have seen her face, E. The kids took her under their wings and showed her the basics before swapping numbers so they could practice during to the week to make sure she knows our routine before our next class. She fits into our group dynamic so well."

"I get it, Will, really, I do. I'm just..." He fixes my low-hanging bra strap before raising his eyes to mine, letting them say the rest of his sentence. He's worried about me.

I return his stare with both wonderment and shock. Our interactions today have been nothing like they were the night we met. We gushed over Dalton and Becca's gorgeous baby girl when we visited them after our tea towel whipping competition this morning, then we picked up some fried chicken on our way home before vegging out on his couch the past three hours.

If you were a stranger peering in on us, you'd swear we've been friends for months—if not years. Electricity has been bouncing between us nonstop, even more so when Becca asked about us showing up together, but for the most part, we've set aside the spark to form a deeper, more tangible connection. It's been amazing, and the fact it was done without mentioning the incident that led to me arriving at his house at midnight makes it even more phenomenal.

I swirl my wine around my glass when Elvis asks, "What's the worst thing that could happen if this blows up?"

"For me or Chelsea?"

He stares me dead set in the eyes. "Both of you."

My teeth rake my lower lip as I contemplate. "For me, I'd most likely get fired."

I can handle being fired; my pay is half what Skylar gets at the bar gig she picks up each weekend to cover her "luxuries," but I understand mine and Chelsea's circumstances are very different. No matter how much she wishes it were true, she can't divorce her parents and pick up a weekend job serving drunken baboons to put her through school.

"Chelsea would most likely get grounded; she'll probably be forced back into ballet and lose internet privileges for a month." I raise my eyes to Elvis's, ensuring he can see the honesty in mine when I say, "But I truly believe she'd say the sacrifice was worth it. She has so much passion for dance, E. She reminds me of myself when I was her age. She doesn't care if it is classical ballet or busting moves on the trampoline in her backyard, she just wants to dance. Have you ever had a passion so great, no matter how bad the odds are stacked against you, you'll never stop fighting until you achieve your dreams?"

He nods without pause.

"That's all I could see when I peered down at her tear-stained face. I couldn't deny her the opportunity to reach her dreams because I was scared of the consequences. Fuck consequences; they're barely a blip on the radar when you're endeavoring for greatness."

My eyes bounce between my wine glass and Elvis when he removes it from my hand. He places it on the coffee table before tilting closer to me.

"Whatcha doing?"

I choke on the spit sliding down my throat when he replies, "I'm going to kiss you," as his sexy dark eyes dance between mine. "I've been dying to kiss you since you murmured my name when I carried you upstairs to my room. I've been dying to kiss you since you skidded across the tiles in my living room because you were trying to sneak out without saying goodbye…" I attempt to interrupt him, but him tugging my wrist until I straddle his lap stops me. "…I've also been dying to kiss you since I spotted the cutest pool of tzatziki sauce in the corner of your plump lips, but I was waiting, hoping you'd make the first move so you wouldn't think I was a dirty old man who brings home drunk college girls with the hope of making out with them on my three-thousand-dollar couch."

Three thousand *dollar couch?*

Believing he's showing off, I say, "You *are* a dirty old man hoping to make out with a college girl."

He continues talking as if I didn't speak, but the curve of his lips as they arrow toward mine reveals he took my comment as me being playful. "But your speech inspired me. If you want something, you've got to go for it, right? No matter the consequences."

My breath fans his mouth when I reply, "That's right." When I breathe in and out three times to settle the ruckus in my stomach, my nipples brush against his chest. His eyes when he stares up at me

—my god, they're enough to unleash a tsunami of butterflies ripping through my gut. "Is this what you want, E? A kiss? A couch grind-up? More?"

Please say "more." Please say "more."

My silent prayers kind of get answered when he murmurs, "How about we start with a kiss and see where it goes from there?"

He drops his delicious mouth to mine, his tongue darting out to clear away the smudge of sauce he referenced earlier. I taste it on his tongue when he slips it between my parted lips. He kisses me fiercely, his tongue fucking my mouth as greedily as his fingers grip my ass to draw me closer. He pulls me in close enough that my earlier fear of him having a cheerio for a cock is a distant memory, but far enough away the half-inch of air between us is teasingly frustrating.

His kisses are hungry and bruising, with the perfect combination of speed and control. I'll never forget being kissed by him, but I'll also be begging for more long before his taste leaves my lips.

I kiss him with the same fierceness. I want to step up to the plate sooner next time, to not wait for me to make the first move. *I want him to fill the last damn snippet of air between us.*

"Yes," I breathe over his mouth in a throaty groan when he answers my question by slipping his hand under my shirt to tug me in the last half-inch.

I swivel my hips and drag my skirt up my thighs without needing to remove my fingers from his shaggy mane before I execute an earth-shuddering grind down his thickened shaft. "Sweet baby Jesus. Is that thing legal?"

I stammer back with a squeal when a deep voice on our left says, "I've been wondering that same thing myself." A man with more style than a straight man could pull off saunters into the room. "Any time he gets accused of using steroids, I tell him to whip out his cock." He snaps back, holds his empty hand in the air, then clicks his finger three times. *Snap, crackle, pop, Motherfucker.* "Never once has he listened."

After giving Elvis a *you're no fun* look, he continues his sashay across the room. The bag of takeout in his hand swings as heavily as the tension brewing between Elvis and me, but before I can act on it, I spot the three Blu-ray discs our interrupter is clasping in his overloaded hand. A giggle bubbles in my chest when I recognize the cover of the top Blu-ray. It's *What Men Want* starring Taraji P. Henson.

Someone is eager to find out how his own specimen thinks.

After adjusting his cock so it's no longer digging into my panties, Elvis tugs down the hem of my skirt, deposits me and my pouting backside on the spot next to him, then stands to his feet. I can't see his face, but he's clearly giving his uninvited guest his best *fuck-off* look as he clambers backward with his hand held in the air and his mouth gaped only two seconds later.

"It's Sunday afternoon. We always have a movie marathon on Sundays. It's how you recover after——"

"A long week at work." Elvis's tone is sterner than I've heard it before. "Yeah, that's right, but I have a *guest* over."

The uninvited hottie asks, "Does she not like Chinese?"

His eyes snap to mine when I groan. The last time I ate Chinese, I nearly died. "N. O. Say it isn't so. You can't be Willow *my farts smell like a moldy potato chip sandwich* Willow. Surely not. You look nothing like the fire-breathing witch I handled last month."

His eccentric voice fills me with happiness. Unfortunately, that's where my giddiness ends. I thought Windy Willow was horrid, but the nickname Elvis has shared with his friends is ten times worse.

"Thank you for a great day, but I think it's time for me to leave."

I freeze, unsure if I am coming or going when Elvis threatens, "If your ass moves an inch off that couch, Will, I'm gonna spank it."

Confident he has squashed my eagerness to leave, Elvis refocuses his attention on his friend. He looks as excited by Elvis's warning as I am. "I gave you that description to ensure you delivered the goods to the right person, not to use it against her."

"Ohhh." The blond drops the takeout and Blu-Rays on a table at his side before kicking off his shoes. He doesn't care how stern Elvis's glare gets, he ain't leaving. "I thought you wanted it included in the package." He shrugs. "My bad?"

Elvis's fists clench so fast, a blood vessel nearly bursts in his wrist. "You put my description in the package?"

"Yeah." He rolls his eyes, as if to say *duh*. "How else do you think I'd find her? There were over thirteen Willows just in the co-ed dorms. I needed something to work with."

Elvis drags his hand down his face as I finally understand. His guest is the man who brought me the pharmacy products the morning following my embarrassing escapade.

"And here I was thinking she didn't call me because I was cracking jokes when she was five minutes from death."

"Thank you! Finally!" I stand to my feet to bridge the gap between us. "No matter how many times I told Skylar I was dying, she didn't believe me."

I slap Elvis on his chest. My whack has a double meaning. I'm annoyed as hell that he told his friend what my gas smells like, but I understand his dilemma. Without an in-depth description, I may have never been found, which means I wouldn't have had access to the medication I needed to get better.

"I'm Willow *I try not to fart on first dates* Underwood. It's a pleasure to meet you..."

"Danny." The eccentric blond thrusts his hand toward mine, his greeting delivered with a mammoth smile. "I think you and I are going to be very close friends."

Elvis looks more petrified now than he did when Dalton told him he'll be on diaper duty if he didn't get his lips off his wife earlier today. It was only a peck, but Elvis's lips lingered long enough Dalton couldn't help but react.

I'm glad Elvis is uncomfortable because I'm confident Danny is the key to unlocking all his innermost secrets.

"**C**an you lose points for performing a lewd act while driving?"

Willow's wide eyes stray from the road to me. They're darker than usual with the low hang of her eyelids hiding their sparkle. "I guess it would depend on the charge?" She sounds as unsure as her facial expression. "Why? What lewd act are you willing to lose your license for?"

She rakes down my body, missing the thousands of replies streaming from my eyes. The sexual chemistry bristling between us is so intense, if I could drive without any hands on the steering wheel, I'd have more than just her thigh covered. Danny was great; he made Willow feel at ease all while keeping my career on the down low, but the guy is a cockblocking motherfucker.

His corny jokes, stories from our high school years, and his ability to always place himself between Willow and me meant that little taste of her mouth I had at the start of our evening was the *only* taste of her mouth I've had. I'm dying over here—like seriously dying. This is worse than food poisoning, and I'm nearing months of abstinence since I broke my back. I swear, I've never craved something as badly as I'm craving another taste of her mouth.

The sexy moan she released when she grinded down on me stops replaying through my head when her giggle takes its place.

"It's lucky you asked before leaping." She nudges her head to my rearview mirror, which shows a decked-out state trooper sedan following closely behind us. "Did you want to test the theory?"

I almost swerve onto the wrong side of the road when she pulls her seatbelt far away from her chest so she can tilt my way. She is inches from the zipper biting my cock. So close, I can picture her hot breaths leaving beads of condensation on the crest of my cock after she whips it out of my pants.

When she arrows down even lower, I really want to say, *Willow, don't be such a fucking tease. Take my dick between those pillowy lips like I've been dying to do all day.* Instead, I say, "Willow, god damn it, don't be stupid. I don't want to be forced to prove my muscles aren't just for looks when we get arrested."

Laughing, she pulls back. "People think your muscles are for show?" I lose the chance to answer when she adds on, "I can understand their error. They're very pretty to look at." Her shoulder pops up two inches as a lightbulb inside her head switches on. "Oh my god. How did I not think of this earlier? Underwear model?"

"Huh?"

My eyes bounce between hers and my speedo. The trooper is still following us, meaning I've got to make sure I keep it under the limit. I'm not worried about a speeding ticket; I just don't want my cover blown if he's a 69ers fan.

"Sexy body. Panty-wetting face. You sell undies for a living, don't you?"

"Undies?"

Her tongue peeks between her teeth as she strives to hold back a grin. "Undies. Jocks. Briefs. Nut-huggers. Trunks. Boxer shorts. Whatever you call them." She folds one of her ankles over the other before twisting her torso to face me. "You do the seedy, head-sloped-to-the-side grins that make women like me think you lost your cock somewhere between the makeup chair and the photography studio, don't you? You know, the *oh shit, who stole my penis!* expression every magazine in America is running with these days."

"I'm not an underwear model." *Anymore.*

Five years ago, I wore the exact expression Willow mentioned when Lillian forced me to do a shoot with her. The agency wasn't interested in the fiancée of the top quarterback in the country; they wanted the real deal. With Lillian's ego at stake, I manned up and did the gig.

Worst decision I ever made.

I don't care if you're hung like a donkey, when you're poked and prodded by over a dozen spectators before being stripped bare in front of an additional thirty people in an air-conditioned room, you'll have shrinkage issues. Not even Lillian's playful grind-up had my cock popping up to say "hello." He was down for the count, preferring to have me paraded around America as if I had a corn kernel for a penis than pretend it was showtime.

That hoopla saw me swearing off underwear gigs for the remainder of my life. Although, I don't see shrinkage ever being a problem if I were partnered up with Willow. She's got enough curves for the nation to pay attention to. The photographer would need an extra-wide lens to capture them all.

Jeez, would you listen to me? The pompous head on my shoulders is nearly as big as the one between my legs.

Hating that parts of the man I was when I was with Lillian are creeping out of me, I switch our conversation to something that will help ease the throb between my legs. "I gather dance is a vital part of your life, but what's your major?"

Willow appears stumped by the quick change in our conversation, but my mention of her first love quickly secures her attention. "It was dance—"

"You can major in dance?" I'm not being an ass. I'm truly shocked.

She smiles, loving my surprise. "Yep. It's a Bachelor of Arts."

My lips quirk as I nod. "Nice. So why the 'was' part of your statement? Your passion for dance is all over your face, so why did you give it up?"

She taps her knees as if it's the answer to everything. It isn't. She has a nice kneecap, but I'm not seeing the issue.

"I had a knee reconstruction two years ago. I was landing the most perfect grand jeté when my knee gave out from underneath me." She's not being showy. I can't see anything but genuine honesty in her eyes. "I spent a week in the hospital and another six on crutches, then..." Her words drift off when disappointment takes them hostage.

I'm not as willing to end our conversation. This isn't the first chat we've had today, but it is the most interesting. "That was two years ago, so what's stopping you now?"

Willow's brows stitch as she stares at me like I'm a moron. "I had a *complete* knee reconstruction."

"So?" I reply, unsure why that would stop her. I broke my back, yet, here I am, playing the game I love. "Wasn't it you who said 'fuck consequences, they're barely a blip on the radar when you're endeavoring for greatness'? Maybe you should listen to your own advice?"

"My knee can't withstand the endurance needed for ballet." She looks like she wants to say more, but she holds it back—barely.

"You can't say that if you haven't given it a chance. Besides, even if that were true, when one part of your body can't stand the pressure, teach the ones around it to take up its slack. Your thighs, your ankles, train them to support your knee, then, over time, give your knee a shot to prove its strength."

I take a mental note to kiss the shit out of my physical therapist for her once unwanted advice when a staunch glint forms in Willow's eyes. She's not entirely with my proposal, but she's not shutting it down either. That's good enough for me—for now.

"Okay. I'll give it a go. There's no harm in trying, right?"

My heart tap-dances on my ribs as excitement roars through me. I never realized how good it feels to help someone. It's nearly as rewarding as achieving the seemingly impossible yourself.

"Until then... what's occupying your time?"

Her first reply is unvoiced. Her glance at me through lowered lashes adds an extra beat to my already thumping heart. Her second reply shocks me, "If I play my cards right, by the end of this academic year, I'll graduate with a bachelor in sports medicine."

"Sports medicine?"

I apologize to anyone within a ten-mile radius of the parking lot of Willow's school. I just damaged your hearing, didn't I?

"Yes!" Willow leans over to whack me in the arm. "Why are you so surprised by that? Sports and dancing are one and the same."

Spit gargles in my throat when I fake a gag. "That's not true, because you *hate* sports."

"I don't hate them! I just don't love them. Those are two entirely different things." After smacking me for a second time, she sinks into her chair before folding her arms over her chest. "I didn't have the means to throw two years of study down the drain. It was either pick a major that worked with the credits I already had or quit altogether." I chuckle under my breath when she murmurs, "It was a close call."

The playfulness fueling our conversation does a complete one-eighty when she discloses, "I'm unlikely to graduate anyway. If I don't find a placement next month, I'll lose fifty percent of my grade this term."

"You need an internship to graduate?"

She jerks her chin up. "Yeah, and no one is eager to let a novice get within an inch of their 'superstar client.'" She air quotes her last two words. "I'm weeks from setting up a massage table outside my local gym and requesting volunteers on their way out."

I'd laugh if she didn't sound so serious.

"Do you want me to have a word with some contacts I have in the industry?"

She peers at me in shock. "You know people in the sports industry?"

"I can if you need me to."

Asking favors in my field is the equivalent of signing a verbal contract to be their ass-kisser for the remainder of the season, but I like Willow, and I really like the flavor of her mouth, so I'm more than willing to put in a word for her if it brings back her smile and increases my chance of kissing her a little more.

Like she can hear my private thoughts, she leans over to press her mouth to mine. Her kiss is as innocent as I wish her face wasn't, but it's full of tenderness. After drawing back, her grateful eyes dance between mine. "Thanks for the offer, but I'll find a placement. You can only be knocked back so many times before you eventually get what you want, right?"

"Right."

Not willing to part with her mouth just yet, I pull her lips back to mine by the back of her head. We kiss until my windows are foggy, and I'm struggling to figure out why I didn't participate in backseat make-out sessions more frequently during my college days.

Oh, that's right. Lillian didn't like me messing up her hair when we were in public. Come to think of it, she didn't like me messing with it at all. Unless there were sharks circling the carcass she was planning to milk for all it was worth, she didn't hand over a simple peck without whining.

Talk about giving a guy a complex. I was so convinced I sucked at sex, I used the six months following our breakup to do in-depth studies of the female anatomy. I'm not proud to admit I fucked my way through half the population of my hometown when I returned there after our separation, and even with having numerous verbal affirmations, much less a handful of publicized ones the media had a field day with, I still let Lillian's lack of interest play with my thoughts.

Such as now, when I'm withdrawing from Willow way sooner than I'd like. "Not yet. Need more," Willow speaks over my lips before reattaching them to hers. "Got to get enough to last me three weeks."

Like my mood could sour any more, she reminds me of my three-week away game schedule this month.

I still as shock stuns me. *What the fuck is this woman doing to me?* I love football. I eat, breathe, and sleep football, but now I'm whining like a bitch because it's taking me away from a woman I met only weeks ago.

Someone pass me a bag of concrete because I need to harden the fuck up.

The little whimper Willow makes when I pry her back by her shoulders has me regretting every decision I've ever made. Who needs a career that lines your pocket with millions of dollars when you can make a woman whimper like that?

I'd reattach our mouths and see how many times I could make her moan if we weren't being eyeballed like freaks. My Aston stands out in the parking lot of Willow's college, but only because she lives in a dorm instead of one of those fancy sororities Lillian begrudgingly lived in.

Pissed at my third thought of Lillian in one day, I soothe the volatile waters. "Do you have any plans the Saturday night I return?"

"The twenty-third?"

When I nod, the disappointment spreading across Willow's face grows. "I have the kids' recital. I can't skip it; they'd be devastated—"

I muffle her excuse with my finger. "I wouldn't expect you to give that up, much less ask you to." Only a douchebag wouldn't understand she loves the children in her class as much as she loves dancing. "Can I swing by and pick you up after the recital?"

"Will you be *that* desperate you can't wait until Sunday?" Her ear-to-ear smile kills the mirth in her tone. Before I can make a fool out of myself, she adds on, "Pick me up at ten. I'll text you the address."

After a final peck to my lips, she slumps back into her side of my car, throws open my door, then slides out. She completes three long strides down the sidewalk before I call her name. When she spins around to face me, I ask, "Can I get the show now? I'm not sure I'll make the Mickey's parking lot in enough time."

With a smile that reveals she knows exactly what I'm referring to, she sexily saunters to within an inch of my car. I expect her to give me some sass, or at the very least, flip me the bird. She does neither of those things. She proves why she is as playful as the glint in her eyes and as wild as the kinks in her hair.

To the beat in her head, she balls her hands into tiny fists, raises them to her chest, sticks out her delectable ass, then bump and grinds down the pavement like she's in the middle of a nightclub.

She shimmies and shakes until she reaches the front of her dorm, and she's gained an audience of admirers.

She's not the least bit embarrassed. She's loving the attention as much as I'm loving the confidence beaming out of her. She is in her element, beautiful smile and all.

After a curtsy to her wolf-whistling fans, and an air kiss blown my way, Willow slips into the safety of her dorm, leaving me breathless and with the biggest hard-on I've ever had.

That, what you just witnessed right there, is why I asked Dalton to keep her away from me the night we met. I could see the wild spark in her eyes, the one that warned she'd drag me away from my dreams kicking and screaming. Not because I was giving in, but because she'd move the goal posts to a place I swore I'd never strive for again.

She has me seeking the unattainable.

She makes me want to open up my heart to the possibility of loving again.

I can only hope she doesn't crush me when I do.

CHAPTER FOURTEEN

Willow

Chelsea's big blue eyes peer at me in awe when I pull back the tissue paper on the box I placed in front of her. They're welling with as much moisture as mine, equally sad and excited.

"These were your shoes?"

"Uh-huh. They were the last pair of ballet slippers my mom purchased for me before she passed."

Chelsea blinks excessively during my last sentence, fighting to keep her tears at bay. I understand her plight. My mom passed away years ago, yet I still struggle every day to remember she is gone.

"Why did you bring them? I thought you taught hip hop?"

After removing my ballet shoes from the box and placing it to the side, I drag over a second box. "I teach hip hop, but my first love has always been ballet."

Chelsea's face lights up as she nods. She wants to dance no matter the cost, but her first love is ballet too.

"I was talking to a friend recently, and he got me thinking that just because we're told we can't do something doesn't necessarily mean it's true."

"He sounds smart."

I laugh. "He is smart. Very much so."

The smile on Chelsea's face doubles when I crack open the lid on the second box to reveal an identical pair of ballet slippers as hers, just a few sizes bigger. "I couldn't sleep the night he left for a trip—"

"Because you were sad you were going to miss him?" Chelsea interrupts.

I run my hand down her sweet face. "Yes, that, and..." I stop, wordlessly building the suspense. Only once she looks seconds from peeing her pants in anticipation do I say, "I was thinking about you, and how you really wanted to do ballet."

She tries to rebut, but her words fall short.

"It's okay. I understand hip hop isn't your first choice." I lean in close to make sure no little ears hear my next set of words. "It's not my first choice either, but that doesn't mean we can't love it as well, right?"

She nods her head, a little eagerly.

"So what I was thinking was..." I carefully pull off her glitter-coated shoes and replace them with my old ballet slippers. "... if you really want to do ballet, maybe I could show you some moves?"

She stares at me with her lips quivering and her eyes watering. "You'll do that for me?"

"Uh-huh."

Who knew two little words could be so hard to get out without choking? You can't hear how she expressed her question. She's truly stunned someone would go to bat for her. That's sad and shows how far society has stepped away from the "it takes a village to raise a child" logic most of our parents were raised with.

I drag my hand across my cheeks to ensure they're dry. "We don't have much time, but if you're willing to put in the effort, I have a ballet routine you could perform at the recital."

Chelsea's spine straightens as her breathing lengthens. "Really?"

When I nod, she leaps into my arms. The hug she gives me...oh! You can't explain perfection. Warm enough to melt the coldest heart and jam-packed with emotions.

"Thank you, Will."

I draw back far enough to look down at her tear-stained face.

"You're very welcome. Now how about you go and tell everyone your exciting news, then we'll sneak in some moves before your mom arrives to collect you?"

Nodding, she stands before charging for the children still packing up after our lesson. While she updates them on her news, I send a quick text to Elvis.

ME

Thanks for the tip; she's on board and ready to learn.

A smile stretches across my face when he replies.

ELVIS

And you? Are you ready to trust your body to tell you when it's reached its limit?

After waving goodbye to Brock, my fingers fly across the screen of my phone just as swiftly as he races into his father's arms.

ME

If you don't hear from me by eight, send a medic to this location.

I fake coordinates at the end of my sentence.

ELVIS

LOL. Just remember to brace your knee and take it easy.

I'm smiling like a cat staring at a bowl of tuna... until his next message arrives.

ELVIS

Don't forget I have a meeting tonight, so I'll be out of reach for a couple of hours.

Several curious eyes pop up to me when I stomp my feet like a child. My schedule has been extremely wonky the past few weeks. With school requiring I be alert and awake during daylight hours, my phone calls with Elvis every night have me burning the candle at both ends, but I've loved every single moment of it. We talk about anything and everything. Dalton and Becca's daughter, Danny's failed attempt at finding love on an online dating site; even Chelsea has come up a handful of times. It's been a wonderful flirty few weeks, but I am a damn wreck.

ME

I remember. I'm using your absence as an excuse to have an early night. I'll call you before your meeting xx

I stare at the double x's at the end of my message for several minutes, wondering whether I should delete them before hitting send. If it weren't for Chelsea racing back my way with a smile a mile long I would have; I just don't have time to dawdle... *yeah, right.*

I'm glad I couldn't hold back when I see Elvis's reply flash up on my screen just as Chelsea leaps into my arms.

ELVIS

I look forward to it xx

"My knee held up better than I thought it would."

Elvis's scrumptious chuckle barrels down the line. "I told you it would. It just needs retraining."

His knowledge on injury management has me extra curious about his job title, but before I can ask, a much higher-pitched voice comes down the line, "Did you kick it, girl? You did, didn't you? You totally worked that stage."

My girly laugh gains me a handful of spectators. They abandon whatever the hell they do while hanging around the quad to stare at me. "You know I did. Heard your date wasn't as spectacular though. What happened?"

I hear Elvis grumble a moan about it being "my fucking cell phone" before Danny's voice clears his gripe. "He was a full-blown closet case. Like not *a little, I could pretend it was a phase.* He wasn't coming out of the dark any time in the next century."

I gag, loving the eccentrics in his reply. I also love how comfortable he is in his own skin. The only time Danny has ever been in the closet is when he was seeking his next haute couture outfit. That boy has style that puts the pages of *Vogue* to shame.

"But I hear things aren't so dire for you? Do I need to schedule Elvis in for a Danny's special? Could check him over for warts or just make sure he's measuring up to expectations?"

The last half of his sentence comes out in a flurry. He's either being chased or he just discovered the Back Street Boys are doing a revival concert, and he's racing to get tickets.

I realize it's the former when Elvis's deep timbre sounds down the line. "You know the more you encourage him, the more he'll hang around. He's worse than the annoying cat I tossed a chunk of fish at four months ago. He's at my doorstep every night at precisely six."

"You love it."

I twirl on the spot, my happiness at being included in their unique duo too intense not to respond. I've been friends with girls who have had gay male friends before, but this is the first instance where two men have such a profound relationship when they're not chasing the same interests: women.

"I do, but that doesn't mean he needs to know it. He might ask for a pay raise if he thinks I like him." He suddenly stops talking, worried he's said too much.

He has, and I'm not going to let him off lightly.

"Danny works for you?"

From what I witnessed in person last weekend, it's clear Elvis is slightly higher on the totem pole than Danny, but I thought that was their dynamic. It's the same as Skylar and me. The attractive, more popular one always ranks first, then the second more subdued one is a few steps behind them. Not by much, but enough for society to take notice.

I hear Elvis scrub the stubble on his chin before he murmurs, "He doesn't really work for me; he works with me on mutual goals."

"Like a partner?"

"Ah... I guess you could call it that, although I'd prefer you didn't. Danny has separation issues as it is, let alone you calling him my partner."

My laugh is cut short when someone calls Elvis's name from across the room. He muffles his phone, advising he'll only be a minute before focusing his attention back to me. "I have to go. My...*meeting* is about to start."

"Okay. Go get 'em, old man." I roar like a tiger.

I thought he'd laugh at my playfulness, but his gargled reply is more pained than joyous. I'm not surprised. Whatever we've got going on is extremely new, but I'm already well aware how much he hates me mentioning our age gap, which is still a mystery to me.

After slinging open the front door at Mickey's, I enter the foyer. Parmesan cheese, garlic bread, and the imaginary scent of Elvis's aftershave smack into me when I pace to the counter to order a much-needed calorie replacer. With Chelsea's eagerness to learn fueling my eagerness for a comeback to ballet, I put in a few hours longer at the dance studio than usual today. My muscles are aching, but my heart is the biggest it's been in two years.

"I'm about to gorge on a slice at Mickey's, so I'll be out cold in a food coma in around thirty minutes. I'll talk to you tomorrow?"

"Alright, and Willow?" Elvis waits long enough for me to prompt him to continue before saying, "I'm proud of what you accomplished today. Just getting your mind to focus on anything but the pain it expects is the equivalent of climbing Mount Everest. But you did it. You took the first step. Now the world is your oyster."

Wow. I didn't expect his words to knock me so fiercely, but they have. I'm truly speechless.

I'm snapped from my trance by a loud grumble. Elvis is either walking into a lion cage with a thousand hungry investors waiting to eat him alive, or a subway train just roared past him. Whatever it is, it is near deafening, and I have a hard time hearing him when he asks, "Will? You still there?"

"Yeah, I'm here, but will you be by the end of tonight? Sounds like you're walking into a gladiators' ring."

He laughs. "It's not quite the colosseum, but it's pretty damn close." He assures someone he'll only be another minute before redirecting his voice to me. "I'm sorry, I've really got to go."

"It's fine. Go." I shoo him as if he is standing in front of me instead of hundreds of miles away. "Bye."

His farewell is more breathless than mine...before it's swallowed by the massive roar of a crowd.

I toss my phone to Danny before wordlessly apologizing to Coach James. He's not impressed I had my cell attached to my ear as we trekked down the walkway separating our locker room and the field, but he's keeping his grumble on the down low since I've chalked up an impressive number of statistics during games and training drills these past few weeks.

I'm not being modest when I say I'm on fucking fire this month.

You'd think my late night talks with Willow would have me slow off the mark, but they've had the opposite effect. While encouraging her to bite the bullet by re-strapping on her ballet shoes, I lit a fire up my own ass. I love football so much, I've done nothing but relentlessly train the past twelve months to get myself ready to return to the field. My determination to return had me missing the most vital part of my revival. I had to be mentally ready more than physically.

I don't remember the hours following the crash that nearly ended my career, but I do remember the pain of taking my first step. I was doped up on pain killers, but I was on the verge of vomiting from the pain shooting down my spine. I couldn't walk without cringing; I couldn't sit down without wondering if I'd ever get back up. Fuck, for those first few weeks, I couldn't even wipe my own ass.

I don't want to go through that again—not ever again—but that fear is what has stopped me from regaining my former glory. I'm so scared of getting injured, I strategized how to stop it from happening, thus not only taking away the love I have for the game, but making me an easy target. I was the best in my field because I was unpredictable. My opponents couldn't read my next move. In a game where plays are rehearsed backwards and forwards, it was unheard of. Some coaches hated it, but Coach James always encouraged me to think outside the box. It's what led to him winning three championships before my career was struck down by a cocky attitude and shield I thought was impenetrable.

I won't let that happen again.

"Are you sure you're good to go?" Coach James' breath is visible in the cool night air. It's colder in this part of the country this late in the season. "If you want to sit out, we can put Foster in for Dalton this week, slowly ease you back to a full schedule."

"I'm good, Coach. I've got this." For the first time in the past six weeks, there's absolutely no hesitation in my tone. I can survive another injury, but I'll never survive giving up my dream.

"Alright then, let's hustle. We want this win, boys, and we want it bad."

And that's precisely what he got ninety minutes later.

"You're fucking back, baby! Do you hear the electricity crackling in the air, smell the scent of your money being printed? Damn, boy! I'm not even the one who heard my name being screamed all night long, but I'm fucking buzzed like a bumble bee."

Foster does an impromptu breakdance in front of me. His Michael Jackson-inspired dance moves have my mind drifting to Willow for the fourth time this evening. The spell that woman has put on me is frightening. Even during the middle of Foster's impressive buttonhook route, my thoughts shifted to her. It wasn't Foster's blistering smile when he convinced the defensive back he was running a deep route that had my mind straying; it was his near fall when he planted hard on the slippery surface. He looked like a giraffe taking its first steps. Thankfully, he dug in his cleats, righted himself, then charged back my way before his defensive mark figured out what play we were running.

After grabbing his crotch enough times for Danny to take notice, Foster moonwalks into the showers. His excitement is understandable. We killed it tonight. Our opponents were left grappling when we hit them with touchdown after touchdown. I'm so buzzing with adrenaline, I reach for my phone to call Willow before I can stop myself.

I may not have any self-control, but my conscience does when my eyes drop to the screen of my phone. Willow sent me a text. She's wearing a pair of fluffy unicorn earmuffs and is snuggling into a pillow that looks like the poop emoji.

The caption of her photo reads:

> Anything to drown out Skylar's screams. I swear if I hear her shout, "Go, Carlton! Run, Carlton! You're the fucking man, Carlton!" one more time, I'm going to puke.

An eyerolling emoji ends her message.

For how much I love football, you'd think her disdain for the game would have me backing away from our friendship with my hands held high and my knees bowed. But, nope, if anything, it increases my eagerness. Everyone has their own passion and quirks. Willow's happens to be dancing and having the ability to pull off kiddie earmuffs like they're a piece of lingerie. Mine are football and being man enough to understand it's not everyone's flavor of the month.

While I'm being upfront, I'll admit, my love of football hasn't always been as strong as it is now. When you're the only son of a football fanatic, you expect to get more than a request to be quiet during game time. I didn't need my father to run me through drills and watch every game I've ever played. I just wanted him to be around.

I'm drawn from my negative thoughts when my phone buzzes in my hand. It's another text from Willow.

> WILLOW
>
> Thank god, the squawking has finally stopped. Now I can get some shuteye. I hope your meeting went well. Talk soon. Willow xx

I'm in the process of returning her message when my phone rings, and since I was frantically tapping on the keyboard, I accidentally hit the connect button. So I have no choice but to answer the call I've been avoiding like the plague the past few months.

"Lillian, how are you?" I don't give a shit how she is, and thankfully, my grinding teeth when I asked my question should advise her of that.

"Great now. I was beginning to fret that you had forgotten to give me your new number. I've left god knows how many messages the past two months. Did you get any of them?"

Her voice is so dramatic, I can picture her lounging on the day bed in her office with her hand splayed across her sweaty forehead. She'll be wearing something satiny and designer. Most likely one of the hundred negligees she was gifted after our disastrous lingerie shoot, and she'll most likely have a flute of champagne in her hand.

"I watched the game. You're almost back to full form."

I huff, equally grateful and annoyed to see nothing has changed. She never complimented me without adding a snippet of hesitation to her voice. She'll never issue straight-up praise without me having to grovel for it.

Not realizing her conversation is one-sided, Lillian murmurs, "I talked to some old contacts I have in your field. They're under the impression you should be back to full contract sooner rather than later. Is Coach James giving you the same vibe? If he is, I can go over the contract for you, if you like? I'll do it for free, for old times' sake."

I honestly don't know how to reply to her comment. Talking money is nothing out of the ordinary for us; I never looked at a contract Lillian didn't handle first, but a lot has happened the past fourteen months, enough that I'm confident in declaring I don't want her anywhere near me or my assets.

"I've got things handled. Danny is—"

"I still can't believe you hired him, Presley. I thought we agreed to have a little break until your head got back in the game, then you'd return here, where I'd continue to manage your career."

She really means manage *me*, not my career. I also don't recall there being any agreement.

"We didn't have an agreement, Lillian." I say her name with the same disdain she used on mine. "Once I was released on bail, I left New York with the intention of never returning. You've only popped back into the picture because you've caught wind that maybe your cash cow isn't as dried up as you thought."

"Now you're just being ridiculous. I 'popped back into the picture' because we had nine years together." I can imagine her pompous turned-up nose screwing up during the quoted part of her statement. "You might be able to push aside a near decade of time, commitment, and feelings as if it is worthless, but I'm not as cold-hearted as you are."

"Oh, please, because only warmhearted women fuck their yoga instructors when their fiancé is in rehab!"

I could lower my voice, but I don't need to. All the men surrounding me are familiar with Lillian and my bickering. They were subjected to it a minimum of twice a week before we separated.

"It was a cry for help! I needed to startle you back to living!"

"By sleeping with..." I pause, hating that I'm stooping to her level, but I'm unable to stop myself. "How many men was it again?"

"It was only ever Josue... and Dean, but he doesn't count. I did that for you."

I scrub my hand down my face as my adrenaline from our victory drains from my veins. "That's right. I forgot you took one for the team that day."

"He was going to let you go, Presley."

"He wasn't letting me go; I fired his ass! That's what you do when your fucking agent works more for himself than he does you! If you had paid any attention to anything I *ever* said, you would have known that, but no, you were all about the money and what you could get out of any deal I made. You didn't care about me or my well-being; all you cared about was yourself!"

Stealing her chance to reply, I disconnect our call by throwing my cell phone onto the ground. I don't know why I'm letting her get to me. For the most part, her affairs were a godsend. I should have called our relationship off years before I did, but I hung on, convinced it was the stress of fame playing havoc with who we were as people.

I was so fucking wrong, and I learned a hard lesson from my mistake. That's why, as much as I hate that my relationship with Willow is being founded on a lie, I need to do this. I need to know she likes me for me. Not a job title. Not the possibility of what I could bring to the table for her. If she wants it, she'll strive to achieve it herself. I see that in Willow. I see her determination and drive, but it took me nine years to see through Lillian's tricks, so I need a little longer than a few weeks before I can make a final assessment.

My deceit could blow up in my face, but I don't see it being any worse than what I went through with Lillian.

CHAPTER SIXTEEN

Willow

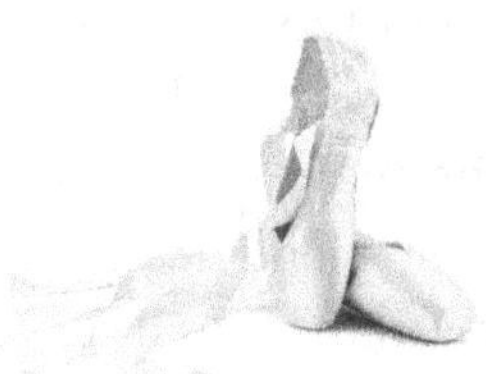

$\mathcal{B}$utterflies take control of my stomach as the hum from behind the stage curtains increases with every minute ticking by. Tonight is recital night at the dance studio I've worked at the past year. My hip hop kids killed it. They not only had the kids in the audience up on their feet joining in, they also received a standing ovation from their parents.

Now it's Chelsea's turn. I swear I'm more nervous than she is. She dodged one grenade when her mother questioned why she wasn't on stage with the other ballerinas. I told her only the most exemplary students are given a solo on recital night. She bought it. For how long, I don't know, but for now, Chelsea's smile is the only thing that matters. She's worked hard the past few weeks. She trained between six and seven every evening, then she practiced her routine from sunup to sundown on the weekends. She's nervous, but she's more than ready.

"Just remember, *glissade*, then *sauté*. We tried the other way, but your landing is perfect this way, so we'll stick with what you find easiest." I ensure every strand of Chelsea's straight blonde hair is pulled back into her bun then stand to take in the entire picture. "Perfect."

"Thank you, Will." She wraps her arms around my thighs to hug me tight.

"You're very welcome." I guide her to the stage with my hand on her back. Her excitement is as palpable as the energy in the room. I can feel it brimming from her even though I'm barely touching her. "Big smiles, Chelsea. Show everyone how much you love dancing."

When she nods and smiles, I signal to the music producer that she is ready. I swear the entire world blurs when she darts onto the stage to take her spot on the taped X in the middle of it. I can't see anything through the tears in my eyes and the blinding smile on her face. She is in her element, her heart more fulfilled than the people packing the dance hall to watch their loved ones perform.

My focus only shifts from her when the quickest flash of a smile stops both my feet and my heart. Elvis is slipping through a side entrance of the hall. Even though the sun went down over an hour ago, he wears a cap sitting low on his face, hiding his trademark wonky grin. Once he is ushered to a seat by one of the senior students who won't perform until next month, he removes his cap. He should have left it on, as his smile when he spots me gawking at him is more blinding than the spotlight following Chelsea's every move.

I wave at him like a giddy idiot before refocusing my attention on Chelsea. Tonight isn't about me and the crazy strong feelings I'm developing in an extremely short time period. It's about a little girl proving to the haters that she can dance despite what anyone thinks. Weight, height, and agility don't matter when you have passion, and Chelsea has that in abundance.

At the end of her performance, there's barely a dry eye in the house. Chelsea keeps her cool though. Her prima ballerina attitude is out in full force. She struts off the stage like a super model walking the catwalk, her first tear not shed until she's in the safety of the stage wings.

"Well done! I'm so proud of you!" My claps are barely heard over the uproarious ones coming from the hall, but I can't help myself. Her bravery tonight deserves more than a round of applause, but it is all I have to offer, so it is what I give her.

By the time all the classes have worked through their routines, two hours have ticked by. I've checked on Elvis regularly from my post backstage, and not once has he shown signs of boredom. He has watched every child's performance with the same pride of the parents surrounding him.

He appears thoroughly entertained, and even more so when I sashay up to him with my hips swinging and my booty shaking. "Did you see Chelsea's performance!? My god, E. The smile on her face will light mine for years to come."

I'm still so euphoric, I throw my arms around his neck and plant my lips on his without giving him the chance to protest. He doesn't seem to mind. His tongue lashes my mouth a mere second before my coat is tugged.

"Excuse me, Ms. Willow, we're going home now."

I smile against Elvis's lips before pulling back and dropping my eyes to Xane, up and coming dance prodigy. He's only six, but his talents are undeniable.

While I bob down to Xane's level, Elvis advises me he will wait for me outside. It's probably for the best. Behind Xane are another two dozen students waiting to wish me farewell. Most are clutching flowers.

As I step out of the dance studio wrangling roses and baby's breath like I'm hacking my way through the wilderness, Elvis fights through an even more dangerous wasteland. He hasn't just caught the single mothers' eyes, he's wrestling back a handful of fathers as well.

"Look at you, Mr. Popular. If they're not moaning about me confiscating their cellphones, I barely get a grunt out of them."

Smiling, he removes three-quarters of the flowers from my grip before heading toward his car parked halfway down the parking lot. "They were a little overfriendly, but nothing I can't handle."

"Handled more than one groupie at a time previously, have we?"

When his smile grows, I know he took my comment as I intended. I'm not bothered by the attention he gains. I dragged my ass out of bed at 5 AM every Saturday for nearly two years just to get the daily dose of man-meat my diet requires, so I can't blame the dance moms for getting their hit any way they can.

Elvis removes the remaining flowers from my grasp and places them into his backseat before opening my door for me. "Such *old* school charm," I tease while sliding into the passenger seat.

I can't see his face, but I can picture his grimace from the grunt rumbling through the tinted window near my head. After unclenching his fists, he jogs around to the driver's side door and slips inside. He fastens his belt, checks mine is latched, then fires up his engine before swinging his dark eyes my way. Damn, I've missed seeing his eyes in the flesh. We've FaceTimed many times the past three weeks, but a screen can't show the sparkle his eyes get when the moonlight bounces off them. His dark and mysterious features only heighten the anonymity surrounding him.

We've talked an average of six hours a day the past three weeks, yet I still don't know his job description, what he studied in college, or how old he is. We got the basics out of the way in the first week. He is the only sibling to his older sister, Syndi. His parents have a rocky relationship, but with their steaming moments far exceeding their screaming matches, he doesn't see them splitting anytime soon. He's known Danny since he was six and met Dalton as a freshman. When I asked how long ago that was, he skirted the question like he did any time I've tiptoed around his age.

If I were desperate to find out his age, I'm sure there are ways I could, but I'm not concerned. They're can't be a ton of years between us. His face is too youthful for him to be older than mid-thirties, and he's never mentioned an ex-wife or the slew of kids most men in their forties have. If I had to guess, I'd say he is late-twenties, perhaps inching towards his thirties, but I wouldn't go much more than that. That puts him a good six to ten years older than me. Not enough age gap to be frowned upon, but plenty for me to feel guiltless when calling him "old man."

My stomach grumbles at the exact moment Elvis asks if I'm hungry. "I'll take that as a yes."

I nod. "What do you feel like? There's a Vietnamese restaurant not too far from here, or Skylar swears by Chino's on 42nd Street."

My interest piques when he mutters, "I think I can top both Italian and Vietnamese. What are your thoughts on an Elvis special?"

"Swinging hips and all?"

He throws his head back and laughs. His deep grumble adds to the sexual energy teeming between us. "If you're lucky."

After saving my lip from my teeth, he throws his gearstick into first, then hightails it out of the parking lot. It doesn't take me long to gather my bearings. With me house-sitting for Becca and Dalton during her short stay in the hospital, then their trip home to show off their new bundle of joy, the streets surrounding their home are as familiar to me as the ones around my university.

"Couldn't wait another hour to get into my panties?" I scan the manly hedges sheltering Elvis's condo from prying eyes. "Where's Danny? If he knew you were planning to bring me home, he would have rocked up with bells on."

"That's why I didn't tell him." There's no humor in his voice. He's being dead serious... until he helps me out of his car. "I'm not trying to get into your panties—"

"Like a dirty old man," I fill in on his behalf.

His teeth grit, but he nods all the same. "I just want to spend some time with you—alone. Is that okay?"

I answer his question by asking one of my own, "Why wouldn't it be?"

He waits for me to shimmy my skirt down to a respectable level. "This is new."

"Yeah, and...?"

"You don't really know me. That might be scary to some women."

I quirk my lips. "True, but that doesn't really apply to me, does it?" When he looks at me in confusion, I add on, "I'm not a woman. I'm only a college girl, remember?"

His cheeks flame with heat as his pupils dilate. He looks seconds from coronary failure.

"I'm joking." I slap him in the chest, my mood extra playful. I love that he wants to spend time alone with me. "I am in college, but I'm one hundred percent legal. Do you want to see my license? I'll show you mine if you show me yours."

My promise doesn't ease the worry on his face. It continues to grow every second we spend standing across from each other in silence.

Fearful he's minutes from taking me home and tucking me into bed like the good little girl I'm not, I climb the stairs of his condo. "Which rock do you hide your key under? Dalton said it was by the door; he just failed to mentioned there's over a dozen of them."

Grumbling about how he's going to rearrange Dalton's face, Elvis takes the stairs two at a time, jabs a key from his pocket into the lock, then swings open the door.

"Don't be grumpy. He wasn't aware of our conflicting schedules when he suggested I surprise you at home by wearing nothing but a bow." I scrape my recently grown nails across his chest before sauntering into his foyer.

Wanting to see if my tease had the effect I was aiming for, I spin around to face him. He's looking at me with so much heat, I miss the first step into his foyer. Lessons from previous incidents save me from doing the flappy-armed chicken dance. I'm going to fall with dignity even if it kills me.

Thankfully, Elvis isn't as clumsy as me. He seizes my wrist and tugs me forward with barely a second to spare. My crash into his torso most likely sustains me more injury than my fall would have, but in a good, *I can't wait to recreate it* type of way. He's right there—in front of me. A six-foot-four brick shithouse of muscles with a sexy smirk and an angled head. You can't get any sexier than what I'm facing right now.

When he notices me drinking him in, he smiles his crazily

gorgeous grin. It's the catalyst of an avalanche. Lips crash, hands wander, and moans not appropriate for an outdoor environment rip through my lips.

My moans aren't the only things being shredded. So is my skirt from Elvis hoisting me up his body so I can curl my legs around his thighs. My god, just stretching to span the width of his hips adds to the exhaustion of my overworked muscles, much less the growth I feel in his pants. His cock is throbbing against his zipper, begging to be released from its tight confines.

As he starts our climb up the stairwell to his bedroom, I attempt to muffle my giggles with his tongue.

It does me no good.

"You better not be laughing, Willow."

"Me, laughing? *Never.*" I snicker over his stern, snapped-shut mouth before lashing his succulent lips with my tongue.

He's not having any of it. He stops our climb halfway up the stairwell before locking his more-blistering-than-the-sun eyes with me. "Why are you laughing? Is it because I'm walking stiffly? I can't help it. My therapist said it will take years before my spine returns to its normal agility."

"What?" I'm more confused now than amused. "I *was* giggling about your stiffness—it just had nothing to do with your back. When I felt how hard you were, all I could imagine was The Hulk breaking through a brick wall, but since your penis shouldn't be green— *if it is, I suggest you consult your doctor*—all I saw when he burst through the wall was one of the snakes on Medusa's hair. Do you know the ones I'm talking about? The hissing, cute, penis-colored ones?"

I'm rambling because I'm nervous, and the fact I'm nervous makes me even more nervous. I don't get nervous. I'm not a cocky person, but I can't be accused of being shy either.

"We should have just fucked in the foyer, then I wouldn't have made an idiot out of myself."

When I wiggle my hips, silently demanding for Elvis to put me down, he stays holding on firm. "Look at me."

Feeling as deflated as I'm sure his cock is now, I shake my head.

"Willow..." The roll of his hips is more effective than the demand in his voice. The only deflation issue in this stairwell is mine.

When I lift my eyes to his, he winks. "You think my cock is The Hulk?"

"Seriously! That's all you got from that?"

He throws his hips forward two times, increasing the dampness in my panties. "I'm a man, Will, so your confession has me wanting to Hulk-smash your ass."

"Settle down, big boy. Hulk-smash and ass should never be mentioned in the same sentence. How about we start with my front hole, then, when you've aced that test, we'll discuss the possibilities of extracurricular activities?"

Now I'm not the only one laughing—*thank god.* A little bit of playfulness puts our exchange back on the track it was traveling before I stupidly laughed, although it's a little friskier now. The way he tosses me onto his bed reveals the fun I'm about to have—and then there's the removal of his shirt.

"Still not fair," I murmur to myself. I didn't think it was possible for his body to get more spectacular than what it was, but if my mental calculations are anything to go by, his body is more rigid now than it was three weeks ago.

Insecurities plague me when my eyes take in the deep carves of his eight-pack, the indented lines of his formidable V muscle, and the brawny span of his hips. His body isn't compact, but it's not squidgy like mine. The bumps in my stomach aren't muscles. The girth of my arms isn't from the gym, and my thigh gap isn't natural. It's from Elvis's knee bracing between my legs as he leans over to reacquaint our lips. We couldn't be any more opposite if we tried. I'm soft and fluffy, and he's hard and firm, but his mouth tastes really, *really* good, and I don't want to give it up for anything.

Before any of the stupid thoughts in my head can make me pull away, Elvis withdraws his mouth first. He stares down at me with hooded eyes as his hand moves to the hem of my shirt. I love what I'm seeing in his eyes so much, I curl my hand over his to aid in his endeavor to strip me bare.

The air hissing between his teeth when my breasts fall heavily on my chest tells me I did the right thing, much less the throbbing member I feel tensing on my thigh. He likes the bra I selected with the hope this is how our night would end up, but he's more interested in what's happening underneath the velvety red material.

"I'm like a kid in a candy store. I don't know which goodie to sample first."

I wiggle my breasts in his face. "Go for the gobstoppers. They're more than a mouthful, but they last the longest since they never tire."

His laughing breaths tickle my neckline before his lips, then his teeth join the party a few seconds after that. "You don't need to worry, buttercup. By the time I'm finished with you, it won't be just your jaw aching."

He tugs my earlobe with his teeth before lowering his mouth to suckle on my skin. He bites and kisses my neck, collarbone, and chest. His movements are slow, like he's cherishing every moment, but fast, like he doesn't want to lose the chance to sample every inch of me.

Like that will ever be a possibility.

When he reaches my panties, which are red and completely soaked through with my desire, he raises his eyes to mine. He stares at me for ages, his breath fanning my panties, his eyes arrested on mine over the globes of flesh on my chest.

He waits and waits and waits until I am at the point of desperation before slipping my panties to the side and slicing through my heat with his tongue. I call out as my back arches. Unlike the kisses he cherished my body with, he consumes my pussy with greedy licks and frantic sucks. He takes me to a place of hysteria within a matter of minutes. It is a beautifully twisted ride that treads the fine line of insanity.

My ass lifts from the sheets with a groan tearing from my throat. I feel like I'm spiraling out of control, like I'm on the verge of either a panic attack or reaching the highest crest I've ever climbed.

He devours me fast, eating me expertly with grunts as feral as mine. I come undone when his hand slithers up my stomach to cup my still-covered breast. His hand is so large, even my natural DDs pale in comparison.

I shatter like a glass, my orgasm rushing over me, pulling me into the darkness weighing heavily on my chest. While quivering through the pleasure blasting through every inch of me, my moans ramp up to a never-before-reached level. He should stop now. He should be pulling back. Instead, he circles his lips around my clit before slipping two fingers into my clenching core.

"Oh God. Oh God. Please, no. Oh god, no." My orgasm has no end in sight. It keeps pummeling into me, taking every bit of energy I have left. "I can't do this... Holy fucking... Christ."

I dig my toes into the massive muscles on the top of Elvis's shoulders and push back. I free my pussy from his mouth for barely a second before he snares my ankle and drags me back. He eats me like the Beast eating porridge, a sloppy, messy consumption that has my second giggle of the night rumbling in my chest cavity. Damn Skylar and her obsession with Disney movie GIFs. I've never seen the Beast in the same light since she showed me a GIF last year with comments way too rude for the movie's PG rating.

My laughter is pushed aside when Elvis's growl roars through my pussy. "Willow..."

"I'm not laughing. I swear. I just need a breather. Just for a second."

I drag the curls sticking to my face out of the way before crawling across the sticky sheets. After wiping evidence of my arousal off his face with the back of his hand, Elvis watches me span the distance between us. He's still wearing trousers, but I know he is hard. I can see the massive bulge in his crotch, much less the wetness at one side.

"How about I return the favor? You've eaten, so it's only fair I get to have a little nibble as well."

Little is not the right word for me to use while freeing Elvis's cock from his trousers. There's not a single *little* thing about him. *Not a single fucking one.*

"Do you hear that? I think I hear my mom calling."

I slip off the bed and charge for the stairwell, running away from a penis I have no doubt will snap me in half. My bung knee gives me enough issues, so I sure as hell ain't volunteering to become a cripple.

A panicked moan—*or is it a turned on one?*—rolls up my chest when Elvis bands his arm around my waist and draws me back. "Where do you think you're going?"

"I thought I could whip you up a sandwich? Egg and lettuce on rye with a large side of lube coming up!"

His laugh doubles the wetness between my legs, but I'm still not convinced I can take him. There should be a law against men with penises as large as his—or at least a warning label.

"What are you looking for?" Elvis asks after dropping his boxer shorts to huddle around his ankles with his pants.

"They have warnings about small parts being a choke hazard, so where's the one warning me I risk asphyxiation because a penis is too large to fit down my throat?"

When Elvis laughs for the second time in under a minute, I raise my eyes to his, taking in his splayed thighs, a cock too perfect to massacre my lady bits, eight rock-hard bumps, and a set of pecs I intend to burrow my face and cry into when he claims a virginity I didn't realize I still had.

Faking annoyance at his ruggedly handsome grin and lust-filled gaze, my eyes slit. "Are you laughing at me, Old Man?"

Ha! Take that.

"Holy guacamole!" My bra strap rolls up my back when Elvis hooks my ankle, drags me down the bed, then flips me over as if I'm weightless.

"I'm not smiling. I'm preparing."

"To die a death more painful than a thousand if you hurt me?" I question through quirked brows.

Excited quivers shimmy down my spine when he arches over my back to whisper in my ear, "I'm not going to hurt you, Willow."

His voice is so fucking sexy.

"I'm just gonna Hulk-smash your ass."

Not anymore, it ain't.

I crawl across the sheets on my hands and knees, my endeavor to get away only halting when Elvis chuckles, "I'm joking. I've heard this angle makes Hulk Junior a little easier to take."

It isn't just his words bringing me back. It's the image of him rolling a condom down his cock. My god, there is nothing sexier than a thick, hot, virile hunk of a man prepping to get down and dirty. I can hear Christina Aguilera's "Dirty" song in my ear right now. It brings out my naughty side, my filthy side, my *I'm so goddamn horny, I'll take his dick like I was born to ride it* side.

I've been wanting to get frisky with Elvis since his Tarzan-ass walked into my life, so why the hell am I cowering away like a baby who can't handle a big chunk of man-meat? I eat my steak practically raw; you can't get more prepared for battle than that.

Although I'm ready, willing, and able—*finally*—I can't help but ask, "What do you do during a drought?" When Elvis looks at me, confused, I give him a flirty wink. "There's no need to stock raincoats in a drought, so do you buy condoms in bulk during the wet season, or do you rinse them out once you're done and hang them outside to dry?"

CHAPTER SEVENTEEN

Presley

*I*f you ever told me you had more gut cramps from laughing during sex than sexual exertion, I would have told you you weren't doing it right. Now I'm being forced to eat my words.

Willow.

Willow.

Willow.

What can I say about Willow? Divine body, gorgeous face, and a pussy that drizzles like honey on hot toast when she comes. Fuck me, she's damn near perfect... once I get her mouth occupied with something other than rambling.

I was right about her lips, soft as a cloud but as greedy as a woman about to be locked in a nunnery. She took my dick like a real pro, her eyes only bulging when I got a little eager with my pumps. I couldn't help it. Her eyes darken when she's horny, and her sweet scent intensifies. Add those two factors to the image of her naked body plastered on the mattress as I fed my cock in and out of her mouth... sweet lord, that's what dreams are made from.

I will never take anything unwillingly given—the last thing I need is a sexual harassment claim—so I had no choice but to tease

Willow to the point of begging before consummating our union in one of the many ways I've dreamed about the past six weeks.

I'm hard now recalling how her lips parted when I notched in the first four inches of my cock. Her pussy sucked at me ravenously, her desire to be claimed overtaking the worry her eyes held when they first landed on my cock. Even with only an hour of sleep, I'm not eager for more—sleep that is. Who needs sleep when you've got a woman like Willow warming your sheets?

Well, she was warming my sheets. Now my hands are coming up empty.

While scrubbing the sleep from my eyes, I rise to a half-seated position. Unlike the morning she tried to sneak out, her clothes are still spread across the floor, and her shoes are tucked nicely under my drawers. The purse we dumped halfway across the room remains where it fell. Even with all the evidence stacking up in my favor, I didn't need it to know she is here. I can sense her closeness in my gut. It's that same tight tension I feel in the seconds leading to me running onto the field, the one a mere nanosecond from my breaking out of the walkway and the crowd spotting me. It's excitement and anticipation with a dash of fear.

That's what I feel every time I think about Willow.

After tugging on a pair of sleeping pants, I make my way down the stairwell. My muscles are feeling the aftermath of a night of exhausting activities, but my steps are silent. It's a trick my physical therapist taught me. By lightening the load on my ankles, I lighten the load on my spine.

With the faint hum of a tune coming out of the living room, I head that direction first instead of toward the kitchen, which has a light on. I recognize the music Willow's iPhone is playing. Not because I'm a fan, but because Danny forced me to watch all three movies in a movie marathon only last week. This song was featured in the last movie we watched. It was actually my favorite out of all three—not that I'll ever tell Danny that.

I spot Willow when I enter my dining room. She's standing next to an antique table covered with photos of my family and friends. Her hair is a mess from how tightly I gripped it while fucking, and the stage makeup she had on has all but vanished. She's wearing the shirt I discarded earlier, and from the lack of panty line, I can assume it is the only article of clothing she is wearing.

The more Julia Michaels' "Heaven" flows out of the speaker of her phone, the more her hips sway. I watch her from afar, mesmerized by how she can make such a simple movement look so sultry. She's barely moving, yet she has me feeling like I'm watching a performance worthy of the biggest audience.

When the song reaches the chorus about bad boys bringing heaven to you, she glides across the wooden floor of my living room. Her toes peak and her shoulders roll when she gets lost in the music. The generous gap between my couches and dining table gives her the perfect stage to perform on, and I'm more than eager to have a front row seat.

When her sexy one-legged twirl leads to her spotting my stalker watch, I assume she'll stop dancing. She does no such thing. My sleeping pants can't hide my enjoyment of her show, much less the smile on my face. She floats toward me, her dance moves a cross between ballet and the modern dance Danny is fascinated with.

Just before she reaches me, she pulls out a chair from beneath the dining table. She even does that sexily, but it's nothing compared to how she uses it to enhance her performance. She prances around it, her arms and legs weightless and free as she tumbles over it, under it, and around it. I'm reasonably sure this isn't the type of dance she teaches the kids in her class, or last night's performance would have had a lot of angry parents. This dance is especially for me, a one-of-a-kind show that doubles my fascination of her—*like it could get any bigger.*

I groan and adjust myself when she lifts her leg well above her head. I learned firsthand how flexible she is only an hour ago, but my fucking God, seeing it outside the bedroom is as fascinating as using it for better angles beneath the sheets. Recognizing the song is seconds from finishing, she clasps my sweaty hand in hers, then guides me to sit in the chair in the middle of her makeshift stage.

Her sweet scent streams through my nose when her hair slaps my face. She dances around me at a slow, seductive pace. It's like a private lap dance minus the seedy, *I've paid to have a woman grind against me* factor. It's fucking hot and has me conflicted. I want the song to hurry up and finish so I can check if she's as turned on as me right now, but I also don't want this to ever end.

Seconds from my last thought entering my mind, Julia Michaels' song switches from a promiscuous tone to a sweeter one, but nothing can dampen the sexual tension brewing between Willow and me. She's straddling my lap, and her thrusting-with-exhaustion chest is rubbing her erect nipples up and down my pecs.

As they did earlier tonight, her eyes have me coming undone. The lust in them is too intense to ignore. They have me acting reckless, almost caveman-like. I tug my shirt off her body violently before yanking down the waistband on my pants. My hand slides up her sticky back to grip her hair in a firm fist when her heat hits the crest of my cock. She's as turned on by her performance as me.

As I tug back her head far enough for a bead of sweat to glide down her nape, I thrust my hips upward. The moan that shreds from her throat steals my worry that I'm fucking her without protection. This is worth more than any amount she could siphon from me with a paternity challenge. I'm acting reckless, but after the fucked-up two years I've had, I need to let go of the reins. I need to be the man I once was. I need to fuck her so hard and fast, nothing but me is on her mind even when I'm not around.

Willow murmurs my name in a throaty groan when I stand from my seat, taking her with me. I'm not going far—I'm also not withdrawing my cock from her snug canal. I'm simply planting her naked ass on my dining table so I can see her beautiful body while I fuck it to the brink of insanity. After I un-wrangle her arms from around my neck, I gently push her back by her shoulders. The speed of my pumps quicken when her sweat-slicked back braces against the sturdy wooden material. The visual is better than I was hoping. The generous mounds on her chest are bouncing, her tight slit already red from my poundings, and the satisfied look on her face... Pure. Fucking. Heaven.

There's no giggling this time around. No jokes about my cock poking her ass when she took it in her mouth. She's taking as good as I'm giving, a fuck that's happening on the very table I had planned to feed her on. What I said earlier was true. I didn't bring her here to fuck her. I just needed a quiet location away from prying eyes.

With my game picking up right alongside my attitude the past six weeks, the attention from the public and sports reporters has returned to pre-Lillian breakup levels. I couldn't even attend Willow's recital without being hounded by fans wanting an autograph. Don't get me wrong. I don't like 69ers fans. I love them. I just don't want them screwing up whatever it is I have going on with Willow. I can fuck up things perfectly fine myself, thank you very much. I don't need additional help.

Like now, I certainly don't need any assistance taking Willow's throaty moans to an ear-piercing level. I've got that on lockdown. She's screaming as effectively as her pussy is sucking at my cock, and trembling all over when I shift some of my focus to her clit. I rub my thumb over the hardened bud while increasing the tempo of my thrusts.

The wooden legs on the table begin to shake when the image becomes too much. She's rocking her hips in rhythm with mine, which have taken on the speed I'm flicking her clit. It's a brutal pace, faster than the one earlier tonight. We're not fooling around or having sex; we're fucking like animals. My grunts are one hundred percent proof of this.

"Fuck, Elvis. Fuck. Fuck. Fuck."

Willow's frantic moans reveal she can feel the table legs coming out from beneath us as well, but just like me, she's not willing to end this for anything. She'd rather encounter a brutal blow with the floor than give up the climax I feel preparing to roar through her body. She's heating up everywhere. Her clit is scorching my thumb, and the warmth surrounding my cock has reached boiling point.

The intimacy I've gained with her body in a short period of time is proven without a doubt not even two seconds later. She stills as her back arches off the table. I hear my name in a breathless moan as violent shudders charge through her body. I thrust harder, filling her with every inch of my cock. She is slick and wet, her entire body trembling. She's fucking me as much as I am fucking her, ensuring her pussy strangling my cock won't slow down my pace.

"Don't stop. Don't stop. Don't stop," she begs over and over again, her pussy tightening around my cock with every word she speaks.

Her face in the haze of climax pushes mine toward the finish line. Her lips part with want as my mouth waters with need. I pump into her faster, the heat inside of me roaring like a wildfire.

Feeling the veins in my cock pulsating as my own release closes in on me, Willow says, "Pull out before you come."

I give her a look, one that exposes there's no fucking chance in hell of that happening. I can feel cum sitting at the crest of my cock, begging to be released into the slickness causing its demise.

"You either pull out or spend the next two weeks panicked out of your mind you went and got a college *girl* knocked up." She overemphasizes the word "girl," but her voice is still husky from the ferocious climax she just endured. "I'm not overly good with keeping a schedule, so I may occasionally skip a pill or two each month."

You'd think her confession would have me yanking my cock out this very instant, but for some fucked-up reason, that's the last thing my fucked-up mind considers doing. It considers the idea I could get her knocked up, toys with it for several long minutes as my thumb does her clit before it finally succumbs to the glare Willow's giving me through lust-wild eyes.

"I'll pull out, but I'm not fucking happy about it."

Willow flashes a grin that nearly has me breaking the pledge I made. "I'm sure I can make it up to you."

Her dismount from my cock makes the first leg on the table buckle under our weight, but I hardly notice when her mouth arrows toward my cock.

"Get on your knees, Will. If you want to suck my dick right, you need to be on your knees."

Sparks of excitement rain down my shaft when she does as requested with a moan. She swivels her tongue around my knob, tasting herself on my dick before lowering her pillowy lips down my twitching member.

"That's it. Just like that." I gather her hair to the side, gaining the leverage needed so I can fuck her mouth as eagerly as I did her pussy. "Stretch your throat before I coat it with my seed."

She murmurs something in a gargle, but I don't hear what she says. My cock is too busy plunging into her mouth for my ears to follow any commands from my brain.

The wider she opens her mouth, the more of my cock I feed her. She draws me to the very back of her throat, triggering only the slightest gag before drawing me back out. Her eyes water from taking me so deep, but she pushes past the pain, her excitement too strong for something so minor to impact it.

I inhale sharp, quick breaths as a tingle works up from my balls to the crest of my cock. I could have come the instant she wrapped her lips around my dick, but I held off, certain the reward would far outweigh the penance. I was right. She's sucking me more fiercely now than she did earlier tonight. Not even tasting her climax has slowed her down.

"I understand why I couldn't come in your tight, drenched, fucking wet slit, but do you have any objections to me coming down your pretty little throat?" My grip on her hair tightens with every word I speak. I can feel the wheels jumping off the track, feel the hysteria coming on. "You've got two seconds to answer me, Willow, or I'm going to come in your mouth like I've been fantasizing about since the day we met."

When she answers me with a groan, I come hard and fast down her throat. She takes everything I'm offering, her swallows as frantic as her sucks, and she does it all while staring up at me with wild, lust-blitzed eyes.

"You liked that, didn't you?"

She extracts my cock from her mouth with a pop before running her finger over her lips to soothe their burn with a bit of moisture. "Very much so..."

Her last word comes out with a groan, but not like the groans she was making only minutes ago.

"What's wrong? Are you hurt?"

She shoos off my worry with a wave of her hand as she gingerly rises to her feet. "It's nothing I can't handle."

"Will..." I let the worry on my face express the words my climax-hazed brain can't articulate.

"It's my knee," she confesses, her tone annoyed. "After standing on it for hours unbraced during the recital, I shouldn't have danced around on it—"

"Or gotten on your knees to suck my dick?"

Jesus, I'm an A-grade fucking moron.

She tugs my shirt back over her head before snagging my pants off the ground and bridging the gap between us. "Believe me, I wasn't feeling anything close to pain then..." Her glistening eyes dance between mine. "Except perhaps wondering how I could stop you coming out my ears."

Her playfulness lightens the tension between us, but it does nothing to ease the weight on my shoulders. "How about we take a look at your knee?"

Not giving her a chance to protest, I yank on my pants before scooping down to gather her in my arms. She remains quiet, but I can feel her excitement thrumming through her veins as we weave through my living room to the kitchen on the other side.

"What's your pain scale? One is non-existent; ten is you're seconds from ripping out the nuts of any man within a five-mile radius?"

While she comes up with a suitable number, I move into the foyer to grab my gym bag from the closet. It has tape, stitches, bandages, and enough pain medication to cover the highest number on her list.

When I reenter the room with the goodies in my hand, Willow's teeth catch her bottom lip. "You've got a whole pharmacy there, don't you?" She drops her eyes to a nearly empty bottle. "Is that sugar-coated oxycodone?"

Smiling, I nod. "Makes them easier to swallow."

"No shit, Sherlock. Anything coated in sugar tastes ten times better." I feel my cock pulsate like it didn't just release when she raises her eyes to mine and murmurs, "Except perhaps you."

"Knee first." I dump my medical equipment next to her naked backside that is sitting on my kitchen counter. "Then we'll discuss back-breaking positions that don't require knee strain."

"I'm going to pretend I'm not pissed at your extensive knowledge of sexual positions, but you should take note that I am pissed—so much so, I'm considering switching my rating from a seven to a ten just so I can rip your nuts off."

Like many male specimens, I hear only what I want to hear. "Your pain is a seven?"

When she halfheartedly nods, I bite out a string of curse words. Even if she had said a two, I wouldn't be happy, but a seven; that's high.

"Pick your poison while I get your knee wrapped."

I nudge my head to the ten or so containers of pain medications displayed near her thigh before dragging over a barstool so I can sit between her legs. Not the smartest thing I've ever done in my life, but her puffy knee keeps my focus on the task at hand instead of an area much more appetizing. It's well past dinner and way too early for breakfast, but dessert is a meal that can be consumed at all times of the day and night.

Willow rifles through the box until she finds one that is the equivalent of Tylenol. "Are you sure you don't mind? I don't want to stuff up your prescription schedule."

"They're not current." I raise the hem on my shirt before straightening her knee. She hisses in pain from me bending it to its natural position. Wanting to keep her focus off the pain, I say, "They're old scripts I keep around in case they're needed."

"In case you hurt your back again?"

I do a weird, shruggy thing. "My injury isn't like yours. The chances of it occurring again are low, but the worry is always there."

My low tone reveals more than my words ever will. I'm not scared of breaking my back. I'm scared of severing my spinal cord the second time around. I'm walking proof you can do anything you set out to achieve, but if my break had been mere millimeters from where it was, we wouldn't be having this conversation. I'd be holed up in a wheelchair at an old folks home with a nurse wiping my ass every day. That scares me. It scares the fucking shit out of me.

I freeze my taping of Willow's knee when she asks, "How did you hurt your back?"

I begin taping her leg again, hoping it will hide the shame my eyes get every time I recount my story. "I was an idiot who thought nothing would bring me down. I learned the errors of my ways when I got behind the wheel of my car drunk and crashed into a minivan, nearly killing all the occupants inside."

Willow's hand darts up to cover her gasp, but she remains as quiet as a church mouse.

"The driver of the minivan spent four weeks in the hospital. I was there for twelve. It doesn't change what I did, but I'm glad his injuries weren't as dire as mine."

I cut the tape with aggression, my anger still paramount. I'm not angry at the driver; I'm pissed that no matter what I do to fix my errors, the guilt never fades. The driver forgave me; I call Mr. Beckett every Monday to see how he's doing, and we even got together last Fourth of July, but the frustration remains heavy on my chest. I was an adult; I knew the consequences of my actions, yet I still got behind the wheel after drinking because I thought I could do no wrong.

"Survivor guilt is horrible, isn't it?"

After fixing the last piece of tape into place, I stand to my feet to face Willow. She didn't ask her question like my therapist did numerous times the months following my accident. She asked it as if she has experienced it herself.

My thoughts are proven correct when her quick brush of her cheeks misses the faintest tear slipping off her chin. "My parents died in a housefire when I was nine. It was a bitterly cold winter that required more heat than our little house could handle. My dad got me to safety before he went back for my mom. They both perished in the fire."

"Oh, Willow." I don't know what else I can say. There are a thousand condolences in my head, but none I'm sure she hasn't heard before. So, instead of offering her words of comfort, I use my body. I grip her head as firmly as I did earlier before drawing her into my chest.

Her tears soak my pecs when she whispers, "I was so sure they were going to be okay, I stood on the footpath, panicked out of my mind that my dancing trophies were melting. I never considered the fact they might not make it out. My dad was so strong, I didn't think anything would take him away from me."

Now her bigger-than-life personality makes sense. When you've been hurt, you either become a recluse who hates the world and everyone in it, or you bring out the sunshine, certain your worst days are behind you.

Willow is the sunshine, and I was the blackness determined to keep everyone at arm's length.

That all changed when a ray of sunshine I never knew I wanted shone down on me.

CHAPTER EIGHTEEN

Willow

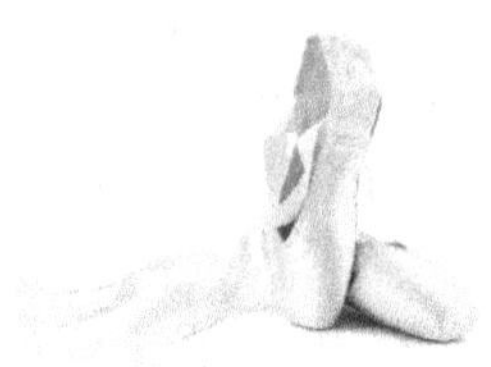

"Are you sure you don't want to stay another night? I can drop you at school before your first class tomorrow. I'll even set two alarms to make sure I don't sleep in."

I giggle, loving the cheek in Elvis's voice. If I could explain this weekend in only one word it would be outrageously-fucking-fantastic.

What? When it's hyphenated, it's only one word. I found that out the hard way when I submitted my English essay earlier this month. It had to be three thousand words. I delivered an amazing piece of literature that was exactly three thousand words. Supposedly I lost a few points because I didn't reach the minimum required word count. It's a crock of shit excuse as far as I'm concerned, but my B+ averaged out my score to a A-, so I pulled up my big girl panties and copped Professor Smith's disdain on my chin like a nearly graduated student.

I'll be honest, after our outrageously-fucking-fantastic (*still one word*) fuck on Elvis's now buckled dining table, I thought things were going to get awkward very quickly. I cried. I'm not talking a few little tears I could blame on a lash in my eye. I'm talking *cry me a river, I just watched* My Girl *for the hundredth time* cry. It wasn't pretty.

Not in the slightest. But do you know what? Elvis handled it like a pro. He just held me, then when I stopped slobbering over him like a kid eyeing the latest electronic game, he wiped away my tears and proceeded to cook us dinner.

No, I'm not joking.

He knew I didn't want to break down in front of him just as much as I believed my dad was coming back the night he perished. It took a crumbled house, seven firefighters, and a social worker ripping a pair of ballet shoes I had grabbed in haste out of my hands before I realized what was happening all those years ago. If it weren't for the social worker trying to remove the last piece of my parents I had, I would have never left the footpath.

I haven't been back to Melbourne since that night. I was shipped to Bundaberg, Queensland to live with my Aunt, grew an unhealthy obsession with dance, then the instant I was old enough, I moved to another country to pursue my dreams.

I didn't realize how far I had strayed from my dreams until last night. It wasn't the smiles on my students' faces when they performed at the recital causing my turmoil. It was Elvis's face when I danced for him. Last night was the first time I've danced for pleasure in a very long time. The moves came from inside of me, from a place I didn't think I'd ever have relit again. I was dancing purely because I loved it, and not for what it could give me.

That's why as much as Elvis's invitation is tempting, I can't accept it. With me finally gaining a work placement, and Elvis's schedule keeping him on this side of the country the next six weeks, this afternoon is my last chance to enter and prepare for a competition I've been eyeing the past four months. Every time I was about to sign up, I convinced myself not to be stupid, that I am only a dance *instructor*, not a dancer. Last night proved I was wrong. I am a dancer before anything; my passion was just a little misguided the past two years. But it's back now, stronger than ever.

I stop curling out of Elvis's flashy ride halfway when he says, "Hey, Willow?"

My chances of peeling out of his car uninjured are cut in half when I peer at him over my shoulder. My god, he's gorgeous. He's got the casual, *I'm made of money, but I won't flash it in your face* look going on. Designer jeans, nicely fitted shirt, recently showered hair, and a smirk that reveals he is the devil his eyes portray.

"One, can you wait for me to come to a full stop before exiting my car? You're giving me a complex." His smile doesn't convey that. He loves my eagerness, as I'm reasonably sure he knows what it centers around. "Two, you're never to leave my side without your lips first touching mine." I grin when he taps his puckered lips.

"And three?" I murmur over his mouth after kissing him with much more feeling than a newly formed relationship should have.

He doesn't seem bothered. He lashes my kiss-swollen lips with his tongue, enhancing their wetness before muttering, "Take it easy on your knee." I pull a face like a child being reprimanded by a parent. "If your kneecap pops out under the strain, you'll spend the next six weeks on the sidelines in crutches. Which would you prefer? Crutches or slowly easing back into competitive dancing?"

I hide my excitement that he already knows me so well. "I'd prefer neither."

"And I'd rather have your backside heating my couch instead of Danny's, but we all have to make sacrifices."

I kiss him some more. "Don't act upset. Danny could have arrived twenty minutes earlier, thus not only ruining your breakfast, but he would have also seen my kitty."

I giggle against his mouth when he replies, "He would have died, and not just by my fists. He's a platinum gay. He's never been with a woman." He runs his hand down my heated cheeks, doubling the energy teeming between us. "But I'm sure one look at your pretty pink pussy would have had him jumping the fence."

After rolling my eyes, I kiss him some more. His compliment was delivered in a roundabout way, but at the end of the day, it was still a compliment.

Once I'm confident he's been thoroughly farewelled, I slip out of his car and head toward my dorm. I make it three steps before he calls my name. I already have my playlists rolling through my head, prepared for the bump and grind routine he has requested every time we've seen each other or FaceTimed the past three weeks, so you can imagine my surprise when he simply asks, "Can I see you tomorrow?"

"Don't you have that thingy tomorrow?" "Thingy" is code for the numerous business meetings he attends at all times of the morning, day, and night.

"I'll have that all wrapped up by four."

He flashes me a flirty grin before jerking up his chin. *There's the request I was waiting for.*

Acting like one of the many Neanderthals at my school, I bob across the concrete, dancing to my own tune... and perhaps the fire burning in Elvis's eyes.

"It's a knee brace." My voice clearly relays what I think about Dr. Peter and his request for me to remove the flesh-colored brace supporting my knee. "It's barely visible, but even if it were, I don't see the issue."

Dr. Peter's eyes stray from the road to me. I'm sitting in the passenger seat of his car, my assurance that I can drive myself to my workplace not confident enough to save me from a highly embarrassing situation. "This institution is extremely important to the athletic department at our university. With this being the first time a student has been granted a placement at this establishment, I want to ensure you don't mess it up."

"And a knee brace could be the possible cause of that?" When Dr. Peter nods, I screech, "How?"

"The people you're being entrusted with are gifted athletes. Their bodies aren't like mine and yours. They're conditioned to perform, to succeed, to have people like us marvel over them. You're wearing a knee brace, which not only insinuates you don't take care of yourself, but it means you're not at the same level of fitness as the people you're preaching peak physical fitness to. Some may say that makes you a hypocrite."

Although our conversation started in regards to my knee brace, Dr. Peter's glance down my body shifted our conversation. He's not staring at my knee brace; his focus is locked on the bulge that will take months of dance classes to budge.

"I eat healthy—"

"I'm not saying you don't, Willow," Dr. Peter interrupts, "but this is about showing balance. Ensuring the output exceeds the intake. That you know the correct nutrition for your body type and size. You are a representation of my skills in sports management and nutrition."

He doesn't say it, but I know he's giving himself a big fat F for failure.

"I want you to not only represent yourself during your internship, but I want you to represent our university as a whole."

"A whole bunch of assholes."

If we weren't entering the parking lot of a place I despise more than appreciate, I would have said my comment louder. Unfortunately, my lungs are too busy amassing air to force it out in anger.

"You got me an internship with a football team?" I don't sound impressed because I am far from it. "I requested over two dozen placements; the 69ers were never listed on any of my forms."

"Don't worry, I was just as surprised by their call as you. " He still sounds shocked, like all his Christmases have come at once. "I'm just grateful they granted my request to supervise your placement here. I've been looking for an in for years."

"Great, so you're using me to unleash your fantasy? I'd rather have you picturing my tits while you wank in the shower than be subjected to this."

Dr. Peter's eyes pop up from his wallet to me. "What was that?"

"Nothing," I lie with a shrug. "I didn't say anything."

Can you smack a professor without punishment? I'm asking for a friend.

No? Well, you suck.

I remember how far I am down the totem pole of wealth when the guard hands back Dr. Peter's license before directing him to park in the employee side of the parking lot. There are pricy rides stretching as far as the eye can see, and I doubt one of them is under a quarter of a million dollars to buy.

"Nope. Not happening." I fire Dr. Peter a stern finger point when his spit-loaded hand comes within an inch of my face. I don't care if I have vegemite smeared from one ear to the next, he is not licking and spitting my face clean. "They're antibacterial wipes. Look them up sometime." After snagging a wet napkin from the packet in my purse, I fling the packet into Dr. Peter's chest.

I scrub my face like I'm scrubbing off any possibility of this nightmare being true. It does me no good. Even with my cheeks raw and my face sparkling, we're still sitting in the 69ers' parking lot.

Goddammit!

Like a child being guided to the principal's office after placing tacks on their teacher's chair, I follow Dr. Peter through the underbelly of the 69ers stadium. It's not as bad as I was anticipating. The adrenaline-laced sweat I expected is in abundance, but the rowdy players, half-naked cheerleaders, and the walls lined with photos of toothless, muscle-bulked players are missing.

Oops. Nope. Here they are. I jumped off the blocks too early. The cheerleaders might be clothed, but their outfits don't cover much of their teeny tiny *how the hell is it possible to be so small?* bodies. And although the pictures lining the walls are most definitely filled with Hulk-inspired men, most also have their teeth.

I store each name and face into my memory bank for future use. Skylar will shit her pants when she finds out where I'm "working" the next six weeks—if I tell her. I don't want to lie, but imagine the whining that will come with my confession? She'll demand I accept her as a volunteer in a job I'm not getting paid at. If that doesn't work, I have no doubt she'll rig every button in my clothes with hidden cameras. She wouldn't leave my side for the entire six weeks. That could be both a catastrophe and a godsend.

I lose the chance to work out which when someone calls my name. We stop down the wall of photos approximately four-fifths of the way, meaning I miss the last six faces. I guess it's lucky I have a whole six weeks to memorize them.

Six. Whole. God. Damn. Weeks.

"Coach James, this is Willow Underwood."

That silly feeling I get in my belly every time my cell lights up with a message from Elvis tap-dances through my stomach when the man I'm being introduced to sinks himself deeper into his leather chair before dragging his eyes down my body. His prolonged gawk isn't overly bothersome; it's the way Dr. Peter introduced him. You'd swear I was sitting across from Barack Obama. Man—that would be cool.

"My friends call me Will. It's nice to meet you."

I thrust my hand over Coach James's desk in greeting. He doesn't accept my gesture. Instead, he nudges his head to a chair across from him, demanding for me to sit. I do, albeit wonkily. He's got the stern, *do you think I give a fuck you're only a girl* look down pat, and it has more than my heart rate quickening. I've got a sweaty mustache as well.

"It says here that your internship is for six weeks; is that correct?"

"Yes... if that's what you want? I don't mind either way." Dr. Peter's cough reminds me that without this placement, I'll be without the credits needed to pass this semester. "Yes. Six weeks. Not a day more, or a day less." I flash Coach James a grin that reveals my cheekiness. "Unless that's what you want?"

He doesn't appear to appreciate my humor. "You'll work with Amara. She's stern, but it appears as if you need a tight lead."

Ah, there it is. I saw the glimmer in his eyes he tried to stuff halfway through his sentence. He might not be Mary Poppins, but he's got a funny bone hiding in there somewhere.

"Amara will supply you with a uniform. You are to wear it every day. If it doesn't fit, we can arrange to have it altered." I'm about to snicker under my breath about him being an asshole when his next sentence snuffs my anger to a point of no return. "The seamstress the team uses is great at taking in dresses. Fixing ruined jerseys... not so much."

I fold my hands over each other in my lap, feeling better about our arrangement already. "Okay. Thank you."

Several painstakingly long seconds pass without a word being uttered. I can tell Dr. Peter is dying for the chance to speak; he's squirming like a kid busting to use the bathroom, but his jaw is hanging too close to the ground to produce speech.

When the silence becomes too much to bear, I ask, "Anything else?"

Coach James flexes his fingertips together as he silently contemplates. After what feels like a lifetime, he murmurs, "My job here at 69ers camp isn't just to have the best performance stats and highest win ratio in the country; I'm also here to protect my boys." He stands from his seat, walks around his messy table, then plants his backside a mere inch from my shoulder. "In saying that, I think it's important we establish a non-fraternization policy during your stay here. It's nothing against you; I just want to protect both yourself and your university, as well as my players from any unnecessary heartache."

"That's perfect; I think that is a fabulous idea."

"You do?" Coach James's voice is as high as mine. Shock is evident all over his face.

"Yes!" I jump up from my seat, more than ready to start my placement. "This is a place of business, not a frat house, so I have no qualms whatsoever about following your rules."

"That's very mature of you, Willow." Dr. Peter's praise isn't needed, but I'm glad to be on his good side—*for once.*

Once we have all the insurance forms filled out and a brand-spanking new non-fraternization policy signed, Coach James takes me to meet Amara. With her cubicle at the back of the locker rooms the 69er players are in the process of filling up, we take a shortcut down the corridor of photos. I don't mind. It gives me the opportunity to take in the photos I missed earlier, including one I couldn't miss even if I tried.

Presley "Elvis" Carlton

You son of a bitch!

CHAPTER NINETEEN

Presley

"Great practice. We need to hit up a few plays Chester designed tomorrow, and you need to practice on your reach." Coach James points to Mitch. "But other than that, we're good to go." He claps twice, signaling the end of our four-hour training session.

Thank fuck. I'm exhausted and have kinks in places I didn't know could kink. Not all of them are from practice, though. I'm in a whole lot of pain for an entirely worthwhile reason.

Willow.

Willow.

Willow.

No other words needed... except perhaps these five: *it's time for a massage.*

My sluggish steps into Amara's dungeon of torture slow when the flash of a murderous pair of blue eyes stops me in my tracks. Willow's backside is propped on the massage table Amara usually tortures me on. She has her arms folded under her chest, and she's chewing gum like she's crushing my nuts with every bite she takes.

I play it cool, acting like I haven't just been busted for being a lying piece of shit. "Hey, Will, whatcha doing—"

My question is cut short from her pegging a rolled-up towel at my head. She doesn't stop when her hit has perfect aim; she continues pegging towels at me until Amara's usually overstocked shelf is depleted of stock other than heated bottles of massage oil.

"Jesus Christ." I duck, barely missing being smacked in the head by a missile filled with gel-like liquid. "Calm the fuck down and give me a chance to speak."

Willow freezes with a second bottle midair. "Oh, you want to speak?"

When I nod, she squeals, "Like you didn't have plenty of opportunities the past three weeks!"

She releases the bottle from her hand, not without first giving it a good flick for mileage. It hits me in the chest, adding to the burn stretching across my pecs. It's a muscle burn, just not one I used at training today. It's compliments of the hurt look in Willow's eyes. She's mad I deceived her, but not as angry as she is at herself for opening up to me. I understand her pain. I wanted so bad to fess up yesterday, but every time the opportunity presented, my head pulled rank over my heart.

That's not happening today. She's hurting too much for my head not to hear the pleas of my heart. "I was planning to tell you—"

She glares at me with pained eyes. "When, Elvis? When I worked it out for myself? Or via a text message after you fucked me then dropped me home?"

"Hey, that's not fair." I step into her path, blocking her only exit with my body. "I wanted you to stay last night; you're the one who wanted to leave."

"Only because you felt sorry for me." She slaps my chest, seemingly more angry at herself than me. "That's what this is all about, isn't it? I tell you I'm an orphan, so you give me an afternoon pity fuck session before pulling strings so I get an internship with a team most sport therapists would cream their pants to get."

I feel my anger festering. It's bubbling in my gut, begging to be released, but I keep a cool head, understanding she has every right to be angry.

"For one, I didn't arrange this. If I did, why would I walk into battle without adequate protection? I'm not a fucking idiot. If I knew you were going to be here, I would have entered in full defensive getup."

There it is, the smile I've dreamed about more than I've seen in person. It's only half her usual smile, but it's better than the vicious snarl I was getting only seconds ago.

"Two, when did you get the call about this placement? Was it before or after you sucked my dick with more power than the world's most expensive vacuum?"

I can tell the exact moment the truth smacks into her. Her pupils widen as the angry sneer coloring her cheeks drains.

"It was before we fucked, wasn't it?"

She refolds her arms in front of her chest, hoisting up her fantastic tits until they sit an inch under her chin. She's hoping her bountiful bosoms will distract me. They do, but not enough to end our conversation. They just make me want to take a slight pause, to slip into the void where all married couples go when they can't be fucked to bicker about the same old shit for another day.

Thankfully, I've learned from the mistakes I made with Lillian, and I refuse to make the same ones with Willow. "It was before, wasn't it?"

"Yes," she finally relents. "But that's not the point."

"Then what is the point? I get I lied to you. I get I fucked up, but this seems more than that." She didn't smile at my vacuum comment, so I know it's something more than a lie that has her panties in a twist.

"It's just... It's... Argh!"

I save her bottom teeth from menacing her lip, fight with all my might not to replace her teeth with my own, before dropping my hand to my side. "Say it, Willow. Express whatever is on your mind. I'm a big boy. I can handle it."

I feel like she punches me in the nuts when she mutters, "Coach James made me sign a non-fraternization policy."

"Huh?"

That's it. I have no more words.

Except, "When? Was it notarized? Did you sign it?" I yank on my hair like I've just been told I'm being pulled from the team when I read the confirmation in her eyes. "You signed it. Why would you do that, Will? Fuck me..." I glare at her. "Oh, that's right, you can't!"

"Don't blame me. This is your fault." She socks me in the stomach, making my pain real instead of imaginary. "I didn't know at the time that you...*worked* here." She chokes on the "work" part of her statement, like she's unsure my job is work. "I wouldn't have signed it if I had known—" She suddenly stops, swallows, then starts again. "Actually, I probably would have to teach you what happens when you're a lying piece of shit!" She yells her last four words in my face.

"Okay, I deserve that, but you're not seeing the entire picture here. If I'm missing out, so the fuck are you."

The earlier anger I mentioned works up from my gut to my throat when she does a weird shruggy thing as if to say, *why am I missing out?*

When she steps past me, I'm too shocked to stop her.

"You chose to lie, E, so you're the one left to suffer the consequences of your actions." She waves her fingers to the first man in the line outside her cubicle. "Who's ready for a rubdown?"

I swear to God, the line doubles in under a second when they realize Amara has been replaced with a much younger and much more attractive masseuse.

I point to a now empty bench at the side of the locker room. "Sit the fuck down, Foster."

He licks his puffy black lips that get all the cheerleaders' heads in a tizzy while rubbing his hands together. "It's all good, man. I'll wait right here. I don't want to miss my place in line." Not once do his eyes leave Willow's tits during his entire sentence.

They finally lift to mine when I snarl, "Sit. *The fuck*. Down. Or find your ass on the bench for the rest of the season."

"Hey, brother, calm down. I'm not saying you can't go first. I'm more than happy to wait my turn."

When I growl, Foster holds his hands up in defeat while moving back to reclaim his spot in the line that grows longer the more

Willow stands at my side smiling a shit-eating grin. She's not the only one smiling, though. Dalton has his shoulder propped against the wall separating the massage chamber from the locker room. He's only just returned to the field after taking a few weeks off to introduce Jayla to his family, but his smile tells me everything I need to know. He's not only forcing me to confess my line of work to Willow. He's forcing me to confess my feelings for her as well.

Fuck face.

I lock my furious eyes with Dalton. My snarled words are for Foster, but Dalton can have the wrath of my vicious glare. "Amara will be back any second to *serve* you." The way I sneer "serve" leaves no doubt to what I am referring. "For the rest of you, if I hear so much of a murmur that you're thinking about Willow massaging your schlong while you're in the shower, my cleats will be so firmly planted up your ass, you won't sit for a week. Do you understand me?"

Dalton smirks like a smug fuck, impressed by my arrogant macho-headed warning. Willow looks shocked, and I'm still harboring so much jealousy, my clutch on her arm is a little firmer than I'm comfortable with. I don't mean to hurt her; I just want to get her into Coach James's office before I switch from offense to defense.

It's the fight of my life not to tighten my grip on Willow's arm when she murmurs, "Do you really think they'll play slippery sausage while thinking about me? If your answer is yes, can you add a location and a time to your answer? You need to hook a girl up!" She raises the arm I'm not clutching in the air like she's waiting for a high-five.

"I'll give you five; it just won't be your hand I'm smacking."

Her smile doesn't slacken in the slightest. She's loving the douchebag routine I'm working even more than I fucking love the way her tight white dress clings to her curves. I hated when Coach James requested that Amara wear a uniform. Now I'm loving it.

Coach James swivels his big leather chair around to face us when we enter his office unannounced.

"You know how you've been recommending I get my own physical therapist?" When he nods, I nudge my head to Willow. "I've got one. Mine exclusively. She's not to touch the other players. Do you understand?"

I swallow some of my attitude when Coach James raises a brow. He can squash my dreams as quickly as he made them come true. He's not a man I should be bossing around, but I just can't help it. I'm pissed, hackled with jealousy, and five seconds from gouging out Foster's eyes for how long they lingered on Willow's tits. My career is the last thing on my mind right now.

"Now it makes sense." Coach James's dark eyes dance between Willow and me as he stands from his seat to pace around his messy desk. "I knew something was off when Dalton requested we take on an intern. He has a wife and a new kid, so he shouldn't be messing with one. But this..." he gestures his hand between Willow and me, "this makes sense."

I don't know what pisses me off more. The mirth in his tone, confirmation that Dalton set me up, or him calling Willow a kid. I'm confident it's the latter when I snarl, "She's twenty-two." I curse a thousand times in my head. "In a couple of months."

Willow glares at me in shock. Her jaw is hanging open, and her eyes are bugged, but her stunned expression doesn't detract from her murderous glare.

"Hey, don't be pissed at me. Dalton snooped in your purse, not me, so if anyone deserves your anger, it's him."

Her eyes narrow into thin slits. "Oh, don't worry, he'll get his."

I smile, loving that I have an ally on my side to take down Dalton. I may have pulled a similar stunt on him and Becca, but that was years ago, pre *millions of dollars at stake* days.

My smile is wiped right off my face when Coach James says, "Willow signed a non-fraternization policy. It applies to *all* members of our team—players included."

"Yeah, but that was only because you thought she was going to break up your golden couple. Now you know she isn't, there's no need for the policy."

Coach James pulls a face. "The policy wasn't just implemented for this instance. It's something the directors have been looking at implementing for a while now. Willow's placement here just presented the perfect opportunity to bring it into play. You know what the media is like; if they catch wind of anything fishy, they run with it—no matter if it's true or not."

I know what he is saying; I understand what he is saying, but I still fucking hate what he is saying.

My tongue swivels around my mouth so I can ease out my next set of words. "It's too late. We've already…"

Willow bumps me with her hip at the same time Coach James coughs, wordlessly advising me he gets the gist of my confession.

"The policy was only signed today, so anything that happened before it was signed is invalid." Coach James's amused gaze locks with mine as his lips tug into a smirk. "But…" He delays the inevitable, loving the way he's making me squirm. "It is very much valid now, and it will be upheld by *all* staff members."

"I didn't sign anything, so it's only Willow left dateless for the next six weeks—" I chuckle under my breath when Willow's fist whacking into my gut steals my words. It's nice to see I'm not the only one handling jealousy issues today.

"We're very sorry to have interrupted you, and I assure you we'll have no issues adhering to your rules."

Willow waits for Coach James to dip his chin before dragging me out of the office as forcefully as I dragged her into it. Once we're halfway down the hallway, free from prying eyes, she relinquishes my arm from her grip. She looks like she wants to smack the living shit out of me, so the last thing I expect her to do is give me an out.

"You're right. You didn't sign anything, so you don't have to follow Coach James's policy. You're free to do whatever or whomever you want." The anger in her eyes hides her devastation, but it does nothing to lessen the tremble of her lips.

"You're giving me a free pass?"

"It's six weeks, Elvis. To a guy, that's nearly a lifetime." She does her trademark half-eyeroll-twitchy-spasm thing. She's so fucking cute when she's riled with jealousy. "So if you can't wait that long, yes, I'm giving you a free pass."

Her eyes snap to mine when I murmur, "What if I don't want

one?" I move closer to her, crowding her between the wall and me. "What if I want to contest Coach James's ruling on the terms that non-fraternization policies are supposed to minimize the impact of things going wrong in the workplace while maximizing positive employee relationships? I've been playing the best ball in my life since you entered it, so if anything, your introduction into the 69ers family should be a positive, not a negative." When surprise crosses her features, I murmur, "Not as stupid as you thought, hey?"

"I never said you were stupid."

"No, you just thought I was a dumb fuck who chases a football around a field for money."

Having no defense, she groans. "I'm a cow."

"A really pretty cow."

The grimace on Willow's face jumps to mine. That was not the best compliment I've ever given, but thankfully, she doesn't seem too upset by it.

Well, not enough she needs to deliver her scorn via her fists. "Things could be worse." She bobs under my arm and moseys down the corridor backward. Her swinging hips and blistering smile make it appear as if she has the world at her feet. I realize it isn't the world she's stomping on when she mumbles, "I could be rubbing out the Marshall players' kinks instead of the men you class as family." She air quotes her last word before spinning on her heels and racing down the hallway.

I stand frozen, unsure of my next move. Do I go back to Coach James and force him to not only rip up the stupid policy he had Willow sign, but to make Willow my private masseuse? Or do I re-establish my stance at the front of Willow's cubicle so any man who dares to enter it knows what the repercussions will be?

I know, I'll do both.

"Coach?"

Coach pops his head into the hallway too quickly for a man not in the process of spying. "Yeah?"

"Follow me."

CHAPTER TWENTY

Willow

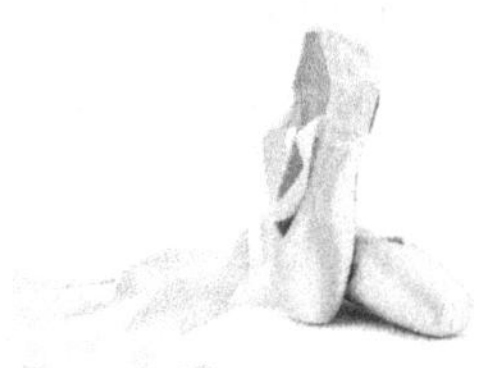

"No way. No. Fucking. Way." Skylar's big cornflower blue eyes shift from the front row, plush leather seats to me. "You got front row seats? How!"

Although she's highly doubtful I can afford such pricy seats, she shimmies past the handful of players' wives and girlfriends who prefer to be up close with the action than have access to unlimited mini hot dogs, spring rolls, and beverages the skybox seats offer that come comped with their relationship. Two Barbie doll-looking, designer-clad, *Botoxed within an inch of their lives* wives eye us with suspicion when we saunter by, but the rest flash friendly smiles. They've seen me around 69ers' bunkers the past three weeks, and know I'm no danger to their positions in the 69er family. As far as they are concerned, I'm only Presley Carlton's private sports therapist. What danger could I be?

Although Elvis got his way with his demand I not touch any players bar him, nothing he said would convince Coach James to remove the non-fraternization policy from the table. He was adamant it needed to be implemented, and from what I've witnessed my first three weeks of my internship, I'm inclined to agree with him. There's a very slippery slope between flirting with a team member and acting on it. Many of the players and a handful of the entertainment staff have yet to work out the difference.

The first week was pure torture. Elvis drove me home every day, kissed me as if he was dropping his daughter off to school before rocketing out of the parking lot like his ass was on fire. I thought we'd keep our distance on the weekends to save temptation, but Danny's closeness has kept us on the straight and narrow. When the second week began, things got a little easier. Elvis's exemplary stats on game night, and above-par training sessions made Coach James relax, meaning we got in lots of sneaky kisses and a handful of heavy-petting sessions.

This week, Coach James is turning a complete blind eye to our antics. He believes Elvis's claims that I'm his lucky charm so it's bought me a near empty front row with two tickets that cost the equivalent of a semester's worth of schooling. Coach James is testing a theory—a highly stupid, *he has no clue how much I despise football* theory. For the past two games, I've camped my backside on the massage table Elvis refuses to use, turned on one of the many TVs around the locker room, eaten cheese and bacon ball Cheetos by the bagful, and pretended I wasn't smiling every time Elvis's mug flashed up on the screen. It was a routine that worked well for me. I was still mad at Elvis for not telling the truth, so I couldn't let him think I enjoyed watching him play.

It all came tumbling down when Coach James entered the locker room second-quarter last week. He never leaves the sideline, so for him to abort his mission while the game was in progress didn't just surprise me, it scared the shit out of me. I thought my college dorm makeover of his domain was going to get me fired. It had the opposite effect.

"You, with me, now."

I jumped to his command, unladylike fumble and all.

"Ohhhh, no, no, no," I stammered when he directed me to the corridor that leads to the field. "You don't want me to go out there." The last time I went anywhere near where he was directing me to, I knocked a man out cold, but considering I couldn't tell him that, I made up a pathetic excuse. "I'm scared of crowds. Like poop-my-pants scared."

I'm a terrible liar, but my acting skills aren't too bad. Coach James didn't force me onto the field, but he did make me stand just outside the bleachers. My view of Elvis was worse than what I got inside, but the atmosphere was electric. The crowd was eating up his performance. They loved his return to the game as much as Elvis did. It was a beautiful thing to witness; so much so, I wasn't as quick to shoot down Coach James's suggestion for me to sit closer to the action this week. He blocked out the two seats beside me and three behind to help with my supposed phobia, so how could I say no?

"No." I grab Skylar's arm when she waves it at the drink attendant. "You were right; you don't want to touch anything he's serving."

She pulls a face like she's seconds from vomiting before it's replaced with suspicion. "How do you know that? I thought our game was the one and *only* game you've attended."

"It is."

I hate lying to her, but her level of craziness has grown tenfold the past six weeks. She's not just obsessed with all things 69ers; she's crushing hard on one of their star players—the star player I get driven home by every day. I want to tell her what's going on with Elvis and me, but I feel like I'd crush her dreams even more than a knee reconstruction squashed mine. Furthermore, my internship came with a confidentiality clause. I can't discuss the players, coaches or staff in any way without prior consent. I'm confident Elvis would give me consent, but who wants to have that conversation?

"Hey, Elvis, I know things are new between us, and I don't even know if we are an 'us,' but would you mind me telling my roommate all about our escapades—monster dick and all? She only falls asleep after kissing your picture every night, and she's pledged to name her firstborn son after you. That's cool though, isn't it?"

Ugh! No thanks.

It's better this way. Elvis kept quiet about what he did for a living because he wanted me to see the real him, and I'm keeping quiet because, away from the hoopla, that's precisely who I see. Off the field, he's goofy, a little jealous, and as sweet as the pie he scarfed down last night. On the field... he's cocky, arrogant, and so fucking sexy I can't get annoyed at the number of women flashing their tits at him.

Well, I can, I just fake that I'm not annoyed.

When Skylar ribs me with her elbow, prompting me to fess up on the lie she sees in my eyes, I murmur, "The lady I aided in the YouTube video is a wife of one of the players. He was so grateful for my help, he threw some perks my way." Because my reply isn't a total lie, Skylar buys it. "I could have sold the tickets, but I figured this would make up for the way I ran out on you that day."

"Oh, it does." She waggles her platinum blonde brows. "But it doesn't explain how you know Mr. Magoo has been cooling his balls in the drinks cooler." Like a perfectly planned skit, the drink vendor pivots around to face us. Skylar's nose screws up when she spots the sleazy look on his face. It answers all her questions and then some.

I stand from my seat and set down my jacket and backpack like they'll guard my seat better than the security personnel at the end of our row. "What do you want to drink?"

"No, it's fine. I'll grab something later."

Skylar stops shooing away my offer like a fly when I say, "You either tell me what you want to drink, or I'll waterboard you with Cherry Coke."

She gags loud enough that people three rows over hear her. "I'll have a Diet Pepsi, two pretzels, and a hot dog." She freezes, purses her lips, then starts again, "Actually make it two hot dogs, one pretzel and a bag of chips. I'm super hungry today."

I act like it's unusual for her to order for an army. "Alright. I'll be back in a minute."

When I exit our row, I'm tempted to climb the stairs to the pavilion I know serves cheaper food, but I veer to the right instead, deciding not having to climb stairs is worth a few dollars. There should be less queue as well since most people can't access this part of the stadium without the bank balance to support personal assistants and bodyguards to fetch their grub.

Just as I'm about to gallop down the six stairs separating me and the delicious-smelling canteen, a roaring voice captures my attention. There are many shouted words surrounding me, so that isn't what gained my notice; it is recognizing the deep timbre shuddering through my core. Elvis is pissed, and he's more than happy for the person he is shouting at to know it.

Keeping my snoop on the down low, I pad closer to the railing. I can't see the person Elvis is shouting at, but I have no trouble figuring out it's a woman. If his constant mention of the name "Lillian" isn't enough of an indication, the low slant of his head is a surefire sign.

"I didn't not answer your calls because I was playing hard to get. I didn't want to talk to you! My silence isn't an invitation for you to come and visit me, Lillian; it was a request for you to back the fuck off."

I see the quickest flash of a blonde head, but I can't hear a word she is whispering.

Whatever she is saying irritates the shit out of Elvis. "That's not true! This wasn't a temporary thing." I would laugh at his air quote of the word "temporary" if his face wasn't etched with so much pain. "You don't get to fuck whoever you want then say you're sorry and expect it to be done and dusted. That's not the way things work."

The blonde steps closer to Elvis. She's clearly slim; she barely casts a shadow in the late-hanging sun, and she's well put-together. Designer pants hug her tiny bottom; she's wearing killer high heel shoes, and every strand of her dead-straight locks are in perfect placement on her head. I don't need to see her face to know she is a knockout. The appreciative rake of her body by the men surrounding her reveals she is stunning. They're so busy ogling her, they failed to hear Elvis's accusation that her insides are nowhere near as sparkly as her outsides.

"For fuck's sake, give me a break. You're here for one thing and one thing only: money. A year ago, I would have fallen for your tricks, but not anymore. I'm smarter than I was back then."

After giving her a final sneer, Elvis thrusts his helmet under his arm then jogs onto the field to join the players already warming up. The crowd spots him in an instant. They jump to their feet, their roars of excitement enticing him to spin around and thank them for their support with a wave. That's when he notices me spying on him. He slants his head as his squinted eyes dart between me and the blonde frozen where he left her.

I try and play it cool with a wiggle of my fingers. He doesn't buy my act. The anger barely receding from his face returns stronger than ever. It's so blistering, I dash down the corridor, needing something more than an icy-cold drink to settle my skyrocketing temps.

My assumption on the queue being smaller at the pricier canteen was right. It also cost me less money. Not because Skylar went easier on me, but because the pass that grants me backstage access to the stadium every day also gives me a staff discount. It wasn't mammoth, but enough to convince me I could fluff up Skylar's order with the grilled sandwich she missed out on last time. It takes twenty-five minutes for them to fill my order, but plenty of time for me to put on my game face before returning to my seat. I don't think Coach James will be pleased knowing he forked out premium seats only to have me piss off his star player minutes before the game.

"Hey, what's going on?"

I hand Skylar her order, minus my hot dog and coke, before shifting my eyes to the field. The last time the crowd was this boisterous was when the opposing team recognized Elvis's play before his receiver did. It's just lucky his misread occurred at the same time the defense awarded the offense an automatic first down penalty or who knows how many yards they would have lost.

I freeze as a disturbance makes itself known in my gut. *What the hell was that? I don't do football talk.*

Hoping it will remove the disdain on my tongue, I chug down half my bottle of Coca-Cola. It sits heavy in my stomach when Skylar launches to her feet and yells, "Come on, Carlton! Where's the magic you had last week?"

I grimace. "Things not good?"

Huffing, Skylar plops back into her chair. "We're barely into the first quarter, and he's fumbled the ball twice. Coach is going to pull him." She sounds more frustrated that he'll be out of her sight than benched.

"Maybe he just needs some encouragement?" I curl my hands around my mouth to ensure my words extend further than the mumbled gripes around me. "Come on, Ref, let 'em play!" I doubt the referee has done anything wrong, but tell me one football fanatic who doesn't love complaining about poor refereeing. "It looks like swiss cheese out there. Tighten up the holes."

"Yeah!" Skylar joins me in heckling both the referees and the players. "You have one job, Lee: protect your QB. If he stops getting slammed, maybe he'll stop dropping the ball."

I cringe. That's not quite the encouragement I was hoping for, but thankfully, her comment inspires many others. They stand to their feet so their words can be accentuated with the stomp of their shoes. "Hut! Hut! Hut! Hut!"

I get in on the action too. Before I know it, I'm stomping my feet and clapping my hands in rhythm with the crowd. I'm not suddenly a fan of football; the energy is just too intense not to swallow me whole.

"Come on, Elvis, show them why you're the King!"

"Oh my gawd!" Skylar's scream sets my hearing back by a decade. "Did you see that? Presley, *I'm so fucking hot I'll get you pregnant just by looking at you* Carlton, winked at me!" She dances on the spot, her bump and grind gaining her more than a few admirers. "I'm going home with him tonight. We're going to make cute babies, buy a Porsche and a ginormous house with no picket fences. Oh yeah, I'm going home with him tonight."

I don't have the heart to tell her Elvis's wink wasn't for her. He was responding to the frisky one I gave him when my shout reached him halfway across the field. His smile, though... that's for Skylar. He's more amused by her invisible cowboy lasso routine than me. He can be. He can't hear the naughty things she's whispering while galloping around the seats generous enough to give her ample dance space.

I'm not so lucky.

"Yeah, baby! Did you see that? Our boy is on fire!"

I jump forward two steps when Foster slaps my backside. I want to blame the adrenaline pumping through his veins for the strength behind his frisky tease, but that would be a lie. Foster is either stronger than he realizes, or he thinks my generous curves can withstand rough-handling. They can, but I don't think Elvis appreciates his knowledge of this.

His eyes squint when they lower to the area Foster spanked. They narrow even further when he realizes what I'm wearing. I could have dressed in the uniform I've donned every day for the past three weeks, but I thought that would look a little suspicious to Skylar, so I opted for a more casual look with a miniskirt and a fitted shirt that says, "I'm only here for the beer."

"Do you like my shirt?" I ask him when he stands in front of me. My words are a little huskier, the smell of his heated skin too invigorating for my body not to respond. If you can take away the scent of fresh-cut grass, he smells like he did after a night of fucking. It's a virile, manly scent that has my thighs squeezing together.

"Your shirt is okay. Your skirt..." He bites on the edge of his hand as he makes a groaning sound.

I bump him with my hip. "So it's good then, yeah?"

He ignores my question, instead choosing to ask his own. "Where's Skylar?"

I want to reply, *most likely waiting for you in the parking lot,* but instead, I opt with, "She's gone to celebrate the win with your other super fans." I swivel on the spot. Excitement is brimming out of me.

"You killed it tonight, E. I don't think I've ever seen you play so well."

He saves my lower lip from my teeth before murmuring, "I can think of one time I brought out all my best tricks. It wasn't on a playing field though; it was on a much more appetizing playground."

Someone pull the fire alarm because I'm burning up like a witch on a stake. His hot breath on my ear is too much for me to bear. It reminds me of when he was kneeling between my legs, preparing to devour my pussy. His eyes are holding the same spark they did that night as well. He looks like he's about to ravish me at any moment, like the rules no longer matter.

I wish that were true.

"We can't." Pulling away from his lips is pure torture—torture I'm not sure I'm strong enough to endure. "Coach James is watching."

"Coach James thanks you for our win tonight, so I doubt he'll care about a little grind-up in the hallway." Elvis drags his crotch against me to emphasize certain parts of his comment.

I pull back for the second time. It's even more torturous than the first since I can feel how erect he is. "Coach James might not care, but fifty percent of my grade is relying on this internship. I can't give that up for anything or anyone." I lock my eyes with his. They're brimming with lust. "Not even The Hulk."

The truth in my statement settles some of the spark in Elvis's eyes. Not entirely, just a smidge. "So no ass smashing for The Hulk, so what about a rubdown?"

"You want a rubdown?" I swear half the continent hears my question. After lowering my voice to a more acceptable level, I ask more calmly, "You want a rubdown?"

"Yeah, my back is killing me." He arches his back while pulling a face that has every man around us paying careful attention to him. Their concern isn't needed when he adds on, "I think a large kink in my crotch has thrown off my balance, so if you work on that first, my back will feel much better as well."

I punch him in the stomach before pushing off my feet. "I'm a sports therapist, not a Chinese masseuse."

He overtakes me, his wish to get to my cubicle at the back of the locker room the reason for his lengthened steps. "I'll call you anything you want to be called if you fix my *issue*." I don't care if you're as old as dirt or as new as Dalton and Becca's daughter, you couldn't have missed the innuendo in his tone when he said "issue."

The vibe in the locker room is the most intense it's been since I started at 69ers camp. I wasn't lying earlier when I said Elvis played the game of his life tonight. I was in such awe, it was the fight of my life not to yell out, "That's my man!" every time he did something spectacular. I shouldn't have held back. There were at least a dozen women yelling precisely that. It's lucky I don't get jealous...much.

Worries I'm one of many women in Elvis's life fly out the window when I enter my little domain. He's sitting on my massage table, eating the bag of Cheetos Coach James confiscated from me last week. He tugged off his jersey somewhere between the locker rooms and here, and he has a twinkle in his eyes that reveals under all those layers of muscle is a teen boy drunk on the high of a win.

His impish glint turns lethargic when I nudge my head to the carpeted floor beneath his feet. "On your feet, old man."

I snatch the bag of chips out of his hand, dump them next to his thigh, before moving to stand in front of him. He doesn't appreciate me calling him old man, but with adrenaline still thick in his veins, he lets it slide.

"Spread your feet to the width of your shoulders, then raise one knee to your midsection."

Elvis's brow pops up. "Why?"

"Just do it." I kick his cleats with my shoes to widen his stance. "I want to check your balance."

"I was joking about my balance being off. I just wanted you to rub my schlong—"

He swallows his words when I glare at him. "Just do it. *Please*."

"Fine." He does his right leg first, and it's a nice, straight movement. His left raise is nowhere near as balanced.

I grab his file off my desk to take notes before asking, "How is the pain in your lower back?"

He waits for me to pivot around to face him before answering, "I broke discs in the thoracic area of my spine. That's nowhere near my lower back."

I give him my *duh* face. His entire medical history is set out in front of me, but even if it weren't, I'm aware the spinal cord he nearly severed is in the top half of his spine. "Your balance is unsteady, meaning when you're lifting weights or doing squats, you may not be evenly distributing the weight. That, over time, will cause lower back pain." I step closer to him, ensuring he knows our discussion right now is between a sports therapist and her client. "So, truthfully, how's the lower back pain?"

His cheeky smirk reveals things will always be personal between us, but he plays along with my endeavor to keep things professional. "It niggles occasionally, but it's nothing I can't handle."

I place my file on the massage table before taking two big steps back. "What starts as a niggle can flare into something much worse. With that in mind, hit the deck, old man."

He growls at my age reference again before doing as instructed.

"Lie on your side. I'll show you a trick that will instantly eradicate the pain in your lower back, then I'll pass on some notes to your weight trainer to make sure he checks you're evenly distributing your weights during sessions." I position him how I need him before moving his hand to sit just above his ass. "Place your thumb on the gluteus medius muscle; it's on the surface of the pelvis. Can you feel it?"

"Uh-huh." The grunt that comes with his reply reveals his pain is more than just a niggle.

"While placing pressure on the muscle, bring your knee forward until it touches the carpet." I smile when he does as asked without hesitation. "Okay, good. Now extend your leg back until it is level with your thumb."

We do ten repetitions before adding an abduct to the move. He grunts even more, showing how much pain there is in his hip region. For a man known for his fitness, his wobbling thighs as he struggles to hold his leg in the air is hilarious. From how red his face is, anyone would swear he was doing the splits.

"Willow..."

I stuff my laughter into the back of my throat with a deep swallow. "What? I wasn't laughing. It's just..."

My words trail off when Elvis sweeps my hands out from underneath me, causing me to topple onto him. I'm not strong enough for this. I'm lying on top of him. My hands are splayed across his mouthwatering pecs, and he's sweaty and panting. No woman would be strong enough for this.

He runs his finger down my cheek before tucking one of my wild locks behind my ear. I assume he is feeling the sentiment in the air the same as me... until he says, "I'm sorry about what you witnessed today."

"Don't be. You didn't do anything wrong."

He angles his head to the side and arches a brow. He appears utterly confused.

It clears when I murmur, "If I had walked in on something like this, then I'd have a problem, but words mean nothing without actions to back them up. I'm sorry you busted me spying. I shouldn't have; I was just worried about what had gotten you so worked up."

Nothing but honesty rings in his tone when he grumbles, "She frustrates the shit out of me."

"And I don't?"

I hope my question will ease the tension radiating out of him. It does exactly that when he murmurs, "Only on Tuesdays." He rolls over until the lower half of my body is pinned to the carpet by his hips.

"Thank god today is Saturday."

With a smile that proves he appreciates my sass, he rocks his hips three times. He's pretending he's testing out how well my exercises reduced the pain in his lower back, but in reality, he's teasing me as only he can. "Oh, you're right, that does feel better. There are barely any spasms. Can you notice the difference, Will? Am I more evenly balanced now?"

I'd answer him if I could. It's a pity the roll of his hips didn't just steal my words. It pinched my morals as well. "I doubt you can tell it's truly effective with only three pumps. Maybe you should add a few more to the mix."

I throw my head back and grunt when he does as requested not even two seconds later. He grinds against me, the movements of his hips anything but innocent. He knows he has me at his mercy, and if my needy moans don't shut the hell up, so will the rest of his team.

"E, we shouldn't," I mutter in a breathless moan when his lips arrow toward mine. "I don't want to break the rules."

"If that were true, you wouldn't have called me 'E.'"

He's right. I'd lie on a bed of nails if it guaranteed our kiss would occur. Thankfully, Elvis doesn't require that level of commitment for his mouth to continue its expedition to mine. He lowers it slowly, his pace as tempting and as devilish as the half-smirk he's wearing. I'm so caught up in memorizing how delicious his mouth tastes, I don't realize we have company until it is too late.

"Oh my goodness, I'm so sorry. I was looking for the washroom."

A blonde lady quickly retreats, but she's not quick enough for me not to put a face to her designer pants, unruffled hair, and the tension her voice caused to Elvis. He stiffened even faster than he did when I landed on top of him with a bang. Fortunately, none of the stiffness was to his lower regions. This must be Lillian.

"It's okay. There's a washroom in the far right corner." I point in the direction I'm referencing. I doubt the tiny facilities will be up to her standards, but when it's the only bathroom that guarantees a lowered lid, you take what you can get.

When she heads for the washroom, I stand to my feet. "I'll send a message to your weight trainer on my way home."

"Will—"

"It's okay," I assure Elvis, more than eager not to be stuck between two battling powerhouses. "This gives me the opportunity to get a head start on practice tomorrow."

More than a niggle in his back echoes in his voice when he mutters, "I don't want to talk to her."

"Then tell her that." I squeeze his hand in support before snagging my backpack from behind my desk and ambling toward the locker room.

I'm barely halfway across the room when Elvis shouts, "Wait up! I'll give you a ride."

When he stops at my side, I raise my eyes to his. "Running from your problems won't solve anything."

"Who said I'm running from trouble?" He slings his arm around my shoulder and tugs me into his side. "Maybe I'm striving to tackle the storm head on this time around. Wasn't it you who said I should be able to both give and receive tackles? Figured I should give it a shot."

"I was talking out of my ass, but I guess when you're a guy who does nothing but dribble shit all day, that's the equivalent of liquid gold."

Elvis laughs. It is such a beautiful thing to hear when my stomach is twisted up in a tight, jealous ball. I thought I had a handle on my neurosis. I took Skylar's numerous proclamations that she's moments away from bedding the "King of Quarterbacks" like a champ, and I didn't even ruffle a feather when a group of female fans wanted Elvis to sign more than a jersey at the end of his game, but this, I'm struggling with this. Danny has mentioned a Lillian a handful of times the past six weeks, but Elvis quickly shut his comments down.

It doesn't take a genius to realize Elvis and Lillian have a past; I'm just unsure how deep their ties run. Skylar and Elvis's many fans can dream of being with him, but the chances of their wishes coming true are basically non-existent. Lillian doesn't have to clutch at the same skerrick of hope as them. I'm confident she's already had her wish granted, and I'm even more confident her resurrection in Elvis's life at this very moment isn't a coincidence. The hype around him at the moment is mammoth; so much so, I really hope he doesn't see my attention as mooching. I almost kissed him because I like him, not because of what he could bring to my life.

"I'm going to catch a cab. It's late, and I don't want you going out of your way to take me home."

Elvis's words trap in his throat when I briefly press my lips to his mouth before making a beeline for an idling taxi. The drivers always hang out at this entrance of the stadium with the hope of driving one of the idols home. My driver's face lights up like a Christmas tree when he notices me approaching. His excitement doesn't linger for long when I slide into the back seat before slamming the door shut, leaving his preferred passenger at the private entrance of the stadium looking as dumbfounded as I feel.

CHAPTER TWENTY-ONE

Presley

I wait until Willow's taxi blurs into a sea of many before kicking the steel trash can in front of me. The high of a win is being quickly overshadowed by a low, and I can't even blame the woman evading me for the drop of my mood. It's the one I'm trying to avoid like the plague. The one watching me right now like a hawk, hiding in the shadows like she never would during our relationship. She always wanted to be the center of attention, at the front of every campaign. My victories were her victories, no matter what they were.

"What do you want, Lillian? Is the penthouse getting too dated for you and you're in need of an upgrade? Or has that hideous pink Barbie doll car you drive around gotten too many miles on the odometer?"

I hear Lillian swallow before she steps out of the shadows. She doesn't speak a word, but I don't need to hear them to know what they are. She's about to run with the same excuse she used on me earlier tonight. The ones where she pledged she can't live without me, and that she's never stopped loving me.

She stops wordlessly pleading with me when I swipe my hand through the air. "As I said earlier, I know why you're here, and I've learned from my mistakes. We're not going down that road again, Lillian. I've moved on. It's time for you to do the same." I try to hold in the rest of my scorn, but Willow's eagerness to leave me stranded on the sidewalk weakens my campaign. "Oh, that's right—too late. You moved on months before me." My brows furrow. "Or was it years? I can't remember all the details."

"Everything I did was to help you and your career."

Over her using the same pathetic excuses, I curse into the cool night air before pushing off my feet. I've got as much knowledge of these streets as a taxi driver but more enthusiasm than one hoping to fleece a student of money she doesn't have by taking her the long way home.

"It's her, isn't it?" I can't see Lillian, but I'm certain she's pointing in the direction Willow's taxi just went.

Not having the time nor the patience to deal with her antics, I continue for my car. The parking lot is as empty as my bank balance after I paid for my angry outburst the last time we were in the same room as each other. Not willing to part with more of my hard-earned money, leaving is the best thing I can do.

"When I said you needed to find yourself again, I didn't mean you should go back to who you were before we met. She's a child, for crying out loud! How is anyone okay with this?"

I take in a deep breath, then continue walking.

While Lillian persists with her belligerent rant on how we're destined to be together, I remind myself time and time again how much I lost because of her. I repeat *twenty-three million dollars* over and over again while my mind replays the unsure expression Willow's face held when she slipped into the cab. If I needed any more proof on how toxic my relationship with Lillian was, I just got it. None of my thoughts center around our time together—not one of them.

As a security guard cautions Lillian to calm down, I slip into my driver's seat. The purr of my engine matches the havoc twisting in my gut. Lillian didn't arrive tonight for no reason. She's up to something. If my eagerness to beat Willow to her dorm wasn't on the forefront of my mind, I'd look into her sudden unwanted return.

Alas, I only have one woman on my mind. She isn't the one who makes my blood boil. Well, not in anger anyway.

I make it to Willow's school a whole two and a half minutes before her taxi. I didn't run a single red light or floor the gas; I just used my knowledge of the streets to my advantage. It paid off for me tonight; Willow doesn't look like she's enjoying the change in our plans as much as me.

"Regretting your decision now, aren't you?"

Willow stops counting the small change in her purse. Instead, she scoops them out and thrusts them at the taxi driver, pretending she wasn't counting his fare to the very dime.

"Not really; it was a nice night for a drive." With the wink of a woman who doesn't know the phrase "back down," she pivots on her heels and stalks to her dorm.

Her steps slow to barely a snail's pace when I say, "Lillian is my ex-fiancée. We were supposed to wed three weeks before I walked in on her in our bed with her yoga instructor."

Willow swivels around to face me. "*Ex*-fiancée?"

"Very much so," I answer without hesitation.

"Does she know that?"

Determined not to lie to her again, I shrug. "I don't know." When she turns and walks away from me, I rush out my next set of words, "But I plan on confirming she's well aware of that fact no matter what happens between us. I didn't postpone our wedding the first time for no reason. I've always known deep down inside that she isn't the girl for me. Then when I broke my back, I was saved from the fire for the second time."

I rake my fingers through my hair while cursing the cool fall air. That was not a good analogy for me to use. Mercifully, Willow is as strong as the woman I see in her eyes.

"You postponed your wedding before you injured yourself?"

I step closer to her. "Yes. I made an excuse about it being the end of the season and that I needed to keep my mind focused on the game instead of wedding hoopla."

"And Lillian bought that?" Willow sounds equally sickened and humored.

I nod. "She was happy for the postponement. Not because she needed more time to plan our wedding, but because it gave her plenty of opportunities to seek out the highest bidder to broadcast our ceremony to the supposed two million people who signed up to watch it live."

"Yet, you still asked her to marry you. What kind of man does that make you?"

Ouch! Take that, ego.

"Sorry." Regret fills Willow's eyes when she spots the shock in mine. "I'm dealing with a whole heap of emotions I'm not used to handling. I'm also hangry. Nobody likes a hangry Will."

The smile stretching across my face makes it hard to get out my next set of words. "Join the club."

She cocks her hip and drags her teeth over her lip in an undoubtedly sexy way. "Which part? The hangry part? Or the whole heap of emotions?"

"A bit of both." I nudge my head to the right. "We could work through both issues over there."

Her eyes stray to Mickey's for a few seconds before they return to me. "Who's paying? I'm living off coupons until Tuesday." She doesn't sound the least bit embarrassed. During our conversations the three weeks I was on the road, I verified my college days were just as dire as hers.

"I'll get this one; you can pick up the next."

I sling my arm around her shoulder to guide her to Mickey's, only to have her pull away from me two seconds later. My panic subsides when she murmurs, "You may not want to hug me when you learn how many appetizers I'm planning to order."

"Does Danny know?" A string of tomato-loaded spaghetti wiggles up Willow's chin, flicks her nose, then gets lost in her O-circled mouth before she locks her light blue eyes with mine.

I'm tempted to lick the smear of tomato paste from her nose but keep my focus on the task at hand. It's a fucking hard feat. "Know what?"

She swallows her mouthful of spaghetti before replying, "That you hired him to lower the possibilities of 'it' happening again." She air quotes "it" like she's afraid to say the word "affair" out loud.

"You think I hired Danny because I'm worried about being cheated on again?"

I scrub pizza sauce from my face with a napkin, no longer hungry, when she shrugs. "It's understandable. Being deceived really screws people up. You didn't just have it happen once; by the sounds of it, the two men you know of aren't the only ones you're suspicious of."

"I hired Danny because he is a lifelong friend, not because he's disinterested in the same body parts as me." I screw up my napkin and dump it onto my half-eaten plate of food. "I also hated seeing him go through what I had experienced only months before."

"Danny was cheated on?" She sounds like I just told her her puppy died. Her eyes are welling with moisture, and her cheeks are whitening.

I nod. "Yes, but why is that more concerning to you than hearing my stories of Lillian's infidelities?"

She smiles, loving the jealousy tainting my tone. Perhaps she is right? Maybe I did hire Danny so I didn't have to worry about him sniffing around my turf?

"Danny is a sweetheart, but he isn't you." Willow waves her hand down my body, which is still embarrassingly outfitted with my team uniform—cleats and all. I was in such a hurry to track Willow down, I didn't bother getting changed. Thank god my head was screwed on enough to throw on a smelly shirt I found in my gym bag during my drive.

"You handled Lillian's... *indiscretion*..." –that sounded as awkward as you'd expect—"...by beating the pulp out of a man before losing yourself in..." She taps her sauce-smeared lips with her index finger. "What did you say again... ? 'All the girls I didn't get to tap.' So, yeah, Mr. Wave My Dick Around Like It's A Magic Wand, my heart is pained for Danny. I feel for him so greatly, I wish to nuzzle him into my bosoms so I can wipe away his tears. You..." A sudden urgency to protect my nuts hits me when she rakes her eyes down my body, only stopping when she reaches the section of my pants my groin protector is usually guarding. "You don't get any of my sympathy."

Although I'm loving her jealousy, I can't help but defend myself. "She cheated on me. I'm not the one in the wrong here."

"No, you're not. What she did was wrong, but your actions since haven't been any better. You let her play you tonight."

I attempt to argue, to blame my fumbling hands on the wet conditions, but I can't. She's right. I let Lillian fuck with my head so badly, I was seconds from being benched. Until I heard Willow cheering for me, I didn't think anything would get me out of the dark hole my conversation with Lillian pushed me down.

When I tell Willow that, she cups my jaw with her tiny hands. "Then remember that anytime she riles you up. She arrived tonight to get a reaction out of you—good or bad. You played right into her hand." She screws up her face as if her next set of words are scorching her throat. "As did I. I shouldn't have run like I did. I was just..."

The scared expression on her face says way more than her words ever could. Just like me, she's unsure what we are, but unlike me, she's not yet hellbent on fighting for what she wants. Running is less complicated but nowhere near as effective.

With that in mind, I ask, "Do you have any plans two weeks from Friday?"

Willow peers at me in shock, stunned by the sudden detour in our conversation. It went from being sentimental to being electric in less than a nanosecond.

When she shakes her head, I disclose, "Coach James hosts an annual costume party every year. It's nothing fancy, just the players' family and friends all in one spot before the playoffs. I'd love to take you as my date."

"Date? I doubt Coach would be happy with that."

Her breathing quickens when I run my finger along her lips, incapable of ignoring her messy mouth for a second longer. It was either wipe it away with my finger or scrub it with my tongue. I went for the one less likely to be filmed by the several phone cameras currently facing us.

Once her mouth is clear of sauce, I sink back into my side of the booth. "If I run it by Coach first? Would you be up for it then?"

She hears more in my tone than I meant to display. "Just a date? The standard *pick me up and take me home with the hope of a peck at my door* date?"

I twist my lips. "These things can run late, and Coach James does live around the corner from my condo, so..." My words are stolen by her fist landing in my stomach. Her anger is all a ploy; she's more excited at the prospect of me going to bat for our relationship than anything.

"*If* you get approval from Coach James, I'll pick you up. Then, if you play your cards right, I might let you touch my boob during our goodnight kiss."

She scoots out of our booth, her smile as raging as my heart rate at just the thought of getting a bit of boob action. It's been three weeks since I've felt her up, so I'm more than dying to get reacquainted with her body.

Her lips tickle my earlobe when she leans over to whisper in my ear. "Look at you getting all excited, and I didn't even mention which part of your body I'm planning to kiss."

CHAPTER TWENTY-TWO

Presley

"Surprise!"

My deep gasp almost lodges my toothbrush down my throat. I choke on a mountain-load of minty spit, my near death adding to the humorous image confronting me.

While gesturing for Willow to enter the foyer of my condo, I talk around my toothbrush. "What the hell are you wearing?"

"A costume. Skylar said it's un-American to go to a costume party without a costume, so here I am." She places her hands on her hips and rocks them forward, thrusting an oversized set of udders my way. "You know how I said if you got Coach James to agree to our date, I'd let you touch my boob?" She gyrates her hips in a circle, swiveling the gigantic udders on her cow costume with more agility than a real cow would have. "I've got all the bases covered."

My mouth opens as my brow cocks. "Are you telling me my shameful, nearly tearful beg at Coach James's feet was all to feel up cow udders?"

After nodding, Willow follows me into my bathroom. I spit out the foam in my mouth, rinse my toothbrush, then spin around to face her. "That wasn't a part of our deal. I kept my side by letting you pick me up, so you're not reneging on your half of our deal. I want boob action—goddammit." Yep, I sound like a teen boy who's never slid past second base.

Willow's cow ears slant as much as her sexy lips when she drops her head to the side. "Don't let the sexiness of my outfit deceive you, E. If you've got the right m*oooo*ves, you won't need milk to get to the udder side of it."

I grin at her spunk. "That took you all day to come up with, didn't it?"

When she nods, I weave my hand through her hair, tug her head back, then plant a minty kiss on her smiling lips. I can do that now without looking over my shoulder. Not just because we're in the safety of my home, but because the better I play, the more lenient Coach James is becoming. I have him so convinced Willow is my good luck charm, I'm certain the *no sex before games* rule he mandates for all the players during championship month would be null and void if I asked. He might even book hotel rooms and stage them for intimacy if it guaranteed his players would keep thrashing our opponents as we have the past eight weeks. Alas, Willow signed a legally-binding contract. Fortunately, it's over in a little under two weeks.

I stop counting down the hours left in Willow's internship when she asks, "I had a few to work with. Wanna hear them?"

I nod before heading back down the stairs we just climbed. As I move through my condo to gather my wallet and keys, she hits me with her best cow jokes.

"What did one cow say to the other cow? Got milk?"

"What do you call a sleeping cow? A bulldozer."

"What are grumpy cows called? M*ooooo*dy."

"What do you call a cow with a nervous twitch? Beef jerky."

That one gets me laughing. I like that one.

Once she is out of jokes, I slip my wallet into my back pocket before pivoting to face her. It's not hot today, but she's feeling the heat in her getup. Sweat is dribbling down her neck, and her shoulders are hanging as low as her udders.

"Hot?"

She blows a rogue curl out of her eyes before murmuring, "As boiling as curdled milk in a saucepan. It's totally worth it though. I'm udderly adorable."

She is. She's so fucking cute, even a ridiculously hideous outfit can't take away her appeal. I like seeing her like this, fun and happy. She's been loving life as much as me the past eight weeks. Excluding our little hiccup two weeks ago, things couldn't be better. Lillian flew back to New York on her broomstick; Coach James agreed to let me "date" Willow as long as we keep our relationship on a Disney movie level, and a big chunk of the endorsement deal Danny negotiated on my behalf months ago will land in my bank next month. We're scheduled to start shooting the first commercials next week. Life is golden at the moment... so perfect that I'm waiting for the other shoe to drop.

Taking a page out of Willow's book, I look for the positives instead of the negatives. "In all seriousness, though, where are your clothes? You should probably get changed; Coach James's house is forty minutes away."

Willow stops at the side of my dining room to glare at me. "Whatever do you mean?" She's trying to act coy, but I can see the panic igniting in her eyes. "For one, you said Coach lived around the corner, and two, you're the one who needs to get changed, right?"

I follow her wide eyes when they glide down the rolled-up sleeves of my dress shirt, over my black trousers before coming to a stop at my recently polished boots. When I hear her forcefully swallow, I raise my eyes back to her face. She's as white as a ghost, her lack of coloring not compliments of the heavy costume she's wearing.

She peers at me in shock. "It's a costume party."

"It is," I agree with a nod.

"An American tradition more important than Christmas, Halloween, Thanksgiving, and Super Bowl Sunday."

I grimace. "You had me until your last comment."

"You need to wear a costume, E! Skylar said!" She stomps down her foot in a way that shouldn't be sexy, but is.

As quickly as her tantrum arrives, it disappears. Her eyes widen like she has a brilliant idea as her finger rises in the air. "How fond are you of your rug in the living room?"

I lose the chance to reply when she pushes off her feet and charges for the fur rug we wrestled on weeks ago. Her cheetah speed slows when I murmur, "You're not hacking up my rug to make me a costume."

She huffs. "Why not? You'd make the perfect Tarzan. You Tarzan, me Jane." She makes a face likes she's seconds from orgasming before murmuring, "You have no idea how long I've wanted to say that."

"You're not Jane; you're a cow." She pokes her tongue out at me. "And its cold out there. I'm not having any dick shrinkage pictures of me uploaded to the internet."

"Any *more* dick shrinkage pictures," Willow corrects.

She takes a moment to fan her heated cheeks from my growl before she restarts her endeavor to make me look as ridiculous as her. "What about an old football jersey? Surely you have one of those lying around."

She stops racing across my living room when she reaches my fireplace. With her hands splayed across her tiny waist, her head flops back. "Where's the pompous, *I'm a football star* jersey every player has framed above their fireplaces at? That would work."

"I had Danny put it in storage when I was trying to deceive you into believing I was regular folk..." My words fall short when her narrowed eyes snap to mine. "Too soon?"

"Don't be a m*ooooo*ron, E. It doesn't suit you."

Laughing at herself, she makes a beeline for my coat closet. She's seen me dump my gym bag in there many times the past few weeks, so she knows there's a high possibility of finding what she's chasing in there. "Oh my god, E. Have you heard of a washing machine? Send in the battle crews; I'm fighting back a stinky sock army in here."

My chuckles are sliced in half when she emerges from the coat closet with one of my team jersey's in her hand. "Bingo."

I take a step back, exasperated. "I'm not dressing up as myself!"

"Why not? It will be cute." She pulls a cutesy face, fluttering eyelashes and all.

I'm not buying it. "I'll look like a fucking idiot. Who rocks up to a party held by their coach in their team uniform?"

Willow perks her lips. "A person too cheap to buy a damn costume for a party." She thrusts the jersey into my chest. "You either wear this, or I hack up your rug."

"I can't believe I'm doing this."

The bus driver peers down at the hundred I'm attempting to feed into the machine at her side before lifting her eyes to mine. "Correct change only."

"Yeah, I know. It's all I have." That, and a really annoying girl-friend who makes me dress up as myself and catch the bus like "the regular folks" do.

When the machine finally accepts my fare, I join Willow on one of only a few vacant seats. After plopping into my spot, my eyes scan the bus. We're the only riders wearing costumes, and we stick out like sore thumbs.

Halfway down the block, the lady next to me angles her head to the side to stare at my outfit. "We're going to a costume party," I inform her, panicked I'm seconds from being mauled by an overzealous fan. She's giving me a look, one I'm not a fan of when I'm off the field.

My fear subsides when the gawker says, "Your outfit is the bomb. You look just like him." The flash on her phone blinds me when she snaps my picture. After tapping her fake nails on the screen of her cell for a few seconds, she spins it around to face me. "See? Your resemblance is uncanny."

She has a picture of me next to a picture of me.

She uploads her photo to facechat, snapbooky, whatever the hell it's called before leaning across me to tap Willow on her shoulder. "YouTube tutorials?"

Now I'm not the only one panicked. Willow's dilated eyes and thrusting chest have me taking a mental note to look into her YouTube infamy a little more intently tomorrow morning.

"Excuse me?" Willow's voice is as high as the unnamed lady's penciled brow.

"His face? It's makeup, right? You can make anyone look like anyone with the right amount of makeup."

She'd know. She's wearing five pounds' worth on her face.

The longer Willow delays answering the stranger's question, the more inquisitive glances we gain. The bus riders arrow in closer, more intrigued by our choice in clothing than concerned.

After a quick swallow, Willow murmurs, "Oh, yeah. Awesome stuff. I contoured and shit, and shazam, look what happened?" She leaps to her feet, filling the air with her sweet scent. "Oh, look, it's our stop!"

Nice try, buttercup, but you're about to be taught a hard lesson. "No, that's not our stop. We've still got thirty miles to travel."

Willow slaps me with her udders when she jackknifes my way. That shouldn't have my dick paying attention, but for some fucked-up reason it does.

"Shut up and walk, E."

I fold my right ankle over my left before sinking deeper into my seat. "Not until you say it." The smirk tugging my lips high wipes the last of the worry from my face.

Willow folds her arms in front of her chest as the lady watches our exchange with enough interest to be deemed creepy. "I'm not saying it."

"Then sit your ass down, buttercup, cause we've still got another thirty miles to travel." I scoot over, giving her plenty of room to sit on the bench seat we're sharing with Ms. Stalker and another two travelers.

Willow makes a face that looks like she's a chicken about to lay an egg when my thigh brushes the unnamed lady's. "Fine! I'll say it." Her ribs expand and contract three times before she murmurs, *"You were right."* Her words are so soft, I barely heard them.

I tuck my feet under my seat before leaning closer to her. "What was that?"

"You were right." This attempt isn't any louder than her first.

Tilting my head to the side, I tug on my ear. "Still didn't get it."

"You were right!"

Jesus, and now I'm deaf as well.

With a smile on her face, she watches me wiggle her words from my ear before adding a few more. "Now can we go? Please."

The strain crinkling her forehead eases when I wave my hand across my body, indicating for her to lead the way. Once she's out of earshot, I twist my torso to face the lady sitting mute next to me. "Can you forward me that photo?" It's not a good shot of me, but the look on Willow's face when I was being bombarded with the unnamed female's attention makes it a real keepsake. "Here are my details."

I hand her my business card before tracing the steps Willow just took. I barely make it onto the sidewalk before the bus doors slam shut, almost drowning out the lady's high-pitched screech, "O. M. G! Presley Carlton's thigh touched my thigh!"

Shoving my hands into my pockets, I rock back and forth on my heels. My mood is at an all-time high, my smirk just as large. Willow and I argued for twenty minutes straight this afternoon that I'd be recognized within a minute of getting on the bus. Don't quote me, but I'm reasonably sure she said something along the lines of, "You're not *that* famous, E."

I don't want to say it, but I must: "I was right."

Willow's bouncy hair flings in her face when she glances at me over her shoulder. She's standing on the curb, holding open a taxi door. "Shut up and get in the cab, old man."

Her taunt doesn't have the same effect on me tonight. "Don't get m*ooooo*dy, Willow. I was just playin'. I've got no beef with you."

With a waggle of my brows, I slip past the door she's holding open for me.

🏈

"What do you get when you cross a Smurf with a cow?" Dalton moseys up to my side, his smirk as big as the one he was wearing when he noticed I came dressed as myself. "Blue cheese. Or in your case, blue cheese balls." He ribs me with his elbow, his Aladdin outfit not emasculating enough to lessen his scorn. "Get it? Blue balls, as in your balls since Coach James put a stop to all your fun."

"I get it. Very funny." It's not, but I'll give him a B for trying.

Taking a sip on my bottle of Coca-Cola to hide my smile, I return my eyes to Willow. She's in the middle of a makeshift dance floor, surrounded by all the players' children. They honed in on her the instant we entered the room. They loved her outfit, but more than that, they were smitten with her personality.

I can understand why. Within ten minutes, she took a usually dull affair and made it the place to be. We've been here for over three hours, and I've yet to see one person leave. That's unheard of. Don't get me wrong; my team is a rowdy bunch of fuckers, but with the majority of them being single, the last thing they want to do is hang out at the Coach's house with their shacked-up counterparts. Willow changed that. She's bridged the divide between the players like Coach James has been trying to do for years, and all she did was be herself.

I'm a lucky fuckin' man.

Dalton must feel the sentiment in the air as much as me. "All jokes aside, how are things? I feel like I hardly see you now you've *moooo*ved on to greener pastures."

The neck of my bottle can't hide my smile, so I don't bother trying. "Things are good."

"Yeah?" Dalton only says one word, but his eyes ask a lot more.

I wait for Willow to finish twirling Ben's four-year-old around the dance floor before answering, "Yeah. She's good. Different."

"Different is good. Different works."

Dalton sounds like he's trying to convince me there's nothing wrong with different. I don't need convincing. I'm well aware how good a change can be. I'm playing the best football of my life while also enjoying my life. I've never had this type of balance before. Five weeks ago, I wanted to strangle Coach James for his non-fraternization policy, but now I'm not so opposed to it. Willow and I have had chemistry from the get-go, so to have to set that aside for six weeks has allowed us to discover we have a lot more in common than mutual sexual attraction. We're both striving to return to the glory we once held, me with football and Willow with dance. We love carbs like they're going out of fashion, and she's as dorky as I am moody. It's a nice balance, one I'm very much looking forward to exploring for several months, if not years to come.

I crank my neck to Dalton when he mutters, "I'm glad things are going well for you, Elvis. She's worked quite the number on Becca as well. She wants to ask her to be a godparent to Jayla."

"Really?" I don't know why I'm shocked. Willow's numerous daily chats with Becca have revealed the extent of their immediate bond. I guess I'm more frustrated than anything. Like why is Willow a prime candidate to be Jayla's godparent, but I'm not? I've only threatened to take Jayla for a cruise down main street in my car with the top down. Doesn't mean I'd actually do it.

Dalton laughs at my grumbly expression. "You're already set to be Jayla's godfather. I just have no plans to ask you since I have no intention of taking no for an answer. But that's why I wanted to clear Willow's involvement with you. I don't want it to get awkward if things don't work out between you two. We know it's still early, and I don't want a lifetime commitment forcing you into something you're not ready for."

"Like when I attempted to take Becca home for some magic between the sheets?"

Any happiness on his face fades. "Yes, like that." He straightens his spine as his eyes seek his wife and daughter across the room. "She wouldn't have gone with you."

"Dude! Seriously? She was ready, willing, and able until your dumb ass turned up."

Coke jumps from my stomach to my throat when Dalton punches me in the gut. "She wasn't like that."

I arch a brow, bullshit written all over my face.

"She's not—*now*." He barges me with his shoulder, his knock more in anger than in jest. "Kiss your godfather role goodbye, Elvis. I don't want an asshat who can't tell the difference between a girl letting him down nicely and one eager to take him home being responsible for the care of my daughter if anything were to happen to me."

I know he's only joking, but I play along. "Ah, come on, man. You know I'm just playin'. Becca only talked to me because she knew you were my friend." That's not true, but if it makes him feel better, I'll pretend it is.

"Damn straight." His words aren't as confident as he's hoping, but like our entire conversation tonight, he plays it cool. "So what do you say? You up for a co-parenting role with a girl too young to know how to parent?"

Malted liquid sprays through the air when I whack him in the guts. He wheezes on the beer trapped halfway between his lungs and his throat, acquiring us many eyes in the room, two pairs more notable than the rest: Willow's and Becca's.

"She's twenty-two—"

"In a couple of months." He's chuckling so hard, I can barely make out his words.

If we weren't entering the playoffs, I'd stomp on his foot. Luckily for him, my head is already in game mode—and no, I'm not entirely referring to the game of football.

"Ask her, but don't mention I've already been recruited. If Willow wants to do it on her own accord, let her."

I wait for Dalton to nod before pushing off my feet and heading to Willow. We turned up; we partied; now it's time for the real entertainment to begin.

My stride shortens when Dalton calls out my name. When I spin around to face him, he quotes, "I'm just playin'." He has the smirk down pat, even his stance is accurate, he's just missing one thing: the fire in my eyes every time I quote my infamous line.

CHAPTER TWENTY-THREE

Willow

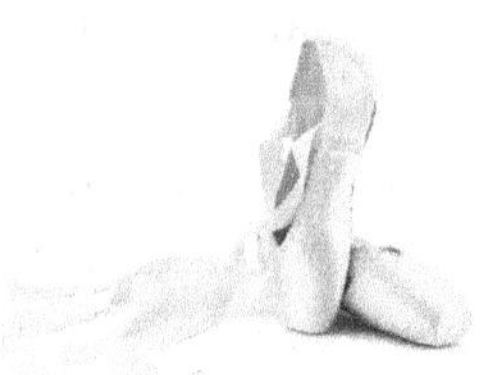

"*I* cross my heart and hope to die; I won't stick my fingers in your pie."

I throw my head back and laugh. "I don't recall *ever* hearing that version before."

Elvis climbs out of the cab idling at the front of his condo before shifting on his feet to face me. "Wait until you hear Danny's version." He tugs on the collar of his shirt as his face screws up. When he hears my laugh, the plea on his face turns rampant. "Come on, Will. I'll keep it Hannah Montana clean."

"Hannah Montana pre-'Wrecking Ball' days? Or *grinding her ass on Robin Thicke's dick on stage* Hannah Montana?" When he makes a face like he's leaning toward the latter, I murmur, "No deal. We have less than two weeks, E. It's not that long."

My tone relays my disappointment. I was handling our abstinence from sex okay until tonight, but seeing Elvis woo the shyness out of a handful of girls who flocked to my side tonight makes me despise events that haven't even happened yet. It was a struggle for me to keep my hands off him during our thirty-minute trip home, so I know without a doubt that I won't be able to hold back when we're safe from prying eyes.

Hearing the devastation in my tone, Elvis increases his odds. "What if I agree to keep my hands to myself? I won't touch you in the slightest." His brows furrow as confusion washes over his face. "Is spooning classified as touching?"

I try to play it cool, act like his question didn't make my heart rate triple, but the high squeak of my words gives away my true composure. "You want to spoon with me?"

"Yes." His smile does wicked things to my insides. "Very much so."

"And that's it? Just spooning?"

He nods while holding his hands up like he's about to be arrested. "My hands will remain above board at all times."

His smile enlarges when I grumble, "You don't have to sound so happy about it."

"What were Coach James's stipulations when he altered your contract?"

Pretending the cab driver isn't watching our exchange with an eagle eye, I reply, "Lip kissing and handholding are okay." Recalling the mortified expression on Coach's face when he read out his newly drafted rules has me laughing. "And by lips, he means the ones on my face."

Elvis's laughter joins mine. "I still can't believe he included that."

"I can. He knows every man on your team as if you are his sons." I lift and lock my eyes with Elvis's glistening gaze. "That's why I don't want to disappoint him."

He yanks his cell out of his pocket. "I'll ring him now. Get the go ahead. He'll give it to me."

When he dials a number he knows by heart, I launch out of the cab to snatch his phone from his hand. "You can't call him now! It's 2 AM."

I realize the error of my ways when Elvis flings a bundle of notes through the lowered passenger side window, slams the door I just dove through shut, then bangs on the roof of the taxi, signaling for the driver to leave.

He waits until the taxi's taillights blur on the horizon before facing me. "Oh, jeez, would you look at that? It's 2 AM. I don't like your chances of getting a taxi willing to come out here this late at night."

I give him the cutie pie face I used to give my dad seconds before causing trouble. "I guess it's lucky my boyfriend doesn't drink, so he has no excuse not to drive me home." I prop my hip against his pricy ride before my eyes stray to Elvis.

He screws up his face. I don't know what has him more worked up: me referring to him as my boyfriend or the honesty of my reply. He doesn't drink. I haven't seen him touch a drop of alcohol the past five weeks.

Tired of fighting a desire bigger than Elvis's biceps, I give in to temptation. "Hands to yourself at all times. We can kiss, but no tongue." He looks like he wants to protest, but I continue talking, foiling his attempt. "I can't do tongue, E, because then I'll want more. It's a given. Just like neck kisses. Neck kisses turn into chest kisses. Chest kisses turn into kitty kisses, then kitty kisses turn in—"

"I get it." He adjusts his crotch like he's in pain. He's not the only one. Just thinking about how many naughty things we could do behind closed doors has me panting.

Elvis's eyes widen as he steps back. If I could see inside his head, I imagine there'd be a light bulb switching on. "Hands to myself, right?"

Even though I'm shocked by the eagerness in his voice, I still nod.

"Alright. Deal."

Clasping my hand in his, he guides us into his condo. The sexual tension that forever radiates between us is still in abundance, but there's an edge of excitement surrounding us. I have the same nervous butterflies I got every time I was waiting for the song to start when standing on a dark stage, but it's stronger, almost palpable.

The reason behind my jitters comes to light when Elvis guides us straight up the spiral staircase separating his loft-like bedroom from the rest of his home. But he doesn't move toward the bed to start our spooning escapades. He heads straight for the bathroom, the one big enough to fit us both at the same time without needing to share a showerhead. It has two.

"I'm not strong enough for this, E. I'm seconds away from throwing years of study down the toilet already. I can't endure more temptation."

He doesn't answer me. He just steps into his master bathroom, turns on both of the showerheads full pelt, then commences stripping. *Fuck the world. I'm not giving this up for anything.* My hands instinctively dart out to trace his rock-hard abs. I'll start there before following the trail of dark hair that flows from his belly button to the bulge even a lack of lighting can't conceal.

Before I get within an inch of his stomach, Elvis slaps my hands away. "No touching, remember?"

My fingers itch to tiptoe over his skin when his pants are the next article of clothing he removes. He drags them down his muscular spread thighs before kicking them to the side. With his eyes locked on mine and mine locked on his sculptured chest, he tugs down his boxer shorts.

Good lord! Someone send up the medic. I'm going into coronary failure.

We're standing so close, there's barely an inch of air between me and his erect cock. If it weren't for a ridiculously large set of udders, I'd fill the gap... before filling *any* part of my body with his painfully erect cock.

I stop staring at the veins pulsating through his manhood when Elvis murmurs, "Your turn."

"Huh?" I raise my eyes from his cock to his face. Wetness pools between my legs when I see the predatory gleam in his eyes.

"Your turn," he repeats, fully knowing I heard him the first time.

I hesitate. I could never be accused of being shy, but this is different. I'm wearing a cow suit, for crying out loud!

"Cows don't bathe inside. They wait for it to rain."

An absurdly large grin stretches across his face before he says, "Okay. Suit yourself."

The noise that tears from my throat when he steps under the water is one I've never heard before. It isn't the image of watering pelting down his gorgeous face before rolling down his glistening pecs causing my near stuttering state. It's him fisting his cock in his big, manly hand.

"Hands to *myself*, right?"

"Uh-huh." I have no more words—not one.

After watching him glide his hand all the way to the tip and back to the base, I raise my eyes to his face. His parted lips and hooded eyes reveal he's enjoying himself, but they're missing the cocky gleam they held when we fooled around weeks ago.

I find out why when he murmurs, "This would be a lot more fun if you joined me."

My hand skates across the furry material of my costume without a negative thought entering my mind. Coach James was very adamant with his rules, but not once did he stipulate I couldn't participate in an activity like this.

Elvis's strokes on his cock quicken when the cow suit slips off my body in one fell swoop. He seems to like that I'm wearing the same bra and panty combination I wore the last time we had a sleepover. As my hands unclasp my bra, I lick my lips. The visual in front of me is too glorious for words. You'd think the size of his thighs would detract from the magnificent girth of his cock. But it doesn't—not in the slightest. And the length... I groan. I might need to change his nickname to tripod.

"Come on, Will, give me something to work with..."

His words trail off when my bra falls to my feet. When my panties quickly follow, his thumb skids across his knob to gather a glistening drop at the tip. Before he can use it to lubricate his pumps, I seize his hand and raise it to my mouth. His groan rumbles straight through my core, and his taste frees me from any modesty inhibiting me.

After stepping back to drench my unruly hair with steaming hot water, I cup my breasts in my hands. When I twist my nipples, jolts of electricity dart down to my sex. I roll and fondle them at the same pace Elvis strokes his cock. I pretend he's tit-fucking me, my tongue instinctively darting out to lap up his goodness like I did in this very room five weeks ago.

When the slither of my hand halts halfway down my stomach,

Elvis gives me a final push of encouragement. "Go on. Show me how much you're enjoying this."

His dick throbs in his hand when I roll my fingertips over the hood of my clit. The sensation is overwhelming, the show nearly over before it even begins.

"Sit on the hob and rest your foot on the shower screen."

I'm more than happy to oblige... until my new position adds rolls of fat to my midsection.

"No, no, no. Stay there. Just like that. It's fucking perfect. You're fucking perfect." The fire in his eyes reveals the truth in his statement, but if it didn't, the amount of precum pooling on the end of his cock would soon clear up any misconceptions. "That's it. Nice and slow."

He slows the speed of his pumps, matching them to the grind of my fingers. We fuck as one, as if there isn't three feet of air between us.

"I can feel you squeezing my cock, sucking at it." Elvis tightens his hand, strangling the vein feeding his manhood with every stroke. "Can you feel me, Willow? Can you feel me pumping into you, taking you in the shower like I've fantasized about every day since we met?"

I nearly jest that my fist couldn't replicate his cock, much less two fingers, but I keep my mouth shut, finally recognizing that sexy time is not a place for jokes.

"Uh-huh. I can feel every inch of you. You're getting thicker, harder, seconds from release."

"And I'm going to release inside you, aren't I, Will?"

I shouldn't love the way he sounds desperate to fill me with his seed, but I do.

After locking my eyes with his, I nod. The hope in my eyes causes an avalanche of excitement. I grind my fingers into my pussy harder before lowering my second hand to toy with my clit. Elvis adjusts the spread of his feet before leaning close enough to me, his virile, manly scent activates every one of my hot buttons.

While one of his hands pumps his cock, his other braces against the tiles above my head. The heat in the room turns excruciating as we bring each other to climax without laying a finger on one another. This isn't the first time I've pleasured myself, but it is the first time it's been this exhilarating. My entire body is coiled tight, ready to shatter at any moment.

I do when Elvis raises my head to his with his spare hand before planting a kiss on my quenched mouth. Recalling my demand for no tongue, he keeps our kiss innocent, but it gives me the final push I need to freefall into orgasmic bliss.

He follows closely behind me.

"I can walk, you know. I have legs."

Elvis smirks as he continues strutting across his bedroom. His footing seems lighter than it was thirty minutes ago, his happiness at an all-time high.

"Pick a side, buttercup. I have no preferences."

When I peer at him in shock, he nudges his head to his bed. "Left."

"Right it is."

He laughs when I punch him in the bicep. "Ouch." After adjusting me so he's carrying me with one hand, he rubs his arm, feigning injury.

"Serves you right."

"What? I can't help that I want anything you want."

He drops his head to the side and flashes an adorable smile before dragging back the sheets on his bed. As requested, he places me on the left side.

When he slides in behind me, I roll over to face him. "Do you think we should get dressed first?"

The boyish grin on his face doubles as he replies, "Why? Afraid I'll maul you in the middle of the night?"

I nod. "I'm concerned you only see that as a possibility instead of a given. I thought my fate was already decided, but I guess if you've had your fun, I may as well head home."

He ends my scoot across the mattress by grabbing ahold of my arm. "We have nine days, three hours, and twenty-seven minutes remaining on your contract. Once that's done, I'll maul you as often as you want, but until then, get your fine ass back here to heat my cock while I sleep."

"Are you sure you're not Tarzan?" I roll over then shimmy back, purposely grinding my ass more than necessary. "You went all caveman on me, and although he's more a *Jungle Book* type of guy, I'm certain I heard some Tarzanish twang in there."

"I have many ethnicities in my bloodlines, but we missed out on the African jungle lineage, I'm afraid."

I stick out my bottom lip. "That's a shame. You sure do have the cock for it."

His laugh vibrates through my chest. "I'll take that as a compliment."

"You should. You have a very splendid penis." *Which happens to be digging into my ass more with every word I speak.*

After reminding myself that nine days isn't really that long, I shift our conversation to less dangerous waters. "A little birdie told me your birthday is coming up."

"Dalton?"

"Huh?"

Elvis cranks an elbow to peer down at me. "Was the little birdie Dalton?"

I nod. With an overworked gasp, his torso flops back onto the mattress.

"I know it's before a big game month, but did you want to do something? We could grab a slice at Mickey's before watching a movie. Or try out that new go-kart track that opened up recently?"

He groans as if nothing I'm serving sounds appetizing.

"We have to do something, E. You only turn sixty once—" I squeal like I'm twelve when his hands dive into my ribs. It isn't a little tickle I can push off as an accident. It's one of the torture methods sick, sadistic people use on poor, unsuspecting victims. "Alright! Alright! Alright! We don't have to celebrate your thirty-ninth 21st birthday."

While dragging my hair off my face, I scoot back half a foot.

"But we've got to have cake. It's cake. You love cake." I actually don't know if he does, but I sure do. "Can we do cake?"

I gain back some of my maturity when he murmurs, "We'll do cake, but I can't sign up for anything else. I've got plans in the works."

"Oh." *Well, that sucks.* "At least there'll be cake."

His confession puts a damper on our exchange. Not from Elvis's side; he's more than happy to pull me back to his side of the bed, roll me, and spoon me like I'm his own personal body pillow. It's only me left wondering who's so vital in his life, he can't spare an hour of his birthday to grab a slice with me.

CHAPTER TWENTY-FOUR

Presley

"No. Don't move. Not yet." I scurry across warm sheets to secure Willow back into my arms. We've only been sleeping for five hours, but it's been the most restful five hours I've ever had. "Just a few more hours."

I stop chewing on air to replenish my mouth with spit when Willow whispers, "Someone's in your house."

"What?" I jackknife up so fast, we nearly bump heads.

"Listen." She tries to calm the frantic beats of her heart as she cranks her ear to the noise. "They sound like they're in the kitchen." Her brows lower down her face as her lips twist. "Making pancakes?"

A blistering smile stretches across my face. After flinging off the sheets, I climb out of bed. Willow watches me like I'm insane. I guess that makes sense. Who interrupts an intruder brandishing nothing but a smile? Only one man would be stupid enough to do that. A sister's baby brother.

"It's my sister, Syndi. She and her son, Emerick travel down every year for my birthday."

My love for my sister is clear in my voice. Don't get me wrong, when we were younger, we shared the typical sibling hate, but once I got older and realized exactly how much Syndi did for me, that became a thing of the past.

Syndi was a professional dancer like Willow. She just didn't dance for her pleasure. She did it for the men willing to fill her bikini bottoms with crinkly dollar bills, then she deposited that money into a bank account and paid for my schooling. If she hadn't put her body on the line for me, I wouldn't be the man I am today. Can you understand my appreciation now?

"Get dressed and join us downstairs. Syndi makes the best pancakes."

Willow looks excited until her eyes scan my room. "I don't have any clothes."

"Borrow some of mine." I nudge my head to my walk-in closet.

Her eyes snap to mine. "I can't wear your clothes to meet your sister. She'll think I'm a hussy."

"Syndi isn't like that." I lean down and brush my lips against hers. "She'll love you." *Nearly as much as I do.*

Panicked by my inner monologue, I yank back, pivot on my heels and race down the stairwell. It must be the massive morning wood I have draining my brain of blood, because I've never had a thought like that before. Not even once during the nine years I was with Lillian.

"You better hurry before all the good pancakes are gone."

As I stomp down the stairwell, I reprimand myself. *What the fuck was that? Even if it's true, it doesn't mean you can just blurt it out like that. You're the guy, the man, the alpha-fucking-male; you don't declare that you're in love first, especially not to the girl you're crushing on. You're supposed to hold out, tap her nose like she's cute the first time she says it before eventually saying it back a good few weeks later, but no, Sir Fuckface nearly blurts it out while assuring her his sister's pancakes are worth wearing one of my shirts as if it's a dress.*

"Presley!" Syndi's squeal draws me from my rant. "Happy birthday week! We're making your favorite." She wiggles her batter-smeared spatula at Emerick, who is adding chocolate chips into the banana mix.

Her hand falls to her side when I return her greeting. "Why do you smell like..." She takes in a deep whiff of air through her nose, not the least bit embarrassed that she's smelling Willow's skin on mine. "Honey?"

"Sweet, right?"

Before she can answer, a soft voice over my shoulder whispers, "It's the oat and honey shampoo I use."

"You dog." Sydni's words are only loud enough for me to hear, but her whack in my gut would be sufficient for ten men. "I'm Syndi Carlton. It's a pleasure to meet you."

When I spin around to witness their introduction, a chuckle rumbles in my chest. Willow is wearing the cow outfit she had on last night, and Syndi is doing her best to pretend she's not. Only someone with as much confidence as Willow would think wearing a costume instead of a man's shirt is the lesser of two evils. That's one of the things I love about her the most...

There I go again, and I don't even have a stiffy this time around!

As my skin grows clammy with panic, Willow offers up her own introduction. "I'm Willow, or Will as my friends call me." She glances over my shoulder, her smile picking up when she spots Emerick sitting on the kitchen counter. "And who's this handsome little guy?"

"That's Emerick, my son." Syndi sounds as proud as I do anytime I introduce her and Emerick. "He's making banana chocolate chip pancakes. Would you like some?"

My panic recedes when Willow replies, "I'd love some." It's quick to return when she adds on, "But I have to go. I have dance class in an hour, and I really don't want to turn up in this." She points to the udders poking out from her midsection.

Taking Syndi's laugh as playful instead of scornful, Willow locks her eyes with mine and mouths, *"I'll see you later?"*

The worry on her face eases when I nod.

After promising to test out Emerick's "fantastic cooking" next time, she spins on her heels and heads for the front door. Her already slow steps taper when I call her name.

I wait for her to glance my way before asking, "Are you forgetting something?"

I mean a goodbye kiss, but with her brain still not firing on all cylinders, she doesn't get what I'm asking. Emerick jumps off the kitchen counter when Willow breaks out the moves she used to fill the dance floor last night. They aren't moves I learned when I was in school. The funky chicken dance was the only one I knew by heart, but this generation uses video games to get their funky dance moves.

The unexpected feelings I had for Willow earlier hit me full force for the second time when she extends her usually thirty-second farewell dance by a minute and a half so she can teach Emerick how to floss. He had most of it down pat, but his hips were swinging out of sync with his arms.

Once Willow is confident he's got it, she and Emerick groove across the kitchen like they've known each other for years, their happiness uncontained.

At the end of their performance, which is a good five or so minutes, Willow holds her hand out in front of herself. "High-five, Emerick! You did so well."

When he disses her high-five for a hug, Willow raises her eyes to mine. "Aww, can I keep him?"

Not waiting for me to answer, she drags Emerick toward my front door. Once they're out of sight, Syndi shifts on her feet to face me. "She's so damn sweet. I've never seen Emerick instantly smitten with someone like that before. How quickly she got him to open up was phenomenal."

Her gushing ends when I say, "You know she's not joking, right? If you don't get out there fast, she'll kidnap your son."

It takes Syndi two long heart beats to see the truth in my eyes before she sprints out of the kitchen. It doesn't take me nearly as long to realize why I slept so well last night.

I'm falling in love with Willow Underwood, a twenty-one-year-old college student who doesn't have two dimes to rub together, and I couldn't be happier about it.

What the fuck?

CHAPTER TWENTY-FIVE

Presley

My heart is still skipping to its own tune Wednesday afternoon, a whole four days after a revelation I thought would knock me on my ass. Don't misconstrue. I'm shocked about how quickly I'm developing feelings for Willow, but for the first time in my life, I'm not scared about them. The past weekend was good. The team closest to us on the ladder was defeated, meaning even with our bye last week, we're still in top position. I'm lighter on my feet—I'm sure you already know why—and after she wrapped up her dance class, Willow returned to my condo to spend the rest of her weekend with Syndi, Emerick, and me.

I hardly saw her since Syndi and Emerick hogged her time, but the slices of peace we snuck between family obligations and work strengthened my belief that I'm falling in love. It feels so obvious now, I wouldn't be shocked to be accused of walking around with love hearts in my eyes.

Tonight will only make matters ten times worse. It's my birthday. You know that celebration I wasn't looking so forward to only a few months ago because it will put a ten-year gap between Willow and me? I'm not as worried about it now. Dalton was right: age doesn't matter when you stop seeking its expiration date.

Foster's lips purse as he bobs his head. He's impressed by how fast I scrub up when my game plan goes from on the field to off.

"I clean up alright, eh?"

He awards me a frisky wink. "Not bad at all. What're your plans for tonight? I heard Berkley say something about—"

I stuff his question into the back of his throat with a tap of my knuckles on his shirt. Willow may not be in my sight, but I can sense her presence.

"Come on out, Will; your cover has been busted."

Foster chuckles when she emerges from the shadows with a sexy pout on her red-painted lips. "I tried. Your boy is too smart to fall for our tricks," Foster explains when her narrowed eyes glare at him.

I'm about to have a go at Foster for ganging up on me with Willow, but my scan of her body has me choking on my words. She's wearing a dress. A fuckin' smoking hot dress. Its flirty hem sits high on her scrumptious thighs, and the cropped jacket keeping her warm from the late hour is fitted to accent the generous swell of her tits.

"Damn, Willow."

She swivels on the spot, fanning out the hem of her sexy all-red number. "Too much for cake?" Because she's nervous, her Australian accent is on full display.

Before I can answer her, Foster rejoins our conversation. "There's no such thing as too much." He leans in to press a kiss to her cheek before his eyes drift my way. "If you don't snatch this girl up soon, you're gonna need to move aside so a real man has a chance to seal the deal."

He moves aside when I shove him out of the locker room. Grabbing his crotch, he laughs. His old gangster lifestyle is never forgotten when it comes to brawling over a fine-looking lady.

I hear his throaty laugh for another thirty seconds before it's swallowed by the freeway that roars along one side of the 69ers home stadium. His lengthy departure gives me time to settle my erratic heart rate, but it does nothing to ease my sticky palms. Sweat is practically dribbling off my hands.

After dragging them down my pants, I curl one of them around Willow's. Because the heat roaring through her body is as boiling as mine, she only slightly grimaces when she feels the wetness of my hands.

"It's weird being here after hours. It's a little spooky." She pauses, seeking a ghoul in every dark corner we pass.

"This is my favorite time to walk the halls. There's something euphoric about being in a space which is usually such a hive of activity. I swear when I just stop and listen for a few seconds, I can hear the crowd chanting my name."

She smiles before raking her teeth over her lower lip. "You should probably get that checked. I don't think that's normal."

"I had my hearing checked last week, thank you very much. It's perfectly okay," I tilt down close so my lips brush her ear, "for an old guy."

Her giggles overtake the thump of my heart from her sugary scent. "Who is now *another* step closer to the grave."

When her hand digs into her bag, no doubt seeking the present she tried to give me before practice today, I place my hand over hers. "Not yet."

"I've been waiting to give this to you all day, E. How much longer do I have to wait?"

I tweak her protruding lip. "Whose birthday is it?"

"Yours. It's your birthday." She huffs as her shoulders sag. "Doesn't mean you get to be a party pooper, though."

The low hang of her shoulders barely lingers for a minute. They inch up high when we walk through the corridor the players charge through a minimum four times a week.

"E..." I can tell she wants to say more, but the picnic blanket, a basket loaded with wine, cheese and grapes, and two boxes of Mickey's pizza steal her words.

I give myself a mental pat on the back when she raises her welling eyes to mine. "It's not my birthday."

"No, it's not. But it is mine, and I couldn't think of a better way to spend it than with you."

Her brows become tighter the longer her confused gaze bounces between mine. "I thought you had plans...without me?"

I try not to smile at the uncomfortable delivery of her last two words. I fail. "I said I had plans in the works, but I didn't say who they were with. You wanted to go out; I wanted to stay in. This is my compromise. "

Taking her hand in mine, I guide her onto the spongy green field. She giggles when her heels are swallowed by the thick grass. It turns into full-blown laughter when I scoop down low to gather her in my arms.

"So strong and manly," she drawls in a fake American accent while running her fingertips over my bicep. "Do you work out?"

"Only on Tuesdays."

Her husky laugh has my dick becoming super friendly with my zipper. "You need to add a time and a location to your answer. Hook a girl up!"

She stops waiting for the high-five I'm never going to give her when I place her back onto her feet on the picnic blanket. "Wow, E. How do you not get scared every time you step out here?" She spins in a circle, taking in the thousands upon thousands of empty seats. "I feel like a worm being eyed by a million kookaburras."

Her eyes drift my way, preparing to explain to me what a kookaburra is. I beat her to the punch by making the kookaburra mating call.

Well, I thought that was what I was doing before she bursts out laughing.

"Not quite right?"

She holds her thumb and index finger an inch apart. "Close. You kinda sound like a kookaburra being strangled, but I appreciate the effort."

Smiling, I gesture for her to sit. She does, cross-legged. Her eyes float to mine when I ask if she'd like a glass of wine.

"Please."

After filling her glass and handing it to her, I crack open a can of soda. She freezes with her wineglass pressed against her lips to watch me take a mouthful of soda.

"What?" I ask, wondering why she's peering at me funny.

She lowers her eyes to my can of soft drink. "Is it hard?"

"Not drinking?" When she nods, I add on, "Shockingly, no. I just get my highs in non-alcoholic ways now."

She bats her long lashes. "Such as?"

I wave my hand over the pizza boxes; the cheesy scent is wafting up more than fond memories. When she does her cute eyeroll, I rake the back of my index finger down her cheek. "Neither are good for my heart, but what doesn't kill me will only make me stronger."

Assuming I'm playing, she nudges me hard enough some of her wine sloshes out of her glass. It only takes her peering into my unamused gaze for three seconds to realize I'm being forthright. With the vein in her neck thrumming, the remainder of her wine is upended onto the grass before she returns the plastic flute to the picnic basket. "I'm feeling daring today. Hand me a lemonade."

"You don't have to do this."

"No, I don't," she agrees, peering straight at me, "But I want to."

We spend the next two hours eating, talking, and depleting half a dozen soft drink cans. We discussed everything you can imagine: my surprise when I scored the number one draft pick, how she used ballet to get over her grief, Emerick's unexpected arrival into my family, and how she wants to drag her roommate around the Australian outback with nothing but a backpack of clothes.

The only time our conversation veers into uncomfortable territory is when my mention of the upcoming playoff schedule unveils a disastrous conflict. Her dance recital is scheduled for the same night I'll helm my teams' campaign to play in the grand finale.

"I'll cancel my recital. My score won't reflect on the national title tally, so it's not important."

"Maybe not on a competition level, but it is for you personally." When Willow fails to rebut, I know I'm right. This is her first competition since she busted her knee, meaning it is as important to her as the day I strapped on my cleats for the first time after breaking my back. "You don't have to cancel; we'll just work around it. What time are you down to perform?"

"7:30."

"AM?" I ask, hopeful.

Guilt taints her eyes before she shakes her head. "PM. But that's okay. Don't worry about it. I'll just cancel."

I impede her haste to pack our now empty picnic basket by snatching an empty pizza box from her grasp and Frisbeeing it across the field. "You're not cancelling. You've worked too hard for this, and I'd never ask you to give up a part of who you are for me. I might be arrogant at times, but I'm not a complete fucking asshole."

She swipes her hand across her cheeks to ensure none of her tears have fallen. When she's confident her face is dry, she locks her moisture-filled eyes with mine. "Then what's your solution? I don't want to miss watching you play."

"Says a lady who hates football with every fiber of her being."

My gibe has the effect I was aiming for. It brings our exchange back onto playful territory by easing some of the tension strangling it.

"I don't hate football." She catches her eyeroll halfway before her eyes twitch back to their original position. "I just don't under-stand it."

"I wouldn't say that too loud. If Coach James hears you're seeking knowledge, he'll include you in every team strategy meeting for the remainder of your internship."

A chuckle breaks through my lips when she glances over her shoulder with wide, panicked eyes. Only once she's confident we're alone does she return her devotion to me. "Sheesh, you nearly gave me a heart attack."

I ease her erratically beating chest by lying down on the blanket, taking her with me. With the sky free of clouds, a million stars twinkle above our heads. Our star-gazing pushes us into our first bout of silence for the night. It's not awkward. It's more necessary than anything. It also strengthens what I thought last week. This whole abstinence thing has as many good points as it does bad. Although, I may not have been saying that if our weekend didn't end the way it did.

Willow breaks the silence first. "I really wish I could watch you play." She rolls over to balance her chin on my chest. "I may not understand anything happening, but I still like supporting you."

"Just as I do you, but it's rare to get everything you want." *I'm still learning that the hard way.*

I grow worried I said my last comment out loud when Willow's head pops off my chest. Her brows furrow as she scans our location. The worry darkening her light eyes makes me follow the direction of her gaze. We're alone, for the most part. The stadium is rarely empty. Excluding the players and management staff, over half a dozen janitors work during closing hours to keep its world-class facilities looking new even though they're nearly as old as me.

I prop myself on my elbows when Willow suddenly leaps to her feet. "Wait here. I'll be right back."

She races three steps away from me before spinning around and coming straight back. "Sorry, I forgot." With her hands slapped on my cheeks and a grin a mile wide, she lowers her mouth to mine. Her kiss is innocent, but the excitement blistering out of her... *dyna-fucking-mite.* "I'll be back. Don't go anywhere."

She charges across the field like Foster outrunning a defensive linebacker before she is swallowed by the darkness of the stadium bleachers.

I'm still staring in shock at the direction she bolted when she reemerges approximately ten minutes later. She's still wearing her knockout dress, but her jacket and shoes have been removed, and she's carrying a football.

What the fuck?

"What are you up to?"

She presses her finger to her lips before dumping the football onto the blanket next to me. After taking four steps back, she raises her arm into the air. My heart beats at an unnatural rhythm when the stadium lights switch on two seconds later. The brightness is closely followed by the soulful voice of Ed Sheeran. I can't remember the name of his song, but he performs it with Beyoncé.

Equally excited and filled with anticipation, I scoot to the very edge of the blanket. The hope blazing through my veins is answered in the most brilliant light when Willow starts dancing to the song blaring out of the stadium speakers. She floats through the air, her movements similar to the ones she made the first time she danced for me, but more refined and graceful. Her variety makes her performance so riveting, I can't take my eyes off her. I just stare in awe, smug as fuck about my private show.

With her wish to keep her routine under wraps from her competitors, she hasn't shared any aspects of it with anyone—not even me. She wouldn't even say what style of dance she was performing. I'm going to call her dance the "Willow Effect" because I've never seen this style of dance before. She has the elegance of a ballerina but with an edge of fierceness that can't conceal the years she's spent teaching hip hop to rowdy children.

She's in her element, and I'm loving every fucking minute of it.

As the song fades, I stand to my feet, clapping and hollering like a loon. I'm not lying when I say my grin is brighter than the stadium lights. "That was fucking awesome! My god, Willow, I'm so hard right now. That was hot, sensual, and way better than any of the shitty shows Lillian dragged me to in New York."

I didn't mean to bring up my ex while flattering my current squeeze; it just slipped out during my excitement. Mercifully, Willow doesn't seem to mind. "Was it okay? I'm trying something different by merging traditional with new age. I think it gives it more depth."

"It was perfect. You're going to kill it."

Smiling, she snags an untouched bottle of water from the picnic basket. She's panting so hard, her expanding chest catches the little droplets of sweat rolling down her cheeks. "Damn, I didn't realize how hot those lights are." She takes a generous sip of water before screwing on the lid and dumping it next to her bare feet. "Alright." She claps her hands together like Coach James does at the beginning of every quarter. "Your turn."

My confusion grows when she bobs down to snag the football

off the blanket. Stepping back, she flashes me a grin that has my cock getting friendly with my zipper before tossing the football into my chest. "You saw mine; now show me yours."

She tucks the hem of her dress into her panties before huddling down low like she's primed to tackle me. I realize I have the situation all wrong when she shouts, "Roger 73, Green 98, Red 62!"

I laugh at her attempt to impersonate the plays I use on field before shouting. "Hut-hut!"

Hearing my command, she pushes off her feet with a grunt, her sprint down the sideline remarkably fast for how hard she is panting. When she's a good distance from me, I lean back and send the football sailing through the air. I don't throw it with as much force as I usually use, but my accuracy is perfect.

The look on Willow's face when she catches my throw is priceless. She stops frozen in the middle of the field with her mouth hanging open and her eyes wide.

She snaps out of her trance when I cup my hands around my mouth to yell, "Run, Willow, run!"

Her lack of footballs skills can't be missed when she races back my way. "Not this way. That way." I point to the end zone behind her. "We're on the same team."

"Not anymore, we ain't." Holding her arm out like Foster does any time a linebacker is charging his way, she sidesteps me. "Oh, did you see the skill? Underwood outplayed Carlton. She's making a break for it. Stand to your feet, ladies and gentleman. We're in the midst of greatness tonight." She sounds just like the commentators do when I'm charging down the sideline... until she picks up that I'm on her tail. "No, E, no!"

"Less talking and more running, rookie." I catch her on the twenty-yard line. Her squeals come out with a giggle when I band my arm around her waist, hoist her from the ground, then charge for her end zone like she's my football.

"Boo-yah! Touchdown!"

After slamming down the ball on the orange-painted ground, Willow wiggles out of my hold so she can imitate the moonwalk *leg kicky chest whacky* thing Foster does every time he crosses the line.

Through a hearty bout of laughter, I mimic the noise of a boisterous crowd. I swear I've never laughed so hard in my life. My gut is cramping, and tears are leaking from my eyes.

Willow shakes her ass from one side of the field to the next before regathering the football in her hand and moving to stand in front of me. She is red-faced, but the most beautiful I've ever seen. "Alright, next?"

"Next?" I'm truly confused.

She angles her head to the side and spreads her free hand over her cocked hip. "That wasn't championship play, Carlton. I want to see the magic. The intensity. The plays that will lead to you getting a championship ring on your finger."

She stops when I interrupt, "I'd rather make out."

"Oh, don't worry, we'll do that as well." She awards me a frisky wink before tossing the ball into my chest. "After you've shown me every play I'll miss next month."

The truth smacks into me like a freight train. She danced so I could see her performance without needing to attend the recital, and now she wants to watch me play ball so she won't miss any of the action. It's not the same as it will be in front of thousands of people, but more special since we get the exclusive, never-before-seen material before anyone else.

I jerk my chin up. "Step back; I'm gonna show you a few tricks."

She tugs her dress back into her panties before bending down low and raising one hand into the air. She's got the play all wrong, but before I can tell her that, she charges for me. Her body's impact with mine is the equivalent of a drop of rain hitting my shoulder, but I pretend it's more.

With my arms flailing, I fall backward, taking her with me. I angle my body to ensure she lands on top of me without injury. Willow comes out of our exchange okay, but my crotch isn't as lucky. It didn't endure a reckless knee or the ball lodged between us. It's fighting to ignore how good it feels having Willow grind against it.

I'm not the only one noticing the shift in the air. Willow's bouncy curls fan her face as she stares down at me with dilated, needy eyes. Her prolonged glance changes our exchange from playful to greedy in under a second. Hands slither over sweaty skin as lips collide. Our kiss is hungry and ravenous, an embrace that reveals how attracted we are to each other.

I could stay in this moment forever... if we weren't interrupted by a stern cough.

CHAPTER TWENTY-SIX

Presley

As play-by-play of Willow's response to Coach James busting us making out like teens flows through my brain, I stroll down the nearly isolated corridor of 69er Stadium. My strut is so cocky, my hips are swinging as much as the Elvis car air freshener Willow gifted me for my birthday. Usually, I'd scrunch up anything Elvis-related and toss it into the trash within a second of the gift-giver leaving my presence, but since this gift was from Willow, it's hanging off my rearview mirror, rocking and rolling with every bump in the road.

I clutch at my chest to keep my heart in its rightful spot when Danny unexpectedly steps in my path. He nearly gave me a damn heart attack. I'm more surprised by his unexpected arrival than I was Coach James's last night. He threatened to bench me, but I know he didn't mean it. No coach in the history of coaches would bench his star player a week out from finals.

"Sorry." Don't let Danny's apology fool you. He's not the faintest bit sorry. "You looked spaced out, so I thought I'd give you a kickstart."

He fiddles with the collar of my shirt before attempting to lick and spit my hair into submission. I say "attempt" as my glare freezes his spit-loaded hand an inch from my recently washed hair.

"We're good?"

I nod. "We're more than good."

He hears something I didn't want to relay in my tone. "You said you were keeping it PG!" He wiggles his finger in front of my face. "This is *not* PG. What is this?"

He leans in close and sniffs me, like he can smell indiscretion on my skin.

That's exactly what he accuses me of when he takes a step back and drops his jaw. "Presley Wilson Carlton."

"Don't you Presley Wilson Carlton me. I didn't do a single thing your eyes are accusing me of. We ate pizza and played ball. I kept my hands to myself." *More than you'll ever know*, but I keep that snippet of information to myself.

Danny cocks his hip, his dramatics not unusual. "You're five minutes early. You're never five minutes early."

"I had to drop by Willow's school. Traffic was good. Sue me."

His jaw hangs even more profoundly. "Willow spent the night at your condo?" He slaps my chest more times than acceptable for a man who relies on me for his income. "You have five days to go—"

"Four, but who's counting?"

Me, I'm fucking counting.

"Then why screw this up now? It's four days, Elvis. Four goddamn, *why has it been eleven long months for me?* days." His change of topic isn't uncommon either. Even if a conversation has nothing to do with him, it soon becomes about him.

Happy to keep the focus off me and what he assumes I did wrong, I ask, "Has it really been eleven months since you... you know?"

Danny leans his head on my shoulder like a dog wanting a scratch behind the ears. "Yes. I'm hurting, Elvis. I can barely squeeze my balls in my y-fronts anymore."

"Well, there's your issue. Who wants to date a man who wears Y-fronts?" I question through a bout of breathless laughter.

When he pouts, I rub his head like he's a dog. "There, there, it'll

be okay. If things get too bad, take matters into your own hands."
Trust me, it's a lot of fun when done with the right person.

His head pops off my shoulder, his eyes widening like he's never considered the possibility of taking care of business himself. "You're right! Who says I need a man? I've got everything I need right here."

"He means himself," I assure two of my teammates walking past us, eyeballing our exchange with a curious glance. "Not that there is anything wrong with being gay. I'm just not."

Danny rolls his eyes as his shoulders slump. "Thanks for the reminder. I thought we were starting something beautiful." He laughs when I shove him away from me. "What? You were raking your fingers through my hair, Elvis, what did you expect me to think?"

I give him a stern finger point. "You're... You're..." *I've got nothing.*

He clasps his hands together, rests them on his chest, then swivels on the spot like he's just been crowned Mr. Gay 2020. "Beautiful? Perfect? The man of your dreams—?"

"Have two seconds to point me in the direction of the shoot before I donate your portion of our negotiation to the charity bringing *Love Boat* back on air."

He pauses for a moment to consider my terms before reluctantly dragging his hand across his body. "This way, Mood Killer."

Like he can talk. I was walking on clouds before I bumped into him. Now I feel like I'm walking into a storm head on, and I don't just mean figuratively. Lillian is standing in the middle of a conference room that has been transformed into a studio. She's wearing a microscopic tank top and running shorts. Her outfit—*if you can call it that*—leaves nothing to the imagination. She may as well be wearing nothing.

"What is she doing here?"

"I don't know." Danny's shock is as high as mine. "Let me find out?"

He waits for me to nod before making his way to the lady who headed up our negotiations months ago. I can't recall her name. It starts with a D. *Danielle. Daphne. Delilah.* That's it—Delilah! How could I forget? I always thought Delilah sounded sweet until I discovered a face behind the name. Don't get me wrong, Delilah is attractive, but her personality could certainly use some polish.

When Danny makes his way back to me, I meet him halfway. "What's the deal?"

He swivels his tongue around his mouth like his words are hard for him to deliver. I understand why when he mumbles, "Lillian's doing the shoot with you."

"What? That wasn't part of our arrangement."

"I know." His eyes beg me to calm down. "But this is separate from our deal. Lillian forged her own negotiations with Delilah after bumping into her last month."

"Then we'll shoot them separately. Easy."

Danny drags his hand down his face, his expression pained. "Delilah wants this to be a joint collaboration. She thinks consumers will respond better to a couple than they will you as an individual."

"No!" I hit him with the same stern finger point I gave him earlier. "It's not happening." I shift my finger to Lillian, who's pretending not to watch our exchange as she completes a handful of reps under a set of bright lights. *Who warms up to shoot a commercial?* "She was not a part of our deal. If they want to add her name into my contract, they'll have to remove my name first."

Danny shadows my brisk exit from the conference room. "We can't do that. You signed an agreement to endorse their product."

"Yeah, that's right. Me." I bang my fist on my chest. "*I* would endorse their product. Not her." I once again point to Lillian, who has abandoned her deception. She stares straight at me, stunned as fuck that I'd rather lose a ten-million dollar endorsement deal than work alongside her. "Tell them the deal's off."

"I can't."

I jackknife back, certain I heard Danny wrong. I didn't. The truth is all over his face.

"What aren't you telling me?" My words are minced by the tight grinds of my jaw.

"When we began negotiations—"

"Don't pussyfoot around, Danny. Get straight to the point."

His Adam's apple bobs up and down before he forces out, "If you walk away from this deal, you'll be liable for any loss in revenue the pharmaceutical company sustains from your failure to uphold your contract."

"Are you fucking kidding me!" My roar bellows down the corridor. "That's not the way these things work. I've never signed a contract with a clause like that before."

"That's because this is the first contract you've negotiated since your DUI."

"What?" I heard what he said; I just want to see if he's game enough to repeat it.

He is, but not in the manner I expect. "When you went on your bender, you cost a lot of companies a lot of money. No one wanted to touch you with a ten-foot pole."

"I've been sober for two years, Danny."

He steps closer to me, his eyes watering. "Yes, you have, and I'm very proud of that, but you were a drunk for years longer than that."

His words hurt to hear, but they're true, so there's no point denying them.

"How much are we talking?" I hate that I'm even considering the possibility of doing this, but my contract isn't due for renewal with the 69ers for another two years, and I'm not getting any younger, so there's no guarantee they'll even re-sign me.

Danny shrugs. "I don't know. Rumors around the water cooler are that they're looking at tripling their investment, so you'd be close to the figure cited on your contract, if not more."

"Ten million dollars? I could possibly have to pay them ten million if I don't follow through with our arrangement?"

It kills him to do, but Danny nods.

"Fuck!"

I drag my fingers through my hair, adding a few tugs to the pain already rocketing through my head. This is literally my worst nightmare coming true. I can't do this, but I can't afford ten million dollars either, so I have no choice. I have to side with the devil.

CHAPTER TWENTY-SEVEN

Willow

Slinging my head back, I peer over my shoulder when a deep voice rumbles down the nearly isolated corridor I'm walking. "Willow, can I see you for a minute?"

I swallow numerous times in a row to relieve my parched throat when I realize who's requesting to see me. It's Coach James. This is the first time I've seen him since he caught me getting frisky with his star quarterback three nights ago.

"Sure. Just give me a sec to put down my things, then I'll be right in."

I don't even get half an inch down the hall when he grumbles, "Now, Ms. Underwood."

Pouting like I'm being sent to the principal's office, I spin on my heels and stomp toward his office, my steps sluggish and slow. Including today, I have only two days left on my internship, but I swear to god, it feels like a thousand. You'd think seeing the light at the end of the tunnel would fill me with eagerness. It did until Thursday. Something is off with Elvis. He's moody and withdrawn; even our kiss goodbye when he asked Danny to drive me home Thursday afternoon was cold. I know it's playoff week, which stresses out even the cockiest men in the country, but he seemed to be handling it well.

Wednesday night was magical. We laughed, and danced, and I gave my best performance pretending I'm a fan of football. Well, I can't really call it a "performance" when it's true. I'll eat glass before I ever don the getup Skylar does, but the game is growing on me... *as is one of its stars.*

I stop hunting for clues on what happened between the grinning Elvis who dropped off the textbooks I left at his house to the one who kissed me goodbye two nights ago without a single spark igniting between us when Coach James gestures for me to take a seat in the chair opposite him. I'm truly lost in Elvis's swift change in composure. It's like turning thirty-one flipped his personality switch to grumpy. I've heard of a midlife crisis, but this is ridiculous. He truly is a grumpy old man.

My worry for Elvis switches to myself when Coach James closes his office door. He only ever closes it during a crisis, and considering most of those calamities are about his players, I'm shitting bricks as to why I'm being given the royal treatment.

My delusions of believing I'm one of the team clear when Coach James props his backside on his desk before lowering his worldly eyes to mine. "Have you spoken to Carlton today?"

I shake my head. That's why I'm filled with so much confusion. Elvis and I communicate multiple times a day... until yesterday. I was so convinced my cell had crapped itself, I made Skylar call it to check it was in working order. It appears to be functioning fine, but I've yet to receive a single returned call or text from Elvis in nearly forty hours.

Coach James scrubs the stubble on his chin. "I know I was a little hard on you two Wednesday night. If that's the cause for his mood of late, I'm sorry about that."

I'm grateful I'm not the only one noticing Elvis's switch in personalities, but I hate it as well.

"He mentioned his accident was around this time of the year; do you think that could be affecting his thoughts?"

Coach takes a few seconds to deliberate on my question before shaking his head. "He's close with Mr. Beckett and his family. He even paid to fly them out here for the playoffs."

The sludge my heart has been sitting in the past forty hours clears a little from his confession, but my confusion remains. "Then I am at a loss. He was fine Thursday morning, then poof, he turned into a bigger, grumpier version of you." My pupils dilate to the size of saucers. I was meant to say my last comment in my head.

I start breathing again when Coach James laughs. "I wouldn't have minded him being a mini-me if we weren't heading into the playoffs, but I don't have time for theatrics this week." He gathers my hands in his. His are much warmer than mine. "Can you talk to him, see if you can find out what's going on?"

"I'll give it a shot, but I don't see it doing any good. He's more likely to open up to you than he is me."

Coach pulls a face like he doesn't believe me, but he keeps his thoughts to himself while guiding me out of his office. "He's in the conference room. Down the hall and on the right, then follow the scent of bagels. You can't miss it."

He crashes into me when I stop walking. "You want me to talk to him now?" I ask through the lump in my throat. When he nods, I choke on my spit. "But it's game night. You have *very* strict rules on game night."

I'm not lying. If I so much as breathe on the players, Coach breathes fire down my neck. He wants the team to enter the field with nothing but the game on their minds. That's why he makes them hand in their cells at the start of every game. For the two hours before kick-off, he has a zero disturbance statute. If I wasn't interning as a sport therapist, I wouldn't be allowed within six hundred feet of the locker rooms.

"I need Elvis's head screwed on right for tonight's game. If you do that, I'll get those tickets for your friend."

My jaw drops as my heart rate climbs. I asked Coach James last week if he could put me in contact with someone who could grant Skylar cheaper tickets to any 69er home games. Her birthday is coming up, and I want to get her something I know she'll love. He was apprehensive until I showed him the sneaky picture I took while

Skylar wasn't watching. She was dressed head to toe in 69er gear, and it had her specially-made bedspread in the background of the photo.

"I'll give it my best shot."

I glide down the corridor with more spirited steps than only minutes ago. I've never been in the "business" part of the stadium, but with my intuition about Elvis guiding me, I soon find him. It's just not how I hoped. He's in a storage closet at the side of a conference room. With all the equipment moved out, it looks more like a walk-in closet than a room housing the mugs and glasses board members use on a regular basis.

Unfortunately, he's not alone. Lillian is standing next to him. She's leaning intimately close to his shirtless torso, and her index finger is tracing one of the veins in his thick bicep. I can't hear what they're saying, but Lillian's smile reveals everything in sickening detail. She's in her element... and I'm swimming way outside of my depth.

Not willing to watch the nauseating event for a second longer, I pivot on my heels, preparing to race back down the hallway. Like things could get any more awkward, I crash chest-first into a cooler.

While clutching my bruised boob in my hand, I raise my eyes, confused as to why there's a cooler in the middle of a walkway. My stomach swirls when I'm awarded the same seedy grin Skylar and I witnessed a group of cheerleaders getting last month. It's Seedy-McWeedy, the drink vendor who cools more than cans of soft drink in his cooler.

"Excuse me." I push him out of my way, my eagerness to leave spurred on by a deep voice calling my name. I know who the voice belongs to. I've heard it shout, chuckle, and moan my name multiple times the past three months, so you can sure as hell be guaranteed I know what it sounds like when it's full of deceit.

"Willow, wait up!"

Just before I break through the door separating the underbelly of the stadium from its fancier counterpart, I sling my head back. Elvis is following me as suspected. His usually fast pace is slowed by him yanking a shirt over his naked, sweat-slicked torso and buttoning his pants.

When I enter the locker room, things go from bad to worse. Elvis's teammates have covered his locker with high-resolution photos. That's nothing out of the ordinary. Whether it is birthday week or a bad photo shared by a fan, if it is embarrassing, it's displayed. This is both embarrassing and devastating. They're photos of Elvis and Lillian—intimate photos. Neither of them appear to be wearing any clothes.

The players' boisterous laughter dulls to barely a hum when Elvis storms to his locker to rip down the photos. His movements are so aggressive, the vein Lillian was toying with earlier protrudes as far as his nostrils. "This isn't fuckin' funny."

After pointing his finger to the aggressors, he dumps the now ruined collage into the nearest waste bin before spanning the distance between us. Although his broody, temper-filled frame sends excitement sparking down my spine, I flee as quickly as his teammates pretended to act busy when subjected to his wrath.

I make it all the way to my cubicle before a blistering hunk of fury catches up with me. Elvis pins my arms behind my back with one of his hands before using his other to raise my weighted head. He peers down at me, the baby oil slicking his skin more concerning than soothing.

"It's not what you think."

My eyes roll skyward, and for the first time in my life, they make it all the way around without twitching. "Geez, could you be any more original?" My voice is as vile as the vomit creeping up my esophagus.

Elvis is about to respond when a deep rumbling rolls into the room. "Two hours until kickoff; let's get this room on lockdown."

Coach James claps two times, sending the usually quiet room into a hive of activity. The only player ignoring his demand is Elvis. He continues staring down at me, his concentration only breaking when Coach James taps him on the shoulder. "Room is on lockdown; you can finish this later."

Coach James gives me a look, one that reveals he's panicked that my attempt to talk Elvis from the ledge has instead inched him closer to it. Refusing to accept the shit shovel he's handing me, I return his glare. I'm not the one in the wrong here. If anyone needs help digging themselves out from the stench, it's Elvis, not me.

My eyes shift back to Elvis when he says, "I'll be a minute."

His remorse-filled eyes stop bouncing between mine when Coach replies, "No, Carlton, now or find your ass warming the bench during playoffs."

I take his threat as idle, but Elvis doesn't. He frees my hands from his tight grip before taking a step back. He's barely lodged an inch of air between us when Coach James fills the gap by thrusting the bucket he stores the players' phones in at the start of communication lockdown. I forget every silent plea Elvis's eyes gave me the past five minutes when he removes his cell from his pocket to place it in the box. The screen is clear, meaning not only did he see the dozens of text messages I sent him, he also ignored them.

"We'll talk about this after the game."

Stealing my chance to tell him to break a leg—*figuratively*—he runs his index finger down my flaming-with-anger cheek before stalking back to his locker. His steps are as heavy as mine when I was ordered into Coach James's office, but they have nothing on the weight that hits my chest when Coach James requests I stay in my cubicle until after the game.

He'd never say it, but supposedly I'm no longer Elvis's good luck charm.

I can't help but wonder who stole my title.

"Ugh! Come on, E!" I rake my fingers through my hair when Elvis foils his third play of this quarter. He's playing like shit, and that's putting it nicely.

With how worked up I was, I hadn't planned on watching the game. I only switched on the TV in the locker room when the roars coming from the crowd vibrated under my feet. I've never heard them so frustrated before. Now I understand their pain. The plays the team is running are complex, but their opponents are responding to them as if they're child's play. They seem to know Elvis's game plan before he's even decided which play he's pursuing.

When Elvis's throw is intercepted by the opposition, I switch off the TV. I'd rather not know what's happening than see the onslaught firsthand.

I've barely restacked my supplies cupboard when a flurry of noise bursts into the locker room. My eyes drop to my watch. There are still eleven minutes left in the third quarter, so it can't be the players making a ruckus. But if it isn't them, who is it?

My curiosity is satisfied when a blast of air hits my face. Three big burly men throw open my door with so much force, it nearly comes off the hinges. I leap to my feet when the urgency of their visit breaks through the fog in my head. They're carting Elvis on a stretcher. His face shows an immense amount of pain.

"What happened?"

While lifting his stretcher onto my massage table, a range of answers are flung at me. From what I can gather between breaths, he was illegally tackled midair, went down and never got back up.

"The team's doc is on his way. He went in the ambulance with Terrence when he got a concussion." This comes from head assistant coach, Mick Salter. "We were going to keep Carlton field-side, but he insisted we bring him here. Can you watch him until Doc arrives? We're getting slaughtered out there."

I'm shaking my head, but Coach Salter doesn't notice. He just gestures for the men who brought Elvis in to exit before locking me in a room with a man grunting more in frustration than pain.

"Willow?" Elvis's one word takes him almost ten seconds to articulate.

After breathing out my nerves, I spin around to face him. "Yeah?"

Holding his left shoulder in his arm, he shuffles to a half-seated position. "I've popped my shoulder out."

"No shit, Sherlock." I'm surprised I can talk with how much I'm cringing. The low hang of his shoulder makes horrid memories race to the forefront of my mind.

My eyes snap to Elvis's when he says, "I need you to pop it back in."

"Nooooo." I shake my head while drawling out my short reply as if it is an entire sentence.

He jumps off the massage table to pace closer to me, the plea in his eyes doubling with each step he takes. "Please. It's only a partial dislocation, but if you don't put it back in its place, it will keep hurting like a bitch."

"The doctor is only a few minutes away—"

"I don't have a few minutes. Please, Willow. You're trained to do this. You can ease my pain."

I'm about to say no again when he adds a final "please" to his reply. He truly needs my help, and he's right, I am trained to handle dislocations, not just from my studies, but in my private life as well. My knee has popped out a handful of times the past two years. It's why I was apprehensive about returning to dance. I nearly vomit when my knee cap dislocates. Aside from losing my parents, it's the worst pain I've ever experienced.

With that in mind, I instruct, "Remove your jersey and lie down on the table, face first."

Relief crosses Elvis's features before apprehension overtakes them. Since he's holding his arm into his shoulder socket, he has no way to remove his shirt.

I guess that leaves the task up to me?

"Sorry," I murmur when my endeavor to remove his shirt causes him more pain.

After standing on a chair so our difference in height doesn't hinder my ability to undress him, I dump his muddy jersey on the ground then warm up my cold hands by rubbing them together.

Air hisses between his lips when I press around the area that is swollen and red. "I need to check the possibility of muscle damage before I can guide it back in. More times than not, popping a shoulder back in can make matters worse."

He doesn't reply, and I don't mind the silence. Furthermore, I'm comfortable with my assessment. His shoulder has popped out of its socket, but only barely.

"I'll need to apply pressure to your arm to see if we can slip it back into place." I lower myself onto my knees before flattening my back on the carpet beneath Elvis's dangling arm. Because we have such contrasting heights, I have no choice but to use this method. "Tell me if it hurts too much."

I wait for him to grunt in agreement before circling one of my hands around his elbow then clamping his wrist with the other. When I pull down, the groan that tears from his throat fills my eyes with tears. I know I'm hurting him, but with this being the lesser of two evils, I don't have much choice.

"Keep going," he pleads when I back off. "I can feel it sliding back into place. You just need to pull a little harder."

I'd laugh at the double-meaning of his words if they weren't laced in pain.

"We're supposed to slowly guide the ball back into your shoulder, not ram it in there." I'm grunting, the strain I'm placing on his arm felt by both of us.

I stop weighing down his arm when a familiar pop sounds through my ears, closely followed by Elvis's relieved sigh. When he moves to a half-seated position, I shout, "Wait! I need to make sure everything is in the correct position before you can move."

"It's good. It's fine. I'm good."

When he heads for the door, I clamber to my feet. I barely beat him to the exit a mere second before he charges through it. "Where are you going? Your arm needs to be placed in a sling."

"No, it doesn't." His wild eyes bounce between mine, his chest movements frantic. "It's fine. Look." He rotates his shoulder, his expression blank. I would have believed he wasn't in any pain if his eyes didn't flare with every rotation.

"You need an ice compress, a sling, and a full work-up by a *proper* doctor. You're not going back onto the field tonight, E, and perhaps not for the rest of the season."

My strides to the ice bin halt when he growls, "Give me a shot of Toradol, and I'll be good to play."

"You can't play! You're injured!" I pivot to face him, my twirl slow since I can feel the anger radiating out of him. Fury is rising from my gut as well. The images of him and Lillian broadcasting through my head on repeat are too frustrating to stay on the back burner where I placed them when he was injured. "I'm sorry to be the bearer of bad news, but you dislocated your shoulder. That's an instant sideline for six to eight weeks."

Devastation fills his eyes as he steps closer to me. "It's playoff month. I can't be sidelined for six weeks. Just give me a shot of Toradol and keep your mouth shut. That's all you need to do."

"You want me to lie? To say we didn't just pop your shoulder back in?" I thrust my hand to the massage table holding his dirty jersey. It trembles as badly as Elvis's thighs did when I showed him my trick to minimize back pain. "I can't do that. It's morally and ethically wrong. Besides, it's just a game, I'm sure your team will survive without you for a few weeks."

"This isn't just a game! It's my fucking life! Everything I've been working my ass off for the past year is out there, waiting for me, but you're standing in my way! This isn't a stupid dance recital, Willow. It's my fucking career! It means more to me than anything."

I take a step back, physically stunned by his words, but before I can fire off a rebuttal, the ruckus I expected earlier breaks the silence between us. Players pour into the room Elvis is blocking from my view with his brooding frame, their mood hanging as low as my heart rate.

"Hey, what's the deal? One minute I see you charging down the sideline; next minute, you're being carted off the field on a stretcher." Elvis acts like Foster's tap on his shoulder isn't hurting him. "Don't worry, man, you're not the only one wanting to hide your face in shame. We're getting slaughtered tonight. I'm glad you're up and moving, or we'd have no chance of a comeback."

Elvis raises his brow, silently demanding I remain quiet. He shouldn't waste his precious time. I'm too stunned by his scorn to say anything.

"What was it? A cramp?" Foster slips through the thin gap between Elvis and the doorframe so he can see his face. "You should eat more bananas. They're full of potassium."

Staring right at me, Elvis lies, "Yeah, it was a cramp. I'll be sure to take your advice on the bananas."

Happy he's helped his fellow teammate, Foster backhands Elvis's chest before returning to the locker room. "Elvis is alive and ready to rock this place! Now the rest of you fuckers need to get your heads in the game! We can win this; we've just got to fight for it."

His excited cheer inspires a joint one from the players surrounding him. It also doubles the grit in Elvis's eyes. They're no longer brimming with pleas. They're arrogant and cocky, as confident I won't rat him out as he is about winning tonight's game. That's all that matters to him, right? The game. Not me. Not my dancing. Just the game.

"Is it true? Was it just a cramp?"

In his excitement, Coach Salter yanks Elvis back far enough to help me hatch my escape plan. After snagging my bag from my desk and my cell from the top drawer, I hightail it out of the room. I make it three steps out of my cubicle when a hand clutches my elbow, stopping my hasty retreat. I pray it is Elvis, but there's no zap shooting up my arm, crushing my dream as quickly as it surfaced.

I bite the inside of my cheek, warning my eyes to hold in their tears before slinging them to the person accosting me. Coach James's hold isn't firm, but the concern in his eyes is.

His lips twitch as he prepares to speak, but I beat him to the task. "I'm done."

"For today?"

He doesn't need me to spell it out for him, but I do. With a shake of my head, I murmur, "No. I'm done for good."

Ignoring his quick intake of air, I charge down the corridor, not the least bit concerned when my tornado-like speed has me careening past a grinning Lillian.

CHAPTER TWENTY-EIGHT

Presley

Fans huddled around the entrance of the stadium clear a path for me when I kick a waste receptacle in anger. Tonight was my worst game on record. The difference in the figures on the scoreboard leaves no doubt of this. The pain zooming through my shoulder isn't to blame either. I fucked up long before Willow popped it back into place.

My head hasn't been in *any* game the past forty-eight hours, much less the one I just played. Lillian's return to my life has been as toxic as always. Just being around her reminds me of why I drank so much when we were together. She does my head in, but instead of putting her in her place as Willow suggested, I have to cozy up with her to film infomercials.

They're not even real fucking commercials! They're going to be shown on those TV shows that pry people's hard-earned money from their grasps at 3 AM when they're as high as a kite or wanting their lives to end prematurely. Then, after embarrassing myself on national TV, I have to wear their company logo on a cap, shirt, and pants during the live broadcast before the preliminary final.

That's their money-maker. Advertising firms pay upwards of five point one million dollars for a thirty-second slot during breaks during the final game, but they'll get my ass sitting in a chair for thirty minutes at the greatly discounted rate of ten million dollars only a week before.

I got short-changed—in more ways than one.

Hoping to get things wrapped up quickly, I've been working my ass off from sunup to sundown the past two days. I figured the quicker I got this part of my career over, the faster I could return to my post-Lillian life.

If I still have one after what Willow saw.

What Willow witnessed earlier today wasn't as it seemed. Lillian and I were rehearsing a scene the advertising executives want filmed tonight before I spend the next three weeks on the road for away games. Since Delilah had a prior arrangement, she wanted to check our placements to ensure we understood her "vision." She stepped out to take a call a mere minute before Willow arrived.

The look Willow gave me just before she entered the locker room was exactly how my insides were feeling. Every time Lillian touched me, I honestly felt ill. That's why I've been such an asshole the past two days. My temptation to drink is at its highest; I've not had a single minute to speak to Willow, and my opponents seem to have telepathic powers to read my subliminal thoughts. Tonight, they knew every move before I even decided which one to make.

Stopping by my locker, I run a towel over my sweat-drenched head before heading for Willow's cubicle. I'm not a fan of rubdowns after a match, especially not from Willow, but with my shoulder still aching like a bitch, I'm willing to face the embarrassment if she gives me a boner. Furthermore, any excuse to have her hands on me is the right excuse.

I halt midstride when Danny unexpectedly steps in front of me. I really wish he'd stop doing that.

"Amara is waiting for you upstairs." His tone is clipped and firm, nothing like I've heard it before.

"Thanks, but I'm good."

When I sidestep him, he darts back into my path. I'd shove him out of my way, but with my right arm needed to hold together my left arm, I'm not willing to risk it.

"What's going on with you today? You're not yourself."

Air rushes out of Danny's nose in a hurry as the sternness on his face grows. "I could ask you the same thing." He holds nothing back when he slaps me across the chest. "When I find out what you did to make her leave, I'm going to...to..." His nostrils flare as he struggles to think of a threat worthy of his anger. He finds one two seconds later: "Release the images of you dancing with me at Mardi Gras to the media!"

"So? I was there as your support person, and I wasn't the only celebrity there." I quit arguing when the entirety of his reply smacks into me. "My pissy attitude worked? Lillian got the hint we're *never* getting back together?"

"What? No! I'm talking about Willow. Coach James asked me to drive her home after she left here in near tears."

My brows furrow, certain I heard him wrong. It's only after the movie of my night rolls to our exchange after she popped my shoulder back in does the truth smack into me.

Fuck!

I snatch my gym bag out of my locker before hightailing it out of the room. My heart is thumping as hard as my cleat-covered feet.

"You have that final scene to shoot tonight."

Danny's confession doesn't slow me down in the slightest. "This is more important."

It could be my raging heart wreaking havoc with my hearing, but I swear I hear someone shout, "Damn straight, it is!" seconds before I break into a sprint down the hall.

The fans I scared earlier part like a river when I race toward them, but one isn't as eager to get out of my way. The fear on Lillian's face when I continue charging for her standing firm halfway down the corridor increases my speed. I'd never hurt a woman, but I have no issues showing them how good my skills are.

Blonde hair whips up around Lillian's face when I sidestep her with the skill that led to me being drafted as the number one pick out of college. I've slipped into the seat of my car and torn out of the parking lot before the shocked expression on her face can subside. A man of my size shouldn't be able to move with such agility, but you'll be surprised how lithe someone can be when their movements are being commanded by their heart instead of their head.

I pull into an empty space at the front of Willow's dorm twenty minutes later. Not wanting to look like a complete moron, I swap out my cleats for a pair of running shoes and my jersey for a plain T. My pants will have to do.

The hard close of my door gains me numerous sets of eyes, but with the locals as pissed about my performance tonight as I am, none approach me. Good, because I don't want any witnesses for the groveling I'm about to do. I didn't mean the words I shouted earlier. I was frustrated and tired, but instead of taking my frustration out on the person responsible for it, I lashed out at the only one available.

While running my sweat-slicked hands down my pants, I climb the stairs two at a time. I've never been inside Willow's dorm, but I know which room is hers. I doubt she shakes her ass in any random's room.

The whiteboard hanging on her door rattles when I bang my hand on it. I hear a commotion like feet scuffling before a loud shriek. "I can't believe he found me!"

Before my brain can decipher that the voice was missing Willow's Australian twang, the door flings open. A pretty blonde with big blue eyes and a face full of 69er fan paint stands just inside the room. Her skin-tight 69er jersey and the number on her cheek is recognizable, as is her face. She's Willow's friend, the blonde who excited the fans alongside Willow when I let Lillian play with my emotions as much as she has the past two days.

The blonde bats her lashes at me as her tongue delves out to moisturize her top lip. "What can I do you for, Mr. Presley Carlton?"

"I'm looking for Willow. Is she here?"

Her throat works hard to swallow, her face shocked. "Willow?"

Shit, maybe I didn't get the right room.

I step back to gather my bearings. There's another door a few feet up, but half of Willow's building is covered by the thick shrubbery Mickey's planted as an environmentally friendly fence, so this has to be her room.

I return my eyes to the blonde. "Yeah, Willow Underwood. She's around this tall. " I hold my hand up to my nipples. "Has light blue eyes, crazy curls. She's real pretty."

"I know who she is; I'm just wondering why you're looking for her." The blonde sounds more annoyed than she was seconds ago.

"She's my girlfriend." *I hope.*

My ears ring when she squeals, "Your girlfriend? Willow Underwood is your girlfriend! For how long?"

Before I can answer, the blonde is pulled away from the door by her shoulder, and Willow takes her place. Her eyes aren't red and puffy like Lillian's got every single time she cried, but her cheeks are white, and her nostrils are red like she's holding back the urge.

I want to break straight into a grovel but her friend's eager eye has me playing it cool. "Hey—"

"What do you want, Elvis?"

Her friend shoves her hand under her arms and huffs. I'm not as quick to judge Willow's snapped tone because I know what I said to her, and I'm man enough to admit it. "I made a mistake—"

My apology is cut short when she interrupts for the second time, "Yeah, you did."

She blinks excessively when I fill the gap between us. "But not in the way you're thinking. Nothing happened between Lillian and me. I'm not interested in her like that."

Willow takes a page out of her friend's book by crossing her arms in front of her chest and huffing. She doesn't need words to call me out as a liar. She's happy for her actions to speak on her behalf. She thinks I'm being dishonest with my disclosure that I have no interest in Lillian whatsoever.

"Why is that so hard for you to believe?"

She contemplates for barely a second before dragging her hand down her body. "Because I'm this..." She thrusts her hand at me before doing the same gesture she did to her body. "And you're that."

I feel anger rising from my gut to my cheeks. "That fire in your eyes better be there because of what I *stupidly* said in a moment of anger, but if it isn't, and it's what I think you're trying to say, you better step the fuck back and take a goddamn hard look at yourself."

I can tell my words hit her like a ton of bricks, but she plays it cool, acting as if the last three months haven't transformed us from strangers to something much more fucking complicated.

"Do you want to know why I have no interest in Lillian?" Although I'm asking a question, I continue talking as if I didn't. "Because she's not you. She's not a girl who'll shake her ass like no one's watching, or who is clueless about the number of admirers she gets when she enters the room. Everything I wished she could have been, you are. That's why I have no interest in her. That's why what you *thought* you saw isn't close to what it actually was. And that's why I'm going to step back and let you work this out for yourself. Because if you haven't already figured out why I'll *always* choose you, maybe I was wrong, and maybe we aren't right for one another."

As hard as it is for me to do, I walk away.

CHAPTER TWENTY-NINE

Willow

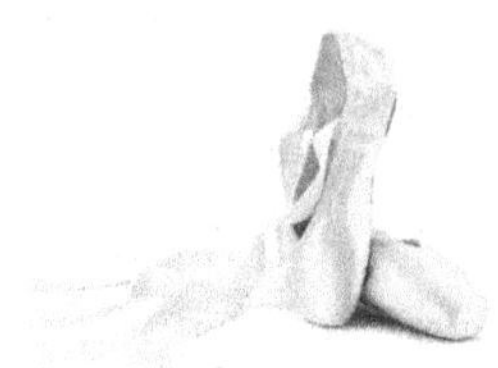

I watch Elvis's retreating frame with my heart in my stomach and tears in my eyes. I want to go after him. I want to pretend the words he yelled at me were just his way of dispelling built-up anger, but something stops me. No matter how much my heart commands my feet to move, my head shuts it down. I'm not in the wrong here, so I'm not the one who should be groveling.

With that in mind, I close the door as tightly as I plan to lock down my heart. Resting my head on the door, I suck in several deep breaths, only spinning when the heat of Skylar's gaze becomes too much for me to bear. Her eyes have narrowed into thin slits and her hands are on her hips. She looks as upset and as angry as me.

"How long?"

"I wanted to tell you—"

"How long?"

Her voice is so loud, it rattles the first tear from my eye. This is the exact reason I didn't want to tell her. I knew she'd be upset. She's so infatuated with Elvis, she could sense his presence through the door. He didn't even speak, yet she knew it was him by the way he knocked. Like, what the hell? So how wrong would it have been for me to shatter her dreams over something I didn't even have a grasp on?

I have feelings for Elvis—way more than I care to admit—but we're on opposite ends of the spectrum. He's moody, handsome, and successful. I'm eccentric, average, and poor. We'd never work out in the long run. I guess that's why I stopped myself from chasing after him. This day would have eventually come, so why not get it out of the way before words are spoken that I can never take back?

Furthermore, his comment about my dancing career cut through me like a knife. His words utterly gutted me. I grew obsessed with dance after my parents died because when I twirled really, really fast, I swore I could hear my mom's giggles in the wind wafting into my ears. So for Elvis to treat it like it's worthless truly devastated me. If it weren't for ballet, I wouldn't be half the person I am today.

I'm snapped from my thoughts when Skylar storms across the room. Unappreciative of my delay in answering, she throws the doors of our shared closet open. My brain scrambles for a response when she yanks down her overnight bag to pack.

"It didn't mean anything. It was just a bit of fun." Even if Skylar weren't my best friend, she'd still hear the dishonesty in my tone. "I wanted to tell you. I toyed with the idea for weeks, but this, right here, is what stopped me. I didn't want to hurt you, Sky."

My use of her nickname doesn't weaken her frustration in the slightest. "Weeks? So it's been weeks?"

Having no plausible defense, I nod.

"Jesus Christ, Willow. I thought we were sisters?"

"We are," I defend myself, stepping closer to her.

I lose any ground I gain when she locks her eyes with mine and sneers, "Family don't lie to each other."

Her reply pains my heart, but it doesn't stop me from saying, "This isn't about me lying. This is about me finally getting something you wanted. Why can't you be happy for me? For years, I've cheered you on from the sidelines."

"This is different, Willow, I didn't place you on the sidelines. You put yourself there with that stupid 'oh pity me' excuse you just gave him." She slings her arm to our dorm door. "You think your bubbly personality hides your insecurities, but guess what, it doesn't! You're just as insecure and self-doubting as the rest of us, but up until ten minutes ago, you did a better job of hiding it."

I don't have a reply. Not one. She's right. I didn't have a personality before my knee replacement, much less the eccentric *I love life* one I have now.

When Skylar moves to her bed to gather her electronic devices, I trace her steps. "I didn't mean to hurt you, Sky. That was never my intention. I love you like the sister I never had. Look, I'll prove it."

Her hand freezes halfway to her cell when I hand her the playoff finals tickets Elvis gifted me before he realized our clash in schedules.

"I don't want stupid tickets, Will. I want my best friend back, the one who'd never lie to me like this." Her quivering words reveal she's mad, but also hurting.

Her hurt is amplified when she snatches the tickets out of my grasp and dumps them into the bin. After swiping her hands across her cheeks, she locks her moisture-filled eyes with mine. "I think we need some distance. I can't think straight with you right there." She thrusts her hand my way.

"Okay. How long?" I adored solitude until a little firecracker with blonde hair and cornflower blue eyes stormed into my life. Now I'll do anything not to be alone with my thoughts.

Skylar shrugs. "I don't know. Maybe a few days, possibly a few weeks."

"Weeks?" I pace closer to her, my eyes begging. "Not weeks. I can't do weeks without you, Sky."

She squeezes my hand, her words not malicious when she says, "You should have thought about that before lying to me. I'll always love you, Will, but I don't have to like you right now."

🏈

As you can imagine, the next two weeks are an extremely lonely time for me. Skylar is so mad, even with our RA rooming her with

Michelle Lester, she's maintained her distance. No one wants to bunk with Michelle because everyone over the age of six knows it's gross to pick your nose, roll your boogers then fling them across the room—everyone but Michelle.

Add Skylar's distance to the dismal losses her beloved 69ers team has endured the past two weeks, and you've got the ultimate recipe for disaster. I'm hating life so much at the moment, dread fills me instead of happiness when I strap on my shoes.

Some of my anguish could be fixed by answering one of my heart's many pleas to make contact with Elvis, but with my inbox as empty as my heart, I've yet to give in. I want to call him—more to tell him to pull his head out of his ass than anything—but I won't. I'm not stubborn. I'm too jealous to throw tenacity into the mix— and perhaps a little bit insecure.

Elvis's claim that what I saw two weeks ago wasn't true was proven accurate early one morning nine days ago. While bunkered down with a hot water bottle and a bucket of cookies and cream ice cream, an infomercial interrupted the black and white movie I was watching. I nearly lost my cookies when Elvis and Lillian pranced across the screen. The only reason I held them down was when I watched Lillian's finger trace the exact vein she did in the storage closet days earlier.

I was so relieved, I snatched up my cell in an instant to call Elvis. I didn't care that it was 3 AM. I had made a mistake, and I was woman enough to admit it.

Just before I hit the connect button, the product Elvis was endorsing flashed up on the screen while he murmured, "Be the best you can be by being the slimmest you can be."

A man without an ounce of fat on his entire body was selling a weight-loss supplement. It was stupid of me to do, and even now I'm angry at myself for doing it, but I pulled off the blanket around my shoulders and stood to my feet, then padded to the full-length mirror in my room. Like all paranoid girls do when they stare at themselves in the mirror, I pinched the roll in the middle of my stomach and shook it before spinning around to assess the love handles I thought Elvis loved gripping. I wiggled my ass and watched it wobble before flapping my arms like a chicken. I loathed everything I saw, but even more than that, I hated that Elvis's commercial made me feel that way.

So, as you can tell from my confession, my confidence isn't just the lowest it's ever been, it's basically non-existent. If it weren't for my upcoming recital, I doubt I'd leave my room. Don't get me wrong; I'm not ashamed of who I am. I'm just too hurt to work through the confusion clouding me.

The cloud thickens when I enter the dance studio in preparation for an all-night practice session. Francesca's ballet class is thankfully void of a crying child being excluded from the activities, but its partially cracked open door can't hide the travesty occurring inside.

Not thinking, I throw open the door and enter Francesca's domain when she's in the middle of a pirouette. "It's my choreography! I created it."

She lands her twirl with perfection before twisting her neck to face me. "Any routine performed in public is fair game." She counts herself back into the beat.

I'm not as willing to let things slide. "I've never performed my routine in public!"

I'm not stupid. I know how competitive dance is, so I'd never freely give away choreography I plan to wow the judges with. That's why I've only ever practiced on a closed stage...

My inner monologue trails off as the truth smacks into me. *No, he'd never.*

When Francesca gives me a smirk, one I'm certain I've seen before, I storm out of her dance studio like a swarm of bees is chasing me. I don't bother picking up the snacks I lose when I rip open my backpack in search of my phone. I don't do anything but dial a number I know by heart and press my cell to my ear.

A player is about to be benched. It's just not the referee calling a penalty. It's me.

CHAPTER THIRTY

Presley

Another week, another loss, and that's not even the reason my shoulders are hanging. I thought I knew Willow. I thought I understood what made her tick, and that stepping back and letting her make her own decision about our relationship was the right thing to do. Clearly, I fucked up. I haven't heard from her in two weeks.

Not a text.

Not a voicemail message.

Nothing.

It's killing me. I can't say it any more simply, but that's exactly how I feel.

I could call her, but that's another mistake I'm trying not to remake. Lillian played the defensive card any time she could, and I fucking fell for it like the naïve idiot I was. If I so much as looked in the direction of another girl, she called it quits.

If I were smart, I would have run for the hills the first half a dozen times she used it, but it's rare to find a college student who thinks with the head on their shoulders. Every man within a five-mile radius of our college told me I was a fool to give up what Lillian was offering—every man except Dalton. He saw what the others didn't. The antics that went on behind closed doors were enough to fill the most angsty romance book. It would just need to skip the romance part because there was none of that.

So why did you ask her to marry you? you wonder.

I didn't.

We spent the weekend of Dalton and Becca's wedding at Dalton's family ranch. Lillian arrived at the reception with a large rock on her ring finger. With Dalton's wedding being covered by a handful of press, rumors of my "supposed" engagement were also circulated. I should have set the record straight, but for some reason I didn't. I don't know why. It might have been the whiskey in my veins or a lack of maturity, but I let the story run, and Lillian started planning our wedding. You know how the rest of our story turned out, so I'll save you the boredom.

"I know, Coach, I know," I assure him when he gives me a look, one that reveals not only his disappointment but his worry. It's lucky we started our playoff campaign so high on the leaderboard, because we would have been tossed to the curb by now. "I'll play better next week."

He wants to believe me. He just doesn't know if he can.

Slumping on the wooden bench in front of my temporary locker, I drag my gym bag until it sits between my feet. I don't need to look up to feel Danny's eyes on me. I can feel them burning my skin. He's still pissed at me. I understand. I'm still pissed at myself. I had wondered if I handled pressure well; my piss-poor performance two weeks ago reveals I don't. I've always been a bit of a hothead who speaks before thinking, but I'm doing everything in my power to change that. Including accepting Danny's anger on the chin like the man I'm supposed to be.

"Delilah sent over the script she wants you to use during the press conference."

My eyes lift to Danny. "Script?" This is the first I'm hearing about a script. As far as I was aware, all I had to do was wear her company's logo.

He thrusts a large document my way. "It's all written down here. In the contract you signed the *only* night you remembered there was more to life than money and chasing a football around a field."

I almost retaliate to his snapped comment, but I hold back, remembering my pledge to be a better man. "I'll take a look at it later after I've hit a salt bath." I thought I kept my tone neutral, but the flare of concern Danny couldn't tuck away before I noticed it has me doubtful.

The reason for his worry comes to light when he asks, "Your back?"

"No." While shaking my head, I stand to my feet. My shoulder is aching like a bitch, but since no one is aware I'm playing injured, I keep that information to myself. "I'll be back in a few."

I'm halfway across the away team's locker room when the shrill of my cell phone halts my steps. I almost let it go to voicemail until a trickle of hope has me racing for the bucket Coach James is carrying into the room. Danny watches me with interest when I search for my phone. It's most likely Lillian calling, but what if it isn't?

The small bit of hope I'm clutching triples when I finally find my phone. With her face lighting up the screen, there's no mistaking who is calling me. It's Willow.

After exhaling deeply, I slide my finger across the screen, then raise my phone to my ear. I play it cool, hoping it will weaken the hammering of my heart echoing in my voice. "I was beginning to think you had lost my number. It's good to hear from you."

Her reply is nowhere near as flirty. "Why would you do that? Why would you take something so precious to me and treat it as if it's meaningless?" Her words are as chilly as ice, but they have nothing on the coldness skating down my spine when she sucks in a shaky breath like she's seconds from crying.

"What I said was stupid. I was talking out of my ass."

Danny makes an agreeing noise, alerting me to the fact that he has his ear pressed against my phone so he can overhear my conversation.

After pulling away from him, I say, "I love the way your eyes light up when you perfect a move and how your lips itch to sing along to the tune when you get caught up in music. I love that you love dance so much you can see it all over your face when you talk about it." *But I doubt it will ever match the love I have for you.*

"Then why do this? What benefit do you get from it?"

I wait for her to catch the sob her hiccup is barely holding back before replying, "Because I was being selfish. I wanted you to fight for me."

"What?" She sounds truly confused.

I try to ease it. "The reason I walked away. I wanted you to fight for me—to fight for us. I needed to know you were in as deep as me. That you understand I want this to be long-term, not a college fling you'll forget in a few months. I wasted nine years of my life trying to hold on to someone who never wanted me. I don't want to do that again, Willow. "

When she fails to respond, I drag my phone from my ear. Our call is still connected; she's just as quiet as a mouse.

Just as I say her name, she whispers, "I wasn't talking about our relationship."

I lick my dry lips, confused. "Okay. Then what did you mean?"

Some of the angst in her voice is pushed away for anger. "My dance routine, the one I performed for you, the moves I created are now out there for the entire world to use." I hear her throat work hard to swallow. "I know you think dance recitals are stupid, but this one was really important to me, and you went and ruined it."

Before I can respond, she disconnects our call.

I immediately redial her number.

She doesn't answer that call or the thirty-seven that follow it.

I spend the next week wading through my confusion. I'm honestly lost as to what Willow meant by her comment. Was she saying I stole her routine, or that she wasted a routine on a man underserving of it? Most of this week, my opinion swayed toward the latter, but now I'm beginning to wonder if that was the case. She said she was referencing us, so that means she was talking about the dance she was preparing for the recital. And that's why I'm stumped. How could I have ruined things for her? Knowing how important the recital was to her was the sole reason I refused to let her cancel it weeks ago. Dancing is a part of who she is, and I don't care if she never talks to me again, I would never take that away from her.

My confusion gets a moment of reprieve when Danny enters the room. "Are you ready?"

I swipe my hand down my body while fighting the urge not to cringe. The advertising execs either misread the measurements Danny sent them for my clothes, or they purposely ordered them several sizes too small. Every bump on my body is on display for the world to see—I mean Every. God. Damn. Bump. This is worse than being photographed in my underwear, because not only does my dick want to hide in shame, so the fuck do I.

"Shut up," I murmur under my breath when Dalton catches sight of me entering the press conference room.

I would glare harder, but I lose the opportunity when Delilah appears at my side. "Do you have the script?"

"Not on me." When she glares at me, I hold my hands up in the air and spin in a circle. Dalton wolf whistles when I work my disastrous getup like a swimwear model showing off her assets in a swimsuit competition. "Where exactly would you like me to put it? It's not like I have pockets."

Delilah is quiet, but I swear she murmurs, "I can think of one spot."

While I take a seat next to Dalton, Delilah gives me a rundown on how she wants our meeting to go down. It's not about football or the odds of us winning a spot in the grand finale; it's about her clients getting the most bang for their buck.

"No matter what is said or asked, never stray from our motto. Be the best you can be—"

"By being the slimmest you can be," I interrupt.

"Good." After tossing a cap with a giant fat-slimming logo plastered across the front, Delilah moves to a set of chairs behind the half-dozen cameras about to capture my every move.

I lower my cap to hide my flaming-with-embarrassment cheeks before swinging my eyes to Dalton. I realize not all the heat on my face is shame when I'm subjected to his furious wrath.

"Seriously? You're endorsing a weight loss supplement?"

"It's a ten million dollar contract."

He backhands me. "I don't care if it was a hundred million dollars. What's your girl gonna think when she watches this? This goes against *everything* she believes in."

Before I can seek clarification on how this affects Willow, the media contingent preparing to interview us enter the room in droves, twisting the nerves in my stomach into a tangled knot.

The first half of our press conference follows a similar pattern most press conferences do: are there any injuries? What do we think our chances are? And have we heard the rumors that Coach James will be axed if we lose tonight's game?

The first two questions were easy to answer. The last one hit me hard. Coach James has been my coach since I was drafted. I don't want anyone but him leading our team, but before I can work through that issue, something else pops up.

"Do you think your poor performance of late is due to influences outside of the game?" This question comes from Mason, a sport journalist who was a teammate of Dalton's and mine back in college. He had the skills to make it far as we did, but his piss-poor attitude meant they never flourished. He truly is what Willow calls a wanker. "You're a bit sluggish, like your mind isn't on the right game."

I lean my elbows on the table, preparing to answer his question, but Dalton beats me to it. "Carlton isn't necessarily playing bad." Mason huffs with as much disbelief as me, but Dalton keeps chipping away at him. "His fumble count is the lowest it's ever been; he's the passing yard leader in the entire league, and he also holds the passing touchdown record. There's nothing wrong with his skills; it just appears as if our opponents are one step ahead of us. We're planning to fix that error tonight."

Happy Dalton has given them an answer worthy of a front page spread, we move on to another reporter. "So what's with the getup, Carlton? Are we playing who stuffed the sausage? Or..."

This question comes from Jeffrey. He's the goofball at every press conference. I like him... when he isn't comparing my package to a stuffed sausage.

I'm about to break into the script Delilah prepared for me when I'm interrupted by Mason, "He's endorsing a weight-loss product he can't even get his girlfriend on board with." He laughs as if he's cracking a joke. I don't find his type of humor amusing. "Bit of a hypocrite, don't you think? Here, buy my fat-slimming products, but don't look at my girlfriend while doing it."

I scoot to the very edge of my chair, ready to charge at any moment. "I beg your pardon?"

I don't give a fuck about him calling me a hypocrite, but dragging Willow into a fight she doesn't belong in... I have more than a problem with that. And don't even get me started on his insinuation that Willow needs to lose weight.

When Mason smirks a sly grin, I feel my anger reaching its boiling point. I'm not just mad at him, though. I'm furious at myself. He's right. I am a hypocrite. I love Willow's curves, and I'd be devastated if my endorsement of a weight-loss product encouraged her to think otherwise. I didn't consider what she or any other curvy person would think when they saw my advertisements. All I saw were dollar signs flashing in front of my eyes, not the consequences of me telling people they're not perfect because they're not a size zero.

Willow is beyond perfect. I love her sassy mouth, beyond beautiful face, and upbeat attitude. Having all of that *and* something to grip while fucking her... *Pure. Fucking. Heaven!* I love her curves. They're a part of who she is, and one of the first things I noticed about her. She and her luscious body are worth more to me than any dollar figure.

Even ten million of them.

With that in mind, I yank off my cap and toss it on the floor. If Delilah wants to sue me, she can go ahead. I'd rather be poor than have anyone think they're not the best they can be because they're not slim.

Dalton slaps my back in support, but Mason isn't as eager to step out of the ring. "Bit late to back out now, isn't it? They're already paying you to endorse a fat-shredding product while dating a fatty, so why not keep running with it? Milk that cow for all it's worth."

When I spring out of my chair, Dalton jumps from his just as fast. He bands his arms around my torso, stopping my charge to Mason. Pain rockets through my shoulder, but it's got nothing on the fire in my gut. Cameras zoom in on me when I give Mason my one and only warning: "You better shut your mouth before I shut it for you!"

He must have a death wish, because only a stupid man would rile another about a woman he loves. "Well there's a solution. Slap a bit of duct tape over her mouth. That'll shred her excess pounds in no time."

"You'll need more than duct tape when I'm done with you."

My determination to reach Mason is so intense, I take Dalton right along with me. I don't know what I'm shouting as I barge my way through the two dozen reporters recording my every move. I'm too high on the adrenaline to pay attention to the minute details.

It's only once I've silenced Mason with my fists and am dragged into the locker room by Coach James do I realize what I've done. I just threw my career down the toilet to defend a vivacious, eccentric college student who is nearly ten years my junior, and I couldn't be fucking happier.

CHAPTER THIRTY-ONE

Willow

I adjust my backpack when I enter the foyer of my dorm. The textbooks stuffed inside have my shoulders the lowest they've been the past three weeks. Tonight should have been filled with palpable excitement. Instead, it's one of the lowest days I've ever had. I'm not performing at the recital or watching Elvis contend for a spot in the final game. I'm going to hide in my room and eat leftover pizza while pretending my fifth slice is my first for the day. It will be a great night—*not.*

My already sluggish pace slows when I hear a roar come from a group of people huddled around the only flat screen TV in the building. "Come on, Carlton! They're reading you like a playbook!"

I naturally progress toward the disgruntled moaners, my heart moving my legs instead of my head. My sneaky steps halt when a pair of big blue eyes swing my way. Skylar is at the side of the pack. She has on her standard jersey—three sizes too small. Her cheeks are donning her favorite player's number—Elvis's lucky number 11, and her hair is teased out like the cheerleaders' pom-poms. Even though she should look utterly ridiculous, she doesn't. She's as adorable as she's always been.

This is the first time I've seen her in three weeks. She's either been dodging me as well as the opposition just sidestepped Elvis's campaign for a touchdown or she hasn't been around. I really hope it is the latter. I'd hate to think she's purposely avoiding me.

After giving her an inconspicuous wave, I pivot on my heels and leave the lobby. My shoulders are hanging even lower now. I thought losing Elvis was bad, but losing my best friend at the same time is the second double-blow I've been hit with in my short nearly-twenty-two years. When my parents died I was too young to comprehend how much I had truly lost. I'm old enough now, and I confidently declare it hurts—*it hurts really bad.*

I jump out of my skin when a crackling voice shouts, "Willow, wait!"

My hands scrape my cheeks to make sure they're dry before I turn to face Skylar. I swear I nearly blabber like a baby when she pushes off her feet to span the distance between us. "I'm still mad as hell at you, and perhaps a smidge jealous, but you need to see this."

When she drags me toward our room, I dig my heels into the carpet. "I don't need to witness the carnage firsthand. I got the gist of it from the moans in the foyer." I can still hear their gripes now. They're not impressed with Elvis or any of his teammates. "It's nauseating."

Although I'd love to use this opportunity to bridge the rift between Skylar and me, I honestly can't handle any more drama tonight. My plate is overloaded. I'm full to the brim—and I don't just mean from the pizza I gorged down like a fat piggy as I strived to forget what day today is.

With slumped shoulders, I enter the room I used to call "ours" before slumping onto my bed and throwing my arm over my eyes. I've never been a crier, but that doesn't mean I don't have to hold back the occasional sob.

I lower my arm from my eyes when Skylar's glare heats my face. "How is defending you nauseating?" She air quotes her last word before walking over to smack me upside the head. "I'm sorry for hitting you, but I had to check if there's more than dust bunnies in your head lately. This is not the Willow I love." She tugs on the hideously ugly jumper I'm wearing before yanking on an unruly curl in my unwashed hair. "You don't wallow in self-pity. You pull up your big girl panties; you admit your mistakes, then you get your best friend lifetime tickets to her favorite team's home games to soothe volatile waters."

A gleam in her eyes reveals she doesn't need anything more than words to accept my apology, so I test the theory by saying, "I'm sorry, Sky. I never meant to hurt you."

"I know." She bumps me with her hip before moving to my desk to gather my laptop. "Doesn't mean I can't be jealous though."

Sitting up, I sigh. "There's nothing to be jealous over. I screwed everything up."

It took me playing my last conversation with Elvis on repeat for days before I fully comprehended it. Not only was he at a loss as to what my accusation centered around, he didn't have the means to circulate my performance. Don't get me wrong; his eyes were fixed on me the entire time, but even a highly-skilled dancer can't memorize a routine after only seeing it once.

That could only mean one thing: Elvis didn't share my routine with Francesca. If I weren't the wallowing, miserable half a woman Skylar pointed out seconds ago, I would have called Elvis to admit my error. Alas, hormonal college students could never be accused of being rational during a crisis, and my ego is still a little stung from his shredding weeks ago.

"I think you still have some tricks up your sleeve."

Skylar looks like she wants to say more, but a roar projecting out of my laptop speakers stops both her words and my heart.

"You better shut your mouth before I shut it for you!"

My eyes rocket to my laptop screen in just enough time to witness Elvis fighting to get out of Dalton's hold. Confident Dalton has him contained, I drop my eyes to the heading of the video. "Football Bad Boy Back to His Old Tricks."

My eyes dart back to Elvis when he shouts, "You'll need more than duct tape when I'm done with you!" I don't know how he does it with an injured shoulder, but he leaps off the stage with Dalton clinging to his back like a baby koala. "You could only dream of sharing the same air with a girl as beautiful as Willow. She's smart.

She's quick-witted, and when she dances, the world fades into the background. She's fucking perfect, more than I could have ever wished for."

I curl my hand over my mouth to stifle a shriek when he punches a man with greasy hair and an even slimier smile. He doesn't just hit him once. He pounds into him multiple times, his fight only ending when Coach James steps in, showing impressive strength for his age. He pulls Elvis off the man wearing journalist tags, throws him into the locker room, then demands for the room to be put on lockdown.

"What the fuck did I just watch?"

My wide eyes bounce between Skylar's as I struggle to unravel the bundle of confusion in my head. She said Elvis was defending me, but from who and why?

Realizing the answer is right in front of me, I attempt to rewind the video. My laptop pinches my finger when Skylar slams the screen shut. "You don't need to see that." She tosses my laptop onto her bed before pivoting to face me. "You need to focus on how we can get Elvis's head back in the game before they get slaughtered even more than they already are. They can't lose tonight's game, Will. If they lose, they're out of the playoffs. I know you don't like football, but even you must understand how important this game is to him."

"I don't have a direct line to his subconscious, Sky."

When she cocks her hip and spreads her hands over them, calling bullshit without any words, I try another tactic. "How am I supposed to fix something if I have no clue what caused it?"

That stumps her. Not for long, but long enough she fails to notice me yanking my cell out of my pocket until it's too late. While leaping onto my mattress and bouncing to the very far corner, I punch in the title of the video Skylar just showed me.

"You don't want to see that!"

I'm not tall—compared to Elvis, I'm a midget—but I have a height advantage over Skylar, meaning she can't reach my outstretched arm when I hold my cell into the air.

Skylar's demands for me to hand her my phone ramp up when

the video begins playing. The start is the standard conferences you'd anticipate before a big game, but one question completely stops my heart. "He's endorsing a weight-loss product he can't even get his girlfriend on board with. Bit of a hypocrite, don't you think? Here, buy my fat-slimming products but don't look at my girlfriend while doing it."

Elvis stills for several long heartbeats before he yanks off the company cap he's wearing and throws it on the floor. I can't stop the smile crossing my face, so I set it free. He has a long way to go before he'll fix the misconceptions his endorsement instigated, but it's a step in the right direction.

My smile is wiped off my face two seconds later when a male voice off-camera snarls, "Bit late to back out now, isn't it? They're paying you to endorse a fat-shredding product while dating a fatty, so why not keep running with it? Milk that cow for all it's worth."

Recognizing that I've heard the worst of it, Skylar stops springing into the air like Tigger. She returns her feet to the ground before watching me with wide, cautious eyes.

I clamber down from my bed and sit on the edge of it. "The reporter thinks I'm fat?" I'm unsure what's taking hostage of my vocal cords: shock or disbelief.

Skylar slings her arm around me and hugs me tight. "He's an idiot, Will. He's one of those stupid, pencil-dicked wannabes all women handle at one stage in their lives. It's like we can't enter womanhood until we've taken down our share of chauvinist pigs."

Her reply warms my heart, but it can't hide the facts. "He's right, though. I am curvy."

There's no denying who I am. This is me. I'm curvaceous, loud, and sometimes a little wacky, but that's okay, because I am happy with who I am, so isn't that all that should matter?

"I just wish while he was judging me, he picked up some of my other great qualities, like that I'm healthy and work out regularly. That I run faster than the wind and fill a bra like no other."

Skylar laughs. "Unless they get help." She wiggles her double Ds, shifting the mood from tense to playful. "And don't forget dancing, Will," she points out. "Elvis was right; when you dance, the entire world fades into the background. I cry every single time I watch you perform."

Her confession fills my eyes with moisture. It also reminds me of all the things Elvis yelled while charging for the reporter. He defended me during a live broadcast on one of the most important days of his career. He risked everything important to him for me —*for me.*

Now I need to make the same sacrifice.

"Where are your supplies?"

When Skylar stares at me with a stupid look on her face, I'm tempted to return her slap upside the head, but with things still touchy between us, I hold the urge back—just.

"Your 69er body paint? Is it here or in Picky McFlicky's room?"

I'm in her closet digging through a mountain of orange and navy pompoms before all my questions are answered.

"Here, let me." Skylar's hip barge sends me sprawling onto my ass, but it also spreads the most mammoth smile across my face. I'm not appreciating the zap zinging through my wrist from my bad landing; I'm loving the super-sized bottle of body paint Skylar is grasping.

Just before she hands it to me, she yanks it back. "You're not planning to streak, are you?"

Waggling my brows, I snatch the paint out of her hand. "I considered it for a minute, but when I realized you'd *never* speak to me again if I got us permanently banned from the stadium, I gave it a second thought. It didn't sound as good the second time around."

"Lucky, as there's no coming back from a lifetime ban." After wiping her brow like she does any time she's fretting about an exam, she asks, "So what *is* the plan?"

I nudge my head to the waste bin. "Grab our tickets first, then I'll fill you in on all the details."

She gags when she sees how overflowing the bin is. "Seriously, Will! Would it kill you to take out the trash? You're disgusting!"

Although she is joking, her rile makes the perfect idea pop into my head.

CHAPTER THIRTY-TWO

Willow

"*P*ull over here; we'll walk the rest of the way."

Even with the game in full swing, traffic is backed up for miles. The army of navy and orange unable to secure tickets is lining the street. I'm glad to see the 69ers haven't lost any fans from their recent poor performances.

When the cab driver does as requested, I hand him the last of the bills in my purse. It's above the fare cited on the meter, but he deserves a generous tip for getting us to the stadium as quickly as he did. I'm also filled with energetic beans. It's lucky I'm not as wealthy as Oprah, or I'd be handing out cars like they're lollipops.

You win a car! And you win a car! Everyone in the tri-state area wins a car!

Oprah's voice fades from my ears when the ticket attendant's third attempt to scan our tickets fails. "The barcode is damaged." I act innocent when she asks, "Is that pizza grease?" She drags her cheesy fingers down her pants before lifting her eyes to mine. "Do you have an online version I can scan?"

"A what?"

"An online version," Skylar explains. "When Elvis gifted you the tickets, was it via email?"

She curses when I shake my head.

The ticket attendant gives me a sympathetic look before handing me back our tickets. "I'm sorry. If I can't scan the ticket, I can't grant you access to the stadium."

"It's alright, I understand."

"You can't just give up. You've come this far, in that!" Skylar waves her hand over an outfit I swore I'd never wear. I have streamers in my hair and paint on my face. Although my skirt is in team colors, I'm wearing a one-of-a-kind shirt. It screams Willow Underwood, and I can't wait for Elvis to see it.

"I'm not giving up. I'm getting inventive." With a grunt, I pull back a section of cut wire I spotted two teenage boys crawling through when I purchased stale hot dogs from a food vendor months ago. "Our tickets are VIP, so we get our own exclusive entrance."

"VIP my ass," Skylar grumbles before getting down low to crawl through the hole.

It will be a tight squeeze—*for me, not Skylar*—but without the cash to buy tickets from a scalper, we don't have much choice.

The wire scratches my thighs when I crawl through the tight space. I want to say it is because Skylar's strength isn't as impressive as mine, but we all know that would be a lie. I am curvy, and I'm fine with that.

"Which way now?"

"Umm..." I scan the area as I strive to think of a solution. The players' entrance would have been locked the instant Coach James began lockdown, so there's no use heading that way. The tunnel between the locker room and the field is guarded by too many security officers, so that only leaves us one option: the merchant entrance.

"Throw this on." I hand Skylar a discarded apron food service staff left lying around before donning my own. They do little to hide the paint on our faces, but they'll get us close enough to the stadium, we can make a run for it if we get caught.

Which is exactly what happens two seconds later. "Hey! Stop! You can't go in there!"

"Run. I'll cover you."

I look up at Skylar in shock. "If you get caught, you'll be banned for life."

"I'll be fine! Trust me."

She shoves me toward the entrance before shifting on her feet to face the security officer sprinting our way. His wheezing becomes even more profound when Skylar raises her shirt above her head. From the lack of a strap on her back, it's obvious she is braless.

"Run, Will! Jesus!" Skylar squeals when she spots me frozen in shock, stunned she'd flash her boobies to save me.

I shouldn't be surprised. I'd do the same for her.

With the security guard's interests no longer fixated on chasing me down, I make it into the underbelly of the stadium without further protests. After pulling away the hairs stuck to my sweaty forehead, I unknot the apron and dump it in the closest bin. I pray to God my security ID is still active when I reach the first alarmed door. When three green lines beep across the security panel mere seconds before the door clicks open, I kiss my ID card and raise it in the air.

My steps from here are a little uneasy. I'm in a section of the stadium I've only been in once before. It didn't end well for me. Let's hope today is different.

I'm about to take a detour down a corridor that looks like the one I raced down after I discovered Elvis in the storage closet with Lillian when a voice halts my steps. It's a voice I immediately recognize. *Who would forget the man who called them a fatty during a live broadcast?*

Although I'd love nothing more than to give the reporter a taste of his own medicine, with the game already halfway over, I don't have time to teach him some manners... until he says, "Our ploy might not have worked as you were hoping. Carlton didn't get sidelined, but I can see our bank balances getting a nice boost a few months from now."

Someone laughs. I can't tell from its huskiness if it belongs to a man or a woman. I retrace my steps, more than interested in unearthing the rest of their conversation.

My snooping pays dividends when the male voice asks, "How

did you know he had a girlfriend? He kept his relationship well hidden from the media."

"And we know why!" This voice is bitchy, snarky, and 100% female. You can't miss the hiss of disdain from a woman enraged with jealousy. "She's a hideous beast."

I round the corner with my activated cell in my hand just as the male replies, "She's not that bad. Did you watch the video you took? I got stiff watching it."

Annoyed, an elegantly dressed lady with dark hair breaks away from the snickering man. He grabs ahold of her before she can flee the room. His hold is firm, but it doesn't stop her hand from flinging out to slap him across the face. I expect him to react negatively to her violence, so you can imagine my surprise when it has the opposite effect. He throws her against a wall on his right before sealing his mouth over hers. He kisses her hungrily, as if apologizing for his comment with actions instead of words.

His wordless plea for forgiveness does him no good. She chomps down on his tongue before pulling back from their embrace. "Not until you've delivered the goods."

"Come on, Delilah. They can't come back from that." He points to a muted TV in the corner of the room that shows Elvis's team is close to facing their fourth devastating loss this month. "Their bid for the championship is done and dusted."

Delilah runs her finger along his kiss-bitten lips, soothing the deep incline of his brows. "The game isn't over yet. Surely you can wait a few more hours for your reward."

He's a fool if he believes a word she's speaking. I don't know her, yet I still know she's full of shit. As soon as she gets what she wants, he'll be left licking his wounds—alone.

"Did you return the playbook?"

Before Delilah can answer him, a person joins their intimate gathering from an attached room. This participant's entrance boils my blood with anger.

"I swear to god, if I'm forced to fake an orgasm with Coach Salter one more time this season, I'll need to invest in acting class-es." Lillian smirks a grin that reveals her cold insides before joining the duo. "Everything is back where it should be, and Coach James is none the wiser."

Hearing the gripe in her tone as well as me, Delilah says, "You can't complain, dear. We're doing this for you. If you want Carlton running back to you with his tail between his legs, this needs to happen." Delilah steps away from the wall the man pinned her on, the clicking of her heels covering up the gasp I can't stifle. "Then we can switch our focus to more important matters."

Lillian blows a hair out of her eyes like she's about to endure months of heavy lifting. "That's easy for you to say, Aunt Dee; you're not the one flashing her kitty to dirty old men every time she needs a favor."

Eww. I'm never using the word "kitty" ever again.

I slide right back until I'm flush with the doorjamb when Delilah paces to a window on my side of the room. It has a direct view of the sideline. My mouth falls open when she says, "Our plan is working. Look at them. The buffoons don't have the faintest clue Coach Salter has been giving you the playbook for each game."

Lillian's eyes widen sardonically. "I didn't suck his dick for no reason."

They laugh like playing men for fools is a game and they're master manipulators.

Just as their laughter dulls, for the first time the past three minutes, the gentleman speaks. It doesn't improve the situation. "Our campaign is paying dividends. Last month, no one expected a final game without the 69ers; now look at the statistics. Our outlay is minutes from tripling." He reads the difference between the fixed odds they bet on six weeks ago, and what they're paying now. They're going to come out of this shitstorm very wealthy.

"Excellent!" Delilah claps her hands together two times before barking out orders like a drill sergeant. "Mason, continue your campaign of driving a wedge between Carlton and that hideous girl. Releasing her video didn't have the impact I was hoping for, so jazz it up a little. Get her hackles as raised as you did Carlton's tonight." She shifts on her feet to face Lillian, who is waiting further instruction. "Position yourself as close to Carlton as you can. When he's wallowing about his team's losses, convince him you'll do everything in your power to see him through this. Even go as far as offering to pay the restitution we added to his contract after he signed it. He's too stupid to question how you can afford that, but he'll be so appreciative of your offer, you'll be back in his good graces in an instant. While you remind him who's boss, I'll continue schmoozing the Devils' coach. We need as many allies on our side as we can get before you suggest Carlton break his contract with the 69ers."

Lillian's frantic head bob halts when I say, "And me? What would you like me to do?"

I should be scared walking into a room full of people trying to take me down, but I'm not. I'm pissed and hormonal, so if anyone should be scared, it sure as hell ain't me.

When Delilah's attempt to snatch my cell comes up empty, she stands in front of me with her brow arched and her lips in a flat line. "So you're not just fat and ugly, you're stupid as well. It's three against one; how far do you think you'll get?"

I could answer her with words, but I think my fists will do a better job. After sliding my cell into the back pocket of my skirt, I test out my theory.

"Oh my god, are you an animal?" Delilah's hand darts up to cover her gushing nose—the nose I just socked her in. "You can't hit people."

"Really? Then what did I just do?"

I take a second swing. This time, I aim for her eye. My hit has enough force, she tumbles down. Her fake ass hitting the floor is music to my ears, her pained wail the icing on the cake.

Pretending my knuckles aren't throbbing, I shift my focus to her minions. My chest puffs with smugness when Mason steps back with his hands held in the air. His cowardice could be excused because he has a badly battered face, but I'd rather pretend it isn't.

Lillian's eyes bounce between her aunt wailing like a child on the ground and me for several long heartbeats. She makes the right decision when she mimics Mason's movements. She bows out of our fight without words, her spinelessness inexcusable. It's probably for the best, though. I don't have time to dispel all my anger. Instead, I issue them a final sneer before pivoting on my heels and exiting the room.

I make it four steps before Lillian's snicker slows my quick pace. Almost robotically, I turn back around and retrace my steps. "What did you say?"

"Nothing," she denies, her head shaking. "I didn't say anything."

"Oh, I must have heard you call me a 'fat cow' by mistake. Silly me."

I try to convince myself to let it go. I remind myself time and time again that reacting to bullies is as bad as instigating bullying, but I just can't help myself. Lillian needs to be taught a lesson, and who better to do that than me?

"No, please, not my nose. I just had my deviated septum fixed."

Her plea turns into a garble when I undo the hard work of her plastic surgeon with my fist. When she falls to the ground, holding her nose, I bend over her. "Sticks and stones may break my bones, but names will never hurt me, but I will hurt you if I ever see you near Elvis again. Do you understand me?"

I wait for her to nod before returning to my campaign to fix the injustices every person in this room committed—myself included. Adrenaline spurs on my steps as I race down the corridor. I make it within three inches of the field before I'm stopped by a security personnel.

"I have a ticket. I'm just trying to get to my seat." I show him the ticket the attendant couldn't scan.

He glances at it for barely a second before he gestures to a stairwell on his right. "Climb those and go three rows over. Your seat is just above my head." He points up.

"Okay. Thank you."

I kiss his cheek like he told me I'm pretty before darting for the stairs. I've climbed two steps when his rumble rolls through my ears, "I like your shirt."

"Thank you!" I reply, my pace undeterred. "Me too!"

His laugh warms my heart, but it has nothing on the heat that hits me when I finish climbing the stairs. The crowd is on their feet, their anger not just visible on their faces. They're fuming mad. I'd even go as far as saying steamingly angry. The heat bouncing off them is so stifling, I can feel my face paint sagging off my cheeks.

"E!" I shout when I see him in the middle of the field.

I move to the very end of the bleachers before waving my arms in the air. "E!"

My shouts are overpowered by the boisterous boo of the crowd when Elvis's throw is intercepted by the opposition. At this rate, he'll never hear me. Recalling how shouted words can be as good as they are bad, I try a new tactic.

"Come on, Elvis! Show them why you're the king!" My words barely float three feet away from me, but they are heard by the spectators surrounding me. "You've got this! You're the number one quarterback in the country for a reason! Bring the magic! Show them why you're the king!"

"Yeah, come on, Elvis. Show us the magic!" a 69er fan on my left joins in.

His words of encouragement are closely followed by another on my left. "We can still win this. We're the 69ers. We don't go down without a fight."

Excitement slicks my skin when each roar is enhanced by another, and another, and another. By the time my eyes are close to breaking the damn welling in them, every spectator in my section is mimicking my chants. Our roars of encouragement not only gain us the attention of the defensive half of Elvis's team, it gains us the watchful eye of the jumbo screen cameraman.

My eardrums are nearly blasted from the hive of activity around me, but I swear I hear Elvis whisper, "Willow?" when he spots me on the jumbo screen.

When he spins in a circle, looking for me, I wave my hands in the air like I'm landing a jumbo jet. I can tell the exact moment he spots me as the most blistering smile stretches across his face. It's so large, not even his helmet can conceal it.

Coach James manically signals for time when Elvis starts to race off the field. His panicked demand is granted by the referee a mere second before Elvis crosses the sideline. He races my way, his helmet discarded at the halfway mark. The roars of the crowd dull to barely a hum when he climbs up the railing like King Kong climbed the Empire State Building. They're as shocked by his arrival as me.

The delicious scent of sweat-slicked skin with a hint of grass hits me when Elvis stops to stand in front of me. He's dangling a good twelve or so feet from the ground, and the strain from his climb is visible on his face.

"Hey."

Who knew one stupid word could cause an avalanche of emotions? I guess if you add his greeting to the excitement in his eyes, it can be easily excused.

"Hey."

What? You aren't dealing with what I am right now. I'm impressed I managed to get out a single word.

As the crowd hovers to eavesdrop on our conversation, Elvis's eyes dance between mine like he's convinced I'm going to disappear at any moment. When I don't, he asks, "What are you doing here, Willow? I thought you had your dance recital?"

"This was more important." Realizing my error, I correct, "*You* are more important."

His eyes flare with relief as the most gorgeous smile spreads across his face. I swear to god it makes my knees weak and has several ladies behind me collapsing into their seats.

"But right now, we've got more urgent matters to take care of." Pretending I can't feel a million eyes on me, I yank my cell phone out of my pocket. "Your competitors aren't one step ahead of you. They know your plays."

As I log into the videos on my phone, I blurt out everything I just witnessed. Delilah's scheme, how they added stuff into his contract after he signed it, and that Mason purposely goaded him with the hope of getting him benched, before closing with how Lillian secured the playbook from Coach Salter before every game.

The only thing I don't mention is Lillian's plan to play him for an idiot. He's been hurt enough by her, and I refuse to subject him to any more.

"Jesus." There are a thousand words in Elvis's eyes, but he went for the easiest one.

"It's okay," I assure him when I see the bewilderment in his eyes shift to indecisiveness. He wants to update Coach James on what is happening before making his competitors pay for their underhandedness, but he doesn't want me to think he is picking football over me. "I'm not going anywhere. I'll be right there when you're done." I point to my seat three bleachers over.

"Are you sure?"

I nod without hesitation. "I'm sure." I seal my hand over his before giving it a squeeze. "Now go and show them why you're the king!"

While silently praying he has the agility of a cat, I place my phone in his hand before giving him a gentle nudge. He lands on his feet, but they remain planted on the ground.

"Go!" I gesture to Coach James who is seconds from bursting an artery. "Coach is about to bench you."

Elvis's grin does stupid things to my insides. "I'm willing to take the risk."

My already brisk heart rate speeds up when he climbs up toward me. His pace is so fast this time around, a gust of air hits my face a mere second before I'm engulfed by the most delicious set of lips I've ever tasted in my life. Even with the cheer of the crowd strong enough to collapse the grandstand, he holds nothing back. He kisses the living hell out of me. Tongue, lips, teeth, you name it, it's included in our kiss.

By the time he pulls back, I'm as woozy as a drunk after a night out on the town.

"I'll be back. Don't go anywhere."

I think I nod, but don't quote me on it. I can barely stand upright.

I gingerly lean over the railing when Elvis calls my name. When my eyes land on his, he smirks a wickedly devilish grin. "I like your shirt."

"Why thank you." I curtsy. "I made it myself."

After a final wink, he spins on his heels and sprints to Coach James, picking up his helmet on the way. Coach's face pales when Elvis hands him my phone, but he's not upset for long. The natural beige coloring of his cheeks shifts to a vibrant red as he approaches Coach Salter standing on the sidelines.

Recognizing his game is about to be cut short, Coach Salter makes an excuse to leave the field. His hasty exodus is stopped by two security officers just before he enters the stadium tunnel. He should consider himself lucky. Coach James looks minutes away from turning this game of football into a boxing match.

My heart warms when Coach James shifts his eyes my way. He dips his chin, his gratitude coming without words. I return his greeting before accepting the seat the gentleman next to me is offering. I could find my own seat, but since I don't trust my legs to keep me upright, I'd rather not.

"It is a cool shirt," the fan praises.

With a smile as bright as a moon on a cloudless night, I drop my eyes to my shirt. I saw this slogan in a kick-ass reading group I'm a part of and thought it was highly appropriate for tonight. Its lettering is a little wonky since I painted it while we were in transit, but its message is imperative:

Unless I'm sitting on your face, my weight is none of your business.

CHAPTER THIRTY-THREE

Willow

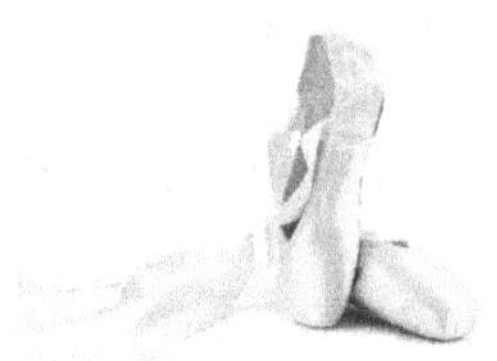

My lungs haven't secured an entire breath the past thirty-seven minutes. Coach James had enough proof to force the opposition into forfeiting the game, but at the request of Elvis and his teammates, he allowed the game to continue as scheduled. Let me tell you, it has been a nail-biting thirty-seven minutes. It took everything the 69ers had to swing the game in their favor, but they did it. After a grueling twelve minutes in sudden-death overtime, Foster moonwalks across the end zone, and the crowd leaps to their feet.

"Yes!"

I hug Skylar, whose impressive rack saved her from prosecution, before turning my affections to anyone willing to hug a stranger. My excitement is too extreme to care that I'm getting friendly with football freaks. I'm one of them now, so I can't exclude myself from the festivities.

I stop celebrating the team's win as if it were my own when the crowd's focus shifts in a different direction. They all turn one way, the joy on their faces changing to wonder. I discover the cause for their slackened jaws and wide eyes when I crank my neck in the direction they're gawking. Elvis has once again climbed the railing, except this time, he's on our side of the fence.

Fans slaps his back in congratulations as he spans the distance between us. I lick my lips, assuming his hurried steps are spurred on by his eagerness to reacquaint our mouth. They are, but that's not the only thing encouraging his swiftness.

After returning air to my lungs with nothing but his mouth, Elvis shifts his eyes to Skylar. "How did you go?"

The love hearts bouncing from her eyes double under his watchful gaze, but she plays it cool. "We're good to go." She grimaces like she got a bit of vomit on her shirt. "If you can get her there in thirty minutes."

"Challenged accepted."

Stealing my chance to ask what the hell is going on, Elvis seals his hand over mine before hightailing it down the stairs. Skylar follows closely behind us. It's lucky we're fit, or we would have died from Elvis's grueling pace.

I take a step back, squealing, when Elvis's car comes shrieking to a halt in front of us not even a second after we burst through the back doors of the stadium. After tossing me into the back seat—yes, he tossed me in there—Elvis demands that Danny scoot into the passenger seat. While he does that, all legs and arms, Skylar drags a damp cloth down my painted cheek.

"That better be water."

She giggles, loving the fret in my tone. She shouldn't be laughing because I wasn't joking. I don't care how much I love her; if her spit is on my face, there'll be hell to pay.

As Elvis zooms out of the parking lot too fast for his car not to become airborne, Skylar dangles a travel-size pack of wet wipes in front of my face. It eases the tension in my shoulders, but it does nothing for the knot in my gut. I'm confused as hell and not ashamed to admit it.

"Will someone please tell me what is going on?"

They all talk at once, meaning I get nothing but blasted eardrums.

I swipe my hand through the air, silencing them in an instant. "One at a time."

Skylar is the closest, so you'd think my eyes would go straight to her. They don't. They seek Elvis's in the rearview mirror.

Although I can't see his mouth, I know he is smiling. His twinkling eyes give it away. "We're going to your recital. Skylar had them slot you in for the final performance of the night. "

My first thought is excitement, but it quickly switches to dread.

"Francesca has already performed. I'll look like a copycat if I use the routine she stole from me."

"Then do something else," Skylar suggests, like it's as easy as baking a pie.

"It's not that simple. Finding the right choreography takes weeks. You can't just throw something together and expect it to look good."

My eyes stray to Elvis's when he says, "You can, Will. Just listen to the music like you did in my condo."

"That was different. That was a private performance for you, not in front of hundreds of spectators..."

My words trail off when Elvis suggests, "Then pretend you're performing for me."

When I huff, more in disarray than anger, he cranks his neck back to peer at me. I'm panicked we're seconds from crashing, but Danny's quick thinking saves us from getting friendly with the cars in front of us. He leans across Elvis to take control of the wheel. His lack of surprise makes me wonder if this is something he often does.

My eyes bounce between Elvis's when he says, "You don't need music or a routine. You need to listen to the beat inside of you. The one that would *never* lead you astray. You need to trust yourself."

His words floor me. Excluding my parents, no one has ever had such faith in me before. Realizing he is getting through to me, Elvis strengthens his campaign. "A beautifully stubborn lady once told me 'the only time someone fails is when they don't try.'" Tears burn my eyes when he delivers my dad's favorite Winston Churchill quote, "Success is not final; failure is not fatal: it is the courage to continue that counts." Nothing but honesty rings in his tone when he says,

"You've got this, Willow. You have too much passion not to have it in the bag. You just need to dance from your heart instead of your head."

Now his team's decision to play tonight makes sense. They could have made it to the finals without any effort, but they wanted to earn it instead of having it handed to them.

"Okay."

"Yes?" Elvis double-checks. My voice was only a whisper, so he could have misheard me.

"Yes," I repeat, louder this time.

Skylar's squeal will ring in my ears for the next twelve months. I just hope the favor I am about to ask her doesn't take me as long to repay.

Nerves tap dance in my stomach as I make my way to the wings of the stage. Elvis is already in his seat. The late hour of the performance didn't hinder his wish to get the best seat in town. He has a prime position—as front and center as you can get.

The butterflies in my stomach settle the instant the drums start banging in Toni Basil's one-hit wonder "Hey, Mickey." As the song breaks into the first verse I clap in rhythm to the beat, encouraging the audience to follow suit. I can't see them through the blinding light illuminating the stage when I dart across it, but I can hear the claps... and a handful of wolf-whistles from the dads in the audience when I leap, bound, and cartwheel across the stage in a super-short pleated skirt and Skylar's beloved skintight 69ers jersey.

They cheer even louder when the spotlight following my gymnastics routine zooms in on Elvis in the middle of the stage in his full football getup. Just like he did during my performance in his house, he is sitting on a dining chair. The smile on his face when I use his thighs as a balance beam encourages my impromptu performance. I shimmy and shake my ass across the stage while using his body as a prop. I grind against him, pivot around him, and use his impressive height to wow the audience with how much leverage I get from the ground when I do leap splits.

It's a fun, invigorating performance that reminds me why I begged my parents to take dance classes when I was only three. I love dance because it frees me from everything around me. It is the one place where I am me and the rest of the world doesn't exist. It doesn't matter if you are a size two or a size twenty-two, anyone can dance, and they can do it well.

By the time my performance is over, I'm straddling Elvis's lap, sweating like a pig, and I have the biggest smile plastered on my face. With my excitement at an all-time high, I forget there are hundreds of spectators behind my back, watching my every move. I'm only alerted to the fact when they break into uproarious applause. They stomp their feet on the ground like Elvis's fans do every time he charges onto the field and shout my name like I'm the only superstar in their midst.

"Go and soak it up, buttercup, cause your ass is mine for the rest of the night."

Elvis's grin turns blinding when I jest, "What is it with you and asses? Anyone would swear you're obsessed with anal."

I vomit a little when he replies, "Only if it's your anus." His shoulder touches his ear when he shrugs. "Too much?"

"Just a little." I hold my index finger and thumb an inch apart before curling my hands around his bristled jaw so I can line up our lips.

After kissing him long enough my heart rate returns to the crazy tempo it beat when I somersaulted across the stage, I stand to accept my praise. I curtsy to the audience, then thank the judges with a dip of my chin and a smile before shifting on my feet to face Elvis. When he waves off my silent gesture for him to join me, I drag him front and center.

I tug on the hem of my skirt when wolf whistles break across the room. My worry that I'm flashing my panties is pushed aside when I realize the squeals of jubilation are coming from the female attendees.

My eyes bug out of my head when I shift them in the direction the women are gawking. Just like he was the first time I performed for him, Elvis is hard. I don't just mean a little outline his football pants can conceal. He's making every seam bulge and sending more than just my head into a tailspin.

"I guess we've taken care of your underwear modeling catastrophe?"

With a giggle, I seize his hand in mine before sprinting for the wings of the stage. His response to my impromptu routine is too good to give up, and I've finally realized that so is he.

EPILOGUE

Willow

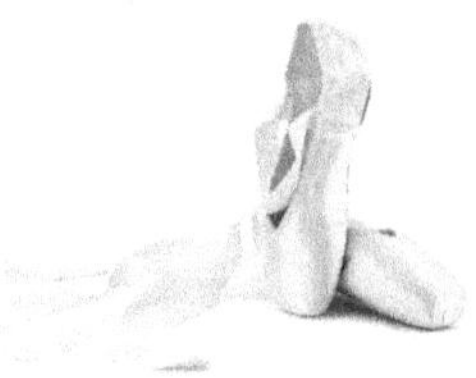

Two years later...

Ignoring the way my jersey is absorbing his milky dribble, I bounce one-year-old Beau on my hip. Just like his daddy, his eyes are as dark as his hair, and his face is downright handsome. He's the cutest 69er fan in the entire stadium.

"Oh, look. There's your daddy. Can you see him?" I swivel Beau to face the recently crowned three-in-a-row national championship team just as Elvis breaks through the huddle.

The crowd shouts his name, encouraging him to do the routine he does at the end of every game. He climbs the bleachers, kisses me like the entire world isn't watching, then demands a private performance to celebrate his team's victory.

Actually, scrap that. Even when they lose, he anticipates some kind of bump and grind. He says my dancing soothes the sting of a loss and enhances a win. I act annoyed every time he asks, but in reality, I love it. Not only do I get to dance for my number one fan, but the moves I've created during our private sessions have benefited me greatly. I've taught them to superstars around the globe and even performed a few of them myself.

I'll never be a prima ballerina; I'm too curvaceous for the ballet world to accept me as I am, but I don't need a tutu covering my backside for people to fork over their hard-earned money to watch me dance. I've done quite well for myself the past two years, but none of it will ever rate higher than my relationship with Elvis. Nothing is perfect, but our relationship is pretty damn close.

When Elvis's muddy cleats land on this side of the railing, I hand Beau to Skylar. I could pass him to his mother, but she has her hands full with Jayla and a seven-months pregnant belly. It's like after her first conception, Becca's uterus finally caught on to the concept it took her and Dalton seven years to achieve the first time around. Becca has been popping out kids like Skylar spits insults at the referees when they go against her beloved team.

Skylar has plenty of time to heckle the referees since she got the lifetime tickets she so desperately craved. They weren't gifted by the person she suspected, though, but that's a story for another day.

My heart beats in an unnatural rhythm when Elvis cocks his head to the side, smirks his wickedly delicious smile before crooking his finger, demanding I meet him halfway. I play hard to get, like my pulse isn't racing a million miles an hour just at the thought of tasting his scrumptious mouth again. I can't help but tease him. I wouldn't if he didn't love it so much.

Lucky for me, he likes being challenged off the field even more than he does on it. That's why I have no qualms riling him about his "old man" sperm having no expiration date every time he asks if I've caught Becca's breeding germs yet. I'll catch the bug one day, but Elvis just asked me to be his wife during an outback adventure in Australia, so we have an off-season wedding to plan before we can add babies to the 69er fandom.

I throw my head back and laugh when a man on my left shouts, "Go on, Elvis, show her why you're the king!"

With a sidestep that exposes why he deserves the eighty-seven million dollar contract he just signed to remain with the 69ers for the next four years, Elvis does precisely that. He climbs the stairs two at a time, grips my hair to hoist my head back, then seals his lips over mine.

Every time he kisses me, I swear it's his best one yet.

This one is no different.

And neither are the million that follow it.

The End!

Disclaimer: *This book is fiction. To avoid legal ramifications, dates and rules were altered so no "codes" were depicted in this story. It's purely for entertainment purposes.*

Did you enjoy Willow and Presley's story? Would you like to hear more about them? **Skylar's** story is available now! Find it here: <u>Ain't Happenin'</u>

Want to stay up-to-date on future books? Follow my social media pages:

Facebook: facebook.com/authorshandi

Instagram: instagram.com/authorshandi

Email: authorshandi@gmail.com

Reader's Group: bit.ly/ShandiBookBabes

Website: authorshandi.com

Newsletter: subscribepage.com/AuthorShandi

Books similar to this one would be The Drop Zone, Spy Thy Neighbor, Lady In Waiting *or* Sugar and Spice*. You can find links to all my books at the end of this book.*

If you enjoyed this book, please leave a review.

ACKNOWLEDGMENTS

I can sit down and write a book, but this, this is hard.

There are always so many people to thank, but not enough page space to thank them adequately, so I'll keep it simple.

Thank you to those who inspire, encourage, and support me. Thank you for buying my books, reading them, and leaving reviews. Thank you for sending me messages of support, and telling me how much you love my characters. Thank you for being there when I wanted to walk away from writing. Thank you for taking a chance on a high school dropout who can't string two sentences together without making a mistake. And last, but not at all least, thank you for seeing past the mess to understand the story beneath it.

Without you, there would be no me, so for that, I'm forever in your debt.

Much Love,

Shandi xx

ALSO BY SHANDI BOYES

Denotes Standalone Books

Perception Series

Saving Noah *

Fighting Jacob *

Taming Nick *

Redeeming Slater *

Saving Emily

Wrapped Up with Rise Up

Enigma

Enigma

Unraveling an Enigma

Enigma The Mystery Unmasked

Enigma: The Final Chapter

Beneath The Secrets

Beneath The Sheets

Spy Thy Neighbor *

The Opposite Effect *

I Married a Mob Boss *

Second Shot *

The Way We Are

The Way We Were

Sugar and Spice *

Lady In Waiting

Man in Queue

Couple on Hold

Enigma: The Wedding

Silent Vigilante

Hushed Guardian

Quiet Protector

Enigma: An Isaac Retelling

Twisted Lies *

Bound Series

Chains

Links

Bound

Restrain

The Misfits *

Russian Mob Chronicles

Nikolai: A Mafia Prince Romance

Nikolai: Taking Back What's Mine

Nikolai: What's Left of Me

Nikolai: Mine to Protect

Asher: My Russian Revenge *

Nikolai: Through the Devil's Eyes

Trey *

The Italian Cartel

Dimitri

Roxanne

Reign

Mafia Ties (Novella)

Maddox

Demi

Ox

Rocco *

Clover *

Smith *

RomCom Standalones

Just Playin' *

Ain't Happenin' *

The Drop Zone *

Very Unlikely *

False Start *

Short Stories - Newsletter Downloads

Christmas Trio *

Falling For A Stranger *

One Night Only Series

Hotshot Boss *

Hotshot Neighbor *

The Bobrov Bratva Series

Wicked Intentions *

Sinful Intentions *

Devious Intentions *

Deadly Intentions *

<u>Coming Soon</u>

Nanny Dispute *

Protecting Nicole (November 23)